BOOKS BY ROBERT PENN WARREN

A Place
to Come To

RANDOM HOUSE
NEW YORK

A Place to Come To

A NOVEL BY

Robert Penn Warren

Library of Congress Cataloging in Publication Data

Warren, Robert Penn, 1905–
A place to come to.

I. Title.
PZ3.W2549Pl [PS3545.A748] 813'.5'2 76–50129
ISBN 0–394–41064–5
ISBN 0–394–41065–3 lim. ed.

Manufactured in the United States of America

24689753
First Edition

TO

my sister Mary

AND

my brother Thomas

No, I'll not, carrion comfort, Despair,
   not feast on thee;
Not untwist—slack they may be—
   these last strands of man
In me or, most weary, cry, *I can no
   more*. I can;
Can something, hope, wish day come,
   not choose not to be.

GERARD MANLEY HOPKINS:
   "Carrion Comfort"

Book One

CHAPTER I

I was the only boy, or girl either, in the public school of the town of Dugton, Claxford County, Alabama, whose father had ever got killed in the middle of the night standing up in the front of his wagon to piss on the hindquarters of one of a span of mules and, being drunk, pitching forward on his head, still hanging on to his dong, and hitting the pike in such a position and condition that both the left front and the left rear wheels of the wagon rolled, with perfect precision, over his unconscious neck, his having passed out being, no doubt, the reason he took the fatal plunge in the first place. Throughout, he was still holding on to his dong.

I know this to be true, for when, on Sunday, well before church time, they brought the body to our house, Mr. Tutwayler, who, coming down the pike in his new Model T that morning, had found the body, explained to the neighbors, now ritually assembled, the original state of affairs as he had observed them. I, then nine years old, had, with a child's curiosity, been hanging around in the bedroom, where they had deposited the body and where now the womenfolks, as they were locally termed, were trying to assuage what seemed to be the nonexistent grief of my mother. She just sat on a split-bottom chair and stared at the cadaver, which had been deposed, insofar as rigor mortis would permit, in a dignified posture. Anyway, the fly of my father's town pants was now buttoned. The womenfolks, some of whom had very probably seen that fly unbuttoned on other less sacrosanct occasions, kept whispering to each other that it was the shock, that my mother would feel better when the shock passed and she could cry—by which now, with the wisdom of years, I presume they meant that they themselves would feel better if my mother would play the game according to the traditional rules that everybody accepted.

But I, even if in my childish and subverbal way, knew that my mother was not suffering from shock. Unless it was the shock she had chronically suffered every Saturday night, and some weeknights too, when my dad came in roaring drunk. Some nights he might just roar around and demand supper, and after eating something, vomit, if it was really bad rotgut, after which he would pass out in a decent Christian fashion. But some nights he would forget to eat, and hell might break loose in Alabama, like the night he took down off the wall above the fireplace the Confederate saber his old granddad had used to fight Yankees, and started screaming *yip-hee!*—which he took to be the Rebel yell—and rising in imaginary stirrups and damning and son-a-bitching the Blue-Bellies and waving the rusty old blade around and performing hideous carnage in that place of the slaughter, as the Anglo-Saxons would have called it, alongside of Marse Robert and Gin'l Forrest. That night it was quite a tussle before the overwhelming battalions of booze got the better of Confederate élan and my father took a header onto the stone hearth and successfully laid himself out like a stunned beef. My mother got him dragged to bed, and found her accustomed chair for such occasions.

She would sit and regard the finished product with a face as noncommittal as a boulder washed bone-white in a creek bed and then dried in the August sun when the drouth came, but the eyes that did the staring, shiny black, burning, and never wavering, were committing themselves to something, even if, standing there watching, I did not know exactly to what. When I was little, I'd see the body lying over there cool-cocked drunk, and her sitting across from it, not close, and staring at it, and it was like holding your breath until your head swam and something was about to explode, and I'd find myself going to her, not meaning to, just there of a sudden, silent and hanging on to her skirt, pulling at it, not jerking, I wouldn't have dared, but with a slow, steady secret pull, to make something happen because I could not stand another second the kind of not-happening that was building up.

But she wouldn't even look at me. Her hand would lift to find me without looking. The hand would find me as accurately as a blind man's hand finds something in his own bedroom, not making a bobble, and I'd feel the strength of that not large but very strong hand, hard too from work, come around my shoulders to press me against her thigh, like forever.

Of course, it was not forever. She was bound to get up and go to bed, for there was always tomorrow to come and the things to do, like milking and cooking breakfast and drawing the water. But the strange fact is, I never remember, even now, how it would stop, or that it ever stopped at all, only the going on, her eyes steady forever, the hand strong around my shoulders, my body pressed against her, my breath coming as quiet as I could make it come, while the coal oil, as though you could see it going down, went lower in the glass bottom of the lamp and the night seemed to get bigger and bigger outside and press on the house, if it was winter, and if it was summer you heard the insects that would not stop.

And that sense of standing there with your breath coming preternaturally quiet while the winter night got bigger or while, off in the summer darkness, the insects would not stop—that is the waiting for the something that I am talking about. But for what? For what? for you I cannot say what—what life can sometimes be, and was to be for me in the time I now undertake to tell about.

Something is going on and will not stop. You are outside the going on, and you are, at the same time, inside the going on. In fact, the going on is what you are. Until you can understand that these things are different but are the same, you know nothing about the nature of life. I proclaim this.

But how do I know that my father was holding his dong when the Dark Angel leaned to pluck him out of the pullulating human swarm?

I had just been sent out of the bedroom where the body was, to get out from underfoot of the womenfolks, and had drifted out to hang on the fringe of the menfolks that were gathered under the big china-berry tree in the middle of the patch of packed red-clay earth stippled with alkali-white chicken droppings that served as a lawn in front of my father's house. It was quiet as church out there, this being Sunday morning and a corpse in the house to boot, and besides, the men would, most of them, be going to church later. Some of the men were already dressed in their Sunday clothes, black coat or maybe blue serge, with starched collars up to the chin, all sweating decorously in the heat except, of course, those who didn't own a black coat or a blue serge suit and were wearing fresh-washed-and-ironed faded blue over-alls, with maybe a gold watch chain anchored to the metal button at the left top corner of the bib of the overalls, the chain disappearing into the bib pocket where, presumably, a gold watch was lurking, but might turn out to be the dollar kind. The men were talking low, and in the pauses between utterance and utterance—that being the proper word for the formality of the occasion—it was so quiet you might even hear now and then a chinaberry pop under some restless foot if the earth was packed hard enough in that particular spot to give adequate resistance to pop it. Furthermore, since it was Mr. Tutwayler talking, people were especially quiet, partly because he had had a throat operation that left him with not much more than a gritty whisper you had to strive and strain to catch and partly because he was the most prosperous farmer in the neighborhood, which in the Heaven's Hope neighborhood meant specifically that he was the only one not engaged in a struggle *corps à corps,* not only with the mortgage, but with the double first cousin of starvation.

Mr. Tutwayler, a very tall thin man, had a peculiarly long stringy neck that, very much like the neck of a plucked chicken, protruded astonishingly above his old-fashioned, stiff, gates-ajar collar, with no tie but with a gold collar button, and I had my eyes fixed on the peculiar bobbling of his dried-out Adam's apple even as he stated that when he had found my father's body in the middle of the gravel of the Dugton Pike, he was holding on like grim death to his dong—that being the phrase he used but with no intention to make a joke. Nobody took it as a joke either, and after the pause in which the information was being communally absorbed, a voice said: "It was about all Buck Tewksbury had left to hang on to, I reckin."

Silence, then another: "Wal, a man ain't got that to hold on to, he ain't got nuthen worth holden on to."

Silence, then another: "Buck—he shore thowed that thing around."

Another: "He thowed hisself away."

Another: "He drunk hisself away."

Another: "Had'n been booze, been tail. Him like he was."

Another: "All his r'aren and skirt-tearen round Claxford County and he ends like tryen to jack off in the middle of the night on the gravel on Dugton Pike."

"Naw," Mr. Tutwayler sepulchrally uttered, "naw, he must of been standen up to piss and—"

"Shush–shsh!" interrupted a sound very much like steam escaping from a locomotive cylinder, a sound clearly intended to invoke silence, and in the absolute silence that did ensue, I found that the group had swung open to expose me. Somebody—one of the men wearing overalls and no black or blue coat—had discovered my presence, and now stood back with his right hand held discreetly low and the thumb cocked toward me, and with his eyes wall-eyed toward me, to indicate, in all this absurd parody of secrecy intended to spare my sensibilities, what had stimulated the warning in the first place: *me*. All eyes were fixed on me.

Suddenly, I found that I had burst into tears.

"Look," Mr. Tutwayler's gritty whisper was saying, "look—the pore little chap, and him a-cryen for his daddy that's dead."

.   .   .

That scene lives vividly for me—more vividly with each passing year—but my relation to it is peculiar. To begin with, it does not seem real. It is like something I might have read in one of those novels about the South, if I had been old enough back then in the time they were being written, or a picture seen in one of those books of photographs

7

of the South published during the Depression years when the region was dubbed the nation's Economic Problem Number One, or a scene from a movie, or a stage set. There is the tree, the bare-packed ground with the white streaks, the about-to-fall-down weatherboard house, long since paintless and with cardboard stuck behind a broken windowpane and one thread of poverty smoke unspooling forever upward from the kitchen chimney, the yellow hound, with moth-eaten flop ears, asleep on the canted front porch and the two tin lard cans with zinnias my mother had planted in them now blooming red and a ferocious orange, one dingy-colored hen collapsed in the shadow of the wood steps, beak parted in the heat, the rusted plow points hung on wire to keep the slat front gate pulled shut but not doing any good now for the gate had long since sagged on its hinges and wouldn't close anyway, the broken-down old Hudson abandoned by the fence, three years unused and rusting away, with no glass in the doors and the seats (as I know) covered with chicken droppings, old-crusty or new-soft, the men with their red, bony, lank-jawed faces looking as though chopped hurriedly out of cedar and left, unfinished, to the weather—the work of a talent untutored but strong, the faces blank, bleak, hieratic, unforgiving, only the eyes alive, and over all, the torrent of gold-bodied August sunlight, perfectly transparent but somehow as substantial as lava, pouring inexhaustibly down from the sky.

As I was saying, the scene does not seem real to me, not even as something imagined seems real, for I have no connection with the weeping child, whose face I cannot see. I always regard the scene as from a distance.

.   .   .

I have crouched in a dugout, during the war—the Second World War, that is—at midnight, in the Apennines, the snow spitting, my lieutenant, a Partisan with the Nazi helmet of a dead man on his head, huddling beside me for warmth, holding the walkie-talkie as the voice comes out, saying: *"Capitano . . . Capitano . . ."*

I seize it, and say: *"Eccomi."* The patrol—the Partisans—have taken five Germans. I say bring them in, be very sure to bring them safe, for interrogation. I know they will not. They rarely do. I know the voice will come again on the walkie-talkie: *"Mi dispiace, Capitano —scusi, Capitano—sono già morti."* Dead. Trying to escape, the voice will say.

I do not blame them. Not after all that happens. I think of how easily the point of a trench knife enters when set at the soft spot at the base of a throat. I think of the men, the Nazis, now suddenly dead. Thinking of them and their way of dying. I look out into the darkness slashed with the white spittle of snow and crouching there in the Apennines I see, far off, as beyond the darkness, the scene under the chinaberry tree, the men, the weeping child, the golden lava of sunlight pouring down. This, as though through a sudden rent in the darkness of night, of distance, of time.

Then it is not there.

I have risen from the open book on the desk in my office at the University of Chicago, and have looked down, far off, over the roofs of that squalid district, which glisten dully with rain, over the jungle of TV aerials. Suddenly, there it is, the scene: the boy under the chinaberry tree. I see it. Behind me the steam clanks in my radiator, but I do not hear it.

In many places, in many unexpected moments, I have seen that scene.

.　　.　　.

At this point, I have reread what I wrote three days ago, up to the scene under the tree. I wrote that part very fast. It came rushing out, my ball-point pen rushing ahead—a new experience for me, who am accustomed only to scholarly and critical composition and who, not being of a quick mind or ready to trust my early notions, am inclined to be painfully slow and careful in my formulations.

Reading that, I was struck with surprise by the tone, what I can only describe as an angry, hard, bantering tone arising from—from what? Maybe from some sense of outrage at that world whose language and dialect I had been now and then contemptuously echoing, and an undefinable sense of outrage at myself—at, to be more specific, my unfended weakness in the face of the way the world was.

9

Well, I have written that down. It surprises me somewhat. But I see no reason to change it. It, whatever it means, is part of the story, too.

That tone represents, I suppose, an unconscious will to detach myself from the scene that is my subject, to deny any sense of identity with the weeping child and the whole reality of the scene. But if I am not that weeping child what can I now be writing about? For what else can I be and where else can I belong?

In any case, the scene was real, in God's truth. The house was there, the tree was there, the men were there, citizens of the Heaven's Hope neighborhood, Claxford County, Alabama, all really alive then and really dead by now—never characters in a piece of fiction nor faces in a photograph nor actors on a stage set nor items in a table of statistics issued by the Department of the Interior: real, existing in flesh and blood, struggling with their lives, full of affliction, weakness, rage, and vice, but somehow capable of love and courage, sustained by hope and irony but in a few years to enter a time of long hunger and despair as the consequence of something that was to happen in New York City, which they had vaguely heard about, in the Stock Market, which was something they had never before heard about or, if they had, thought was a place where people bought and sold cattle and work stock. And now Mr. Tutwayler was saying that I was a pore little chap crying for his daddy.

Then, as I, under all the eyes fixed on me, stood there weeping, not because of the death of my father—certainly not for that as such—but because of some unformulable sense of the way the world is, my mother came out of the house. I did not see her come out—literally, I mean—but I know how it would have been.

She was not a large woman, on the small side rather, and she had a gift for being able to sit motionless with her eyes fixed on something, a nail in the wall, a stone on the ground, a tree on the horizon, or my father's body on the bed, and never shift her gaze, seeing and not seeing, and all the while you knew something was going on deep inside her like a stream in the darkness of a cave. But when she moved, even just to rise from a chair, it always gave the impression of energy suddenly unleashed, of will awakened, of purpose brought to focus. And when she looked at something—even a rock or a tree—or at

---

10

somebody—anybody, but especially my father or me—you had the feeling she was looking right into and right through whatever it was. And sometimes she'd bust out laughing.

Back in the room where the body was, she would have risen sudden from her chair—sudden but not abrupt, for there was never anything jerky in what she did—and not noticing how the women all looked sidewise at her, would have gone out of the room and out to the porch and would have come down the rickety wooden steps of the porch, in perfect balance not noticing the ricketiness, and walked across the open space, in the brilliant openness of light, with her small feet, looking small even in the heavy old work shoes she wore, set lightly but decisively on the packed earth, her head held straight, the dark hair pulled back tight from the straight clear brow, the black eyes on target.

The eyes of all the men were off me now. I was aware of the fact before I knew that my mother had come out of the house. All the eyes were fixed yonder, somewhere. Through the swimming brightness of my tears, she was, all at once, there. She moved directly up to Mr. Tutwayler, and stopped. "Mr. Tutwayler," she said in her clear, firm voice, which always carried further than its softness seemed to warrant, "I'd be kindly obliged if you'd speak to me private."

Ritualistically, the group all fell away, leaving Mr. Tutwayler and my mother face to face under the lacy, rippling gray-green liquefaction of shadow of the chinaberry tree, with the blaze of light all around. After a little, I saw Mr. Tutwayler put out his right hand. My mother took it, and they shook hands. This with a certain rigorous formality beyond social usage—the formality, I would learn, along the way, that was appropriate to the concluding of a bargain between men of honor in Claxford County. But back in that time to me it was only a handshake, mysteriously coming out of thin air, as it were. My mother's hand, as always in that act, made a last sharp, decisive movement before it dropped Mr. Tutwayler's hand—like the brisk, last blow of a carpenter's hammer nicely calculated to set a nail clean and even to the head. She wheeled smartly from him and again moved across the openness of light, now toward the house and the shadowy room.

11

On Monday morning, in the graveyard of the Heaven's Hope Church, they buried my father. Very few people came, Monday being a work day. The remarks of the preacher were brief, less concerned with eulogy of the dead than with the theme of God's infinite mercy. Mr. and Mrs. Tutwayler drove us back home, and my mother took my hand, marched me into the house, told me to put on my old overalls, said something to eat was in the warmer of the range and buttermilk was hung in the well—a method used in that time and place to keep milk cool—and left. She drove off in the Tutwayler Model T. She got back very late.

Shortly after dawn on Tuesday, the wagon-and-team arrived, and my mother and the Negro man who worked for Mr. Tutwayler started loading things. When I asked questions, my mother said shut up, she'd tell me later. In the rush we almost forgot one thing, the saber. As I went out the door, I saw it still hanging on the wall. "The sword!" I yelled to my mother. A second she stood there, already out in the yard for good. Then said: "Git it."

We got on the road by noon.

.   .   .

We were there in the wagon, Mr. Tutwayler's Negro—or black, as is now preferred—driving, me on the seat beside him, and my mother, being a lady and not to sit on the seat with a creature of complexion, on a straight-backed chair just behind us, and behind her all the piled-up and not-too-well-lashed-down household gear.

Before we turned onto the Dugton Pike, we passed Heaven's Hope Church, where I had been just yesterday morning but where I dared only one look now. My mother never gave a sign. The wagon was grinding slow on the gravel and she was looking over our heads and never said a word.

We came to the spot where, according to the story of that Sunday morning, my father had taken his header. My mother, if she had got told about it, made no sign. But when, right away we got on the bridge over Podmore Creek, she did say something. Clear and firm, she said: "Stop!"

The wagon stopped.

She leaned down and reached around in the wagon bed, then stood up. She was holding the saber. It was in the scabbard and she held it a little less than halfway down toward the tip. A saber is pretty heavy, but she had both hands to it as she held it horizontal above her head, stretching up on tiptoe. She was not large but, as I have said, very strong, and so the thing went sailing a good distance before it struck water, splashed, and sank.

I had not believed what I was seeing until the splash. Then I cried out: "But my great-granddad—he fought Yankees with it!"

"If he was like your dad," she said, "he never fought nothing but a bottle"—and I remember, after all these years, my thrill of shock as she said the words, for I knew, even at that age, that there were certain things you never said before a nigger.

But my mother didn't seem to know the Negro was there. Or just didn't give a damn. Her cheeks were flushed and her eyes big and shining.

She turned full on me, shining the eyes at me. "Listen," she said, "yore king-tomfool of a father, he was drunk and he bought that durn thing at an auction for fifty cents which was forty-nine cents more'n it was ever worth new, and comen back in the wagon at night, with me holden the baby—you—he was so drunk he stood up and yelled and waved that king-fool thing in the moonlight, yellen and screamen."

She had stopped because her breath gave out.

All the time the Negro was hunched forward, looking up the pike as though he were driving right on, alone, nobody there. But the wagon, of course, was not moving. He had not been ordered to drive on.

"Drive on!" my mother said, now that her breath was back, and sat down in her chair.

.   .   .

Even without Mr. Tutwayler's report of the condition of my father's body when he found it, I would have known how things happened and of certain details that he could not have known. Earlier in this narrative, I have allowed myself to be distracted, and so add the matter here. It may even belong more naturally here, by association with what has just been told—that night scene in the wagon with my mother and the child at her breast.

What I am about to relate must have occurred when I was about four or five years old, on a Saturday when, because my mother was ill, my father had taken me to Dugton with him to do the weekly trading—that being the old rural word. Returning, we were late getting out of town and, though this was in the years before the drink seriously took hold of him, my father was not steady when we started, and besides, had a bottle with him. Now and then, as the wagon ground along, he'd take a drink, and when he tilted the bottle up I could see, in the starlight, that the liquor was clear as water—what they called white mule, for that would be back in early Prohibition.

Finally, after a drink, he did not drop the bottle back into the side pocket of his coat but, sitting there on the board seat, clutched it in both hands and stared at it. He stared at it as though his gaze were riveted there, shaking his head now and then as though he were trying to detach his gaze but could not. I remember distinctly the retarded, inexorable grind of the gravel under the iron tires, a sound that seemed to declare some irreversible process in which we were trapped, as though we were coffee beans dropped in a coffee grinder as big as the world. I remember the painful movement of my father's head as it jerked from side to side, and the starlight pouring down on us and on the long white road ahead.

Then he burst out: "Jesus—what a man is!"

Then: "Setten in a wagon in the middle of the night with a bottle in his hand and looken at a mule's ass!"

And he shut his eyes and drove his chinbone deep into his chest, shaking his head differently now, with a tight, shuddering motion.

He sat that way a minute, two minutes—how long I cannot know —then jerked his head up and backward so violently that his black felt hat fell off behind into the wagon bed. He was a very strong, fine-looking, handsome man, my father, and the image I carry in my head from that moment is, as I interpret it now, one of a wild nobility. I see, profiled against the pale-starred sky, the head thrown back, with the disorderly unbarbered black hair—the thrust of the chin angled high from the muscular throat, the black clot and tangle of the mustaches, the powerful beak of the nose, the eyes, in glittering rage, glaring at the stars.

Suddenly, he was glaring at me. In wordless command, he thrust the bottle at me. I took it, and he rose, throwing the lines at me, too, and I leaned over to recover them.

When I could look up, with the lines in my hand, he was standing up, fumbling at the front of his overalls to extract his member. He stood there steady enough, it seemed, his noble head again thrown back to glare at the stars, clutching his great member, with a force that must have been painful, waving it at the stars, crying out in manic glee: "Got the biggest dong in Claxford County—and what the hell good does it do me!"

He began to laugh. It seemed that he could not stop laughing. And now, in the midst of the wild mirth, he was relieving himself on the hindquarters of the near mule, playing the stream on that target, a gleaming arc in starlight, while he laughed and laughed.

CHAPTER II

So that was the way we moved to Dugton, on a hot afternoon, with the wagon no longer grinding on gravel and dust clouding thinly white as high as the mules' bellies, but at last moving on tarred pavement so soft with heat it would now and then suck at the wheels, on past the streets of nice houses—not many—with lawns, and on one a spray was whirling to create a rainbow arched over the cool green, across the town square, where Model T's and a few Chevrolets and Essexes were set nose-in around the little patch of Court House park, and a few wagons-and-teams, too, all now looking in my memory as faded and archaic as old photographs found in an attic, and on across the Square now as blank, on account of heat, as Sunday, and sad then to me, who had known it only in the excitement of Saturday afternoon crowds and in my yearning for gumdrops and cap pistols and all the things I could see in the show windows, but now with the quiet so steady you could hear the cooing and simmering of pigeons in the Court House eaves, and on past houses that got dingier and dingier, with paint peeling in bigger patches, and to where you could see the railroad tracks and the boxcars sitting tired, and the tar gave way to gravel again, with half-naked black children playing in yards with no grass, and finally we pulled into a side street, still gravel, and with children, half-naked too but white, and there, my mother said, was our house.

It had a flush toilet in it. It was the first one I had ever sat on or even seen. My mother had to make me stop pulling the flush-chain, and come help carry things.

. . .

We—my mother and I—lived in that house on Jonquil Street for ten years, until I was eighteen, in that racially ambiguous neighborhood of the sort not uncommon in old-fashioned Southern towns, and she stayed on the rest of her life there. It was a tiny sort of shotgun bungalow, white weatherboard—white, that is, when, after a couple of years, we finally got to painting it, my mother and I painting, after work and on Sundays, just as we had worked at other things, to scrub the whole house out with lye and water, to clean the trash out from under it, to get some grass in the yard the best we could, to whitewash the fence, my mother sometimes steeling herself to greater effort by affirming that she was not born white-trash and didn't aim to die that way. In fact, she proclaimed, she did not aim to die till she got that house decent—and wasn't sure she aimed to die at all since it looked like she got meaner and tougher every year trying to keep me straight. But she'd give one of her quick grins and her black eyes would snap.

All those years, my mother worked in the new canning factory— the only industrial development that, even by the bait of no taxes and no unions, ever got lured to Dugton before World War II. She had found a job on her first try, the afternoon of my father's funeral when Mr. Tutwayler, as part of his bargain in buying the falling-down house and thirty acres from her, had driven her to town. That property which, I should add, had been my mother's family farm, had dwindled to forty acres by the time she inherited it, and then, by way of a mortgage, to thirty, this in the early days of marriage when she, little more than a girl and only recently deflowered, had not yet recognized my father for the feckless, vanity-bit dreamer he was, and was drifting through her days and nights still bemused by the enamel-glistening black mustaches and the biggest dong in Claxford County.

She must, however, have recognized the truth in time to fight off another mortgage. The interchanges, hissing or throaty, that I had sometimes heard through the paper-thin walls of the matrimonial chamber, followed by breathy silences filled with what must have been, literally, a grim struggle between two absurdly unmatched adversaries, silences always ending in the sudden, disorderly creak of bedsprings that would settle to a rhythm brutal and brief—all this must have been an index to the rancor of the long financial debate. But my mother held out, against odds of poundage and muscle, and in the end, in the shotgun bungalow on Jonquil Street, where walls were equally thin, there was never a night sound—except, at rare intervals, a voice crying out in dream.

For years after I had left Dugton forever, it seemed to me that nothing had ever happened there. My mother had gone to and from the cannery, to and from cookstove and bed. I had gone to school and come home, had gone to my job, for I always had some sort of job to help out, had worked at my books, had slept. For many years I could, literally, remember nothing except the repetitions of life. It was as though I had moved through those years of my adolescence with never a yearning nor a pang, like a somnabulist wandering a dark house.

At least, looking back, that was the way it seemed to me until the moment, sixteen years after I had left Dugton, when, in Nashville, Tennessee, in my lumpy bed, in my room in a dreary residential hotel, I woke from the luxury of my late Sunday morning sleep, being snatched from the sadness and sexuality of some blurred, unrememberable dream, like so many of my dreams of that period, to grope out for the bedside telephone, which was yet ringing, and to find it and, aware at the same instant of my matutinal erection, to say, questioningly, into the transmitter, "Yes?"

"Guess who?" the voice said, with something like a giggle, but also, it seemed, from some sunlit space, far away, where water rippled, fresh and bright.

"Who?" I demanded almost automatically, that instant being concerned to adjust myself in bed, my pajamas, on account of my twisted position, binding me in the crotch. I was still struggling to get comfortable, telephone in right hand, propped on right elbow to hitch myself higher in bed, left hand down below loosening the pajama string and trying to arrange things—all this while the answer came.

"Rozelle," the voice said, and in that instant, in the great tissue of mystic meaningfulnesses, in the dim forest of symbols and correspondences, in the mist-shrouded fen where the foot lifts suckingly from muck as the *ignis fatuus* of irony lures us on—in other words, in that obscure and merciless logic that life is, as that name came over the wire, out of time and distance, I was clutching my cock.

I dropped it.

"What?" I demanded.

"Yes," the voice was saying, in a burlesque wail of self-pity, "poor little Rozelle—and you never even told her goodbye!"

.   .   .

Indeed, in that instant, that Sunday morning as I lay in my bed in the Old Hickory Arms Hotel in Nashville, Tennessee, all of my past —not only my past in Dugton but my subsequent past—was changed. Here it may be objected that nothing in my past was changed, that only my view of it was changed. In a limited and vulgar sense, this interpretation is valid. There are, of course, certain objectively verifiable "facts" in the world. But even to define the word "fact" is a tricky and shadow-haunted operation, as we must remember, and certainly there is a significant distinction to be made, to say the least, between *fact inert* and *fact operative,* and how does a fact become operative except by the mind's recognition of its relation to a pattern? Here we are dealing, are we not, with the question of the locus of reality? And I intrude here, I must admit, some of my professional concern as a historian—though a historian in a rather backhand way, that of a student of medieval literature.

But, the stultifying lingo aside, the question I raise is a vital one for us all, we are all stuck with trying to find the meaning of our lives, and the only thing we have to work on, or with, is our past. This can be a question of life and death.

In any case, with the sound of Rozelle's name, the past began to loom in a cloudy, burgeoning, undifferentiated mass behind me and over me, a reality that, I knew all at once, had been waiting for me for a long time but that I dared not yet turn to face.

When, however, I had hung up the telephone, the thing that did, after all the years, loom from the undifferentiated mass behind me was a single, specific recollection of the time after we had moved to Dugton. During my first fall at school there, one day at recess time, a big boy, perhaps fourteen or fifteen (who, I learned later, had some kin out near Heaven's Hope neighborhood), appeared before me and demanded: "Hey, you—yore name Tewksbury?" I said yes, or nodded or something. Then he turned away. "Hey, fellers," he said to other big boys behind him, "it's him!" Then yelling: "Hey, ever-body!"

As children, big and little, gathered around, he pointed at me, then announced: "Yeah, him!—and his daddy, he stood up in the wagon and—" and here he dropped a hand down to crotch level, but held out from his body, "—and jacked off—" he made a motion with his hand, "—and fell in the road and killed his-self!"

And with this last statement, he took an elaborately comic plunge, bounced acrobatically off the ground, and again pointed at me, yelling with falsetto laughter. The other big boys were yelling with laughter, and even the very little children hanging on the outskirts, who could have no idea of what the vile word and vile pantomime of my torturer signified, looked at each other in momentary puzzlement, then at the big boys whose faces were contorted with laughter, and then, as though by violence to make up for incomprehension, burst into the wildest merriment of all.

So, in the schoolyard, it was like that Sunday morning under the chinaberry tree—faces ringing me around, while I wept. But with a difference. Now the faces all had enormous eyes that seemed to whirl in their sockets, and great mouths, too big for the faces, with great rubbery lips that were twisting and slickly convolving in laughter, and fingers that pointed at me and were swelling enormously at the thrusting tips like clubs—at least, that was what the scene became in my nightmares. For though the memory had long since been wiped out, now, in Nashville, Tennessee, it was to reappear, just as soon as I had racked up the phone. And waking, that night, I realized that the dream had come many times before, long ago.

———

20

I have mentioned the difference between the original scene of weeping, under the chinaberry tree, and that in the schoolyard. But there was another, of which, in later years, I was to become conscious. In the first scene, I had wept in some sudden, deep awareness of what the world might be. In the second, I wept because of outrage at the contempt visited upon me and the anguishing awareness that it might, somehow, be merited—but also because of rage at the father who had brought it all upon me and left me defenseless. I shook with the discovery of hate.

In a way, however, I should have been grateful to the wicked father. He was, paradoxically, through that very schoolyard scene, in its very pain, to provide me later with the first—I almost said, only—social success I was ever to know, this when I turned twenty-three, toward the end of my first year as a graduate student at the University of Chicago.

In those days, politics, of a more or less leftish variety, New Deal to Stalin, and then the new Stalin-Hitler pact, was the chief extracurricular interest of my academic contemporaries, and even in the face of the war in Europe, a number of them were still deeply concerned over Southern poverty, Southern fascism, Southern lynching, Southern illiteracy, and Southern literature, which, by the way, was regarded as deplorably reactionary. My contemporaries in the Graduate School of the University of Chicago discovered that the hulking, halting, tongue-tied specimen in corduroy pants too short for the legs of a creature that was now six feet one and a half and looking particularly short when hiked high over cumbersome footgear that looked suspiciously like beat-up brogans incompetently dabbed with shoe polish—what I mean to say is that my contemporaries discovered that the specimen was a Southerner of sorts, and now and then asked him to one of their gatherings of sober soul-searching and earnest drinking.

He, in contravention of all promises made to his mother, had begun by this time to drink, and under that beneficent influence and the stimulation of probing questions about the folkways and mores of Claxford County, Alabama, found himself, one evening, giving a character sketch of his father, ending the performance on his feet to enact, in much the same spirit as his old torturer of the schoolyard, the hilarious episode of his father's death, complete with hand on hypothetical dong and the lethal plunge.

It brought down the house. He was a social success. Inflamed by adulation, he began to play the role of Southerner to the hilt. He carefully improved his diction (with some unhappy side-effects on his study of Romance languages), tried to recall folksy locutions, and looted the works of Erskine Caldwell, an especially juicy Southern writer of that period, for material to use in constructing his own family history. He even invented certain episodes, and one of them won special acclaim: his father, returning late at night and plum-tuckered from a lynching over in the next county, didn't forget to leave a little keepsake on the tyke's pillow—carefully wrapped in a piece of waxed paper, a really-truly nigger ear to dry and carry as a luck charm. This episode was, of course, set back in the earlier years of the tyke's childhood, before drink had begun seriously to corrode the natural tenderness of the father's nature as well as family relations on the Tewksbury farmstead.

I suppose that shame accounts for my having put the preceding narrative in the third person, and if so, that shame is justified. Even after the long lapse of time I now feel it. But I am glad to be able to report that compunctious visitings of my nature asserted themselves. One night I happened to be sitting up late to finish Zola's novel *l'Assommoir,* which ends with the decent little girl of a working-class family turned into an absinthe-soaked trollop in a Parisian slum, now and then earning an honest sou for drink by enacting the comic gyrations of her husband's death from delirium tremens—as I had been accustomed to enact the death of my own booze-bit father. I quietly laid the book aside, and mysteriously sad and blank, I took my condition to be a tribute to the artistry of Zola.

But I must have been wrong, for several nights later there was a popular demand that, for the benefit of a new couple, I put on my most admired performance. I had actually risen to my feet to comply. Then, in a very stagey sandhill cracker accent, I heard my voice: "You know, I jest wonders why ain't none of you folks ever told me how any of yore fucken fathers died."

That ended my social success. It also ended my first sexual success
—the first relation, that is, I had ever had with a nice-and-white girl,
this being one Dauphine Finkel, a Jewish girl with a rich father,
fathomless Oriental eyes, a perfect French accent, impeccable Stalin-
ist credentials, an appalling array of A's, even though she was the
youngest member in the Graduate School, and a glittering ass, really
beautiful, a marvelous complex of lavish curves and subtle redundan-
cies, at one moment as soft as a baby's breath and at another as
authoritative as a pipe vise.

On the evening of my first enactment of the death of my father, I
had scarcely sat down before she came to my side, attracted, no doubt,
by the authenticity, the mystery, and the challenge of it all. There was
authenticity in that I really was that creature she had only read about
or seen photographs of; mystery in that from such unpromising beginnings I knew so much Latin and made grades almost as awe-inspiring
as her own; and challenge in that my total lack of political awareness
would test the undaunted mettle of her precocious dialectic. There
was, too, I imagine, some simple female curiosity as to what the Son
of Old Buck—as I had fondly termed my father in my little interlude
—would be like in the clutch.

Thus, all things worked together for the good of Old Buck's Boy
and his social, sexual, and political improvement, and it may even be
said that in the midst of all the confusions of history, the tangle of
dialectic, simple lusts and strong egos, love may have begun to bloom.
But by that evening in the spring of 1941 of which we speak, Dauphine
had so honed Old Buck's Boy's political awareness that he was finding
something peculiar in her international switcheroo and her passionate
defense of Adolf Hitler's virtues and the beauty of his friendship with
Stalin, and on more than one private occasion he had hinted broadly
at her inconsistencies. In other words, the ground was already prepared for a crisis. So when Dauphine, in a sudden access of bourgeois
superiority, took him to task for what she described as his bad manners, and added that he was nothing but a redneck Southern fascist,
he was ready to pour the gravy over his own already cooked goose.
In fact, as far as he could determine, he retorted, he was not the fascist
Hitler-lover in the household, and for a Chicago Jewess, no matter

how rich or insulated from reality and logic, to take up with that cruddy little house painter–turned–mass murderer smacked of a deficiency of racial self-respect.

Dauphine burst into tears and slapped him, and he was really out. For weeks he thought his heart would break. But both logic and pride forbade apology. His only satisfaction was that Dauphine looked very pale and unhappy and began to suffer from sagging grades as well as bust, and was much alone. "Oh, why? Oh, why?" he would wake at night, crying out.

.   .   .

If, in the scene in the schoolyard, I had discovered my hatred of my father, I did not divest myself of such hatred that evening in Chicago when I refused to enact his death for a group of half-drunk but socially conscious graduate students. My feelings about my father were certainly too deeply ingrained, having been, I should add here, so case-hardened for some years after the original scene in the schoolyard by various similar episodes that the full enactment was never required. The first gesture was enough, and the fight would be on.

I had early given up tears for blows, and all an older boy now had to do was to flatter or bully some younger one into making the significant gesture in my presence, and then, at the rallying cry of the schoolyard, "Fight! Fight!" all would gather to enjoy the fun.

As I began to get my growth, however, the dreary routine tapered off, and the last fight was in my freshman year in high school. That time it was the gym teacher (lately a guard on a not very distinguished eleven fielded by the Alabama Institute of Technology), who, apparently liking the way I handled myself, persuaded me to try out for football. Later, it was on a football scholarship that I went to college, but I suppose I would have managed to go anyway, someway.

For by that time I had developed a passion for study. Not a day passed when my mother did not tell me that if I didn't study I'd be stuck for life in what she called "this here durn hellhole," usually adding that if Buck Tewksbury hadn't come along wearing his durn new yellow cowhide boots and with his tomfool self stuck atop a piebald mare and showing all those white teeth he was so durn proud of through those black mustaches, one day when she was walking home from school, she might of finished and made something of herself and got a long way past Dugton, but even if now she was stuck here for life and knew it, she didn't want me to be.

"Dugton," she would say, with a tight, quick shudder of revulsion. She had been to Atlanta once. "Pa took me," she would say. "I was little then, but I got it stuck in my head and recollection."

All in all, it was the shudder, not the words, that did it. Bit by bit, she bleached all reality from Dugton. It was a valley of humiliation and delusive vanities, through which I was to pass on my way to revelation. "Dugton," she would say, shuddering, "do you know how it come to be?" I'd shake my head, and she would give a new version. "One time there was a pigeon big as the Rocky Mountain and he had stuffed his-self on all the pokeberries and cow patties this side of Pikes Peak and the bowel movement hit him about this part of Alabama and they named it Dugton." It was my mother, I am sure, who, day by day, expunged all possibility of any memory of Dugton, who accounted for the fact that for years I could not even remember the life there. It was, too, as a corollary of this, and not by her specific exhortation, that I came to the passion for study.

A Latin book brought it to focus. On our street there was, when I was in the seventh grade, a freshman in high school who was friendly to me, at least when nothing more suitable for his attentions appeared. One afternoon on the way home from school he stopped by my house. I picked up one of his books and opened it. I saw the strange words. They were in what looked like sentences, but made no sense.

"What's this?" I asked.

"Latin," he said, suddenly swollen with information. "What the Romins talked."

"But it don't make any sense," I objected.

"Id-jit," he said, and seized the book, "look a-here!" And he turned a page and showed a column of the words the Romans talked with, opposite each, an English one. "See," he said, "it's like a puzzle, you got to match it up."

I kept staring at the book. "How do you say that?" I demanded, my finger on a word.

"*Agri-cola,*" he replied contemptuously. "Can't you tell by looken? Like Coca-Cola." Then he added: "It means farmer."

"Yeah," I said, bemused. "I see him."

There was a picture of him there, but not like any farmer I had ever seen—wearing sandals and a sort of skirt no farmer in Claxford County would have been caught dead in, and hanging on to what was a strange sort of plow. The plow, I saw, was named *aratrum*.

"Can I borry the book?" I asked.

"I got to study," the boy said, gone greasy with virtue.

"When you ain't studyen," I said.

He inspected me carefully, my hand that clutched the book, my face. His own face slowly assumed a deep, veiled, crafty look. "You got a nickel?" he asked innocently. He knew I had a job helping four afternoons a week at a grocery store.

I nodded.

"You kin have it till Monday," he said. "I already done my lesson for Monday."

So it cost me a nickel every weekend all that year.

For the life of me, I would not have been able to say what drew me on, weekend after weekend, poring over the book, copying out what I meant to learn during the week to come. There was a blind need, that was all. I was hungry and I ate.

Now, however, as I look back, I think I understand things better. It was not hunger, it was magic. It was as deep, as primitive, and as subtle as that. In Claxford County, reality, as I have said, had been bleached away. But if you found a new name for a thing, it became real. That was the magic of the name. And if you found the names for all the things of a world, you could create a world that was real and different. The crazy word on the page was like a little hole in a great wall. You could peek through the hole and see a world where everything was different and bright. That world, I realized with a strange numbness of awe, was not far away. It was just on the other side of a wall.

By the time I got out of high school I had read a lot more than the parts of the *Gallic Wars,* the *Aeneid,* and Cicero's *Orations* that were laid out in Dugton High but never got finished. My reading was due to old Miss McClatty. By Christmas of my first year she got me in Caesar; then on past the *Aeneid* to more Virgil, then lots of Horace, Catullus, Tacitus, and Sallust, not to mention lots of Cicero. "I don't know whatever's come over you, boy," Miss McClatty would say, and shake her old wobbly head. "It'll make work for me, but I won't stand in your way. I'll be honest with you, I've sort of forgot some things, not having any need here in Dugton, but I'll study up as best I can."

So we sat side by side at her desk when she kept study hall, our heads bent over the book, talking low, or we sat in the dreary teachers' lounge in her off-hour, and when she didn't know something and caught herself in a mistake, her thin old parchment cheeks would flush with shame and her finger pointing at something on the page would shake, and looking at me, she would whisper sadly, ferociously, "I told you I'm not right fresh, I just do the best I can." The steam would rustle in the radiators and, if it was in the study hall, pupils would be cutting up, with no fear, in the back of the room.

Miss McClatty had been a student, a thousand years before, at the University of Alabama, majoring in Latin. She had made all A's in it, too. I know, because the last day we ever had a session, just before I graduated, she seemed to brace herself or something, then jerked open her old briefcase and pulled out a manila folder all faded and crackling with age, and opened it out on the desk. There were the quiz papers, the examination papers, and the essays, ink fading away to leave only the spectral calligraphy on the yellowing sheets, and there in a corner would be, in pencil, once blue or red but now gone spectral too, the inevitable A.

She poked at the papers with a forefinger, tentatively, as though exploring some unidentifiable and perhaps unsavory mess. "Long back—" she began, and stopped. Then resumed, with more resolution: "Long back I loved it, Latin, I mean. It sort of—"

She stopped. Tried again: "It sort of took you out of yourself," she declared. "If you know what I mean."

Classes were over, that last day. Somebody came back into the study hall for a forgotten book. The sunlight was bright outside the windows. Boys were yelling out in the yard on their way to baseball practice. Somewhere, far off, a girl was laughing.

After a time, Miss McClatty said, off into the air: "It never came to anything much. But I'm not sorry!" she cried in sudden rapture and ferocity. "I'm really not. I'm glad I did it." She fixed me with her old, pale, bleared-blue eyes, behind the trembling bifocal pince-nez. "I'm glad I did it again, now. These days with you. Even if I forgot so much."

The eyes were no longer glaring at me in their mystic rage. Behind the bifocals, they were sad and beseeching. She was saying: "But I remembered a lot, didn't I?"

"You remembered everything," I affirmed stoutly.

.   .   .

Poor Old Miss Mary McClatty, with her long, thin fleshless legs in twisted white cotton stockings and very high black kid shoes laced up tight—and her long, thin bones, brittle as old spaghetti, shrouded in a white shirtwaist and a long, shiny black serge skirt even originally beyond all fashion, the whole of it topped by the little thin head that always seemed to be trembling, like an aspen on a still day. Sometimes you thought the trembling might shake off the pince-nez—and sometimes it did. The hair on her head was so thin you could see the scalp, and sometimes you thought the scalp was the skull itself, just the old bone with the skin gone but the hair still patchily grabbling on.

All those hours, all those years, Miss McClatty and I seem to be sitting there side by side. Her forefinger shakily indicated the word on the page. I see my own hand on the desk, the broken fingernails, often not cleaned, and the angry hangnail, bitten and not yet healed. I hear, now, the click of dentures in her old mouth, and the hiss of breath through them. I hear the dry, rustling sound of digestion going on in her poor old innards, and catch, perhaps, a faint whiff of the consequence.

We lean over the book together, two deprived ones, two crippled ones, two wanderers in a world of shadows, each trying to set eye to a mystic peephole that may give on a bright reality beyond.

Goodbye, goodbye, Miss Mary McClatty with all your A's.

I never even came to your funeral.

.   .   .

Latin: it brings up Rozelle. The first class I ever had in the Dugton High School, the first Monday, was Latin—and it was, too, the first class I ever had with Rozelle Hardcastle.

We had, naturally, been in the same grade school, there being no other school—for white folks, that is—but she had been a year behind me, just another little girl, eleven or twelve years old as far as I could tell. Which goes to prove that what I could tell was nothing. It meant nothing to me, for instance, when she walked down the hall with her books. I see the main book as the geography, for it had the biggest surface, and was the one closest to her body, pressed tight by her forearms against the place where the breasts would be but were not yet—not even the first sore, little tender-touch buds. She walked with her head slightly bowed, like a good little convent girl, as I would put it now, and the already incredible eyelashes portcullis-ing against the world the lowered eyes, which I did not yet know were of an incredible amethystine light, the color shading from the brightness of sunlit water to an undertint of blue-gray, as when the summer clouds gather above the cliff but the rain has not yet begun.

But in that earliest time, when she passed down the hall, if there were some boys shoving and horsing around—even little not-yet-sexed ones of the sixth or seventh grade—they might stop as suddenly as chicks in a chicken run when the hawk-shadow sweeps across the sky. It was only a little girl passing down the hall, with eyes more downcast than others. The boys hadn't, in fact, even looked at her. They merely felt, for the instant before they resumed their squealing horseplay, the mysterious power of her passage.

But I hadn't felt it. And was not to feel it until high school was over.

By this I do not mean merely sexual attraction. I do not mean the iron automatism of a fixed sexual habit. I do not mean whatever is meant by falling in love. You know about these things as most people do. These things exist in the context of life, and of the world, as we know it. What I mean has no context, it is, in its absoluteness, its own context, the very world in which it exists in its self-fulfilling surge.

Have you ever wandered out too far when the surf is heavy after a storm, and the great breaker booms in at you, heaving above you its tons of slick-sliding mottle of green-gray marble, icy but molten, for that is what it looks like, with its spume-fringe lashing high against the bright blue of sky? The mass towers and teeters against the sky, directly above you. You know that if it catches you in its fall, it will break your back.

But dive under it. Pierce it. Enter it at its depth. Slide slick into its innermost quivering gloom. That is your only hope. Then you hear the crash of the murderous weight collapsing behind you. No, not sound exactly, a deep exacerbation of nerves followed by a silence, and in that silence you hear, now literally, the hollow, whispering grind of shingle beneath you in the deep scour of water.

That is like what I am talking about. If you have been through it, you will recognize it. If you haven't, you are, probably, lucky. You might not have survived to find yourself breathing painful air, cradled weak and slow for a moment in the slow wash of the following trough. As you lie there, after all the strain of holding your breath so long in the depth of the breaker, the sun, swinging high above you, looks black to your eyes.

What I am talking about is Rozelle Hardcastle.

. . .

In those first weeks in the freshman Latin class, Rozelle was clearly the star, as she must have always been, I suppose, just having skipped a grade into high school and caught up with me. Then after six weeks or so, all my unofficial early studying began to pay off, and I was a star too, and I'd catch her looking at me in class in a hard, slow, wondering way, her eyelids lowered a little to shadow the amethystine glance, and I remember how, as she studied me across the distance of desk tops, her full, but not too full, pink-damp lower lip would be drawn slowly up over her lower teeth, then drawn back to tighten, and the upper teeth, glittering white and perfectly formed, would be set precisely and sharply into the tender flesh. It must have been hard enough to hurt, almost.

Anyway, by Christmas I was promoted clear out of the class. Miss McClatty had got it out of me that in my blundering, confused way, I had long since done the *First Year Book* and Caesar on the sly. So now Rozelle was left alone to be the star of her own little first-year Latin class, to her heart's content.

Rozelle was born to be a star, in more ways than one. By the time she was in junior year, she was clearly the Beauty Queen of Dugton High, playing the role with a modesty that was really a contemptuous ease, as though she knew that her being first in this Iberian village was nothing in comparison to what awaited her in Rome. She moved sedately down the hall, always with some girl by her side, for she always had some official lady-in-waiting, devoted, intelligent, and not especially well-favored, who basked in the radiance of Rozelle and had the crumbs that dropped from her table—that is, the company of one of the boys in the entourage, it being well-established that if you weren't nice to the "best friend" you had no place in the entourage.

So Rozelle, with the best friend, each with an arm about the other's waist, their heads bowed together in a slow, intimate discourse, moved down the hall, and the boys free for the duty moved in a sort of shoal on either flank and behind, quiet, reverential, bewitched in humble joy, bathed in the transfiguring glow she shed. Any one of them knew that he would never bury his face in the perfume of that lustrous chestnut hair with the overglow and streaks of sun-bleached gold, hair that lay evenly on each side of the straight, pure brow. That he would never, not even for a moment, cup a hand over one of those ripening but delicately molded breasts even though, when he danced with her, one of them might fleetingly brush him, giving a sudden, sickening sense of nakedness, as though a bare nipple had flickeringly penciled a too quickly broken line across his unfended hide. That he would never kiss those lips.

I can now realize, even if I scarcely knew her, that she was remarkable; and sixteen years later, she was, in fact, more remarkable. That silken hair, with the golden sun-streaks, had not changed, and she had not changed the way of wearing it, parted in the middle to define the perfect brow, and brought almost severely down; but for all this severity, you always saw, on second glance, the little wisps and tendrils curling dewily, from some secret exhalation of the fine-grained flesh, on each side of the brow and at the temples—dewily, coolly, but with some faint hint of a dampness of flesh that might not always be thus dewy and cool, but hot and musky, and a strand of that hair might be wetly plastered, darker for the wetness, flat across a flushed cheek.

Sixteen years later, Rozelle kept the talent for long silences, sitting withdrawn or leaning her head to the words of some single person, inviting, as it were, by silence and posture, a sinking of the speaker's voice into seriousness, even secrecy. She yet had the talent for lowering the eyelids as though to give full value to the modeling of the deep-set eyes and to the spectacular lashes. But the eyes—when she lifted the lids to release the full gleam—always came as surprisingly as joy, or a blow.

Looking back, I should say that the power Rozelle exercised arose from the troubling doubleness which I find I have been unconsciously trying to indicate—on the one hand, the pure brow, the hair drawn severely down, the lowered eyes, the gift of stillness, of loneliness even; and on the other, the vision evoked by the small dewy tendrils at the temples and the unheralded unveiling of the naked glance. Allowing for differences in place and period and that between painted canvas and warm flesh, she exercised something like the effect that the portrait supposedly of Beatrice Cenci and once attributed to Guido Reni —a sick mixture of Counter Reformation religiosity and the hint of goings-on in incestuous sheets—exercised on the Salem-bred gonads of Nathaniel Hawthorne.

Even though my gonads were strictly Claxford County.

.   .   .

I get ahead of myself. Back in Dugton, Rozelle was definitely not for me. Nothing in Dugton was for me. "Ain't nothing here for you," my mother would say. "Yores is waiting for you, somewheres."

Whatever the "yores" might be.

And: "You git stuck here, and I'll kill ye."

Rozelle was not for me, not even in my straining dreams. What was for me was the electric bulb that blazed above my head late at night, the open book on the table, the rough companionship of practice field and locker room (though after the season was over I never passed a word with most of the teammates), the cheers if I happened to complete the pass or make the tackle (but even the cheers always seemed to come faint and tinged with irony), the click and hiss of Miss McClatty's dentures, and the embraces of the little Negro girls whose favors I was introduced to by some of my older and tougher teammates (this when I was sixteen) and enjoyed at the price of twenty-five cents a throw, but with quarters hard to come by in Dugton.

Rozelle was, however, for nobody in Dugton. She was definitely what was called a "good girl," but even the most lumpish brute of the

Dugton High Wildcats—that being the totem animal of the football team—might find himself leaving some talented little tit-pusher and spit-swapper who, in the local lingo, was reputed to "go it dry," or even to "go all the way," for the privilege of walking down the street, merely a nameless one of the group, on the perimeter of the troubling and chastening glow shed by Rozelle Hardcastle.

People said that Mrs. Hardcastle was saving Rozelle for Chester Burton. This was usually said without humor or cynicism. There is no reason to be humorous or cynical about a law of nature, and the particular law of nature here in question is that the richest boy in town gets the prettiest girl.

The law seemed to be operating with Chester and Rozelle, even if she was not quite of his social bracket. Her mother had made the mistake of eloping at a tender age with a young man who had no future, but did have the tact, first, when the only job he could get was as brakeman on the Southern Railroad, to live in another town, where, promptly, she died, leaving the infant Rozelle. The bereaved widower, after turning over the infant to his sister-in-law, had the additional tact to get himself killed off in the line of duty.

Rozelle's aunt, who took her over, was married to the local doctor of Dugton, and lived in one of the nice houses, with, naturally, a sprinkler on the lawn, and so Rozelle had a toehold in Dugton society; and, of course, her looks. To back up the line, she had her ugly aunt's stored-up spite, social condition, childlessness, time-tested wisdom and iron will. As for wisdom, the aunt knew how little place love has in marriage. As for will, it was not iron, it was tungsten steel.

Luck played a part, too. The local Hardcastle kin had all died off or moved away, and so the name was not an ever-present reproach on the social scene. The brakeman was forgotten, almost. In any case, by the time Rozelle was a junior and precociously sixteen years old, Chester Burton, whose family had the only thing in the county that might be remotely termed a plantation and owned most of the stock in the Dugton Bank, was taking her to movies and was her regular escort to parties in the nice houses into which I never got asked.

In fact, I was never asked into any house in Dugton, nice or not.

.   .   .

33

I remember precisely the first time Rozelle ever directly spoke to me—except for the greeting of the sort she always gave everybody, no exceptions, not even me, like old John D. Rockefeller giving away dimes. It was the next to the last Friday in May, 1935, the last week in May being examination week, and both of us due to graduate the week after that, she then seventeen and I just turned eighteen. I could work out the exact date, but it scarcely seems important. I do, however, remember the time, give or take a few minutes, for I had just been doing my very last Latin session with Miss McClatty (the occasion on which she produced all her old examinations and papers), and this would have been about five o'clock in the afternoon. When I came out of the study hall door, there stood Rozelle.

I mumbled a hello, and started to pass. I had, indeed, passed when I heard her voice, not loud, unnaturally low, as a matter of fact, for the big hall and the space between us, say, "Jed." This was a syllable she certainly had never before in her life uttered, at least not in my hearing. But now, in that low-pitched voice edged faintly with a vibrant huskiness, it came charged with deep and secret urgencies.

When I turned to her, my face must have been idiotically gaping. I see the scene as though I am completely outside it. There stands the youth, well over six feet, unbarbered and with unruly dark hair, arms looking gangly because of length and the bigness of the hands hanging irrelevantly down (one clutching a book that in that hand seems trivial), wearing a soiled white shirt with collar open (one of the white shirts his mother always made him wear to school and washed and ironed, at night, three times a week), long legs in blue jeans (this almost two generations and three wars before the garment became the mark of fashion and not of penury), feet in brogans.

The girl—of medium height or a little less—is wearing a peppermint-stripe, sleeveless, cotton summer dress, with a red leather belt and the skirt full and well below the knees in the fashion of the period, bare legs slickly tanned, rising from feet in white, low-heeled, backless slippers. She moves two slow soundless steps toward the youth. Her bare, tanned arms hang down close to her sides, not so much in laxness as in infinite calm. Her face, with the eyes innocently wide, is lifted toward his height, with a look of calmness and trust, like water under a late sky when not a breath is stirring. She seems to be carrying that calm face toward him, like a present. She stops, not very close to him.

She looks up at him for a moment, then, with that hint of confidingness, says, "You're sure a hard sort of fellow to catch."

And adds: "To talk to, I mean."

The tall youth moves a brogan on the black-oiled boards, with a faint scraping sound. His tongue comes out to lick his lips. But he does not manage to speak.

"Two weeks," the musical voice, overlaid with the husky whisperiness, says, "I've been trying to catch you. But see—" She stops, the eyes brightening, the face smiling in a childlike roguishness. "See," she says, "I've outsmarted you. I laid out for you. I'm bushwhacking you right now."

"Yeah," the youth finally manages to say.

"Yeah," she mimics. "Just to ask you a question. Are you going to the Prom?"

The tongue comes out again on the rather coarse and heavy, somewhat parched-looking lower lip of the youth's mouth. He finally says: "No."

"Oh, yes you are!" the girl contradicts him, her face now all aglitter with positive wickedness. "And the joke's on you, because—" She pauses, breaks into a rippling run of laughter, eyes dancing. "Because," she says in miraculous gravity, "you're going to carry me."

"I can't dance," he says.

"I bet you can," the girl says.

She seems closer, but you cannot tell that she has actually moved. Perhaps she has only lifted her face just a fraction more up to him—infinitesimally, but enough to bring her breasts just that little bit farther upward and forward. Perhaps the red-and-white peppermint-striped cloth is now just a little tighter over them.

"I bet you can dance and just don't know it," she is saying. "Dance better than these knock-kneed bums that think they're so hot. Anyway—I could teach you in no time. We'll go to Abby's house—nobody's there in the afternoon to bother us, and put a record on the Victrola, and we'll—"

She stops. She sees that his face is darkening. She hears his breath. He says: "No."

"But," she objects, "school's about—"

"School," he echoes in massive contempt. "I got to *work.*"

The girl's body goes slack. The force that has sustained her is withdrawn.

But, all at once, she lifts her head, in new courage, looking him straight in the eye. "Listen," she says, "I couldn't care less about that old Prom. Let's have a date anyway. We can go to the movies. We can drive round a little—"

"I haven't got any car," the youth says, in a ferocity like pride.

"Hush," she says, "hush." The words rush on: "I'll get my aunt's or one of Uncle George's, he has two. I'll try to get the convertible, and we'll just drop by the Prom a second, just sit out in the car and listen to the music a little, then drive out to Glendora Falls and watch the water coming down and then—"

She stops herself. "Listen," she says, starting over again, "here's graduation, you'll be going away for good—oh, I know you're the kind to do something grand, and here, I've never even talked to you —oh, I know I'm not smart enough for you and all that, but—"

She has kept her distance. But a hand floats toward him in the afternoon light, that is now fading in the dingy hall. The hand is about to touch him—on the arm, on the chest—and if it does he knows that he will jerk back—why, he doesn't know. But the hand stops in the air.

She does not come closer. The sad, humble, fatalistic innocence of her face is lifted toward him, the shadow now falling across it, deepening the color of the eyes. The youth looks down at the face. He looks at the hand poised in the air. It may touch him.

But it does not. It revolves slowly on the rounded wrist. At last supine, it exposes the palm, slightly cupped in its pitiful emptiness. All at once, the hand drops away, as though a cord has been cut. He stares at that motion.

"All right," he utters, in a grating, angry, despairing voice, "all right."

. . .

At 7:15 on the evening of the Prom, dressed in a too-short pair of blue serge pants and a white shirt with collar open but the sleeves down and buttoned to give a touch of formality, and two one-dollar bills in my pocket, ready for the first real date I had ever had, I stood on the cracked cement on the sidewalk of Jonquil Street, in front of my house, waiting for Rozelle—who had not even known that there was a Jonquil Street until I told her how to get there. She had offered to pick me up (I had to work that afternoon at the sawmill), but now I'm inclined to think that, simply, she had not wanted me to come to her house and that she probably had lied to her aunt about the nature of the date.

In any case, I was waiting there on the first evening of summer. At that moment of the season, there is, as evening draws on, no hint of the days of full summer so soon to come, when the Alabama sun sinks squatly toward the horizon, red as molten iron and bulging heavily to one side, and the air has a dusty, sulfurous taste.

But in that region, there is always, just as summer starts, one evening when the light is pure and steady, and the outlines of every-thing, the leaf hanging on the maple tree, the angle of a chimney, the outthrust head and beak of the plunging swallow in saffron light—when everything stands sharp and clear as a revelation, for, in fact, the light seems not to be coming from some distant source but to be calmly unfolding, diffused from the earth itself.

If you shut your eyes, you can taste the air sweet on your lips.

That was the sort of evening it was, as I stood there and did not know the reason for the dry, grinding sensation that was in me.

The car came lounging down the street. It was a big pale blue Chrysler convertible, and it looked very strange on Jonquil Street. On a street in real Nigger Town it would not have looked strange, for some lady might be having to take her cook home. But there were no Negroes on our block on Jonquil, just the next block. So, looking strange, the Chrysler drew toward me, its weight crunching the street slow and steady. It stopped.

Rozelle was on my side, leaning a little, for the convertible top was not back, looking up at me, smiling. "Hi," she said.

"Hello," I said, and started around to the other side.

"No," she said, "you drive." She was already sliding to the other side of the seat.

"See here—" I began.

"Oh, hush," she commanded, lying far over on the seat toward me, smiling up at me.

"But I never drove one like this," I said.

"Hush," she said, "and get in. Ten seconds and you'll be driving it fine. They're all alike—really."

I got in. She told me what to do. I did it, let the clutch out slow, and felt the car effortlessly slip forward. But I stopped. "That house, right there," I said, pointing, "that's where I live."

She was leaning over to look. "It's right pretty," she said.

She kept her eyes on the house, not dutifully, not perfunctorily, all with perfect naturalness. And she had said what she said with perfect naturalness. These factors taken together were what, I presume, made me do it.

"It's pretty," I said, "like—like horse manure."

She was looking at me with a small smile, sweet and a little sorrowful. "That isn't," she said, quite calmly, "the best way to start a nice evening. And—" she paused, then went on: "I've been looking forward to it so."

"I'm sorry," I said, not feeling sorry, feeling something dry and gritty in my chest.

"I wish you'd have asked me in," she said. "To meet your mother."

"She's back washing dishes and mopping up the kitchen floor," I said. "This late, for she was out working today. Saturday or not. It's rush season. At the cannery, I mean. She works at the cannery." I turned full on her. "But you knew that, didn't you?"

"No," she said.

"Well, you know it now," I said, and let the car jerk forward to pull down Jonquil Street with the smell of burning rubber.

We didn't say a word all the way to the movie, which was *It Happened One Night,* with Clark Gable and a woman named Claudette Colbert.

As we walked down the half-block to the theater, after parking the car, I noticed that Rozelle's dress didn't look like something she'd wear to a dance—just a sort of straight up-and-down dress, of what looked like linen, lightish blue, with no sleeves and a white belt. I felt relieved at that, I suppose.

We got out at 9:15 and went for an ice-cream soda at the drugstore.

38

Next we went out to listen to the music, just a little while she said, before going to look at the falls. As we entered the parking lot of the gymnasium, where the Prom was, she said, "Look, there's a good place down by that tree." So we parked under the tree.

There were other places available, however.

.   .   .

We sat there without a word passing between us. I couldn't think of anything to say, and so pretended to be deeply engrossed in the music that wafted out from the gym. "Night and Day" I guess it was, but I could not have cared less. Rozelle, however, seemed wrapped up in the music—so convincingly that I gave a real start when she said: "Do you like your mother?"

For a long instant, I couldn't answer. There was nothing to answer. Literally, the question had never proposed itself to me. My mother was who she was, did the things she did, said the things she said. We were in the house together, as by a fate inscribed in the stars, and that was it.

Finally, I said: "Yeah—yeah, I reckon." And added weakly: "She can make some pretty good jokes sometimes."

Rozelle seemed to sink into the music again, more deeply now, her head lowered and canted a little to one side in the classic posture of critical intentness. For a time, she said nothing.

Then: "I might like a mother—if I had one. But I hate my aunt." She paused a moment. "Maybe I ought to thank God I don't have any mother. It must be awful to have to hate your mother."

That seemed to require no response. Each of us sank into his own silent distance. After a time, the faintest breeze stirred. Then the air fell still again.

The music was now, in irrelevant anguish, proclaiming "Smoke Gets in Your Eyes."

"I've got to ask you something," Rozelle's voice said, coming across the music, from her side of the shadowed seat.

"All right," I said.

"It's a favor," she said.

"All right."

"You don't have to do it," she said.

"Do what?"

She didn't answer. It was as though she had forgotten what we had been talking about, or even forgotten that I was there. Finally she spoke, from her shadow. "It's four years now I've been watching." She paused, resumed: "You aren't like the others. You don't care about the same things. You've got your mind somewhere else. Far off. You walk past things, and don't care."

She stopped, then demanded, across the distance: "Isn't that true?"

"How the hell do I know?" I said, and knew my voice harsh from a great gravelly but fluid something, like phlegm, that seemed to be flooding my chest.

"What makes you always so angry?" she said, in a kind of slow sadness.

"I'm not."

"Like now," she said. "This very minute. Oh, I've been watching you. All these years. In football, when the play is near the sidelines and I can see your face, before the play starts, and they are counting and you are back there waiting—I've seen your face. And sometimes when you're just sitting in study hall, it begins to happen, whatever it is, that look coming on your face."

The swelling in my chest made it hard to breathe. Blood was beating in my temples, too. But at the same time, I felt a sort of panic, a grip of nausea in my guts. Suddenly, secret eyes were all around me, spying.

"That look," she was saying, "it scares me."

I felt the blood in my temples. "Well, don't look," I said.

But she wasn't even noticing me. She had let herself fall back against the big luxurious seat, the bare arms lying lax by her sides, her head falling back on the leather as though tired, far away over there. Moonlight was flooding the parking lot, and all the world beyond, but we were in the shadow of the tree. In the double shadowiness of the car, the convertible top being in place, and against the dark leather of the seat, her face was a scarcely defined patch of paleness.

"The favor," she said at last, not as a question or request, not even a statement, just putting the word out to hang in the air, not even stirring.

"Yes?"

"Kiss me," she said.

"Kiss you!" Nothing could have surprised me more.

"Just once," she said, from her husky, whispery distance, not looking at me. "Just once—but long, slow, and gentle."

I didn't say anything. Different things were going on inside me, but I didn't know what they meant.

"Just once," she said. "That's all. So I'll know."

"Know what?"

"What you are," she said. "For when you're gone. So I can shut my eyes and know that much—anyway."

I couldn't say anything.

"It's so little," she said. "For you, I mean. And a lot for me."

The music had stopped. I could hear her breathing.

"Oh, Jed," she said, over there.

If she hadn't pronounced my name. But she did. There was the sense of my name in her mouth—I can only describe what happened as a physical awareness of that fact, my name in contact, literally, with the softness, the dark, warm, sweet dampness of tissue. And I found myself blundering over the gearshift, not in haste, not lunging; slow, rather, and trying to be methodical, but with the blood beating in my temples, like a savage migraine.

I did not seize her. Did not even lay finger to her. I finally managed to swing over, and braced my left hand scrupulously beyond her, lifted myself with my right hand now braced, and set my lips to hers.

In that instant, in contrast to all the to-do of our conversation, and the deep disturbance of my being, it was comically meaningless. I was aware of the cool, minutely scaling dryness of her lips, as though lipstick were infinitesimally flaking off, then of a faint taste rather like cinnamon.

Was this what all her hullabaloo was about?

What changed things was that the lips beneath my own parted, if only the slightest, with an inaudible little gasp that I felt rather than heard. I felt the exhalation flicker lightly on my own lips.

The kiss, according to specifications, was long, slow, and gentle, certainly not passionate. When I had withdrawn my lips and was sitting beside her, there was no contact between us. We were not looking at each other, but straight ahead, out into the moon-bright

---

41

parking lot. After a little she reached over, found my right hand, lifted it and leaned over to lay her cheek against the back, her face averted from me.

Later came the wetness of tears.

"What's the matter?" I demanded of the back of the head bowed humbly, with cheek against the back of my hand.

Not lifting her head, her voice muffled down there in the deeper shadows, she said: "You don't know anything about girls, do you?"

"No," I said, and wanted to be angry, but my voice didn't come out that way.

Clearly, I didn't know anything about myself, either. Something was happening to me. I had not progressed far enough in my literary studies to know that Helen, as Faustus puts it in Marlowe's play, had made me immortal with a kiss.

But in a way different from that described by Faustus. "Thy lips suck forth my soul," he cried out to Helen. "See, there it flies!" Rozelle's lips, however, did not suck forth my soul. Instead, she breathed one into me, and I now sat there feeling, knowing—even seeing—how a tiny point of light in the dry, roiling darkness of my being was glowing stronger, slowly expanding the bright globe of which it was the center and which was, I slowly and incredulously realized, peace.

Benumbed in the glowing beatitude. I was thinking the one word: *love.* It hung there steady in my mind. This must be what it was, I thought, sunk into myself, marveling. But another thought came: to have love, to feel like this, you had to love somebody.

So I found my head turning slowly, unwillingly, almost painfully, toward the girl leaning down beside me, whose face was averted from me and whose cheek, for reasons I could not fathom, was wet against the back of my right hand.

My left hand was reaching across my body, which was turning slowly and carefully, as though not to upset a precarious equilibrium. I realized, as the hand moved slowly to touch the bowed head, that I was holding my breath. I wanted to lay my free hand on that bowed head. In benediction. In gratitude. Or something.

The hand never got there. By intention or not, the timing was perfect to thwart me.

For Rozelle had unexpectedly straightened up. She was drying her eyes. She was smoothing her hair. She was touching lipstick to her lips, then wiping them in the darkness. She took my hand again, was sliding over the seat, had opened the door, was drawing me, was stepping out of the car, was standing outside the car, firmly holding my hand—all before I could manage, "What?—what?"

"Let's just look in," she said. "Before we go."

"But that wasn't—" I began.

She was drawing me with her. "Oh, just one minute," she was saying, looking intently ahead.

I moved along beside her, still in a sort of daze. Her hand was not gripping mine, but was simply closed on it with a sense of certitude, a grasp cool, firm, impersonal. Fleetingly, I remembered how my mother's hand used to close on mine when I was little, and she would march me along.

We were inside the gym. The music was going, and they were dancing. I cannot remember what the music was—just the swirling bodies, the colored balloons and streamers hanging from the high ceiling, then Rozelle's body all at once against me, her face smiling up at me in what seemed perfect confidence and joy, saying, "Just once—just one minute—dance with me." Before I knew it, my arms were around her, my hand feeling the sweetness of the flow and play of her flesh on her bones as her body swayed, and how, with the grip of her right hand on my left, she undertook, with that and with her body against me, to secretly lead me in the dance.

I was lost in the flood of sensations.

But all at once I was aware of something else. The people nearest were looking at us. They were slowing in the dance to look at us. They were drawing back into a sort of semicircle (we were near the door) to watch us. Beyond them, other people were slowing, too. All their eyes were fixed on us.

For a frozen moment, I stood there, glaring back at the eyes. Then I flung from Rozelle, and was out the door. I heard, in the silence back in the building, the quick, sharp little detonations of her heels across the hardwood floor. As I strode away, her voice calling my name.

I heard her running behind me, felt her hand grip my arm. "Oh, Jed—Jed!" she cried out.

I halted and reached into my pocket. "Oh—the keys," I said, excessively polite.

"Jed," she said.

Tears were brimming in her eyes.

I flung the keys at her feet.

"Here's your fucking keys," I said.

This time she did not follow me.

CHAPTER III

On the first Saturday night in June, 1935, I was through with Dugton and Dugton was through with me. My body, indeed, lingered on there all summer, working in the sawmill for forty cents an hour and exercise, and performing other anatomical actions. But spiritually I had already passed on toward my unspecifiable destination.

What happened, a half-hour after I had flung the keys down at Rozelle's feet, was, I presume, predictable. At a poolroom down near the railroad depot, I found Mel Barkham, a halfback who, if he had ever graduated, would have done so a couple of years before. At the moment he was engaged in his Saturday night drinking and was into a fifth of redeye. Before this, I had never taken even one drink. Tail, yes, but no likker yet. In season I had trained seriously, and after season I had rarely seen my fellow teammates. But now I took a drink —in fact, several.

It was late by that time, but my old companion and earlier initiator into vice thought that he might be able to stir up one of them little girls that would do it for the traditional quarter. He knew which window she slept near in the family shack and nobody gave a damn anyway. He'd just throw a little gravel against the window.

She came crawling right out over that window sill like a little black chicken snake over a deadfall sapling. There was a shed back of the express office, where, according to Mel, they stored tarpaulins, and since he worked there, he had a key. When we came out of that shed door, the moon was westering low behind the coal chute, and there was, as Mel phrased it, shore-God one back-broke but rich little nigger gal.

I had started out that night with two dollars. I had spent the first dollar on a moving picture, two double ice-cream sodas, and the discovery of the nature of love. I had spent the second on poontang. My friend hadn't had but ninety cents, but on the fourth round the little poontang-peddler let him have a dime's worth of credit. I never heard whether she collected.

I remember that we drank some more, but I don't remember how I got home. I do remember lying on my bed, with my clothes on, staring up at the unshaded bulb blazing from the ceiling and laughing fit to kill. I kept on laughing while my mother, wearing some sort of loose white nightgown, barefoot and with her black hair flying loose around her active head, beat on my chest with both fists, which I didn't seem to feel. Nor did I feel it when she hit my face. But I do remember the blood running out of my nose and down my face. She had finally used a shoe, one of mine.

My nose never has been the same.

The next thing I remember, it was near noontime on Sunday. I came out of my bedroom, and stood with one hand on the jamb, not feeling very well. My mother was sitting there sewing. Methodically, she stuck her needle in the cloth, and looked up at me.

"Good morning," she said very calmly.

"Good morning," I said.

"You looked in the mirror yet?" she said.

I said no.

"Well, it'll skeer you," she said. "You look like a hog-killing, and the hog lost."

I made no reply. She studied me.

"I was just waiting here to say one thing," she said in her calmest voice. "Ain't never going to be no drunk come in my house agin. Not yore father, nor yore father's son, nor the Son of God, not even if He takes a notion. Not, and I keep my health."

She continued to regard me critically.

"You look more like him ever day," she observed. "Yore father, I mean," she added. "Not the Son of God."

She kept on looking at me, but what I was seeing was the body of Old Buck, face vomit-smeared and plowed into the stone hearth, with eyes closed and a rusty cavalry saber yet slackly clutched in one hand.

She was saying: "It's time you was out of this durn hellhole. It is time you was out."

.   .   .

I was, as I have said, already, in spirit, far beyond Dugton, and all that remained for me to do was to ship off, as soon as practical, the body too, as soon as it had lived through the summer. I already had my football scholarship at Blackwell College, and by September 12 had drawn my last pay at the sawmill, wrapped and mailed my Latin books to myself at Blackwell, and had my suitcase packed and ready to hit the road to hitch a ride. That night I was already in bed, with the light out, almost asleep, when my mother came in. She sat in a chair well back from the bed, in shadow, for the only light was from the door, which she had left slightly ajar.

After a while, she said, "I'm sorry I made your nose bleed, that night."

I said it was O.K.

"But I would agin," she said.

I told her I knew it.

She waited again, longer.

Then: "You ought never fooled with that girl."

I said, no, I hadn't ought to.

And I meant it. During the summer I had assembled enough data to construct a hypothesis to account for the events of that evening and for, to begin with, my having been invited in the first place.

It had been common knowledge that Chester Burton was going to the University of Alabama that fall, to take pre-law, and that Rozelle, our valedictorian, was to go there, too. But it seemed that Mrs. Burton had begun to have second thoughts about the defunct brakeman and related matters, and a change of plans had been developed. It was decided that Chester Darling would go to Princeton, an institution more suitable to his name and station, and more suitable, too, in that it was strictly non-coeducational. Furthermore, as a preliminary step in the broadening of Chester's horizons, he would be taken, by his mother, to Europe, immediately after graduation, for a leisurely summer-long tour.

At this point I lack a few hard facts. Did Chester know all the time about Princeton and Europe? Or did the parents simply work things out, letting him continue his relations with Rozelle, even making the expected date for the Prom, and then confront him with the *fait accompli?* In any case, it seemed clear that Rozelle herself did not know the truth until the very last minute, when, of course, she broke what was to have been the farewell high school date—no, the date that was to lay groundwork for all the lovely dates at the University of Alabama. Given this evidence, my hypothesis was that she had simply used me.

I was suitable for her purposes. For one thing, I had a certain prestige. I was, in a small-bore way, a football hero, and, to ironically salt that fact, I knew all that crazy Latin. For a second thing, I would certainly be an eye-catching surprise—who had never been to a dance, who, as she put it, had my mind somewhere else and just didn't give a damn and was, furthermore, suspected of seeking pleasure down behind the depot. For a third thing, even my lowly social condition could be exploited. Rozelle would not be content with some miserable second-best (she could, no doubt, have stolen a respectable date, even at the last minute). No, the princess would stoop to the peasant boy and lift him gloriously up to her side.

Rozelle and the peasant boy would tread but a measure at the crummy little Prom in that crummy little gymnasium, she not even bothering to put on a party dress, and then go contemptuously out into the night, and the great Chrysler would lounge luxuriously across the moonlit land, leaving Chester, who, with his thin shanks and little mouse-bulge of biceps, had always been easy to fend off, to wonder what his Rozelle might, in wet-lipped welcome, be now, at this moment, expecting in some shaded glen.

For the summer of 1935, what I had figured out was enough for me. So, that night in my bedroom, with my mother sitting there in shadow, I told her she was right, I ought never have fooled with Rozelle Hardcastle.

"I reckon I can figger out what goes on down back of the depot," she said. She paused, waiting over there in her shadow. "But one thing about a nigger. Maybe they ain't very clean, but they never expect nobody to marry 'em."

She continued to sit there, with no word. At the end she said: "You learn them books now. And remember what I'm here tellen you. For you, it's got to be, git what's to git, then git. Git on."

Then: "It ain't for you to lay by and linger."

With her characteristic impression of purposefulness and energy unleashed, she rose from the chair, and without a word walked out of the room, shutting the door decisively behind her.

I lay there in the dark, trying to think. Or not to think.

·   ·   ·

On awakening next morning, I found coffee on the back of the range and breakfast in the warmer. But my mother had already gone.

I have the memory that during the night she had come into the room and kissed me. If so, it was the first time in years she had done such a thing, but this would have been, after all, a goodbye. I have the distinct impression of a figure leaning over me, dark against a dim light beyond, and cool lips on my brow.

But it may have been a dream.

It may even have been a dream dreamed long years later.

But I cannot believe it only a dream.

·   ·   ·

As for Blackwell College, Alabama, all that now seems a scarcely more substantial dream. I now shut my eyes and try to see the old slate-roofed, red-brick buildings aesthetically redeemed only by decrepitude, the mellowing of the brick and the scraggle of vine, Virginia creeper, that would flame in autumn. The paths between the buildings are gravel, and the grass unmown. In the spring, a few starveling jonquils poke up among the old grass stalks, and wanly bloom. Along the paths I see my fellow students pass almost as spookily unreal in the scene now behind my closed eyelids as they ever were back in Alabama. I hear the drone of a voice leading prayer in the chapel, where we gathered every morning to ask for strength and divine guidance.

That is all. All, that is, except the Greek.

Blackwell was an old-fashioned church college dwindling on into the age of atheism and the internal combustion engine, and one of its traditional functions was to prepare aspiring ministers for the seminary, which stood across the street. This meant that Greek had to be taught, and when I first laid eyes on the chicken-track characters of that alphabet, I knew I had found a magic more potent than the codes of all astrologers or coven masters.

Greek is the only thing I remember of Blackwell College—that and a professor named Pillsbun, who had once spent a summer in graduate study at the University of Chicago (working toward a doctorate that he never finished, not even at the University of Alabama) and who told me that I ought to go to Chicago and study under Dr. Heinrich Stahlmann. Dr. Stahlmann was great, he said; he, Mr. Pillsbun, had had his life changed by studying with him. He had taken Dr. Stahlmann's seminar in the Theory of the Epic. "Yes," he repeated, "the epic"—for emphasis nodding his hairless, pink-skinned balloon head on what would have been his neck if there had been one between the perfectly round hairless bulb of a head and the perfectly round body that you knew was, evenly all over, hairless and of the same baby pink.

For reasons that will later emerge, Mr. Pillsbun always wore, winter and Alabama summer, a suit of pepper-and-salt Irish tweed, with a dark red bow tie which must have been attached to his chest, there being, as I have said, no visible neck, and on the almost nonexistent bridge of the pink bulb of a nose there precariously rode a pair of pince-nez, with tortoise-shell rims and a black ribbon anchored to a clip on his lapel. It was his habit, when he wished to stress a point, to remove the glasses, hold them by one end, shaking them in a threatening fashion, and fix his gaze firmly on the auditor. The trouble was that the gaze was pale and watery.

So I wrote to Chicago for admission to the Graduate School. They regretted that my application had to be rejected. "There must be some mistake," Mr. Pillsbun said. "You have done some advanced study in Latin and Greek, your marks in French and German are excellent, and—" he here removed the glasses, shook them at me in dire menace "—I have written you a very strong recommendation. I propose to write directly to the Dean of the Graduate School and clear the matter up."

With that comforting thought, I settled down for the summer in the town of Blackwell, in my accustomed summer job with the State Highway Department, in construction. Only two events of any consequence occurred that summer.

The first: In late June, I decided to go to cast a last look over Dugton and see my mother. There was a foul-up with my ride, and I did not hit town until three o'clock in the morning on Sunday. At the house on Jonquil Street I saw a faint light burning in the back, not surprised because in the old days it had been my mother's custom, when alone at night, to leave a light on in the kitchen. I went to the back, planning to slip in, leave my gear in full sight to notify her that I was there, and go to my old room and sack up for a long one.

I tiptoed onto the back porch and, with my old key, let myself into the kitchen. I had set my knapsack on a chair before I turned and saw *it.*

Over to one side from the range, on the table where we used to eat, stood what was clearly a half-empty bottle of whiskey. I approached the object. There were, on the table, two glasses, empty. I picked up one of them and smelled it. It had not been empty all night. I picked up the other. I stepped across to the little wall bulb and held up the glass. Yes, there was a smear of lipstick on the rim.

I stood there in the weak light of thirty watts, holding the glass in my hand, telling myself, in a dumb, light-headed, bewildered way, how I had never seen my mother, not in all my born days, put lipstick on her lips.

I happened to lift my eyes from that improbable object, the lipstick glass, and what I saw was, more improbably, a seersucker coat and a straw hat, the town kind with a colored band, hanging on a nail in the wall over beyond the eating table.

My first thought was, in that long moment of floating disorientation, that I had stumbled into the wrong house. The next thought was that my mother, who was no great hand with a penstaff, had sold out and moved and simply hadn't got around to writing me.

Then, standing there with the glass in my hand, I heard the sound. I turned.

There she stood.

She stood there with her long black hair down loose, wearing a new-looking pink silky robe with pink roses sewed to it on the left breast, holding the robe tight over herself with both hands. I looked down at her feet. I wasn't ready yet to look at her face. Her bare feet were stuck in pink slippers, with high heels and big puffy pink pompons on the front.

Then I looked up at her face. There was the lipstick. Even in the weak light I could see that now it was somewhat smeared.

She was looking at me steady, with her eyes black-bright. I looked from her face down to the hands that were clutching that silky-pink robe together, and I knew, quite suddenly and quite coldly, that there wasn't a stitch under it. I knew this as clearly as though, even while I was gazing into her face, she had drawn the garment apart to expose what was beneath, and then, instantly, but somehow deliberately, had again closed the cloth over what I had seen. I could almost feel how that slick, silky pink stuff would slip and slide on the bare skin.

I looked over to the seersucker coat and straw hat with the colored band.

The strange thing about the whole episode was that there was no sense of time to it. What I have narrated must have been a matter of seconds, but it seemed to go on forever. What brought everything back into the dimension of time was the awareness that my mother was about to speak.

I could not bear—I could not, and cannot, say why—to hear any word that she might utter. It was my own voice that took command of the silence. Holding the glass with the lipstick smear up into the light, I said: "I thought it was you who never touched whiskey!"

Then I was roaring with laughter. Then I had released the glass in midair and had simply stepped away from it. Then I was snatching up the knapsack.

I hooked a ride on a big trailer booming out toward Blackwell.

Three weeks later I had a letter from my mother, which, among the others she wrote me over the years, I kept:

Dear Jed you ought not have left so quick you never waited to hear nothing about the truth. No drunk can come in my house now or never and Mister Simms is a hard workin man and has troubles, including wife. About him and me aint nothing I am ashamed of. Till that night from the time yore father had his acident no human flesh ever touched my flesh. I tried to raise you up the only way I knowed good and decent so you could git out of Claxford County and make yoreself a man. Yore father thought if he was so much man in the bed it was a sign everwheres else. It is not so. If the way I raise you was not to yore taste and liking I am grieved in my heart but aint no man can say I did not put meat in yore mouth and keep a clean shirt on your back. I stayed many a night to iron a clean shirt. I try to live decent and aim to die trying. Mr. S. comes to see me but he treats me good and respectful like a decent woman I am. We aim to get married regular when his trouble is fixed. That night you come, was the first time like I say flesh touch my flesh since you know when. I took the whisky to make me relax more I was so worked up and tight like a fiddle string like I was a young girl and didn know what it was like and scart, it was so long since. Mr. S. needed to relax some to, he has got such trouble. I have wrote too long. My hand is not use to it and hurts some. You write me a letter. Yore loving mother,

Elvira K. Tewksbury

PS   When Mr. S. comes now he dont take but one drink maybe two. I do not take *none*, you bet yore bottom dollar.

PS agin   What I want now is to live like folks do and the Lord intend before I get too old and die. I hope and pray you to hold out yore hand to them as is lonesome. I waited a long time and it was lonesome.

I stood there and held the letter in my hand, as though I were trying to make out what it said. But I was trying not to make out what it said.

By middle September I was in Chicago, having hitchhiked up. I had, on arrival, $206.14 left from my summer earnings. I found the University and, in the midst of its grandeur, the Graduate Office. No, there had been no mistake. They were sorry. Had there been a second letter from Professor Pillsbun of Blackwell College, explaining things? No, they had no record of one. Could I speak with the Dean? No, he was very busy. But if I insisted. I insisted.

So next day the Dean saw me. I showed him my diploma from Blackwell. I showed him my grade sheet. I referred to the letter written in my behalf by Professor Pillsbun. Bit by bit, the terrible truth dawned that the Dean had never heard of Blackwell College— or of Pillsbun.

Or, it seemed, of Alabama. Could I take an examination, I asked. Well, that was scarcely regular. And it was already late to enter. Perhaps next year, something might—

I was outside, in the hall, then out the big doors, on the pavement, out on the campus, before I knew it. Fall sunshine gleamed goldenly on all the glory around me. Here and there, far and near, human figures were moving. They all had a place to go.

I stood still. I had no place to go. Not in the world.

It was only late morning, but I went back to my room at the Y.M.C.A. and lay down on my cot. I stared at the ceiling. I felt reality flooding away from me on all sides, like a retreating tide that left me stranded like a jellyfish to rot on a rock in the sun. I lay on my cot and felt a light-headed nausea of blankness—of placelessness, timelessness, of ultimate loneliness. I remember saying out loud: "This is my life."

At last I fell into a sodden sleep. It was dark when I awoke. The rhythmic roar and drone of the city, like the beat of a distant sea, penetrated my room.

From the darkness of my cot I looked up at a reddish glow from below my window that flushed the pebbly plaster of the ceiling. The intensity varied rhythmically. It seemed to be synchronized with the rhythmic variation of the roar and drone of the city. Then it seemed to me that that double rhythm was timed to the beat of my own heart, that it had insinuated itself into my very being. I found tears coming into my eyes at what was so clearly the discovery, at last, of a mystic relation between myself and the world.

I got up, got the light on, and began to count my money. With pencil and paper I worked out that if I ate on only fifty cents a day, and allowed fifty cents for transportation while I hunted work, I would have enough to pay for my room and still last about two months. I ought to be able to find something in that time.

.   .   .

I was almost always hungry, but I stuck to the program. It was clearly not going to be easy to get work. On the night of the twenty-fifth day, I counted my money to be sure I could hold out, and then went to bed. I woke up in the middle of the night. What a fool I had been!

By eight o'clock the next morning I was at the University, in the Library, looking at a directory. In twenty minutes I was at the office of Dr. Heinrich Stahlmann, who had changed the life of Mr. Pillsbun. The office did not open till nine. Then the secretary told me that Dr. Stahlmann's office hours were all filled until next week. Yes, he did have a class today.

I waited in the Library. I found a copy of the *Odyssey* in Greek. I searched out the passage in which Odysseus, at the court of Alkínoös, speaks of his loneliness and remembers Ithaca.

At one o'clock I went out to hunt an eatery of some cheap kind. Then I located the building, and the very room, in which Dr. Stahlmann would hold his class. To occupy my mind, as I lurked in a corner to keep watch on the door of Number 17, I repeated to myself the passage I had just been reading and that long back I had memorized, how, even though Ithaca was nothing but a craggy sea-mark—good for nothing but breeding boys—the world held no place more dear.

Suddenly, with an access of what was like despair, I realized—how late, even after I had learned the rolling words!—that Odysseus, even though guilty perhaps of some dawdling on the way, had been, in his deep heart, lonely for his rocky isle, but that I had nothing, nothing in the world, to be lonely for.

Mine was a different kind of loneliness. Odysseus was a slave to his loneliness, for he was lonely for something. But I was free in my loneliness, for I was lonely for nothing. Was Dugton even a place for breeding boys?

It had bred me.

A wild glee, like a stab of pain, struck me. It was glee at the discovery of freedom. I burst into cackles, right there in my corner of the hall.

Students, early ones, were arriving. Some of them looked at me, and I found myself full of shame. They all belonged here, but I did not. Idly, as though I did not exist, their gaze drifted through me. By ones and twos they were entering the classroom. I moved a little closer to the door.

There he was, coming, and my heart sank.

For two reasons. First, he was escorted by eight or ten students, to whom he was earnestly addressing himself and who were hanging on his words. Second, he was what he was.

He was rather tall, looking even taller than he actually was because of his lean build, but with a little of what a later friend of mine, an Italian scholar from Rome, was to whimsically term the *curvo filologico*. But with Dr. Stahlmann the scholarly stoop gave, rather, the impression of courtesy as he leaned from his height to attend to even the most banal utterance, and, at the same time, of an elegantly modulated insouciance. His frame was draped in a pepper-and-salt Irish tweed, not too well-pressed. He wore a stiff collar—like a dress collar, I later learned—and a dark red bow tie loosely knotted. The head, above the trim but strong-looking shoulders, was long, topped by luxuriant iron-gray hair combed straight back like a mane from a high forehead, and he wore a well-clipped iron-gray imperial tufted on his positive chin. The face, I could observe even at my distance, was aquiline, with a great beak of a nose, and dark eyes capable, as I was to come to know, of casting a terrifyingly incisive glance that now was mollified by the glasses he wore—pince-nez with tortoise-shell frames and a long black ribbon looped to a clip on the left lapel. In his hand was a walking stick with a straight, not curved, handle.

As that figure drew closer, my tongue literally clove to the roof of my mouth at the thought of addressing even one single word to a creature so noble.

But even in that instant, with a sudden sadness and pity—which undoubtedly had also a reference of self-sadness and self-pity—I saw the creature that, in spite of his scrubby height, hairless pink balloon head, round putty nose, soft bulging belly, and never-achieved doctorate, my little Mr. Pillsbun was dreaming himself to be: a figure with that same princely grace and garb, and that towering learnedness.

I lounged in the hall, the whole hour, hoping that I might find opportunity and courage to intercept him after class. The hope was vain. Students moved with him in a swarm, down the hall. I may add that what, over his arm as he approached earlier, I had taken to be a dark topcoat or raincoat, had turned out to be a black cape that now, draped loosely over his shoulders, regally swayed and swung as he withdrew into infinite distance.

And once more I thought of Mr. Pillsbun. The cape, I suddenly knew, was what he had wanted most for his dream—even if it was, sadly, the one accoutrement that, far off in Blackwell, Alabama, he had never dared to get. But after a moment, standing there in the now vacant hall, in Chicago, I knew, too, as clear as could be, that Mr. Pillsbun had indeed, with confusion and embarrassment, bought such a garment. And knew that at night, behind locked door and drawn shades, he would put it on. Standing there in his grubby little rented room, he would regard himself in the mirror. He would deliberately remove the pince-nez and, holding the spectacles in his hand, at one end, would shake them authoritatively, while he bent an eagle glance on the gentleman in the mirror.

.   .   .

I began to spend less time hunting for a job, and more at the University, lying in wait for Dr. Stahlmann, or trailing him, trying to screw my courage to the sticking place. One afternoon, after class, I trailed Dr. Stahlmann to the Library, then, waiting outside till well after dark, when he reappeared, I took up the pursuit. Thus I found where he lived, on a side street not yet deteriorating in that neighborhood where the spores of social blight were already being wafted from block to block. The house stood in a tended lawn, with two enormous maples, and farther back from the street a big hemlock—a fairly large structure in the ghastliest and most grimly whimsical fashion of some half-century before, wooden with a random cluster of Moorish towers and minarets of fish-scale shingling, with stained glass in plenty at the most unexpected places and elaborate scrollwork under the eaves and in every available coign and cornice. Two iron deer, one on each side of the brick walk leading to the steps, stood sentinel.

That first night I hung about under the shade of the maples. Once, I got as far as the steps, with the firm intention of approaching the front door, which was richly framed in the colors of stained glass illuminated from within. But my heart failed me. Several times in the next weeks I was to follow Dr. Stahlmann to this point, hoping always for the miracle of courage.

It was into November before the miracle occurred. I had been trailing my quarry on what I had discovered was his evening walk after dinner, hovering a block behind, watching his vigorous stride pass under the street lights, the swing of his cape, the way he clutched the walking stick well down below the head, handling it more like a marshal's baton than the simple expression of a gentleman's personality. I had decided that it had to be tonight or never, I would overtake him two blocks from his house. Then he couldn't, at least, shut a door on me. He would have to hear me out. For two blocks, anyway.

I hurried after him.

A wind was springing up. Dead leaves slid along the pavement with a dry, scraping sound, the sound of emptiness. Boughs of trees moved, and leaves yet clinging cast their wavering and fluid shadows. I was almost upon him, in such a spot of weaving and flowing darkness when, suddenly, he turned on me.

"What do you want, sir?" he demanded in a firm voice, his stick now grasped at the head and lifted almost to waist level, his right foot a little forward and toward me. And even in the shadows I caught the commanding glint of his glance on me.

I was astounded. I couldn't get a word out. Then, appalled at the very absurdity, I heard my voice:

"*Arma virumque cano* . . ."

The words kept pouring out. Dr. Stahlmann now held his head

cocked a little to one side, listening. The stick touched the pavement and he leaned lightly on it. A full five minutes he stood there motionless as though enraptured by the insane gabble that I seemed powerless to stop. But all at once he shifted the stick to his left hand, and held his right up in a gesture of command.

"Enough," he said. Then: "Your pronunciation is vile. You must be from the South. Nevertheless—"

It was too pitiful, too absurd, but there was nothing I could do about it. The dike had been broken by the *Aeneid* and what came pouring out now was the great chorus from *Oedipus at Colonus* that welcomes the stranger to the land famed for the glory of horses and horsemen, where the nightingales sweetest sing—the chorus now probably being uttered with an even more vile accent.

Dr. Stahlmann heard me to the end, then took off the pince-nez, and standing there in the toss and flow of shadow, with the dry-sliding rustle of leaves about our feet, he fixed me with his glance, as I waited, breathless, sweating, and ashamed.

"What is your name?" he said.

.   .   .

Heinrich Stahlmann was a profoundly kind man, and he was good to me. The goodness was first exhibited when he led me off the dark street into the improbable structure that he called the Castle of Otranto (a reference that, at the time, escaped me) and into his study, set me down, and, observing my shaken condition, summoned a manservant, who fetched me a stout whiskey. Suddenly, my head was exploding into a cataclysmic whirl of thousands of books, green-shaded lamps, and the image, infinitely reduplicated, of a bearded face with piercing eyes.

The next I knew I was in a bed, and a figure, that of a doctor, as I learned, was bending over me. Fifty cents a day had not proved quite enough to keep me going, and agitation and whiskey had done the rest.

That was only the beginning. Dr. Stahlmann got me entered by special arrangement into the Graduate School, arranged my courses. His wife not long since dead, and childless, he lived alone, taken care of by a German couple so old now that they needed help with heavy work, so for this he gave me quarters—quite handsome quarters, in fact—and my keep and tuition. After a few months he paid me a wage for serving as his research assistant in certain simple matters (a privilege for which I would have mortgaged my soul). And he gave me an image of what life could be.

As for the room, it had been, it appeared, originally three—perhaps a library, a drawing room, and a dining room, with a little glassed conservatory off the dining room—now all thrown together, with the old walls still indicated but substantially removed, and the whole place was lined with books from floor to ceiling, except for the longitudinal interior wall.

Here, the big Breughel reigned, flanked right and left by smaller canvases. In another section, in respectful isolation, was the portrait of a severe-looking gentleman with a craggy bald head, wearing a monocle and a handsome decoration, who, it turned out, was Dr. Stahlmann's father; this by Lenbach. In the same section, beyond the Lenbach, were massed, almost solid, other portraits, paintings or photographs, of ladies and gentlemen in the dress of the latter part of the nineteenth century and the early twentieth. In another section hung old-fashioned sepia photographs of the antiquities of Greece and Asia Minor, and beyond them a pair of gorgeous reproductions, in ormolu, of the platters of Mycenae, three sets of foils with masks, a cavalry saber, and an alpenstock.

On the facing wall, interrupting the serried array of books from floor to ceiling, was a fireplace, very large, of glittering greenish tile framed by a massive and marvelously ornate construction of golden oak (in which was set the brass lever that had summoned my lethal draught of bourbon), with caryatids supporting the heavy mantel, various smaller shelves and nooks, and an enormous mirror. On the mantel was a very large Dresden china clock, and on the smaller shelves and in the recesses were inscribed silver cups of different sizes, Dresden shepherdesses, intricate carvings in onyx, *objets d'art,* bibelots, and all the expensive flotsam and jetsam of a vanished world. Around the region of the fireplace were gathered the big leather sofa, leather chairs, and, looking oddly out of place, a straight-backed chair in some dark wood and, beside it, a white enamel contraption like the eating table in a hospital room, the kind that swings across the patient's lap—this, I learned, the chair and writing table used by Dr. Stahlmann when, sitting bolt upright with his right hand slowly executing his precise calligraphy in very black ink on fine bond paper, he composed his works.

Across the upper end of the present room, in the section that must have been the original library, was a sort of freestanding continuous lectern, of dark walnut, in which, deposed at regular intervals, was the vast array of lexicons, dictionaries, and such works of reference, and evenly spaced along the flattened upper ledge, where note pads conveniently waited, a number of brass rods rose to support old-fashioned, green-shaded reading lamps. Dominating that section of the room was the mass of a grand piano.

At the other end of the room, always shadowy except when Dr. Stahlmann was having his dinner or playing host, in what had once been the dining room but was now lined with books, stood a large, heavily carved mahogany table. The entrance to the conservatory was flanked by two mahogany pedestals, on one a life-size copy, in white marble, of the Venus de Milo, and on the other a matching copy of the Discobolus. The conservatory housed a round table, with chairs precisely arranged, a precinct sacred to the uses of Dr. Stahlmann's favorite seminar, which always met at his house. Around that table towered the plants, some branches and great fronds visible even on ordinary nights when there were no guests, in the dimness of that end of the domain, like a wildly improbably surrealistic jungle dream.

I have catalogued the details of Dr. Stahlmann's domain as they existed or as I came to know them in the long hours when, alone there, I would examine every book and every object, trying to penetrate its inner meaning, to grasp its place in the enchanted world into which I had stumbled. I came to know that the photograph of a very young woman with dark hair sculptured high in a most complex fashion, and with great dark eyes that, even on the faded paper and after all the years, looked out, over a feather boa, with a most haunting, smoldering glance quite at odds with the complex and correct coiffure, was Dr. Stahlmann's mother. That the young man with the military tunic, fitted tight as a corset, the splendid epaulets, and the arrogant tilt of the blond head, was his father, who as a captain of hussars had wielded, in a charge at Sedan, the very saber that now hung on the wall. That the foils and masks belonged to the student days of Dr. Stahlmann, and that the silver cups commemorated his triumphs, then and later (even in Chicago he had, for several years assisted in coaching fencing at the University, and even when I was there, practiced every morning before breakfast, in the little improvised gymnasium in the basement and fenced three times a week at the University). That the young man in the photograph of the group of mountain climbers was Dr. Stahlmann, the morning they began their assault on the Matterhorn, and that the alpenstock there in his hand now hung beside the father's saber. That the young man in the white coat in some of the photographs taken in Greece (not the "artistic" sepia ones, of course) was none other than Dr. Stahlmann at digs where he had worked back when he was still wrapped up in classical archaeology. And there were, of course, many pictures, from youth to middle age, of the dead wife, head under coils of blond hair—a face sweet, wide-eyed, innocent, devoted, apparently never touched by time until the last lethal clutch.

Certainly, that first night when, from the rather bare entry hall, I was led into the room, I saw nothing in detail of the thousand things I was later to dwell with so intimately, and had only a most general impression, with shadows lurking mysteriously in corners and distances and the focus of a fire on the extraordinary hearth. But in that moment it was as though everything I later would come to know of the room and its occupant was profoundly distilled into a first impression. It was as though, in a twinkling, by a master-stroke of magic, I had at last, effortlessly, pierced that forbidding wall through which, by this little chink or that, I had been striving to catch a glimpse of the bright reality beyond. And now all that my heart had so ignorantly yearned for was revealed to me in its blessed actuality. I had stumbled upon the magic word and the magic had worked.

I say "ignorantly," for truly I had had no aim in my earlier endeavors, no picture in my head of what I might do or be. I had no conception of gain or praise or fame. I was too uncertain of myself, too contemptuous of myself, if the truth be told, for that. I was, quite literally, without ambition. I had only the blind need: blind, without idea, without image. For what, I did not know, but I did sense that everything around me was generous with mysterious meaning.

But now the image had burst upon me and I stood marveling in the midst of that world, even if I had no name for it—and was not to have until, on the last night I was ever to sit there, Dr. Stahlmann was to utter it: *imperium intellectūs*. I had no name for it, but upon entering it, with feelings compounded by the very namelessness, I was overwhelmed with gratitude, unworthiness, and awe.

Five minutes later, I was, as has been recounted, stretched flat on the floor, colder than mackerel.

.   .   .

For two and a half years that room was the center of my life. There were, too, the occasional parties with other graduate students, the first parties I had ever known. And there was, of course, Dauphine, whose elegantly bohemian little apartment, over an old carriage house, was only a few blocks from the Castle of Otranto. I could, after a little morning tussle, in which the discourse concerning Fourier, Saint Simon, Engels, Bakhunin et al. would be little more than punctuated by the cries and groans of love-wrenched flesh, have breakfast with my juicy philosopher and, with the most recent revelation ringing in my ears, still make it in time to be of service to Dr. Stahlmann's Hans. And as I walked the street my head would hum with the secret of metaphysical bliss—and meaning. And my imagination would be illuminated by the glimmering glory of Dauphine in disarray and my nostrils full of her scent.

That arrangement with Dauphine did not, of course, last forever, ending, as I have said, late in the spring of 1941 shortly before Adolf turned on his erstwhile buddy Joe and thus put Dauphine, no doubt, through another set of anguishing political acrobatics. But, by and large, the place I knew best in those years was not the University or Dauphine's expensive nook, but the Castle, and the person I saw most consistently was its master.

Dr. Stahlmann, indeed, took over a good part of my life. He laid out my program for me. It was his idea that I begin intensive work in Italian to prepare myself for Dante (and his famous seminar in the epic)—this with profound consequences for my life. On certain days of the week, too, he allowed me to speak only German to him, and bore patiently with me. It was his custom to dine out once or twice a week, on other evenings being served a German meal at the big table of the former dining room, and one night a week he would invite me, always quite formally, to be his guest. Every two or three weeks he would give a small dinner party—after which a guest, or perhaps Dr. Stahlmann himself, would perform on the piano—or a supper following the symphony or opera. Sometimes he would include me, to give me, I suppose, some notion of the ways of the great world, which on those late occasions always appeared in the glory of evening dress. Except, of course, for me.

Nothing was too trivial for him to notice. When I began to put on some weight, he made me use the little gymnasium in the basement. He told me that, even if now I could not play football, fencing would keep me in shape. He would teach me, he said. "You should have," he said, with a little ironical curl at the corner of the finely cut mouth, "at least one occupation that is purely gratuitous—completely without any relation to life."

"That first night I chased you down the street," I said, "it mightn't have been me, but another kind of footpad. Then if you had sunk that walking stick in my navel, your fencing wouldn't have been so gratuitous."

"Maybe everything is gratuitous," he said. He paused. "If that is the word for what I mean."

And all at once I realized that he was not even looking at me. He was staring into the coals on the hearth.

.   .   .

Over the period that I knew Dr. Stahlmann I had noticed that the ironical curl at the corners of the mouth was becoming more and more marked. The irony had begun, in a way I found vaguely unsettling, though never with a sense of its being directed at me, to encroach upon the characteristic expression of kindliness, even benignity. He began to sit up late at night. Several times, coming down early in the morning before Hans was about, I found, on the floor by one of the leather chairs drawn up about the fireplace, a brandy bottle and a glass —an ordinary glass, not an old-fashioned snifter of the sort he used for his customary after-dinner drink, a thing I had never, of course, seen before I came to his house except in movies of high life, just as

I had never even heard of brandy (that kind, I mean) until he gave it to me.

Sometimes on the floor I found, too, the daily paper, and once or twice an atlas of Europe. I assumed, then, that the change in Dr. Stahlmann had its roots in the war. But he never discussed the subject with me.

Not, that is, until May 5, 1942. I remember the date because it was the day before the fall of Corregidor.

That night—a Thursday—he invited me to have dinner with him. It was the first time that such an invitation had ever come at the last minute. It was early afternoon, and I was at work in my own room, when he came to knock on the door. He hoped, he said, that I had no other plans, for he would like to have me dine with him.

I said that I had no plans—a lie, but not a significant one.

I did not see Dr. Stahlmann again until seven, the usual hour when, if I was dining with him, he would set out the drinks. Now, greeting me and giving me a Scotch and soda, he was his usual composed and agreeable self. The same impression persisted at dinner, as we sat in our little province at one end of the great table, with its acre of bare mahogany beyond us gleaming in the light of candles in the two massively wrought silver candelabra.

I remember nothing, however, of our conversation before the moment when he, having critically addressed himself to the *Kalbschnitzel* and decided that it was good, took a sip of the great *Schloss Johannisberg,* and turned to me. "The stomach is the best patriot," he said.

"I reckon so," I agreed, without passion.

"Anyway, the least harmful," he said, and I was again aware of the slight curl of the lips.

Then, the trace of irony replaced by the warm directness which he was capable of but which, sometimes, was a little at odds with the elevation of his English, more a matter of rhythm than vocabulary, he said: "I fear I haven't been tender of your patriotic sentiments— gastronomically speaking—in the little dinners you have been kind enough to share with me. But, you see, all Emma knows how to provide me is a little piece of old Germany."

I mumbled something intended to be polite.

"But you," he said, "you must—again, gastronomically speaking—

sometimes feel like the stranger in a strange land."

I had started to say, no—no, I didn't. But, all at once, in a peculiarly vivid and totally surprising way, even with the flavor of the *Kalbschnitzel* on my palate, I was remembering the taste of collards and corn pone, of fried ham and grits, of sorghum and black-eyed peas, and even in that instant I became aware, beyond the stately candle flames and the gleaming mahogany, of the twin statues looming whitely in the dimness and, in the deeper shadows of the conservatory, the great fronds hanging motionless, like a dream. For an instant I was struck with a blind yearning to feel the collards, the corn pone —those substances—in my mouth, the texture, the odor, the taste.

Then I heard, as from a distance, Dr. Stahlmann's voice: "What were the characteristic foods of your childhood?"

Then my own voice: "Greens boiled with sowbelly and corn bread and black-eyed peas and sorghum molasses."

This from some impersonal distance, too, in a throttled timbre, like rage or grief.

Then: "Poverty food."

Then: "When we had it."

I heard my own heavy breathing. Dr. Stahlmann's incisive glance was fixed on me, but there was no curl to his lips.

"Listen," I said, "we were poor. Dirt-poor. My father was a handsome, illiterate fool in overalls who wanted something that was not for him in Claxford County, Alabama, or in the whole goddamned world, and he was a drunkard, and died drunk, fell out of a wagon in the middle of the night when he stood up to piss on the hindquarters of a mule. They found him in the middle of the road, next morning, clutching his prick."

Dr. Stahlmann was still looking at me, his expression unchanged. After a long moment of my silence, he said, very gently: "Do you want to tell me more?"

At that question, rage almost undid me. I felt, to my own surprise, like bursting out at him: *Nearly three years and you've never asked me a question about myself! Except my name.*

But all I said was: "No. There's nothing to tell. We were poor as niggers. We ate like niggers."

"Niggers," he echoed, thoughtfully, turning his attention inward.

I flushed for shame because of the word I had used. I knew that I had used it as an act of aggression against him.

And as a way of asserting myself.

Whatever my self was.

Dr. Stahlmann had begun, very slowly, to eat. When we had finished, Hans removed the plates, brought in dessert, then reappeared with a metal cooler of ice and set it, on its stand, at Dr. Stahlmann's left. In it was propped a bottle of champagne.

Dr. Stahlmann opened the bottle, and with the simple, innocent directness, turned to me and said: "I invited you here tonight to help me celebrate something. A rite of passage. Yes, that's it. You see, only this morning I took my oath as an American citizen."

"Well," I said, "I hope you didn't take any oath as a citizen of Claxford County, Alabama."

He was studiously pouring the wine. Not looking up from his task, he said: "No, not of your natal Claxford County, Alabama—though I should be honored to share it with you—but of another new *patria* somewhat more—"

Now he looked up, and handed me my glass of the pale liquid on the surface of which the myriad beads revolved and glittered in the candlelight.

"A *patria* somewhat more—" he repeated, pausing, looking at me. Then added: "Shall we say—abstract?"

"You mean America?"

"Yes," he said, smiling, lifting his glass, "and let us drink to it—and to my hope to be worthy."

We drank.

"And now," he said, fixing his glance on my face, lifting his glass, "to Claxford County, Alabama!"

"Jesus Christ!" I said.

"Why not?" he asked. "No doubt, in your war—in the last century, your Civil War—men died for it."

"The pore sons of bitches," I said, and drank.

We attacked the *Linzer Torte* in silence, the reflection of the candle flames steady in the mahogany, the carved white marble of the Venus and the Discobolus gleaming mutedly in the dimness beyond. At the end, Dr. Stahlmann said: "I am trying to grow worthy of my new condition. Perhaps you can help me. Can you take me by the hand, like a little child, and lead me into the requisite innocence of heart?"

"I never learned much about that," I said. "Not in Claxford County."

"Look," he said, nodding toward the region of the fireplace, "Hans has set out the coffee."

.   .   .

Suppose I had taken the coffee with him, and a ritual brandy, and then excused myself for pressing work, as I had sometimes done on other evenings when I had been his guest? Perhaps he would then have sunk himself routinely into his own work, or gone for a late walk and then routinely to bed.

But I was there.

He began, after a long silence, over the second brandy. For a long time he had been sitting with snifter cupped in both hands, held up for him to inhale and only occasionally to touch his lips. The narrative came slow and almost as a whispered meditation, as though scarcely addressed to me at all, for, over the snifter, his eyes were fixed on the cold fireplace, now brushed scrupulously clean for the season, with three lengths of birch log laid with mathematical precision on the back bars of the andirons of polished brass.

He was descended on his father's side from generations of Lutheran ministers and theologians of no great fame. But his own father had broken the family tradition, in four ways: he left theology for science (chemistry), gained military distinction (at Sedan), became very rich (by discovering a slight improvement in the process of smelting iron ore), and married a lady of fashion, beauty, wit, and aristocratic connections.

"And I," Dr. Stahlmann said, "was the only child of this couple who embodied the best of their time and world. They loved me devotedly. They leaned over me as over an orchid. Special tutors for English, for Greek. The best instructors in dancing, the best masters in fencing, the best guides and instructors in mountaineering. Discipline. The highest standards of excellence always held firmly in view. Discreet praise. I was the bright star of the *Gymnasium*. I was the finest flower of our *Kultur.* It was my destiny."

Suddenly, he rose to his feet. He slowly poured more brandy, sloshing it in. He looked up at me, snifter in one hand, the bottle still in the other.

"Oh, yes," he said, "we believed in *Kultur!* In the German mission. I believed in it. With, of course, a slight youthful overlay of roseate socialism. It was—"

He paused not to inhale, but to take a solid drink.

"It was," he began again, "a millennial dream."

He set the bottle on the coffee table, switched the snifter to his right hand, then stared down at me.

"Do you know where I woke up?" he demanded, as though in personally directed anger.

"No," I said.

"In the abattoir," he said.

"What?"

"On the Somme," he said.

Very slowly, he resumed his chair. I was struck by a strange creakiness in his movement, as of age coming on. There was moisture on his temples.

"But—" he said. And stopped.

I waited.

"But some dream is necessary," he said. "If a man is to go on at all. Even, as a last resort, the dream that man can live without a dream."

He lay back in the deep leather chair, his gaze angling upward.

"So I dreamed another," he said, at length.

I waited.

"I dreamed," the gently cadenced voice was saying, "of a world not of the nations. Of a timeless and placeless, sunlit lawn, like that of Dante's vision, where the poets and philosophers and sages sit, and where we who are none of those things may come to make obeisance and listen. We may even, if a little grace is vouchsafed, report something of what we have heard. That others may come.

"As the *Civitas Dei,* for the Christian, sheds light on the cities of men, so the *imperium intellectūs* may illuminate and quicken the world of our bewildered body and bestial members. For that was the name that came to me—*imperium intellectūs*—and there the humblest might enter, if—"

The phrase rang in my head. I was not seeing the speaker, not even now aware of what was being uttered, only vaguely aware of the rhythm, for the words that filled my head, *imperium intellectūs,* were like the slow, commanding tones of a great bell, and on the instant, a joy suffused my being.

There is no other word for what was happening. It was as though what had been only vaguely intuited when I first entered this room, now some thirty months back, was suddenly blazing up to fill my sight, and all the slow, sad blunderings of my past existence—the smoldering rage, the aimless and narcotic labors, the self-contempt, the raw and angry pleasures with the little black girls behind the Dugton depot or the moments of ambushing tenderness and undefinable significance with Dauphine Finkel on her perfumed sheets beyond our communal sweat and the subtleties of Marxism, the blind, plunging impact of bodies when the center snaps the ball, the ironical timbre of cheers, the voice of Rozelle Hardcastle calling my name in the June night as she rushed after me from the Prom, dreams and onanism and the cackling laughter of the schoolyard of long ago—all these things, like iron filings that, scattered on a sheet of paper, jerk into a polarized pattern when the magnet is passed beneath, were being redeemed into a perfected meaning of life. Literally, my breath came short.

I knew in that instant what the saints report: that one may be rendered sightless with seeing.

I had not even seen Dr. Stahlmann rise from his chair. Simply, I became aware that he was standing on the hearth, backed by the enormous mirror, the elaborately scrolled golden oak, and on the mantel, shelves, and brackets, the silver cups, the Dresden shepherdesses, the bibelots, the *objets d'art.*

"And then—" he said. "Then out of the beer-swill of München! To make me remember that I was, after all, a citizen of the world of the Body and the Bestial Members. That I was, in short, human. And German!"

Abruptly, he stepped off the hearth, strode past my chair, and even before I could turn my head, called back to me, peremptorily: "Come here!" He was standing at the section of the wall where the photographs were arrayed.

"Come here, please," he was saying in his normal tone of courtesy. When I had reached his side, he jabbed his forefinger at the picture of the dark beauty who looked out over the feather boa. "That is my mother," he said.

The finger came to rest on one of the pictures of the wife. "This is of the time when we were first married," he said. There was the young woman of the wide, devoted eyes and gentle face under the calm, coiled braids of pale hair.

"Look carefully," he commanded, "and tell me which is *la belle juive!*" Then, spitting the word out: *"Die schönen Jüden*—the Jew girl."

I must have unconsciously glanced at his own face, for all at once he had snatched off the pince-nez and swung his head a little to one side, to exhibit his profile, with the beaked nose held high. "Yes—look at me," he said.

Then added: "But you are wrong."

Again he thrust out the forefinger, to touch the dead wife's picture. "She!" he said.

The forefinger touching the glass seemed to weaken. The tip slid down, as by the increasing weight of the hand, slowly across the glass, off the glass. "They killed her," he said in almost a whisper, leaning at me as though to confide a secret. "As surely as though they had put her in one of their camps. She died here, in a hospital. But it might have been in a camp. Like her mother."

He turned back to the picture, studying it.

"Then," he said, still studying the picture, "having discovered that, after all, I was only a mortal man, and a German, I betrayed that homeland. Do you know what I should have done?"

Clearly, the question was not rhetorical.

"I don't know," I said.

"I should have gone back to Germany, to claim my patrimony of honor," he said. "I should have gone back to offer the public testimony of my curse upon what my land had become. And to demand the consequences."

He had turned away from me, was walking across the width of the room, then stopped, turned back to me, and said, resuming: "But I did not."

He proceeded across the remaining space, poured brandy into his snifter, and again stood on the hearth. I returned to my chair. He ignored me, his eyes roving over the room, over all the objects, into every shadow and recess. At last his eyes came again to discover me. "All young men—" he began. Then: "They think they will write the great book. And"—he smiled at me—"I think you will. You have the—the anger, the innocence, the invincible—" He lifted his hand as though to stop me from speaking. "No," he said, "I was not going to say 'invincible ignorance.' No, let me say, with affection and envy, 'sancta simplicitas.' No—to put it differently—you want something and you do not know its name. Only that—that kind of ignorance, my dear boy—can ever lead to greatness."

His eyes wandered again over the room.

"But I did not," he said. "Did not write that book. Oh yes, I have written many books. I puffed up the obvious, like a child's balloon. Or I carved cherrystones. I—"

"But you—" I interrupted.

He lifted his hand again. "Oh yes, I have received parchments with gold seals and great honor and lovely ribbons," he said, and the fingers of his left hand touched the red of the *Légion d'honneur* at the lapel buttonhole. "Yes, look, I once wrote most learnedly of the *Lais* of Marie de France! And I have addressed most reverend assemblies. All that—that is just a game we learned and great ones play with one another. I forgot that it is enough happiness to try to make my report, however inadequate, of greatness. But—"

He made the slightest sad, comic shrug, opened his hands fleetingly in the classic gesture of emptiness.

"The war—" I said. "Do you mean the war?"

"Listen," he said, smiling with curled lips, "that madman Yeats— mad enough, sometimes, to be wise—has a beautiful phrase: 'the murderous innocence of the sea.' Well—" again he shrugged "—as for this little war, I have, you see, the greatest trust in the murderous innocence of the American people."

He moved to the bottle.

"No, that is not quite fair," he said. "America is only a seismograph. With victory, we shall all enter the age of murderous innocence." He poured, drank.

"Listen," he said, "I was in the Tyrol once. I lay on the jut edge of a high crag. It was summer and the sun was hot on my back, through my shirt. I remember the heat of the stone to my bare knees, for, you see, I was wearing lederhosen. Through my binoculars I looked across a profound chasm and down on the opposite slope that, shelving off, a kilometer or so away, from the base of a great escarpment, broke at the chasm lip. The slope was partly in flowery meadow, partly wooded, the upper part. Nothing stirred in that bright champagne air. Nothing stirred on the slope below me.

"I was studying the scree—you know, a sort of long band of talus at the foot of the escarpment beyond the woods. I could not see the whole band, for it lay beyond the woods, but from my height I could see, here and there, over to segments of the band, and in one place the view was open all the way back to the escarpment. There, clearly some years earlier, the scree had broken through the woods in a great land slip that had fanned out over the meadow to the very lip of the chasm. But grass and low growth had now healed much of that rawness. Here and there, I noticed too, along the lower margin of the woods, old detritus was faintly visible under the mask of grass and bushes, and in those spots, one might surmise, long, long ago there had been other land slips, so long ago that the wood itself had reestablished its claim and rooted in the ruin.

"I explain all this so carefully," Dr. Stahlmann interrupted himself, in a faint, ironic parody of his seminar tone, "in order that what happened may be clearly comprehended.

"Looking down from my height, across the chasm—with, of course, my binoculars, I suddenly saw a stone—not very large, probably not much larger than a soccer ball—detach itself, for no discernible reason, from the old heap of scree at the near margin of the wood and roll into the bloom of the meadow. After some hundred meters, it came to rest. Then, a hare lifted up. The hare took a few casual leaps across the slope, then stopped. Another stone came down. It continued beyond the point where the first had stopped. Beyond, a single bird rose from the wood. The hare did not move."

He looked down into the brandy, then up at me.

"Have you ever witnessed a *Bergsturtz*—a landslide?" he asked.

"No," I said.

"I have," he said. "Once. That one. I was well situated. It was like being in the royal box, in the *Stadtsoper,* in München, when the great chorus of Beethoven's *Fidelio* bursts out. The panorama was spread out below me. Only, I could hear nothing. At first. When suddenly a massive flock of birds exploded from the wood, upward, wheeling and gyrating, I knew that their screams were filling the air, but, at such distance, I could hear nothing. I was staring in surprise at the birds, then became aware that, high up the great gash of the old slide, some rubble had begun to dribble down. In the moment before the band of talus began to slip, there must have been the shudder of every bough in that wood."

He drank.

"We are now like those birds," he said.

He drank again.

"Or the hare," he said.

"The hare," he said, resuming, "was motionless in the middle of the meadow. I found with my binoculars the precise little brown patch that at that distance he was, but felt that I could see the very veins, the bright threads of crimson, in his eyes—round eyes, liquid, bulging, unknowledgeable, terrified. It was as though I could hear his heart beat. Then I saw the next stone—a boulder, really—detach itself from the old scree at the edge of the wood. Then another. The hare began to move.

"Then, for the first time, I heard a sound. Not loud, but somehow filling the air. From beyond the far wood. It was like a slow, guttural, grinding exhalation. Like pain. Something was happening at the lower reaches of the escarpment beyond the wood. The tops of the farther trees of the wood began to jerk. Like the coarse mane of a great dog —a shepherd—bristling when he growls.

"By this time," he said, "the band of scree above the woods must have been loosening, moving. The grinding sound rose in volume from beyond the wood. Up there, beyond the wood, was the real thing. As yet I could not see the real thing, but the woods, high up, was in trouble, jerking wildly, while, above, in the bright air, the birds made their circles and uttered their silent cries. Then, massively, it was happening.

"Then it was over. And after all the echoes had died among the peaks, there came what I can only term a sublimity of silence. There was, too, bare rock where the meadow had once been. And the wood.

"You see," he said, in a tone of careful explanation, "there had been so much rain. So soon after the melting of the unusually heavy snows."

"The hare?" I said, after a moment.

"Oh yes, the hare," he echoed, as though in apologetic surprise. "When the few big stones from the edge of the wood began to come, the hare raced over the meadow. But—" and he drank "—he did not make it."

His eyes, as he stood there on the hearth, began again to rove the room, fixing here, then there, then moving on. *"Imperium intellectūs,"* he uttered, into the air, not to me. Then to me, savagely: "Junk! All junk!"

Then, again, calmly: "It's all like a Roman funeral. You have read Polybius?"

"Some," I said.

"You remember that when the illustrious man had died, they carried the corpse around the city, propped in a chair, and set him on the *rostra* in the forum. Well, we of the *imperium intellectūs* prop up a man who, we pretend to think, is so great he must be dead, in a chair, and, like the Romans, make speeches about him. And some of us, again just like the Romans, put on our portrait masks of other illustrious dead and pretend to be them, while others make speeches about us. Oh, it is jolly! That's what we do in the *imperium intellect ūs.*"

He leaned back against the mantel, to one side of the great Dresden clock which dominated that space. He looked very tired. But, of a sudden, he straightened up. He lifted off the pince-nez, and bent his characteristic glance upon me, seated there before him.

Brightly, almost gaily, he said: "You've suffered enough, my dear boy. Get out of that chair. I'm going to send you packing to bed. Anyway, I have a little chore—a letter of recommendation to write.

75

For Montague. He is applying for a post in cryptography. At Washington. He is eminently qualified."

He took a step toward me.

"I have distressed you," he said. "With my—my senile outburst. Forgive me."

"There's nothing to forgive," I said, and rose.

"In any case," he said, and reached out to touch me lightly on the arm, "I thank you for coming to my—celebration. And believe me, I am truly glad to have America as my *patria*. And as for you, remember—if anything I have said does distress you—that you have for a *patria* a land more glowing than even America."

"You mean Claxford County?"

"No," he said, "the country of the young."

In the big mirror behind him I caught my reflection: a large, carelessly contrived face, flushed, heavy lips and pale gray eyes now bloodshot from drink and a slightly flattened, slightly twisted nose—these features under an unkempt mass of black hair. The figure I observed in the mirror was wearing a nondescript and unpressed dark jacket, somewhat too small, and a black knit tie toward one ear, and a once-white shirt, with the top button missing.

All at once I remembered how, in Dugton, my mother had always made me wear a white shirt to school, even with my jean pants. She had stayed up at night to wash and iron it.

"Good night, and again all thanks," my host, smiling, said.

"Good night," I said, "and thank you. It was a great dinner."

He walked with me to the door. Almost there, he stopped. "You know," he said, "there's one kind of American I wish my naturalization papers could make me."

"What?"

"*Ein Neger*—black."

"Jesus Christ," I said.

"You see," he said, "your black man—the black man here—has no history but his blackness. No name but the name stuck on him and not his own. He is the only free man."

"Free?" I said.

"He is the perfect existential man."

He put out his hand again. I took it.

"Even Claxford County couldn't quite do that," he said. Then: "Or could it?"

"It shore-God made one good try," I said. "Me. And me not black."

"Well, good night," he said. He was smiling. It was as though nothing had ever happened.

.   .   .

When I went down next morning to his improvised gymnasium to take my little pre-breakfast workout, I saw his gray suit neatly hung on a hanger, on one of the heating pipes in the ceiling, the shirt on another, the shoes set neatly side by side. It seemed a very strange place to find them.

Then I saw the bare feet sticking out from under the curtain of the little box shower.

There he was.

He was sitting on the floor, wearing his underwear shorts. His head was bowed forward on his chest. The legs, stuck out straight before him, looked very thin and white, as though long submerged in water, with the veins large, slightly varicose, and blue. The old Luger was on the cement bottom of the cubicle. The hole was neatly over the heart.

.   .   .

Later, I discovered, on the hall table, the letter of recommendation, sealed and stamped, addressed to the bureau in Washington, ready to be posted.

Montague got the job.

.   .   .

After the funeral on Monday, I went down to the Loop and volunteered. It was the infantry. This was no sudden access of patriotism. It was certainly no sentimental impulse to avenge the death of my benefactor. The simplest way to put it, perhaps, is to say that, in case of a landslide, I had discovered that I'd rather be a boulder than a rabbit.

．　　．　　．

In reviewing what I have written of this period of my life, I detect two significant omissions. In the summer of 1941, in August, in a big envelope from my mother, but with no covering letter, came a clipping from the *Claxford County Clarion,* describing at length the reception given by the Burtons when, after the honeymoon in the Alps, Chester brought his bride (nee Sylvia Quincy Hempelwhite, of the Hempelwhites of New York, Long Island, and Nassau, Mr. Hempelwhite being a vice-president of the Chase National Bank) on her first (and no doubt last) visit to the family plantation, which must, by the way, have been somewhat a surprise to her. As it may have been to some of what the *Clarion* called the "socialites" summoned from as far off as Birmingham and Montgomery—and Nassau.

On the margin of the clipping my mother had written: "Miss Pritty-Pants was in town. But did not get an invite. Ha! Ha!"

The second significant omission was another clipping from the *Clarion,* dated February, 1942. Rozelle Hardcastle, valedictorian of the class of 1935 of the Dugton High School, and more recently a student at the University of Alabama, at Tuscaloosa, had married, in Florida, Michael X. Butler, a well-known real estate and construction operator of Chicago, now resident at Fort Lauderdale, where, the *Clarion* avowed, he was a prominent figure at the tracks and in yachting circles. The age of the bridegroom was fifty-four.

In other words, Rozelle, it occurred to me, had lost no time in striking back.

CHAPTER IV

In the great checker game in which America, with its murderous innocence, was busy pushing and pulling, hither and yon, its millions of little checkers, Jed Tewksbury was pushed up into the mountains of south central Italy by the brass-bound Blind Doomsters of Washington, D.C., and points east, who had discovered that he spoke well both Italian and German. In a magnificently tossèd, tortured, forested or barren landscape that was sun-bit or snow-lashed according to season, he lived for a time in a ruinous old heap of rubble that was a sheepfold—or rather, in the cellarage recently excavated and lined with cabbage-sized stones set in cement—with the immediate company of some score of compunctionless and louse-bit desperadoes and the intermittent companionship of some four- or fivescore other desperadoes, equally compunctionless, who, unlike the Son of Man but like the foxes, had found holes to lay the head. The desperadoes were under the command of Maggiore Alberto Buonponti, who had early deserted Mussolini's army and taken to the hills, and to this command

Captain Jediah Tewksbury was in liaison (and, in the informality of things, sometimes in combat command of a detachment).

A number of the desperadoes were from the city and zone of Siena, especially from the region of the great volcanic cone of Monte Amiata to the southwest, a region notable for cinnabar mines, intransigence, hunger, brutality, bravery, and forests and ravines eminently designed for the ambush. In this world of fanatical heroism and unspeakable treachery, we were for a time operating well behind the Nazi lines, in an uninterrupted game of blindman's bluff—or rather, of hunter and hunted, in which by day we were the hunted and by night the hunters. Until the Gothic Line cracked and we began to hunt often by day as well as night, and the eyes of my desperadoes brightened and the lips showed more wolfishly their yellowing teeth.

We were almost always deep behind the Nazi lines, but what I remember best is the earlier period before I had become accustomed to the long silent waitings, the hours of crouching in darkness, and the discipline of silence. Anything can become, in the end, a way of life, but then I was still exploring the world I had stumbled into, was even trying to understand why I was in it at all. It was in this period that they brought in as prisoner, taken on a night patrol, the SS lieutenant who, in civil life, as I elicited in preliminary interrogation, had been a classical scholar—an *Assistent* at Göttingen. This was, I should add, only three weeks after my arrival, when the desperadoes regarded me, if I could read those hard, sidelong glances, honed as thin as a knife edge, with more suspicion than cordiality. Besides, I was having some trouble with dialect.

We were in the main room of the cellarage, with a gasoline pressure lamp on a rough wood table a little to one end of the room, and facing it, the lieutenant sat on a stool, flanked by two of the desperadoes—Giacomo Rieti, bald, short, and fat, a painter by civil occupation with a peculiar tiptoe lightness of foot and a quickness of hand like a prestidigitator's, and Gianluigi, with the ruined, once-handsome face, one blind eye, and a partially crippled hand, the left. Seven other desperadoes were in the room, there with rifles and fixed bayonets, pistols loose in holster, watching over three other Germans and an Italian civilian, poor doomed wretch, who had been taken with them, the prisoners on stools against the wall that cut the main room off from the radio installation.

I stood almost in front of the lieutenant, some five feet from him, and saw his shadow and those of the guards splay backward on the stone floor. The other prisoners and their guards were in a farther dimness alleviated by two candles set in bottles. On the wall above them were life-size drawings, charcoal on the whitewashed boards, of wittily obscene figures and graffiti—the work of Giacomo.

I looked down at the lieutenant. He had just finished explaining to me, in the tone he must have used in dealing with dullards at Göttingen, that from my uniform he knew that I was an officer in the American Army and that, according to the Geneva Convention, he need give me no information except his name, rank and serial number.

The desperadoes were eying me.

"Do you speak Italian?" I asked, in German.

He said he did, with an air of complacency, as though he expected me to tell him to go to the head of the class.

"Good," I said, in Italian. "Only one of my men speaks German and I want them to hear all. We will proceed." I turned to Gianluigi. "Come in front of the prisoner," I commanded.

He obeyed.

"Show the prisoner your hand," I said.

Again he obeyed. The nails had been drawn from three fingers and the joints crushed.

"Look carefully," I said to the prisoner, "and tell me if you think that such a condition results from strict observance of the Geneva Convention."

"I answer only my name and serial number."

"Look at his cheek and you will observe that the condition results from a most methodical slicing by a very sharp blade. What about that and the Convention, which you so highly esteem?"

He went into the litany.

"You seemed cheerful enough about telling me how you were an *Assistent* at Göttingen. What's wrong now?"

"I answer only—"

"Shut up," I said. "Three of our men are in the hands of your people, and are no doubt at the SS post. You are going to tell me its exact location. Now. I am going to give you one minute. If you do not speak, I am going to blow your head off."

I saw the eyes of the desperadoes on me.

"You are an American officer," he began, "and—"

"Listen," I said, "after your head's blown off it will be the next man's turn. But I won't touch him, I'll deliver him over to what in the days of the Inquisition was, as you, a man of learning will recognize, called the secular arm. That, my friend, is Gianluigi, who was once—since you are so proud of your Italian—a real *bell'uomo,* that is, a real handsome guy. That is, he was until you SS interrogated him."

"The Geneva—"

"Listen, you pedant," I cut in, "Gianluigi hasn't signed the Geneva Convention."

I took out my revolver.

"I know," I said, "that getting the head shot off is no big business at all. But the man who goes under the hands of Gianluigi will not thank you for your heroism. For Gianluigi always cracks them."

Ostentatiously, I inspected my wrist watch.

"In ten seconds I begin to count," I said.

The prisoner made no reply.

A minute passed. I set the muzzle just back of the lieutenant's left ear. I seemed to remember having read that this was the approved procedure, but perhaps the writer was a man of no practical experience in such matters. Anyway, that was the best thing I could think of.

Then, somewhat to my astonishment, my voice, in a tone of ironic question, was saying: "... *dulce et decorum est?*"

I was hating the bastard.

"*Jawohl,*" the bastard said. Then: "*Heil Hi—*"

I had pulled the trigger.

"Get the garbage out," I said, and nodded to two of the unoccupied desperadoes. To Gianluigi, the one with the ruined face, who spoke German, I said: "Take over."

I went out the underground passage to the cow barn, where our entrance was—this arrangement of a covered trench being necessary, because tramped mud or snow in a cow yard, if observed from the air, seems perfectly natural.

There were scudding clouds, but now and then moonlight broke through. So I went to the shadow side of the barn. There I propped my head against the stone, and vomited.

Afterwards, I washed my mouth with snow, and after a time, I went back in. Fortunately, the next man had cracked, and cracked fairly early. Gianluigi had done a careful, well-modulated job, convincing the subject, at each stage, that the worst was yet to come. Not just more of the same. That is the art of it.

And the worst would have been, indeed, to come: the subject forced to swallow gasoline and then, maddened by thirst, tied up with a pitcher of water in theoretical reach. Or an electrode applied to the subject's scrotum.

But I, personally, was never involved in such procedures.

. . .

Anything, as I have said, can become a way of life. Even death. Even the question why death should become a way of life could itself become a way of life. That question was there continuously and inevitably, like the air you breathe or the bread you eat, but in its inevitability it had long since ceased to demand an answer. It had become, as it were, purely rhetorical.

Even the question as to why I myself was there became, in the end, purely rhetorical.

It took, however, some time for that question to get that way. That is, for me to reach the point where, if I asked myself the question (as I habitually did), I would not make the slightest effort to answer it. To reach the point where I could stare at the question as at an interesting natural object, like a cloud in the sky, or a flower in the hand.

Meanwhile, I had little success in answering it. I would look at the desperadoes and wonder what, beyond the vibrating blue flame of their hatred, sustained them. And when, after I had shot the head off the SS lieutenant and gone out into the moon-flickering darkness to vomit, I knew, even in the midst of heave and retch, that I had hated him. That I had hated him simply because I envied him.

83

I could again hear my voice, in the nastiness of its irony, demanding: ". . . *dulce et decorum est?*" I could again feel the vengefulness with which, at his answer, I had pulled the trigger. I could again feel the upward jerk of the recoil.

One trouble was that I knew too much of the two thousand and five hundred years of history of that peninsula, and it was a blood-sodden drama in which, by my time, one war looked very much like any other. And here I was in the middle of another episode in the blood-sodden drama, the analysis of which, even as early as a century hence, would certainly look very different on the pages of history from the gilded *Dreck* being currently dished out at indoctrination sessions or in the public and well-paid utterances of patrioteers.

Another trouble was that, huddled in my sleeping bag (day or night, for with us they were often reversed) with a candle stuck in a bottle, or sitting on a stool in an off half-hour, I was reading, over and over, my long since battered copy of the *Divina Commedia*. And when I crouched in the dark with snow patting gently at my face, or by day proceeded down some dry *torrente* for cover from prying eyes, I would be saying over to myself the passage I had most recently memorized. The trouble here was that, though this was my program for keeping sane, the book's vision of all-embracing meaningfulness, in the midst of the incessant violence and perfidy depicted there, aggravated, by fundamental and ironic contrast, my awareness of the blankness of spirit that was then my way of life.

I could close my eyes and see the scene of the child weeping under the chinaberry tree, with summer sunlight pouring down like golden lava, and ask myself if I was ready to die for Claxford County. I felt no identity with that child. Sometimes it was as though I hated him. Was I ready to die for the Confederate States of America? They were already dead. For the University of Chicago? Certainly, I was prepared to go back there. But if I died, I couldn't go back. For the Standard Oil Company of New Jersey? I didn't even own a car. I would tick off items of my constantly lengthening list, and all the dying I was ready to do was die laughing.

Yes, I knew all the things people say to themselves, and I could even say the words. They were words, and you could say them. But a man does not die for words. He dies for his relation to them. The words had no relation to me.

But there were the desperadoes. They would, and sometimes did, die, and what they died for, most immediately, was each other. Oh, not in any personal sense. It was just that this way of dying was their way of life. And slowly, very slowly, it dawned on me that this quite unphilosophical and totally unwashed crew was my *patria*. At least, for the moment, the nearest thing I had to one.

Not that I had any intention of dying for them, any more than they had any intention of dying for each other. Nor, certainly, for me. We all knew the great lesson of history; I from reading it and they from living it. And the lesson is: it is more blessed to kill than to be killed.

But if I got stuck?

Well, I'd just have to do the best I could.

Meanwhile, I would pray for grace that I might grow more fully into historical blessedness. For hadn't I said, long back, that in the day of the great landslide I'd rather be the boulder than the rabbit?

The only hitch was, I just couldn't quite achieve the pure and self-contained perfection of the boulder. The boulder has no concern whatsoever with the principles of geology or the law of gravity.

.   .   .

On the night of the death of the SS lieutenant, Major Buonponti, who had been waiting for word from us, mounted a very successful attack on the SS post in question. Unfortunately, it was a little too late to do our fellows much good.

Meanwhile, on the off chance that one of my fellows taken by the SS had cracked, the Major had laid a trap at our sheepfold. When the next night the Nazis did hit, there was, of course, nobody home, and when a sufficient number of intruders were in the cellarage, the desperado detailed to that duty looked at me for authorization, then pushed the plunger of the detonating device and there was no longer any sheepfold. At the instant of its dramatic disappearance, the Nazis aboveground in the cow yard and thereabouts were treated to a very pretty *tir d'enfilade* between the loft of the detached barn and the window of the farmhouse attic.

85

We had, of course, to find a new snuggery. We slaughtered and ate the few head of stock we had around for window dressing, but they had little flesh on the bone. Almost all our radio equipment had been salvaged, too.

.   .   .

Then the war was over, and they all had some place to go. And even I, by August, 1946, was back in Chicago, in mufti.

At the University of Chicago, to which I returned after the horrors of war, I gradually became accustomed to the neurotic shake-up of what Ambrose Bierce once called the horrors of peace; then even they dwindled into nothing more than a way of life. I even persuaded myself that I had found an interesting and important subject for my dissertation. The Great Landslide which was history might still be roaring past, but the roar was now so accustomed that it sounded like silence—and could be called the historical process, and the particular small-gauge boulder called J. Tewksbury had come to rest on its own private little heap of detritus.

I even persuaded myself, in due course, that I had found an appropriate object for matrimony. I had, in fact, persuaded myself that Agnes Andresen was an appropriate object for matrimony well before it ever occurred to me that she might be an appropriate object for getting into bed with. We met in the Library, and in the deepest sense it may be said that we plighted our troth before the high altar of the loan desk.

Working on my dissertation, I occupied a stall—a carrel, we call them in the trade—in the stacks of the Library. For the first two weeks I worked only in the morning and so never caught sight of the next carrel's occupant, who, as I could tell by the books assembled there, was obviously concerned with English literature of the late eighteenth century—a language and a period that I, who now fancied myself as a medievalist in comparative literature, regarded as strictly for women and children. My neighbor turned out to be a woman.

As a scholar, Agnes Andresen was indeed very acceptable, and thanks to her sex, having been relieved of military duty, was on the very verge of her Ph.D., and was already teaching in one of the Chicago universities. As a woman, Agnes was, as I began to notice, despite all the odds she established against such awareness, acceptable, too. She was rather well formed, even if a bit underfed, bony, it might be alleged, and though her idea of what the female scholar should wear was not designed to accent her good points, it could not altogether conceal them. Her face was rather plain—no, severe, well-scrubbed, and unexploited rather than plain—but when she took off her horn-rims, the eyes had a fine celestial Scandinavio-Lutheran blue. Her smile, when it managed to break through the overcast of seriousness and the slight chronic pucker of preoccupation, was a charming surprise—as though it were a surprise to her, too. Later in our acquaintance, she learned to dare, now and then, some small outgoing word or gesture—a joke, a bit of badinage, a touch on the sleeve, even a term of innocent endearment, always shy, always tentative, always a little gauche—and catching herself in the very act, she would be overwhelmed at her own temerity and, like a little girl, would blush to the eyes, and the blush, if she had the horn-rims off, would add glint and depth to that already celestial Lutheran blue.

All in all, it was the shyness, the awkwardness, the tentativeness, the not-quite-prettiness, the little-girlishness, the sense of something defenseless and uncertain, the tender striving, in fear and yearning, to break out into the light and air to bloom—it was all this that touched the heart and made you, in the end, want to reach out. You felt that the blooming would be totally private, totally and secretly your own, totally possessed in a way far more profound and gratifying than might ever be attested to by the mere puncture of a scrap of membrane and the trivial bloodletting thus occasioned. For it never occurred to me that Agnes Andresen was not a virgin, even in the most technical sense.

Again I get ahead of my narrative: these tender and complex feelings and the summarizing notion that it would be a rewarding experience to strip off Agnes Andresen's scholarly garb and get her down to the buff really came to sharp focus only after I had asked for her hand. When I did ask for her hand, it simply seemed appropriate for the thriving young medievalist to have a nice, methodical, well-mannered, not-quite-pretty, and not-very-distracting wife, who, having a Ph.D. of her own, would listen comprehendingly when he talked over professional problems and who would, when occasion arose, compliantly roll over and relieve the cupidity of the flesh when that threatened to disrupt professional concerns. He asked her to marry him, too, because she loved him.

It was a new and agreeable experience to think that somebody loved me. Never before, except perhaps in the luxurious little bohemia of Dauphine, with all its intellectual and sexual complications, had it crossed my mind that any bedmate had been inspired by a motive other than gain or pleasure—or perhaps curiosity, which is a motive never to be underestimated. But to be loved—I really enjoyed the novelty of it. I basked in the unalloyed admiration, which I began to sense even the first time I ever went to her apartment (how different from the bohemian chic of Dauphine's nookery) to a party where (how different from Dauphine's entertainment) the guests drank not-so-dry sherry, listened devoutly to Mozart, Bach and Vivaldi, talked shop, and at the end, under the not-too-subtle prompting of the hostess, talked Jed Tewksbury.

This last inning began when Agnes asked me to tell about Dr. Stahlmann—I had been his assistant, hadn't I? I had lived in his wonderful house, hadn't I? I began to realize that to the new breed of graduate student, who had never known him, Dr. Stahlmann was already a solar myth, a giant from before the flood, and that, to some at least, certainly to Agnes Andresen, I wore the robe of the anointed. So I told about Dr. Stahlmann, and answered modestly questions about Jed Tewksbury and his achievements.

A few weeks later I encountered again, at the loan desk of the Library, one of the guests whom I had first met at Agnes' party, a hearty, hail-fellow-well-met type then miscast as an instructor in English, who now slapped me on the shoulder with the greeting "Hello, you old home-wrecker, you!"

I must have shown my surprise.

"You haven't heard?" he exclaimed, and proceeded to enlighten me. Agnes had been engaged for a long time to a graduate student in English and now she had just given him the gate. "The poor little bastard was sure in a shape," the hail-fellow said. "Came to my place to weep and drink, kept me up all night till he passed out on my divan." Then: "He blames it all on you, so congratulations!"

I told him that any congratulations were, at the least, premature, and probably misdirected, that I didn't know anything about it.

"Nuts," my informant uttered, and breezed on his eventual way toward the cushy job in the advertising agency of Foote, Cone and Belding, which was his natural habitat.

I had told him the truth. I hadn't even known that Agnes had a fiancé. But even at that moment, even as I sardonically criticized myself for the weakness, I heard, deep within me, the faint purr of gratified vanity. After all, I decided, she was rather attractive, in her way.

Not that I had been entirely unaware of certain signs of partiality in Agnes' behavior, and now, inevitably, I began to take a keener relish in the little symptoms of her condition, the improbable touches of color that began to illuminate her drab costume, a hair-do that, in the dusty precinct of our carrels, was even more improbable and certainly cost more than she could afford, the abortive attempts at badinage, the inept coquetries, the miscalculated sallies of learned wit, the not-well-concealed glances of canine yearning that, when caught out, precipitated the painful, little-girl blush.

Then the tears.

The tears came in a taxicab. We had been to a party of the sort enjoyed by Agnes' friends and colleagues, and though I had gone secretly fortified by a flask of vodka in the hip pocket and had made frequent trips to the bathroom, I was, by the time we were in the cab, in torpor rather than exaltation. I blamed this on the sweet sherry that I had been forced, by courtesy, to consume. In any case, I was silent, and Agnes, sitting bolt upright, seemed totally wrapped in her musings. Suddenly, without warning, she burst out: "I can't bear it!"

Before I could rally my dulled wits to ask what she couldn't bear, she was dissolved in tears. *Dissolved* is, I may insist, the *mot juste* for what was happening to Agnes Andresen. She was simply bawling her Scandinavian head off, nothing ladylike or femininely fetching about it, just the plain, old-fashioned, wide-mouthed, lips-drawn-back, tonsil-showing, streak-faced bawling a child does in total lostness and desolation.

"Hey," I demanded, snapping out of the torpor, "what's all this?"

She turned her face to me, managed to get the words out that it was awful, and let off a fresh salvo which, at such close range, was peculiarly unsettling.

"Hey," I said, "hey," and patted her shoulder for comfort, "come on, tell me."

She bawled again, so I patted harder.

"For God's sake," I demanded crossly, "what the hell is it?"

"They just told me," she managed, "just before we left," and emitted a couple of bawls.

"Told you what?"

"Perry—Perry—" she got out. "The qualifying—he busted it!"

"Perry?" I queried, then remembered that Perry—a Perry Gerald —was, as I had picked up from casual gossip, the name of the ex-fiancé, and he had apparently busted the Ph.D. qualifying. So, by way of comfort, I said: "Hell, he can take it over."

"But Perry—he's—he's—" she struggled for words "—he's so— so—"

"He's so what?" I said, beginning to feel considerable distaste for this Perry, whom I had never seen.

"So—so—" she began. "So sensitive," she said. "You see—I— I—" She couldn't go on.

"You mean you sacked this fellow," I said, "and now you blame yourself? Is that it?"

"Yes." She nodded. "Yes—and oh!—he's been working four years."

"God's name!" I exploded. "Four years to get ready for the qualifying? Is he defective?"

"Oh, I hate you!" she cried, and made utterance in a fashion to convince me that any previous achievement had been merely in the way of tuning up.

She let off salvo after salvo, directly at me, and all I felt was that I had to stop the racket. So I put my arm—the left, it was, for whatever significance that may have—around her shoulders, clear around now, patting her more authoritatively. It was as though the center had snapped the ball, for Agnes, in a flash, with the speed and aplomb of an All-America University of Alabama tackle, hunched her head down and plunged. She still had the horn-rims on and drove the sharp corner through fabric and flesh, clean down to grind into my breastbone, it unfortunately being spring and me protected by only a shirt and thin jacket.

I felt the dolphin-heave of the new sobs. I felt the wet weather—I swear it—getting through right to my skin. Then, with my left arm still clear around her shoulders, while she twisted the spikelike corner of the horn-rims into the bleeding wound, I was taking a deep breath, and saying: "Listen, I am as insensitive as a billy goat's foreskull and I made high honors on my qualifying and I have shot men dead with my own hands, but if you can tolerate such limitations what about marrying me and just forgetting the hell out of this little Perry?"

"Oh, you are vile!" she cried out this time, lifting her head for the retort. But she promptly collapsed back into her previous posture and, as I continued the pat-treatment, the sobs gradually diminished in volume and the corner of the horn-rims ceased to exacerbate the carnage already wrought, and the weary were at rest.

.   .   .

Aside, however, from all this horsing around, the strange fact was that, in my relation to Agnes, the usual process of moving through lust to esteem was reversed, and it was only after our engagement was announced to our little circle of acquaintances that I began to become aware of the appeal of Agnes as analyzed above. But Agnes knew how to sharpen that preliminary awareness to high poignancy.

Here, on reflection, I find the word *knew* quite inaccurate. Agnes had, instead of knowledge, instinct—in her as effective as ever the wisdom of the Serpent of Old Nile. For example, what female of guile would ever have chosen a taxicab for the scene that provoked my proposal? Such a female would have chosen some quiet, private, and candlelit nook—and the quarry would have scented danger on the wind. In other words, too smart is dumb. But a taxicab! What could more effectively lull suspicion and certify the sincerity, the depth of genuine feeling, the simplicity of heart, and even the uncalculating stupidity of Agnes Andresen's howls?

And after the engagement, what wiles and expertise could ever have wrought me to the pitch which Agnes managed with no trouble at all? To explain: after the engagement (I had never even kissed her before

—hadn't, in fact, felt any urge to do so), now impelled by a sense of courtesy and social correctness as well as by the first real twinges of concupiscence, I tried a couple of times to come to grips with my fiancée. But it was no dice. She was, in the old-fashioned way, a good girl. Right to the bone and bottled in bond. This was not guile, it was simply that she was from Ripley City.

Ripley City, S.D. (named, I learned, for a brigadier with some minor fame as a Sioux-killer until they outfoxed him), was a town of some thousand souls, where Agnes' father was the Lutheran minister and, in her hierarchy, something like a fourth and not too junior member of the Trinity. It was all arranged that she and I, in June, as soon as she had got her Ph.D., would travel to Ripley City, where her father would administer the marriage rites. To put it bluntly, if her father said it was really all right, then she would go to bed with me. I had the unverbalized, and no doubt slightly resentful, feeling that no other spokesman of Church or State could ever get her to lie and deliver. This was, at last, the classic case of the father giving away the bride.

Meanwhile, I made semiweekly visits to her apartment, where she would serve me sherry (to be secretly and internally mixed with my vodka), cook me a delicious little dinner, while eating which we would talk some desultory shop, and then allow herself to be persuaded to sit in my lap while we embraced with due reservation and dwelt on our bliss to come. Session by session, we developed a picture of what our life would be, our devotion to each other and to scholarship, our three flaxen-haired children, all sharp as tacks, the lovely books we would write, our trip to Europe together, our select circle of intellectual and distinguished friends, our little cottage on a remote lake in Minnesota for summers of health and meditation. All in all, we envisaged a floating island of bliss, cut off from the world.

And privately I observed that, even if our embraces always began discreetly, they might wind up just a little on the far side of discretion, with my hand coming around from under an armpit to hold a breast, her lipstick a little smeary (she had begun to use it, somewhat lavishly if inexpertly, for our semiweekly dates), her attention to conversation wandering, her gaze fixed on some hypothetical point in space, her breath getting short and shallow, and a network of strained white lines

appearing at the corners of the mouth. Once, even, she scrambled off·
my lap, in a kind of desperate awkwardness, and burst into tears, and.
asked me to go—go right away, go please, now, not to kiss her good
night, yes, she loved me, yes, but please go, go now.

I was hoping that, in spite of all my new and interesting feelings,
I would be able to hold out until June 23. Certainly, I was becoming
more and more convinced that there was something worth holding
out for—that, in fact, when Old Dad pulled the trigger of the starting
gun, it would be a little like the great Oklahoma Land Rush of 1889.
With no losers.

. . .

From the air, in June, Ripley City, S.D., was a slight abrasion on
the velvety vastness of the green and purple striped prairie. At close
quarters, it was just another little Western town, with streets wide,
empty, and wind-swept, with the barrooms and bordellos of a more
spacious age long since replaced by Kresge's and Grant's and a minus-
cule branch of the People's Trust Bank, and the buffalo-hunters and
cold-deck artists and high-heeled gunmen and high-heeled ass-ped-
dlers in fancy tight corsets all replaced by grocery clerks and stenogra-
phers, and at the hitching rack the old four-legged mustangs replaced
by last year's models of Ford and Chevrolet, but the sky is the same
as ever and its name, sure-God, is loneliness.

I had never been west before, and it was a new kind of loneliness.
This new kind, I decided, comes because the distance is fleeing away
from you, bleeding away from you, in all directions, and if you can't
stop the process you'll be nothing left except a dry, transparent husk,
like a cicada's, with the ferocious sunlight blazing through it. So
people out there just huddle together like cattle before a storm, but
the storm is not of the sky and the elements. Indeed, it is felt most
dangerously on the stillest day when the visible fleeing horizon shivers
in the brightness of distance. The storm is a purely metaphysical
twister that sucks up the self and carries it away. No, I'll go back to
the other metaphor: a constant, slow bleeding away into the four
quarters of distance.

In any case, this loneliness was, for me, a new kind. For unlike the
bleeding away of the self into distance, the kind of loneliness I had

known so well—the Southern, not the Western kind—is a bleeding inward of the self, away from all the world around, into an internal infinitude, like a pit. This was the kind I had been bred up to, and I had taken full advantage of my opportunities. I was the original, gold-plated, thirty-third-degree loneliness artist, the champion of Alabama.

Western hospitality (I could not then compare this to Southern, no case of which I had ever known) is the direct result of Western loneliness, a desire to add one more chunk of human warmth to the therapeutic huddle. The first day in Ripley City, Agnes and I huddled with the family connection, some score of persons, not counting babes-in-arms and inlaws, all, it seemed, with Lutheran-blue eyes, set, if male, in faces like whit-leather and, if female, in faces much the color of a fine winesap. That day we spent most of the time consuming what must have been a small herd of beeves, a chicken yard full of fryers and capons, a gross of pastries and angel food cakes, and enough black coffee to fill an Esso tank car. The next day we went to church and huddled with the population of the entire community and outlying country (all Lutheran), while Agnes' father preached a sermon, and she (we were on the front row) attended the discourse with rapturous attention while I held her hand. The next day we got married in a simple ceremony in church—me sweating in the first "good" suit I had ever owned, a dark blue creation (chosen by Agnes, who, in her innocence, did not realize that helping a man buy a suit is a more intimate business than getting into bed with him with no clothes on), and Agnes as cool as a cucumber and with eyes as blue-fresh as dew-sparkling gentians. Then there was a reception and social in the church basement, with the whole town on hand (the stores had closed for the occasion, Agnes' father really being the headman of the tribe) to consume an appropriate poundage of marriage meats sluiced down with another tank car of coffee. After Agnes (who had sneaked off with the bridesmaid cousins to the parsonage) had got back with the wedding gown replaced by a regular dress, we, under a storm of rice and well-wishing, drove off in a relatively new Plymouth on loan from an Andresen uncle, to head for Glacier Park.

.   .   .

94

As we tooled along westward, I reflected that, though I had approached Ripley City with dire misgivings, I now looked back on my stay with elegiac pleasure. I was remembering the Reverend Olaf Andresen—cranky-tall and gaunt-boned under the black suit, high pink skull fringed with a tousle of white hair, eyes more immoderately blue than even his daughter's—who, greeting me at the little hedge-hopper airport, had laid a hand on my shoulder and, with all the simplicity in the world, said: "Son, may God bless you as He now blesses us in your coming."

He looked like an Old Testament prophet, but with the gaze of a wise baby, and apparently he had never heard about Divine Wrath, and the words brimmed sweetly out of him like spring water, and I had the grace to blush and stand tongue-tied.

Driving out of town west, I looked back once, and saw Ripley City hull-down on the horizon, only the upper works of the seven grain elevators and the Reverend Andresen's steeple showing pale in the afternoon light. Even if Ripley City had its fine filaments of connection with the outside world—the railroad that drained off the wheat from the elevators now looming bone-white in that light, the highway east and west, and the little hedgehopping planes that passed twice a week—Ripley City was perfectly self-contained, self-fulfilling, complete. Not isolated. Not lost. Simply itself.

I stole a look at Agnes. She was deep in her thoughts. She wore a dress of very light summery stuff, with tiny blue dots sparsely knotted into it. Her feet, in white kid pumps, were set neatly side by side on the floor of the car. Her hands were folded on her lap. Her blue gaze was fixed down the long unswerving highway, where the heat-dazzle flickered and fled.

She looked exactly like a pretty girl from Ripley City, S.D., who had just got married to a very nice fellow with a good job there and they were going off on their honeymoon trip to Glacier National Park, where they had tiptop reservations in the hotel, and then they would come back to Ripley City and live happily ever after.

The wing of rapture brushed my heart. It was, indeed, a new experience.

. . .

We found the nice tourist camp that had been recommended to us for our first stop. Agnes took a bath and changed into a white dress and sandals on bare feet. For our wedding supper, an Andresen aunt had provided a well-stocked picnic hamper and I produced a bottle of Bordeaux and a bottle of sherry. We took a little walk and came back to set out our supper. I ordered ice, lemons and soda from the office and, when that came, boldly dipped into my secret supply of vodka. Agnes looked surprised but said nothing. She took some sherry.

After supper and the quick clearing up, we took another walk, now under a lavish prairie moon in a vast silence punctuated now and then by the faint cry of a night bird. I held my arm around Agnes' shoulders, and we drifted through silence. It was like lying in the bottom of a boat and gazing up at the moonlit sky, not feeling the motion but knowing that the current was sure and steady.

· · ·

Just at the moment of orgasm I broke into laughter that was a token of relief and joy. Agnes went rigid. I realized that she had begun to weep. When I had collected my wits, I said, "Darling, darling— what's the matter?"

She pulled out from under me and huddled on the side of the bed. I had to be very insistent before I could extract, in the midst of tears, an answer. "You're laughing at me," she finally managed to say. "That's what you're doing, and oh, it's awful!"

"Darling, you funny, dear darling," I said, "that's just a laugh of joy—just pure joy—why, it's like the Holy Laugh—you know how the Holy Rollers, or some other Pentecostals, bust out laughing for joy when God's Grace hits 'em."

She said I was blasphemous. She said I was making fun of her father. I said all I meant was Divine Joy, and that said in reverence.

I finally got her calmed down, and she was persuaded to go to sleep with her head on my shoulder. But we didn't make love again that night. I lay awake a long time staring at the ceiling. Next morning I decided I'd better wait until the night stop.

Agnes was, as I had surmised, a virgin, and virgins were something

I didn't know much about. I had never known one—intimately, I mean. Maybe the explanation was as simple as that.

·   ·   ·

In Chicago, in our new apartment, our life was beautiful, calm, and methodical. Agnes was very sweet and very affectionate, generous of attention and sympathy, an extremely good cook, with a good memory for my predilections. We were both working very hard, I trying to get my fool dissertation written, she at a monograph to be entitled "William Blake and Jacob Boehme: Twins of Vision"—a title she rather preened herself on. When, at 6 P.M., I came in from the Library she always greeted me with a kiss, when I went into our bedroom I always found a clean shirt, my lounging jacket (a present from Agnes), and my slippers ready, and when I came out the sherry and glasses were always established. At dinner we talked over the day, and afterwards, cleared the table together. Usually she had a batch of papers to correct or an assignment to review (she was very conscientious), and I read or fiddled with my notes. On Saturday night we had people in or we went out. On Sunday we went to church, and in the afternoon, took a walk, or if a really good cultural movie was available, saw it. On Wednesday and Saturday nights we had intercourse.

Nothing was actually planned that way. No more by Agnes than by me. It was simply that Agnes was the way she was, and didn't have to plan. It is a mystic power. She had a place for everything and everything naturally fell into its place. Including me.

Only once in the earlier period did "me" slip out of pattern. Agnes asked me when I was going to take her to Alabama to meet my mother, and I replied: "Never."

When she got her breath back, she asked why.

I told her that since my departure from Blackwell College in 1939 I had not been back to Alabama.

"But your mother!" she exclaimed.

I told her that the last thing my mother wanted was to see me in Alabama and that when we had anything to say, we wrote letters. I had written my mother of my marriage, I told Agnes, and had sent her a photo of the bride (true), which my mother had greatly admired (not true). What she had written me was this:

Dere Jed, I always figure the more a man waits the bigger chanst he has got of getting a head start but you done it and I hope you git what you want even if it aint what you got a need of. Thanks for the photo. I reckin a school teacher is a good quiet kinda wife to have and she is pritty for a school teacher as far as can tell from the photo. Tell her hello. Mr. Simms and me git on good—2 drinks all he ever takes at a time and that for Sunday. I aint had no call to break no more noses yet, ha ha. I do not mean to make no joke how I broke yore nose. I am sorry I done it. But it seemed like something I had it in me to do at the time. Have you tole the new wife how it is broke and who? I wish I could see her face and you telling her. Your loving mother,

Elvira (Mrs. Perk) Simms.

P.S.   A time back I saw in the paper how that man Rozelle caught in Florida is dead, fell off his boat, with Rozelle steering and drownt and Rozelle is a real rich widder. Rich or not I rather you married a school teacher pritty or not.

When I told Agnes about the letter, she burst out: "But you never mentioned it!"

I told her it was lost (not true, I have it before me this instant, yellow and crumbling), and that it hadn't struck me as of any interest to her.

"But you never talk about anything," she almost wailed. "Like that, I mean, like growing up, like your mother—oh, I don't understand you! I want to meet your mother."

"My mother," I said, "is a woman of great strength of character, and many remarkable qualities, including a trenchant, sardonic humor, but she is of minimal education and no talent for handling abstractions, and you and she would find few ideas to exchange. To characterize her further, she must have been very good-looking in her girlhood, but as is usual among pore white trash—the class to which we, though my mother would hotly deny it, may be said to belong—whatever beauty she had has long since been ravaged. But one more detail. Though she is a rather small-built woman, with small hands, hard work long ago toughened them to the texture of cast iron. And, oh yes, this reminds me that, in her letter, she said I should tell you how I got this broke-nose look. In the nameless college which I attended, I was, in fact, familiarly known as Broke-Nose."

Agnes was regarding me with a slow, painful, and fascinated sky-blue gaze.

"Shall I tell you?" I asked courteously.

She managed a nod.

So, with a gradual intensification of self-loathing, I told her, first giving a brief background sketch of Rozelle Hardcastle and Chester Burton, then moving on, detail by scrupulous detail, to the moment when, next morning, I emerged from the bedroom to confront my mother, who having studied my face and asked me if I had looked in the mirror yet, remarked: "It'll skeer ye. You look like a hog-killing, and the hog lost."

Agnes kept looking at me. Once I thought that she was trying to say something; a faint cloud of sweet sadness, in lieu of the pain and fascination, veiled the sky-blue gaze, and her tongue came out to wet her lips, but she managed no sound.

"So you see," I said then, "the ways of Dugton, Alabama, are not those of Ripley City, S.D."

Well before this remark I had actually tried to break off the narrative, but, finding that impossible, I ground on to the bitter end. Now I went to sit by Agnes' side and take her hands in mine and press my face against them, kissing them. First, I was overwhelmed with self-loathing. Then a secret pride crept over me. She said nothing. Then, after a little, she freed one of her hands and laid it on my head.

For several days thereafter, I was especially gentle with her.

.   .   .

That was our little floating island, cut off from the world; or, to revert to my earlier metaphor, the little heap of detritus on which the small-gauge boulder had come to rest. The silence of the Great Landslide went roaring by, and I was happy. That is, until I got unhappy.

But when I did get unhappy, I did not call it that. I railed at myself for not being worthy of my happiness. The most obvious trouble seemed to be that my dissertation had become dust and ashes in my mouth. I began to regard it as little more than a trick performed by an idiot for the edification of fools, or vice versa. I felt like the prize poodle in a second-rate dog-and-pony show jumping through hoops, or like the pony that could count if you stuck a pin in him. If this dissertation represented the *imperium intellectūs,* then to hell with it. But no man can live without some sense of meaning in life, so I improvised one: I would turn it into a parlor trick.

If doing tricks like my dissertation was in itself meaningless (and I saw myself condemned to a Sisyphean eternity of such tricks), you could still achieve a derivative meaning by getting some fun out of having it taken seriously—and getting paid for it.

With great cunning, I began to plot my brilliant career. I had a firm start, I realized, in a dissertation that involved not a single idea. My next step was to cultivate my supervisor, Dr. Alesbury Sweetzer, who had originally, with furrowed and suffering brow and out of (truly) great learning, proposed my topic. In my earnest search for knowledge, I devised complicated and idiotic questions (which I, by a careful study of his more obscure articles, knew that he could answer), and with a worried expression, took them to him and apologetically begged for help. Soon I heard that my supervisor (who had always hated Dr. Stahlmann with a passion) had fallen into the habit (in spite of my earlier connection with Dr. Stahlmann) of referring to me as a very promising young scholar. So I branched out, cautiously of course, and tried the same tactic on the Chadworth Professor of Medieval History, who also happened to be a Division Chairman.

By this time, too, it got so I simply couldn't stand the dusty carrel and my orderly stacks of note cards, and would sneak out to an afternoon movie, anything, cultural or not, preferably not. I almost got caught once; Agnes asked me where I had been that afternoon, and when I said, in the Library, she told me she had come by and could not find me. A providential lie sprang to my lips. I had, I said, been back in the stacks. I felt no guilt at the lie. Rather, it seemed an inevitable part of a deep mysterious logic that, yet shrouded in mist, had only begun to divulge itself.

Meanwhile, I had grown bold enough to set out a bottle of bourbon beside the bottle of evening sherry. This, on the first occasion (as it had on our honeymoon), evoked a startled look but no verbal reaction. I noticed, however, that when we had our little parties, some of the sherry drinkers began to manifest a marked preference for bottled-in-bond, even though they still clung to Bach and Couperin like grim death. In this I differed, for the more redeye I sipped, the less Bach seemed to mean to me, and I distinctly remember that one night, at the height of the baroque ecstasy of the flute solo of the Brandenberg Concerto, Number 5, having slipped into the bathroom in answer to the call of nature, I stood washing my hands and staring at my flushed image in the mirror and demanding in a firm voice what the hell was Bach to Ole Broke-Nose or he to Hecuba, and thinking that this was very funny.

In fact, I began, more and more often, to feel slightly indisposed on Sunday morning (sometimes for good and sufficient reason, since Sunday morning comes after Saturday night), and so would not be able to accompany Agnes to church. I finally came clean and declared that I knew she would not want me to lead a life of hypocrisy, that though some people could, for various reasons and needs, which I could respect but not understand, fly in the face of the whole intellectual history of the Western world since the Renaissance, I, God help me, could not. So she went to church alone. For a time, that is. But somewhere along the way her own churchgoing dwindled, then ceased.

Speaking of Sundays, I am reminded unhappily of one in particular on which a change was wrought. On the afternoon of that day, with weather too wet and blustery to walk for pleasure and no movie of cultural pretensions within striking distance, a cold-blooded lust, compounded by boredom, frustration, and self-disgust, overcame me, and I went at Agnes tooth and nail, and hell take the hindmost of the three-by-five note cards that were strewing the floor. She made some serious protest, purely verbal, but finally, with an air of what struck me as tight-lipped resignation, succumbed. But only, I may add, in the quite literal and etymological sense of the word, not the spiritual. My victory, achieved on the living room couch (a flat one of the studio variety), with my victim stripped only in the business district and my trousers vibrating around my ankles, was strictly Pyrrhic. Certainly, not the lovely secret blooming which had once possessed my imagination.

Several times that winter (the second of our marriage) I broke schedule, always with the same results. In the end, I decided that it just wasn't worth the trouble. Anyway, Agnes had begun to complain of not feeling very well.

She was not very well. The diagnosis was cancer of the uterus.

.   .   .

In the brief interval between the diagnosis and the admission to the hospital, we still slept in the same bed. The first night I woke around 3 A.M., and became aware that she was staring at the ceiling. I found her hand, and held it. Then, out of the dark, quite calmly, her voice came. "They say it's inside me," the voice, which did not sound at all like hers, but like that of a small, determined child, said.

She jerked her hand free from me. All at once, she was pushing herself up in bed. I tried to put an arm around her, but she shoved me off. I slipped out of bed, came around to the other side, turned on the bedside light there, and sat on a stool, drawn close.

She was sitting bolt-upright in bed. In a slow, probing motion, she was moving her fingers back and forth over her breasts, abdomen, belly. She looked up, in a bright birdlike way. "There's nothing there," she announced. "Except, I mean," she added, with scrupulous factuality, "what ought to be."

The hands, more lightly, more caressingly, were continuing the slow, probing motion over the silky cloth that sheathed her body. I reached out to imprison her hands. I could not bear to watch them. "Darling," I said, as gently as I could, with the raw pain blocking my throat, "it seems almost certain that something is there. But—" and I tried to smile in casual comfort "—that's not important. The doctors, all of them, say that it's not serious. For they'll take it out. And then you'll—"

"But it's not there," she affirmed flatly. "It couldn't be there. There's no way for it to be there." She paused; then, suddenly staring into my face, in another voice, like a marveling, dawning whisper, said: "Unless—"

She jerked her hands from my grip.

"Unless you—" she said, and stopped. Then: "—put—"

102

She stopped.

She wasn't staring into my face now. In pajamas, I sat there on the stool, leaning forward, my hands on my knees, knees wide apart, and she was staring at the formless lump my passionless genitals made under the loose, thin cotton cloth.

She couldn't go on. All at once, she put her face in her hands. Her shoulders were shaking. I was trying to pat her shoulders. As for me, I wasn't feeling anything. My mind seemed to be numbly refusing something, seeking refuge in numbness. All I felt was what I had felt in the taxicab long before—that I had to stop that crying. I kept patting.

She bit her lower lip to make herself stop crying. Then she looked at me in piteous appeal. "Tell me," she begged, "tell me I'm not really crazy. Tell me I was just crazy for a minute when I said that. Tell me I'm not going crazy."

I sat on the edge of the bed and put my arms around her. I sat there that way for a long time, with her head, at last, on my shoulder. The tenseness, bit by bit, drained off from her body. In the end, she fell asleep that way, and I carefully laid her down.

.   .   .

When she woke the next morning, she was very calm. She remained that way, occasionally smiling, speaking quietly to me about trivialities, until the morning when they took her to the hospital. The evening before, she had made me sit by the bed while she told me that she loved me. That she understood me a lot better now. That she wasn't afraid. That we were going to have a nice time together, just the way we had planned. After a while I said that I had to go to the bathroom.

I did have to. So I could cry.

.   .   .

After the operation, the doctor cautioned me against excessive optimism.

I sat by Agnes' bed as long as they would let me. Then I went to the apartment. How strange it looked when I entered. I felt that I had entered the wrong door. Or that all doors, all over the world, are alike.

Enter any door and what you find is both strange and familiar in the communal doom. Look into the mirror and be surprised at whatever face you see.

I took a stiff drink and went to bed. In a bed that was both strange and familiar. In the dark I ran my hands over my own body, back and forth, as she had done over hers. I wondered what truth was lurking in the dark, pulsing inwardness that was body. Body is body, I thought. How silly, how absurd to give any particular body a name. I could not sleep.

So I got up, went to my desk, and found the fool dissertation. My eyes simply would not focus on the words. I had the feeling, all at once, of total entrapment. It was as though I had come to the desk as to a last hoped-for exit. But masonry, quite fresh, had been erected across the aperture. I had been betrayed.

I felt that I was going to vomit.

At last my hand reached out, and with a painful dubiety picked up and arranged before me a sheet of paper. I stared at the blank whiteness. I swear to you that my mind was as blank as the paper. With wonderment, I watched my right hand pick up a pen and begin to write. Each letter, as it took shape on the whiteness, seemed a mysterious achievement, each word a self-generating miracle. I waited with intense interest for what the words might say. The words were in a line across the top of the sheet. Each word began with a capital. When the words were finished, the hand drew a firm black line under them. They said:

DANTE AND THE METAPHYSICS OF DEATH.

The hand kept on writing until 4 A.M.

.   .   .

Agnes recovered rapidly from the operation, bright and cheerful. As I sat by the bed, she talked of how all our dreams would come true. After these conversations, I always went back to the apartment, and the hand would pick up the pen and the pen would begin its slow and often interrupted, but inexorable, progress across the page.

I would think of Agnes lying in the dark, in the hospital room, and would wonder what was happening in her head as she stared up at the ceiling. But the pen kept moving on its secret way that she did not even suspect.

. . .

Then Agnes came home. The first thing she asked for was her notes, a clipboard of paper, and a pen. Propped up in bed, she worked for more than an hour, her horn-rims on her nose, her brow furrowed. Within a week she could work several hours a day. She had some marvelous new ideas, she said. And almost every day she wrote a voluminous letter to her father (her mother had recently had a stroke and was now a vegetable), telling him how well she felt and not to worry for even one minute.

As for housework, she insisted on cooking, even if I had learned so much about it, being on my own. Sometimes people came to see us in the evening to drink sherry and listen to Mozart and Bach and Vivaldi, and Agnes was brighter and more vivacious then she had ever been, and even began to develop a delicious, shy wit, in which the shyness became part of the wit. The guests always went home early now. On the evenings when we were alone, I always cleared things off, after which Agnes would sit in my lap, just as in the days of our courtship, and we would talk of the future. She was getting stronger every day.

Then she began to get weaker.

During the whole period I had never told Agnes about what was in a locked attaché case, on the highest and darkest shelf in the closet of the room I used as a study, but at night, after Agnes was safely asleep (with the mild sedative prescribed for her), I guiltily latched the door of that room, and under the green-shaded lamp, the hand picked up the pen. After a time, it would begin to move.

It might be toward dawn before I put things back into the attaché case, returned it to its dark shelf, undressed and got my pajamas on, and found my way, as silently as possible, to the old army cot beside Agnes' bed, close enough so that she could reach out to take my hand when she began to get wakeful again. I always came to bed before 4

A.M., because that was the time when she would wake up and grope out for my hand.

Then she went back to the hospital. All she said was: "Oh, I'm making such a mess of things for you—you silly, sweet old broke-nose old angel." This was just before the ambulance people transferred her from the bed to the stretcher. They stood around and heard her say it.

But I suppose that they had heard plenty in their time.

What she had said was in an idiom totally foreign to her. I could not believe that a locution like "broke-nose" was in her vocabulary. She would have died before using such an illiteracy. But now she was using it and not going to die until later.

I followed the stretcher, and my head seemed to float, and my fingertips felt swollen and without sensitivity as though they were old-fashioned condoms inflated like children's balloons. That was the image that crossed my mind.

.   .   .

My life now revolved, with mechanical regularity, between two poles: the bed in the hospital where Agnes lay and the lighted space under the green-shaded lamp where the pen might begin to move across the white paper. Between, you might say, my laboratory findings and my studies in the theory of death. In the laboratory I gathered what data I could on the process by which death was defining the relation, past and present, between Agnes Andresen and Jediah Tewksbury. In my studies in theory I undertook to analyze the idea that for Dante death defines the meaning of life, that, indeed, the core drama of the *Divina Commedia* depends upon this idea.

Needless to say, my double concern set up deep tensions. On the one hand, in the laboratory the validity of the work, necessarily involving both Agnes and me, depended upon the reliability of the data; and this meant, of course, a degree of dependence upon the "sincerity" of both of us, the truth of our "reports." As far as Agnes was concerned, there was, I knew, no problem, but for me it was different. Naturally, the fact of "insincerity" would be data, too, but to establish "insincerity" required that some norm of "sincerity" be posited. There was a further complication in that *Jediah Tewksbury*

—*investigator* was thus investigating *Jediah Tewksbury—subject.* In what ways, for instance, might the heart pangs and tears of *J.T.— subject* be modified by his awareness of the clinical eye of *J.T.— investigator?* As I sat by the bed, I yearned for purity of feeling, for a sense of meaning in my experience, but when feeling gushed up in my heart, I caught myself asking if the yearning itself might not be the mother of self-deceit. Or, even, asking if the awareness of the clinical eye might provoke the enactment desired.

Into this problematic situation, a peculiar factor obtruded itself.

One evening, when I came to the visitor's desk of the hospital, the attendant said that the doctors were with my wife, would I please wait for an all-clear. I sat down, and sank into my meditations. From them, a moment later, I was summoned by a voice saying: "Mr. Tewksbury?"

Looking up in a dazed way, I saw a man of some thirty years, dressed in the academic uniform of flannel trousers, brown tweed jacket with leather elbow-patches, blue shirt with button-down collar, one button lacking, black knit tie loosely knotted, all on the shabby side. As for the face that hung above the uniform, it was of a type not unusual above such a rig—handsome in a rather thin, nervous way, mouth sensitive, nose nondescript, eyes large, dark, and liquid ("poetic," impressionable female observers might say), hair dark and unkempt. The young man was, without perfect confidence, sticking out his hand. "I'm Perry Gerald," he was saying. "Agnes—maybe she—"

"Howdy-do, Mr. Gerald," I dutifully said.

He withdrew the hand, and stole a glance at it as though it had been up to some rather dubious and dangerous adventure, and then turned his liquid orbs on me. "It's about—" and he wet his lips. "About Agnes," he concluded.

I had nothing to say.

"You know about me?" he demanded, in a flicker of desperation.

"Something," I said. "Enough, I reckon."

"She—she meant a lot to me," he said.

I waited.

"What I mean is—could I see her?"

The upshot was that I let him come. In fact, in some darker dimension of my being I welcomed his presence. Later, it even occurred to me that in giving him permission I had been unconsciously motivated by the notion that in the laboratory, which was the hospital room, Perry would provide some sort of control for the investigation of *J. T.* —*subject*. In the elevator going up, I covertly studied his good looks, his face lifted yearningly as his liquid gaze was fixed on the shifting gleam of the indicator panel, and I thought that soon, soon now, his romantic, self-indulgent dream of a last encounter, fulfilling and sweet, would be subjected to the shock of reality. I lived with the shock of reality, and I knew.

For in this disease, at this stage, the face of the patient changes rapidly, and it does not change for the better. Each day, there is a new face to define as that of your beloved, and to come to terms with. And, as a corollary, there is, each day, your own new self, facing that face, to define, and to come to terms with.

It may be said that this process is like a much speeded-up version of the process of two lovers growing old together. But with two great differences. First, in the natural process of aging there is time to adjust, bit by bit, to change, to mercifully forget the old norms of beauty and charm in the beloved. Second, in the natural process, your own disintegration, proceeding at an equal rate, can subtly, and in even-handed equity, propose new and less difficult norms. All this in contrast to the situation in which one lover merely suffers the slow diminution of time while the other disintegrates at an appalling pace.

I waited for little Perry to confront the shock of reality.

When it came, Perry almost went down. But he was of sterner stuff than I had surmised. He rallied, made his way across the space to the bed, and took the patient's hand and kissed it. For a moment, then, he laid his cheek against it. All this was accomplished with no word uttered. Then he crossed to the far side of the bed and sat upright in a chair.

I sat in the chair close to the bed and held Agnes' hand. There were few words during the visit. Agnes was now too weak and drugged to make such conversation. So for the appointed time, we three were together, each enduring his private destiny. For ten minutes at a stretch, Perry would stare at Agnes' hand lying in my clasp. I wondered who, in the trio, should envy whom.

We were to spend a number of evenings after this fashion. Sometimes I even invented some urgent excuse to leave early and went back to my work desk and picked up the pen. I would wonder if, on such occasions, Perry came around to take my chair and hold Agnes' hand. Finally I concluded that he would not, that he would be much happier with the pure, abstract emotion untainted by any vulgar contact.

.   .   .

One evening, only a few weeks before Agnes' death, as Perry and I were in our accustomed positions, a knock came at the door, and the nurse admitted an aging man who introduced himself to me as an old seminary friend of Olaf Andresen. Olaf, he said, had written him that his doctor would not let him travel even to the bedside of his daughter and he, Olaf, was asking him to go to Chicago (he lived in south Wisconsin) and pray with her. So he had come to fulfill the wish of the old friend.

Agnes, though dulled by drugs, could respond to him, and so he knelt down by the bed. Remembering certain things, I found this somewhat more than I could comfortably take, so I slipped out into the hall.

I waited what I took to be a proper time, then softly entered the room. The old friend was just getting his cranky bones up from the floor, and it was clear that Perry, on the far side of the bed, had been kneeling, too. I caught sight of the nurse, discreetly behind the screen. Her eyes were red.

I thanked the old friend, and he gave me his blessing and took his leave. I went to sit by the bed, and held Agnes' hand. I told her that I was glad he had come. Her mouth worked in its slow way to get the words out, but she said: "I let him do it. For my father. But you—Jed—you know something."

She stopped and looked very tired with the effort.

After a little, I said: "Know what, darling?"

She squeezed my hand. "You were right." She got the words out very slow. "There isn't any—" She stopped. Then her mouth, working even slower not to make the words, said: "Any God."

"But, darling—" I said, hearing the thin edge of anguish in my own voice.

She was squeezing my hand, hard now, harder than I would have thought she now had strength for. "Hush," she said. "Hush."

So I hushed. There wasn't really anything I had to say.

I thought little Perry was going to crack up. He did go out of the room.

.   .   .

When Agnes was dying, I had to keep reminding myself that the jerking of the body, the hand—thin down to bone now—that climbed the air and made the grasping, groping motion of blindly seeking a rope to hang on to, the mewing or guttural utterances of the distorted mouth, were nothing more than mechanical responses like the twitch of the cut-off frog leg back in the biology lab of Dugton High when the electric current was put through it. Agnes Andresen Tewksbury was, for all practical purposes, I kept telling myself, dead.

But Perry, it seemed, was not having much luck telling himself that. He kept edging closer to me, and I kept edging away from him. "I don't believe it," he kept saying, in a hoarse whisper.

"Believe what?" I finally demanded, not even looking at him, at the object on the bed.

"What the doctor said. That she doesn't feel anything. You know what I think," he said, turning at me, seizing me by the arm, digging his sharp little fingers into me, holding me so that I couldn't edge away, thrusting his pale face at me, sweat on the temples, his poetic eyes awash with tears, continuing: "The pain just got down deeper inside her, it's deep inside now, it's gone where the drugs can't reach it, that's why she may be unconscious on the surface, but not down inside—and oh! she is suffering there—you can see, you can see—you—"

"Jesus Christ," I interrupted, not looking at him, looking at the bed, "can't you see I want to be alone, can't you get the hell out?"

He got the hell out.

It took another forty-five minutes. Long before that, I kissed her on the brow. The flesh was cold as ice and wet with sweat that had, it seemed, an acrid rather than a salty taste.

Finally the nurse emerged from behind her screen, spread a sheet

110

over the mangled face from which the glacier-blue eyes stared in muted outrage.

The doctor came in, and laid a hand on my shoulder.

.   .   .

When I came out of the door of the room, I was vaguely aware of a scurry around the corner of the corridor. Out on the street, Perry suddenly reappeared, as though by magic, at my side. He looked at me inquiringly.

"Yes," I said.

As I moved off down the now deserted street (it was toward three o'clock of a May morning, and in spite of gasoline fumes, the air was soft), he fell in beside me, but at a safe arm's length. After a while, he said: "I'll never be able to forget her."

I made no reply, not looking, holding my stride.

"It almost killed me when she chucked me," he said. "I knew I wasn't worthy, she was so fine, she was so smart."

I kept on walking.

"She needed somebody she could look up to. You had been Dr. Stahlmann's favorite student. People thought you'd do something big."

I kept on walking.

"You aren't even listening," he said.

"No," I said.

"Well, listen to this," he said, and stopped short.

I kept on. He had to run a couple of steps to catch up.

"Maybe you'll be great," he said, "but you didn't come up to her, you didn't even know how to appreciate her. I'll never be great, I know that, but I did know how to love her. But you—"

I stopped. I was now looking at him.

But he went on. "You," he said, "you didn't know how. And I don't think you ever could!"

I was still looking at him, waiting for more words to come out of that sensitive mouth.

"Listen," I finally said, quite gently, "you little half-ass Neo-Platonist. Get out of my sight."

———

111

The night of Agnes' death, I went on to the apartment and sat at my desk. In the end, the pen began to move. I was doing some moderate crying, but it kept on moving.

．　　．　　．

Agnes was buried in the family plot in the cemetery in Ripley City. Her father managed to officiate at the funeral, his voice reedy and weak but never faltering. Later, he stood by the grave as the earth went in. All the town was again at the cemetery, silent in the blazing sun. After the last clod was in the hole, they all passed by to shake my hand. An old man, a-shiver with palsy, who told me that for thirty years he had been principal of the Ripley City school, held on to my hand and told me that Little Aggie had been the brightest scholar that ever came out of Ripley City. As he talked, I hung on to the word *scholar*—that old-fashioned use of it. This was something to hang on to.

That night, in the little ritual parlor of the parsonage, I sat with Agnes' father. He said that he—all the family—had committed the sin of pride. In their pride, they had forgotten gratitude to Him who had made the lovely gift. But oh, she was so sweet, she was so bright! At two years old, she had sat on his knee every night after supper and spelled out the names in the picture book, even big words like "hippopotamus."

Sitting there, his hands in the air as though to support the hypothetical child on his knee, he straightened up, the corners of his mouth lifting in a smile, the fading blue of his eyes clearing, all at once, to sky-brightness. Looking at him, I remembered how, on the wedding visit, all the brothers and cousins and aunts and uncles had hung around Agnes, clinging to her every word, staring at her in gentle bemusement, and how she bloomed gently like a potted plant, too long in the house but at last set out in sunlight.

"We all knew from the first," her father was saying, "she was too much for Ripley City. She'd go out in the world. She'd be a credit to Ripley City. When she went away to college, lots of people went down to the train to wave her goodbye. But," he added, "nothing ever spoiled her."

112

And I felt like bursting out: *Oh yes, something did, I married her!*

I felt for a minute that maybe I was going crazy, but I pulled myself together.

The old man was saying something. About trusting God. He was ashamed to admit, he said, but when his wife had her stroke he had a hard time trusting God. And now, with Agnes. He had to stop there, and wait, then start over. Then he said that he knew I was not a churchgoing man, but he also knew that Agnes would have a good man for her husband. She had told him I was a good man—*Christianus naturaliter*—and that he knew that God in His mercy would not let the prayer of a good man, believer or not, be wholly lost. He wanted, he said, looking at me with a sudden, naked, beseeching gaze, to ask me a favor.

I nodded.

"My son," he said, "I cannot pray. I have lost the gift of prayer. Will you kneel down with me and help me pray? Oh, my son, if you, whose pain must be even greater than my selfish pain, can kneel and utter a silent prayer for me, God cannot turn away His face."

He had slipped from the chair. The knobby old knees were on the thin, long-since-gone-drab carpet. His bony fingers came trembling together in the posture of prayer. So I knelt there, by the marble-topped little parlor table, on which the enormous leather-and-brass-bound Bible lay, and by it, now, the stack of Agnes' yellowing school report cards and the baby shoes dipped in bronze, which had been exhibited to me earlier in the evening, and I prayed.

.   .   .

Past three o'clock in the morning, I was in the cemetery. I had tried to sleep but could not. So I got up and walked all over Ripley City, up and down, knowing all the time that after I had seen it all by moonlight—every street, all the shuttered houses, the store windows, the school building, the wheat elevators, the railroad station and the rails glistening off into distance, east and west—I would wind up here where the hump of raw earth was covered by a rug of artificial grass and by the flowers, whose colors—those that were not virginal white —were bleached by the moon.

I had had to come out to look over Ripley City once more, for the last time, I told myself. For after the praying was over, just as we were saying good night, the old man had laid a hand on my shoulder and said: "My son, you will go out into the world and do what Agnes would want you to do and believed you would do. But after the dust and heat, you, my son, may want to come to this quietness. And a place will always be kept waiting by her side. I promise you that."

I looked down at the moon-bleached colors of flowers, and thought that Agnes Andresen had come home. Maybe she should never have left it.

What would she have been spared, I asked myself.

Me.

So I said goodbye. I did not think that I would ever come back, for as much as I liked Ripley City, its ways were not the ways of Dugton, Alabama. But it was nice to know that there was, somewhere, a place to come to.

.   .   .

I was now deep in debt, and what use was the apartment to me alone, anyway? Preparatory to moving, I packed all of Agnes' things to send back to Ripley City. The business went well until I took down the wedding dress from where it hung in the closet, unpinned the sheet around it, and made ready to pack it in the very box in which it had come from the store. That cracked me.

I had things laid out on newspapers on the floor to get a work space, and when I tried to put the wedding dress back into the box it was like putting somebody in a coffin. I couldn't breathe. I simply lay there by the box, on the newspapers that kept telling over and over all the things that were happening all over the world and that I couldn't have cared less about, with my head hunched and my forehead pressed against the hardness of the floor, and little Perry was telling me again how Agnes should have married him, because I had not loved Agnes, and that was about too much for me to bear.

But that was not the worst.

The worst thing was that now, with Agnes far away, under the not-yet-adjusted earth and disintegrating flowers, in the cemetery in Ripley City, S.D., I knew that I did love her.

So, as expiation for the past or as a counterirritant to the intolerable present, I thrust my right forearm (bare, for I was wearing a T-shirt) under my mouth and set my teeth in the flesh. I lay there, depending on the pain to save my life.

It did.

I lifted my head and stared at the two dotted-line semicircles of blue bruises sparsely oozing blood, that faced each other concavely in my flesh. I remembered hearing that the human bite is almost as dangerous as a rattler's. Then I wondered if you can infect yourself. Then I wondered if I should go to a doctor. Then I wondered what the doctor would say if I told him that I had bitten myself by accident. Then I burst into hilarious laughter, for I had, that instant, had a vision of the newspaper headline:

YOUNG SCHOLAR DIES OF SELF-INFLICTED DOG BITE

I sat there laughing in a wild way that finally died off into giggles. The arm had begun to hurt. Staring at the wound, I thought that if I did die of my self-inflicted bite, this would be one more example of the Dantean metaphysic of death that Dante himself hadn't thought up. I would have to try to analyze its aura of significance.

At that, I went to the bathroom and doused my hurt with iodine, then came back to my task.

When, that afternoon, I mailed the boxes to Ripley City, I also sent, by air mail, my essay on Dante to *The Mediaevalist,* of London.

You might as well start at the top, I told myself. I had never before sent anything anywhere.

.   .   .

It was more than two months before I heard from *The Mediaevalist,* and by that time I had sunk into my new life—or rather, my way of living, for it was sure not life: up at 7:00; in carrel by 8:30; dinner at greasy spoon at 6:30; back to room (a sty) at 7:30; work till 11:00. I had persuaded my supervisor to let me develop my essay into my dissertation, which took some doing since he had proposed the old one. But, with my recently developed cunning, I outmaneuvered him by explaining that the new topic had been suggested (a lie) by a statement found in one of his articles, and cited a passage which simply happened to pop into my head and which, if it had no relation to my idea, was not, at least, in flat contravention of it. My supervisor, though of high intelligence and great learning, was also of boundless ambition, inordinate vanity, and a weak ego-structure, and therefore had an ear cocked to every rathole and a built-in psychoelectronic apparatus attuned to catch whatever slightest pulses from interstellar space that might be construed as a code, Morse or otherwise, for his name. So he made no real difficulty.

Indeed, he beamed when, two months later, I showed him the letter from the editor of *The Mediaevalist,* which began:

> Your essay has been read by one of our most distinguished scholars of Dante and by another scholar of equal repute whose specialty is Thomistic philosophy. Independently, they have concurred with our opinion that your essay is of considerable importance. Their comments (including, as is only natural, certain queries, caveats, and reservations) will be forwarded to you. Meanwhile, permit me to congratulate . . .

At this point in his reading, my supervisor interrupted himself to shake my hand and say, in a stagey English public school accent (he was from Indiana): "And permit me to congratulate you—" here he dropped the accent, but continued "—at the threshold of a most distinguished career. For you must know, my dear Jediah—" he had never before used my Christian name "—that I have always regarded you as—"

He wound up by giving me a job as assistant professor.

.   .   .

Thus I began my professional career. This little success gave me at least something to think about and some sense of purpose, however delusory, for what had to be called my life. But, presently, it was a more substantial success that made my life unendurable.

For my essay, in the December issue of *The Mediaevalist* was quite definitely a success. I received several letters from revered scholars, with foreign stamps on the envelopes, including one from the great Enrico Squadalupi of Rome. He was, in fact, translating my essay into Italian (it was already being translated into German).

And so life was really unendurable, for I began to realize that, in the mystic texture of the universe, my success would have been impossible except for the protracted agony and lingering death of Agnes Andresen. It was as though the essay had been, in the deepest sense of the word, her death warrant.

I had, apparently, on some moonless midnight, on a desolate heath where the rocky, white, reared-up outcroppings grinned skeletally in the dark, struck a bargain with the Prince of This World: her life for my success. And he, like the gentleman he is, had scrupulously fulfilled his contract.

The scene is the action, says a distinguished literary critic, and Chicago had been the scene, and so every day in Chicago meant a reenactment. I had my Ph.D. I had a good job and golden promises. My dissertation was to be published as a book.

So I fled.

.   .   .

In September, 1951, I found myself sitting in the club car of the night train to Nashville, Tennessee, where I had accepted a post as associate professor, at a very good salary with liberal time for research. My supervisor had urged me to stay at Chicago and made flattering promises, but I tried to explain why I had to leave. Finally, putting his hand on my shoulder (he had become more and more paternal as each echo of my little success reached him), he said: "My dear boy, I understand. You have had a tragic experience. I can see why you feel you must go back to your native earth. To touch base. To regain your force. Yes—like Antaeus. Yes, very like him. Yes, I understand."

He paused, gripped my shoulder in a manly way, resumed: "But, my boy," he said, "we'll get you back—you are ours!" He said "ours," but he meant "mine." That is, his. In other words, I was no longer Dr. Stahlmann's. I was Dr. Sweetzer's.

Sitting in the club car, I thought of Antaeus, that poor, blundering giant whose strength had to be constantly revived by contact with the earth, his mother, and how Hercules outguessed him by simply lifting him off his feet to kick and squirm and get weaker and weaker. Well, I reflected rather grimly, for that kicking and squirming and getting

117

weaker part of the picture, my supervisor, in his flight of classical fancy, may have been right in the comparison. But he—innocent Indiana victim of Thomas Nelson Page and *Gone with the Wind* and the Lost Cause—was sure-God wrong if he thought that Nashville, Tennessee, even if it was the Second Cradle of the Confederacy, was sacred and revivifying earth to Old Broke-Nose. Old B.-N. had never even seen the place, had never harbored even a fleeting twinge of curiosity about it. Even if he was, at the moment, on the way there.

"Gee, you'll like it," the young woman by my side in the club car was saying and, in the same motion that jiggled the ice in her glass, was jiggling a couple of kilos of shiny hardware on her charm bracelet. She set the empty glass down on the little table by her side, and the black barman, being a mind reader, set a full one down for her; and one for me, I must confess.

"Now I was born and raised and went to college in Detroit—that's where I studied office management and got a good job like the one in Nashville," she continued, "but I sort of like it down South. The women down there—they aren't very bright and they sure aren't stylish—" here smoothing her long flouncy skirt with pointed talons as blood-red as an eagle's after the kill "—but the men, they're different. They sure know how to make you feel like a lady. You take a real Southern Gentleman and—" She interrupted herself to drain off half of the new glass of Scotch, then, having canted a sly glance sidewise at me, asked: "Now where did you say you are from?"

"I didn't say," I said.

"I bet you're from the South!" she asserted recklessly.

I started to deny, but thought what-the-hell, so said: "Claxford County, Alabama."

"I knew it!" she exulted. "I can always tell!" There was a great clatter of the charms on the bracelet as she celebrated her clairvoyance.

I took a drink to celebrate exactly nothing, and the train plunged on south through the equinoctial storm.

The barman served the last drinks and shut up shop. Everybody else except the woman and me left the car. "You know," she finally said, turning to me, "I really need a nightcap." Then in her most clairvoyantly triumphant vein, announced: "I bet you do, too!"

118

Before I could answer, she exclaimed: "I just remembered! I've got a little in my suitcase. We can take our glasses—they've got some ice left, and just pop into my room. Gee!" she added enthusiastically. "I'm sure glad I thought of that!"

"I appreciate the invitation," I said, "but I really don't think I ought. I'm not feeling my best."

"It'll make you feel better," she rejoined, smiling significantly.

"You see," I said, "I'm all cured, the doctor told me just yesterday, but the side effects of the treatment, they sort of drag you down for a few weeks. For syphilis, I mean."

She grabbed one arm of her chair and bounced out, speedily if unsteadily. Weaving a little, clutching her empty glass to her bosom, she stared down at me. If it had not been twisted in outrage, the face would really have been quite attractive. The figure was good, too. But I couldn't have cared less.

Glaring down, she was finally getting some words out: "You— you—" The clutch slipped again, then caught. "You son of a bitch," she wound up, simply.

I watched her make her way in her flouncy skirt across unsteady space toward the narrow passage by the bar, toting her glass with the last ice in it. She was swaying badly. Then I realized that it was not only the whiskey and the plunge of the train. One of her legs was a little shorter than the other. Or something.

But that was not the point. I had told her the lie before I knew that.

.   .   .

I stared at the white lashing of rain on the glossy depthless black of the club car window opposite my chair, and wondered if it was raining in South Dakota. Or, at that latitude, it might be snow, whipping down from the Arctic. I wondered if the humped earth of the grave had sunk much in its fifteen months. I hoped it was not rain, but snow, if there had to be something off in South Dakota. Snow would cover things up.

I thought of what little Perry had said, why Agnes had married me. He was right, no doubt. The heart of the female scholar—womanly, warm, unselfish beneath the dark draperies of learning—finds its expression thus. What did it matter if, in the beginning, I had been nothing more than a sort of fetish left over by Dr. Stahlmann, and the love had been for a symbol of scholarship and not for Jed Tewksbury? How could it matter what had first stirred a maiden's heart, however scholarly? In the end, she had loved me.

And now, as I knew too well, I loved her. I must have loved her, for my own heart, quite literally, hurt. Then it began to hurt worse; the thought, for the first time, came into my mind that if Agnes had lived I would never have loved her—would, in fact, have killed what love she had for me. Her death had been the birth of love and her life would have been its death.

And where did this thought leave me now? It left me only with a grinding pain and a new vision of the way the world was.

So the train plunged on through the dark and storm toward Nashville, and I thought of my recent drinking companion, who at that moment might well be lying on her back in her berth, naked, with a forearm pressed across one breast and the hand clutching the other, and the other hand reaching down to grasp an ankle to draw up the heel of that foot to grind against her sex, while behind her closed eyelids what fantasia, white as fish bellies in dark water, flickered. That was part of what the world was, and suddenly it was not that poor, sodden, courageous wretch in the berth I was seeing, but old Miss Mary McClatty, with her bone-skinny legs and her fungus-green hair. And then I was seeing the first snowflakes coming down out of the darkness of the Godless sky to cling to the yet imperfectly healed earth under which my darling waited in patient devotion—and that was part of the world, too.

Book Two

CHAPTER V

When Aeneas came to Carthage, he moved, in a protecting cloud provided by Venus, toward Dido the Queen, whom he was to love, and then, in the fulfillment of his mission, leave her to the fate of the flames. Well, when I came to Nashville, my cloud was a ramshackle bar car, and if my progress was presided over by the Goddess of Love, she was embodied in the poor, drunken, courageous female with the clanging charm bracelet and the bum gam. But even if Nashville was scarcely Carthage—only a thriving middle-size commercial city of the Buttermilk Belt—I was to find a queen there.

In any case, all was ready when the telephone bell by my bed in the Old Hickory Arms Hotel jerked me from my murky sleep and the dead-endness of my life, and I heaved my body up in the lumpy rented bed and seized the instrument, and, from its brook-musical, sunlit distance, heard the voice say: "Guess who!"

When I hung the phone up, my hand was shaking. Not because I loved Rozelle Hardcastle. Not because, out of my old outrage, I hated her. It was because I was experiencing a crucial disorientation of my sense of time: time was flowing back upon itself. All the things that had ever happened to me in the flow of time had now an absolute and fixed existence outside of time and were standing there in the room, around my bed, staring down at me. I do not mean that people who had been involved in the events were staring. It was as though, somehow, the events themselves were existences, and had eyes, and the enormous eyes were fixed on me. The eyes knew what I was going to do. They were going to watch me do what I did not know I would do.

To begin with, I had agreed to go to Rozelle's house—Carrington, she said she was now, Mrs. Lawford Carrington—for a quiet little supper, just a little informal pickup supper with a few friends coming in, she said, and now I had the day, blank and aimless, to live through. That sense of blankness was not the result of an anticipation of pleasure so keen that I could not brook delay. I didn't want to go to the goddamned little informal, little pickup supper. If the day seemed blank, it was not because I wanted to go. It was because it was written, I suddenly felt, that I would go, and until I had faced that event and knew what it might mean, nothing seemed significant.

But I lived through the day, and at six o'clock took a bath and put on my good suit, the blue suit I had got married in, but September in Nashville is hot, and since I wasn't getting married in this particular heat, I took off the coat and figured that if I did a little spotting job on my seersucker coat and hung it to steam in the bathroom to get the wrinkles out, I could get by with that and to hell with it, anyway. I tried to read while waiting for the coat to unwrinkle, but couldn't, so lay on my back on the bed, blue trousers, black shoes, white shirt, my get-married tie (with little green dots on black silk), and inspected the ceiling until the telephone rang, promptly at seven, to say that Mr. Cudworth was waiting in the lobby.

· · ·

"Bill Cudworth," he said, and put out a strong, sunburned hand, and when I took it, said, "Welcome to Tennessee!"—and then, when the hand was freed, clapped me on the shoulder, the shoulder clapping not being hail-fellow, not false, not presumptuous, just friendly and natural. As we headed for the door, I noticed that he was wearing a faded blue linen jacket, a sport shirt with no tie, washed old khaki pants, and loafers, with no socks. Well, it did look informal, and the man and the two girls waiting in a rather beat-up Buick station wagon confirmed my surmise, the girls wearing gingham or something of the sort. "Get in front with Sally and me," Cudworth directed, after introductions, and seeing my eye light on the faded lettering on the door—FERNDALE STOCK FARM—added, "Yeah, I'm a farmer."

In his seat, hands on the wheel, pulling into the traffic: "Yeah, a stock farm, specialize in walking horses. A refugee lawyer. New York, the law, and night clubs got too much for this country boy. So I just decided I'd rather talk to horses than to horses'-asses and came on home. Yeah, and you know what, found me this long-boned, lanky beautiful Sally-gal right on the next farm."

He clapped her on the near knee.

She was, in fact, long-boned, and rather long-nosed, too, but had fine brown eyes and a totally engaging smile, which, when she turned on Cudworth, declared that she thought he was great. "Get your hand off my leg," she commanded, "and put it on the wheel. And darling—"

"Yep?"

"You know, darling, one small little thing is getting around, all over Davidson County. Do you know what it is?"

"Nope."

"Just that you talk too much, darling. We have heard your autobiography. Let Mr. Tewksbury talk some."

"Hell," said Cudworth, "you know all about Mr. Tewksbury already. You spent the whole morning reading about how great he is in the *Sunday Magazine Section*—and that interview—"

"It was a great story!" the other young man declared heartily from the back seat.

"We're mighty proud to have you here, back down south," the girl in the back seat said. She got real conviction into her Tennessee voice.

The city was thinning out now, and we drove into the setting sun. "The Carringtons are in the country," Sally said, "but they don't farm. He's a sculptor."

They said that the Carringtons had a great place out there. That everybody always had a great time at the Carringtons'. That Rose (that was how I knew she was Rose now, not a tacky name like Rozelle) made Lawford a great wife. That no girl had ever come to Nashville and just offhand been so popular. That she was so pretty but so unpretending. That all sorts of people liked her, that she brought people together. University people—Lawford taught sculpture there —and—

"Ignoramuses like me," Cudworth cut in.

"You talk too much," Sally said to him. Then to me: "But I'll tell you a secret. He's really trying to signal me to tell you that he's pretty bright himself, that he was on the *Yale Law Review* and was in a fine firm in New York City and—"

"Listen," said Cudworth, "all lawyers are ignoramuses, and if you made the *Law Review* it only means you are a real ignoramus because you put all your time on nothing but law."

"But," said Sally, addressing me, "aren't I a loyal wife. You get the score, don't you?"

I said I did, and by this time the light had the blue tint of dusk and we were riding between two limestone gateposts up a winding gravel lane between beeches and then clattering over a wooden bridge across a vigorous, clear stream, up to the standard Tennessee farmhouse, two stories, white clapboard, square columns, high entrance porch, a big limestone chimney at each end, the whole flanked by a great cedar at each end.

"They'll be back in the barn," Cudworth said, and led the way.

The barn was a big stone structure, unusually big for the region— and, in stone, unusual for a barn of that region—with the barnyard still enclosed by a white board fence, but the fence had rambler rose vines on it now, the hoof-stirred mud and dung of the yard had long since given way to raked white gravel, flower beds ran the length of the building, with hollyhock stalks still standing and some gentian-colored flowers and zinnias still blooming. To one side of the barnyard were two tennis courts, and I saw a high diving board and caught the glint of blue water. Music came from the barn.

"Ye Old Carrington Strength through Joy, Recreation, Sour Mash, and Five-Card Straight Stud Mutual Benefit Society," said Cudworth, and, hard on the heels of the girls, propelled me in.

For a moment we were cut off by a semi-wall from the room proper, a wall with coatracks and cabinets, and then we were in the room. There, in a big space that was open all the way up to the high roof beams outlined against white plaster, was a swirl of people, some dozen or so, dancing, and, suddenly detaching itself from the swirl and coming toward me, ignoring the other new arrivals, was a figure, a woman in white slacks, and then it was, quite definitely, Rozelle, untouched by time, smiling in innocent pleasure, seizing both my hands, exclaiming, "Golly, it's wonderful to see you!"—standing close to me, lifting up her cheek to me, saying, "Kiss me hello, you old bum!"

I obeyed, aware, but only in a distant, categorical way, of the coolness, firmness, and delicacy of texture of the cheek, and of the clean, mown-hay scent of her hair. She led me by the hand, like a hulking, oafish child, toward the people, who, all smiling, had swung into a semicircle to receive me. Music, from an indeterminate source, was still flowing on.

I stood in that blur of smiles and voices, in a strange confusion and interfusion of lights—the subdued lights of the room and the last light of the red sky westward that, through the enormous floor-to-ceiling window on that side, came pouring into the room there. While the music pursued a peculiarly independent, sourceless life, I moved from person to person, and they declared that they were glad to see me, were proud to have me there, had seen the wonderful article that very morning in the Sunday paper, that Rose (that was the name they all used) had called them up to say I would be here tonight, asked me if it wasn't good to be back down home again, in the South again, and one man, a well set-up man, burly but not slack, middle-aged, in jodhpurs, with a red outdoorsy face and unthinning carefully barbered white hair brushed back on the strong skull, greeted me, smiling in amiable half-comedy, with "And then came Alabama!"

At that, I must have looked especially blank, for to instruct me he cheerily sang: "And then came Alabama and took her by the hand!"

Now I must have looked even blanker, for in a very friendly but somewhat embarrassed way, he said, "Just 'The Bonny Blue Flag,' old fella. But I bet I'm the only one here knows it. Mark of my age, old fella." He shook my hand warmly, and I found myself liking him.

Then somebody else was saying something to me, and my host, the sculptor, Rozelle's husband, a tall, dark-haired, theatrically handsome man of about my years, wearing tennis clothes, was thrusting a highball glass into my hand, saying, "Hope you haven't lost your taste for old sour mash. But if you have, there's—"

I asserted that I had not lost my taste for sour mash—not adding, however, that I had never heard the term, much less experienced the taste of the product, until long after I had crossed the Mason and Dixon Line, headed north, the beverage I had known in my youth having been little more than the then recently legalized panther-piss, to use the old phrase.

But I had scarcely sampled the highball before Rozelle was there, taking my free hand, telling the people around me that she was sorry to steal me so quick, but she just had to dance with me for old times' sake, she really had to, for oh!—would you believe it?—she'd never danced with this old bum but once in her life and that time they quarreled before they got a couple of steps, and this old bum had just walked off and left her standing in the middle of the dance floor, but oh!—it had all been her fault, she knew that now, but he was going to forgive her—wasn't he, wasn't he?

She drew my hand up to level of her breast, almost as though to press it there, and clasped it in both of hers, and, in a parody of melodramatic guilt and anguish, fixed her gaze, wide and pleading and, it seemed, about to brim with tears, on my face, crying out: "Oh, forgive, dear heart, forgive!"

All at once, as I slow-wittedly looked down into her eyes, she burst out laughing, and the people around were laughing, and she gaily commanded: "Somebody grab the old bum's glass!"

Somebody did grab it, and she drew me out onto the floor, where two or three other couples were doing what I think was an old-fashioned fox trot, and settled herself into my arms. Settled—no, "nestled" is the word—for, as I was to observe that coming winter, always in the moment when Rozelle entered a man's embrace to dance, the effect she gave was, invariably, of nestling, as though this was the place and time God had, for all eternity, intended, and her life had been moving toward, and so she would lift her face with a little inward, drowsy smile, lips relaxed, eyelids drooping ever so little in a way to remind me of the Biblical words "she taketh thee with her eyelids"—her whole being awash, as it were, in a sweetly swaying, secret tide of fulfillment. This would be for only a fleeting moment, a moment of fulfillment and, too, of promise. Then, the eyelids lifted, and whatever had been happening in the real world began to happen again and went on.

What was happening to me in the real world right then was my discovery that the waist my right hand clasped was not a millimeter greater in girth than in June, 1935, and that the only discernible anatomical change was the slightly increased fullness of the breasts that, now and then, brushed me through the protecting seersucker, and that the body to which the waist and breasts appertained was, in spite of all its fluidity and grace, moving like a well-programmed robot, for the real Rozelle Hardcastle—no, Rose Carrington—was withdrawn into some inner distance. But finally, from an averted face, her voice said: "Yes, it was my fault."

"It was a long time ago," I said.

"That's what you don't ever know," she said, and withdrew again into the inner distance. But after a little, again from the averted face: "That night, I drove around the whole county, by myself. About two hours. Then I went home, when I guessed the Prom was over. I felt awful."

"I imagine that I could tell you," I said, "some of the reasons."

"You don't have to," she said. And, after a moment: "What did you do?"

"Are you sure you want to know?"

"Yes."

"Well, if you really want to know," I said. And told her. I told her in detail.

"Oh, I'm sure it was all very splendid," she finally cut in. "But—" and here she looked up directly into my face for the first time during the narrative, and smiled sweetly and innocently at me "—do you always regale girls—white girls, I mean—about how hot you are on poontang? But oh, I forgot. You real, old-timey, good old Southern boys, you're all supposed to like it, aren't you?"

Abruptly she stopped dancing, seized my hand and drew me toward a young man and a rather thin, dark-haired girl who stood to one side, talking. "Hey," Rozelle said to the girl, "you be nice and dance with this old bum, and he'll tell you all about his boyhood's delights." Then to me: "Won't you, darling? But you all will find lots of other things to talk about, too. Maria is the smartest girl in Tennessee—Phi Beta from Bryn Mawr—and the best dancer—and—"

"Hush!" the smartest girl in Tennessee said, and turned to me: "That Rose is the worst flatterer in Tennessee. But—" and she gave the flatterer a little hug "—we all love her for it, she almost convinces you."

With that, the girl Maria and I began to dance, and as far as the dancing went, the advertised expert was tempering the wind to the shorn lamb, which was Ole Big-Foot me, with blue best pants too hot and black shoes too tight, and saying to me, with what I began to feel was a slightly brittle animation, some very pleasant and courteous things. But she must have noticed that my glance had found Rozelle, who had gone to sit on a hassock by the chair of a somewhat older woman, pushing fifty perhaps but very good-looking in a vital, wind-blown way.

"Yes, look at Rose," Maria said, "she's always so interested in other people. Really, sincerely interested," and I was observing that Rozelle—Rose, I mean—was leaning forward on the hassock to follow with appreciative devotion some narrative the older woman was delivering.

"Not," Maria was saying, "that it takes politeness to listen to Mrs. Jones-Talbot. She's fascinating, she's just great, she's Lawford's aunt, and—"

At which very instant a blast from a country cow-horn fox horn brought silence, and Lawford Carrington announced that anybody who, like him, wanted a quick swim to recover from Carrington tennis or Jones-Talbot riding had better get it now, for supper was coming up.

"Let's," said Maria. "I played two sets and I need it."

When I said I didn't have any trunks, she said that there was always plenty of stuff in the bathhouse.

.　　.　　.

There was a lot of laughing and joking at the pool, but I did not join it. I put on trunks as quickly as possible and began to swim. It was a big pool, Olympic scale, and I felt heavy and dull from lack of exercise all summer and the drink, and my breath was coming short in the first length. But I plugged on, somehow wanting to be alone, a few minutes anyway, now and then hearing laughter or splashing, aware, too, of a swimmer in the next lane who kept lapping me with the contemptuous ease of a PT boat passing a coal barge.

Finally, my wind gave out completely, and I rolled over on my back. A full moon was coming up, and around it a faint salmon pink flush spread over the night-blue of sky. The distant hills were black against that light. I lay awash, forgetting, trying to forget where I was, why I was here, everything. After a little, hearing voices headed toward the barn, I began to kick my way in, still on my back.

When I got to the end of the pool, the swimmer of the next lane was, with a last powerful stroke, gliding to the ladder. He drew off to allow me to climb out. It was Lawford Carrington. Standing on the tiles, he snapped his head to one side, the way kids do on coming up from a dive to whip the wet hair off the brow.

"You're a great swimmer," I said to him.

He gave me a fine, infectious, boyish smile, which would have been a grin if he hadn't been so impeccably, so goddamned Greekly handsome, his perfect musculature, wet and, in moonlight, shining like marble. "Christ," he said, "just a college swimmer."

He smiled again. "But it's great for the appetite, isn't it?"

I said it was.

.   .   .

The Cudworths brought me back to town, and at parting Cud urged me to come to their farm for next Sunday, to ride, "to help exercise the stock," he said, and when I said I'd never even been on a rocking horse, which was sure true in Claxford County non-nurseries, he said he had a little nag so polite and smart she'd teach me in a half-day, and so I said I'd go. As they pulled away from the curb, they all yelled back something cheerfully indecipherable.

I stood there and watched the beat-up station wagon disappear, somehow glad that it, at least, was so beat-up, then looked at the late emptiness of the street, and lifted my gaze to the moon now riding high. When I went up to my room, it suddenly looked, in the glare of the ceiling lamp, grubbier and more constricted than ever.

But, I told myself, I had certainly lived in worse.

Undressing, hanging up the trousers of my good blue suit, hanging up the seersucker coat, which the steam treatment hadn't helped much, I let my mind run back over the evening. The barn—the studio —I could now grasp it in its entirety. I remembered the strange, disorienting confusion of lights when I was first dancing—the subdued lights inside, with deep shadows at both ends of the long, high space, and the light of the red sunset coming over the land, with the little river glinting red in the shadowy valley below us: and how, when I first began dancing with the girl called Maria, a curtain, like the drop curtain of a big proscenium stage, operated by some soundless mechanism, had descended over the enormous westward expanse of glass, and light had suddenly gone up in the room. There, at the south end, appeared a jungle of plants, ten, fifteen, twenty-five feet high, growing out of islets of bare earth and reaching up toward the roof, which directly above them was glass, with the night sky vaguely visible beyond; and at that moment, I had felt a disturbing sense of déjà vu, or reliving—until I remembered what now seemed such a poor little token of a jungle in the conservatory off the erstwhile dining room of Dr. Stahlmann's house.

As for the rest of the barn, about two-thirds of the distance toward the north end rose a sort of stone structure incorporating a great fireplace framed in a narrow panel of cream-colored marble, with the marble hearth stretching well forward and to each side to give a generous space for dancing, but surrounded by a floor of what seemed to be waxed brick or tile. On the other side of the chimney was another fireplace, much smaller, with easy chairs gathered round on a great rug of rose and gray in geometrical design. On the ample space of stonework on both sides of the chimney stack etchings and watercolors were displayed, famous names all, as I was to learn, and on a marble ledge that jutted asymetrically above the fireplace stood a large Giacometti. Big paintings were hung against the whitewashed stone of the walls. Freestanding from the walls were the black, boxy constructions on which were exhibited works of the host.

The working space of the artist was cut off at the north end by movable walls, beyond and above which, if you stood far enough back, you could see the upper part of the big north studio window.

.   .   .

After supper, which was served on a long trestle table of rough boards in the jungle end, with the sound of water from a fountain half-hidden behind leaves and fronds, Rozelle had led me away from the other guests to the north end, to show me the pictures. And Lawford's beautiful things, too, she said. She had majored in art history at Alabama, she said, but now she was really mad about painting, Lawford had taught her so much.

So we stood in front of a painting they had bought just that summer in Italy, and had just that day hung, a work by a man named Afro, whom, naturally, I had never heard of, and I could tell that she was really looking at it, not just pretending. She said, after a bit, that they had just got back from Italy a few days ago, hadn't even known I was to be in Nashville till she came on the newspaper that very morning and then had grabbed the phone to run me down. She'd lost all track of me, she said, didn't even know I had been in the war, and here I had been off fighting with the Partisans, the paper said, which she asserted was wildly romantic, and had got decorated into the bargain, a real hero.

"A decoration for me was a bad joke," I said. "Those guys—those Partisans—they were really tough. Too tough for me, I'll tell you."

She made no answer, again studying the picture. Then, with her eyes still fixed on it, she said: "I was sorry to read about your wife."

"Thank you," I said, looking at the picture, a great splattery blob of colors, which I had been enjoying but now, all at once, found trivial, distasteful in its triviality, and I thought how different poor little Agnes, who would not have liked this picture, had been from this woman—this beautiful stranger—here by my side, thinking this with a kind of bitter, defensive loyalty to the body that was now wasting to a musky nothingness in the earth of South Dakota, with an empty plot beside it.

———

"I know what it's like," the voice by my side was saying. "To lose somebody."

I said nothing.

"My first husband—he drowned before my eyes. It was our yawl. I had the wheel and I was just learning, really, and I must have done something wrong, the wind came in a big puff and the boom swung round."

I was seeing, in my mind, vividly, the waxy-white, bony hand struggling up the air above the hospital bed in Chicago.

I said: "As my wife was dying, one hand rose up in the air. Arm's-length. It just struggled up, it seemed. It seemed to be groping, trying to find something to grab hold of. Like a rope to grab."

"Hush!" the voice said sharply, and even as I turned toward it, fingers gripped my arm.

She was looking up at me. "You've got to stop talking that way, thinking that way," she said, with angry intensity, staring into my face. Then: "People have to go on living, don't you know that? No matter what happens."

Looking down into the face that, in the instant, was drawn and old, I said, slowly: "Yes, I suppose so."

With the same angry, whispery intensity she said: "Yes, and you —you've got to."

"Yes, you seem happy," I said.

"Oh, I am," she asserted firmly. "Lawford, he's so sweet to me. But you can be more than one thing at once. Happy and unhappy. You have to learn to live that way, and just live by the minute, what you can take in that minute is what's worth living for, and—"

"Hey!" the voice said, and there was Lawford.

"Speak of the devil and smell brimstone," Rozelle said, smiling, reaching out to take his hand. "I was just telling Jed," she said, "how sweet you are to me." And to me: "Isn't that true?"

"It's gospel," I said.

"Of course I am," Lawford Carrington affirmed, "but right now Aunt Dee-Dee has to go—some buyer coming early tomorrow—and she wants to speak to you."

So Rozelle ran obediently off, and her husband standing there tall and handsome, no longer in tennis shorts but in white duck pants now and broad turquoise-studded leather belt, and red silk shirt open at the neck, remarked that his aunt, like the Cudworths, bred horses, and discoursed learnedly to me on the virtues of Afro, and then she came back and he went away, and she began to show me some of his sculpture—a female head, that of a young woman, the head arched back so far that the neck was strained to accent the tendons, eyes shut, lips slightly parted and drawn back at the corners, the hair falling straight down, backward—and she had just started to say something about it when she stopped.

"Aunt Dee-Dee," she resumed irrelevantly, her hand still touching the marble of the sculpture, as though she had actually forgotten, abandoned, the hand there, "she's Lawford's aunt. She's had the most romantic history, I'll tell you sometime, and now I just know she's having an affair with that nice white-headed man. You noticed how he left right after supper, saying he had an engagement on business. Well, I'll bet his car is hidden in the woods on her place and he's in the house right now, waiting in the dark, for her to come. And you know—"

She stopped, and looked directly at me, then resumed: "I bet there's nobody knows this but me. Not even Lawford. I just figured it out."

A slow, deep, inward expression of satisfaction grew on her face.

Then, all at once, she was looking at me directly, the eyelids fully lifted. "I want to help you get settled here," she said.

"Listen, girlie," I said, "I'm not in Nashville. I'm just a university teacher and the university I happen to teach at happens to be in Nashville. I'm just a—"

She studied me in her shadowy way. Then she said: "You don't know what you are, Jed Tewksbury."

.   .   .

So, in my underwear shorts and my bare feet stuck in old-fashioned carpet slippers, standing before the bathroom mirror with my toothbrush in hand and foam on my lips as thick and white as a maniac with hydrophobia, my mind came to the moment when Rozelle had said that. I stared at the apparition in the mirror, the heavy, swarthy face, the distorted nose, the maniacal foam-flecked mouth and the big brownish body beginning to sag at the gut, and I knew that what she had said was true.

Then I remembered what, after a silence, she had added: "You never know what you are until you stumble on it."

I saw her, in my mind's eye, as she had been standing when those words were uttered, beside the sculpture of the thrown-back female head, with her hand as though lost or forgotten there, touching the marble. And now, seeing that image in my mind's eye, I knew what had been nagging me all evening for recognition: the sculptured head and that of the woman who stood there touching it, were the same.

Well, what of it?

Maybe I was so dumb I was the only person in Nashville who hadn't recognized the fact right away. Anyway, if a man was a sculptor, why shouldn't he use his wife as a model?

And who had more right than he to know how her face looked in orgasm?

. . . .

I hadn't felt like going to bed. I sat at the lousy, unsteady little hotel writing desk and wrote a letter. To my mother, telling her I was pretty well settled, liked my job well enough, and had met a few people, but not describing them and certainly not mentioning the name of Rozelle Hardcastle—which to my mother was always like a red flag to a bull. Either because she represented the temptation of Dugton to ruin her hopes for her Darling Sonny-Boy, or because the aunt was so toney and cut her on the street. I clipped out the article in the Sunday paper about me (mostly a handout from the university publicity bureau) and the dreary interview, and put them into the envelope with the letter. I wanted to know what kind of crack she'd make.

Still I wasn't sleepy. So I began to assemble the notes for the next afternoon, a background lecture on Plato's theory of love for my graduate seminar called "Love in the Middle Ages: Sacred and Profane," and I remembered all the good-natured joshing at dinner that night (the seminar had been mentioned in the newspaper), how Cudworth had said that they all ought to register for the course, if they could just get the profane part, which was, he declared, the only part that a good country boy like him would understand, and somebody else demanded to know if I was a psychoanalyst in disguise, and so on, and suddenly, now, hours later, I was experiencing a sharp surge of contempt.

Those people, all of them, sitting in that fancy million-dollar fucking barn—what did they know about anything? Did any single one of them, with all their fine fun-and-games, and famous pictures on the wall, know what reality was like?

Then quite coldly, with a sudden contempt for myself, colder than any contempt for those people who had been trying to be so goddamned charming to me, I asked myself if a man who was not afraid of reality would be hiding himself in the Middle Ages. My glance fell on my stack of lecture notes.

It was then that the knock came at the door.

It was the night clerk with a special delivery, an oversize pink envelope addressed in lavender ink, in a large, flowing, florid calligraphy ornamented with curlicues and arabesques. When I opened the envelope, the scent from within struck my nostrils. The letter ran:

Dear Dr. Tewksbury:

I have just read the beautiful tribute to you in the paper and feel it behoovens me to drop you a line to say that from the first time I heard you make utterance on the train when I asked you for a light (which you so genteely provided) I knew you were a real *MAN OF DISTINCTION*, like the advertisement says! And a real cultured *SOUTHERN GENTLEMAN* to boot. Intuition—that is what yours truly has really got!

And just think, we both are in Nashville, Tenn! I feel it in my bones, I and you, we could make some beautiful music together. My intuition said so at the very start. Gee, the lovely tribute to you makes me want to go to school again. Do you take special pupils some times? If they really want to work hard?

With warmest regards and congratulations for the occasion, I remain

Faithfully yours
and
Ta-Ta!
Clairbelle Spaethe

P.S.   It behoovens me in addition to tell you that on the train I was coming from seeing my father stricken with the fatal blow of thrombosis, that was why I was so upset and maybe drunk an extra to help quiet my grief.

P.P.S.   I know it was just a joke you made at the end of our delightful conversation. But I have just narratived what had transpired and how I was upset.

A telephone number was at the bottom of the sheet.

There was a color snapshot enclosed. It showed Clairbelle, in token black bikini, lying on her back on a diving board, arms stretched above her head to ensure a good bust-rise, the near leg (the good one, clearly, and quite pretty, too) stretched out as far as possible with the toes pointed like a ballet dancer's, the far leg with the knee crooked upward, and the heel, invisible of course behind the near thigh, drawn back close to the buttock. No infirmity, certainly in that position, was apparent.

I read the letter again and returned to the snapshot.

All at once, I was overwhelmed by a wave of tenderness for Clairbelle Spaethe, charm bracelet and bum gam and her "behoovens" and deceits and fakeries and all. She was, at least in her way, real. Her anguish, lies, transparent cunning, courage, and yearning flesh—it was all real.

What, I demanded, coldly discovering my great stack of notes on the desk before me, were all the idiocies, lies and irrelevancies that I would begin to utter tomorrow afternoon at precisely 4:10, in comparison to the living and suffering fact of Clairbelle Spaethe?

.   .   .

I looked down at the bulge in the lap of my pajamas that proclaimed the erection. I thought how that prod of erectile tissue, with its blind, blunt thrust toward eternity, had had no contact with flesh for—I stopped to calculate—ten months before Agnes had died, now more than two years in all.

I picked up Clairbelle's letter and tore it across and dropped it into the painted tin wastebasket, shiny black enamel with red roses on the side. I picked up the snapshot and again studied it. Then ditto for it. I got up and paced about the room.

After a while I got into bed. Lying there in the dark, I decided to put my life in order. I decided to take regular exercise. To never have a drink alone. To read newspapers regularly and develop an interest in public affairs. To allocate $100 a month to pay off my debts in Chicago. To shave every day, whether I had a class or not. To never pick at hangnails. To get my clothes pressed and cleaned every six months. To write my mother more often. To settle on a really significant subject and work toward another book to fulfill what one importantly placed review (quoted that very day in the newspaper) of my now published dissertation had called "the glowing promise, scholarly and critical, of this splendid work."

And with that last thought, I remembered the genesis of that splendid work, and thought of the grave off yonder in the Dakota night. Finally, I tried not to think at all.

But one more thought came. I remembered how I had stood before the bathroom mirror that very night and seen the belly I was putting on. I would, I promised myself, sweat that goddamned thing off if it was the last thing I ever did. Then, even as sleep closed down on me, there came, I remember, a pang of uninterpreted guilt.

Now, looking back, I would, of course, find it all too easy to interpret it.

Agnes Andresen, far away in the Dakota night, could not have cared less what kind of belly I had.

CHAPTER VI

By the middle of October I had moved into a little house on the Carrington property, back up a lane on the edge of the woods, some half a mile from the main house and barn-studio. Lawford, a few days after the first party (there had been several since), just walked into my office and said that if I wanted to get out of my fleabag hotel, he had a little unoccupied house, to-hell-and-gone away from him, and I could have it for whatever I thought it was worth. It had been occupied by a man who ran the farm for them, but now they just rented the land out. So, having classes on only three days, I bought a second-hand car and moved in. I could really work here, I told myself.

The academic routine began. I had a ritual round of dinner invitations, from the President's dinner for new faculty members on down through the department head to my immediate colleagues, and my good blue suit began to get slick in the seat from sitting on dining room chairs, and my black silk tie with little green polka dots got sadly stringy at the knot. I was reading a lot, too, trying seriously to find the really commanding subject that would give shape to my life.

Meanwhile, what was giving shape to my life, subtly but decisively, was the parties in the Carrington barn. The Carringtons did have, as Sally Cudworth had said that first Sunday, the gift for bringing people together, and you could hear there some passionate conversation between a young chemist and the old banker (Mr. McInnis, the red-faced, white-haired man, the father of Maria), or between a historian and Mrs. Jones-Talbot on the subject of the politics of Italy (where she, it developed, had lived for a time).

But chiefly I remember the rump-sessions, after most guests had left. Then sometimes the gang of hardy night-sitters broke up into twos and threes, widely separated, one pair over in the shadow of the jungle, sitting at the long board table, with a bottle of wine between them, as though in a café, another by the fire, another two or three in the north end, where the pictures and sculpture were, with voices here and there raised in the intensity of argument, or bursting into laughter. Or sometimes the whole group might stay together around the hearth, with the young assistant professor of English quoting poetry, Baudelaire (he had a fine ear for French) or Hardy, or whatever; or the Civil War—a couple of times at least—became a general topic. Once there was a long wrangle about what would have happened if Jeff Davis had not been infatuated with General Bragg—that buffoon with his sick headaches, as Lawford called him—and another time about the notion developed by theoreticians at West Point that Lee could have won at Gettysburg, and all the time all I was seeing was my father drunk as a moonshiner's hog after a run's been drawn and the mash dumped, and r'aren and waving that goddamned cavalry saber of his hypothetical grandpap and visiting ruination on Blue-Bellies until he took the header onto our rock-hearth and cool-cocked himself, and my mother dragged off the finished product to a hero's rest.

But more often than not the debate of serious topics gave way to taletelling, and here the Civil War might turn into comedy, as when Cud told how over in Gallatin County the United Daughters of the Confederacy decided to honor the only surviving hero of the region, who had been in Pickett's charge at Gettysburg.

The U.D.C.'s arranged a dinner at the Elks Hall and the hero was asked to make a few remarks. He got started off well enough, charging gallantly up Cemetery Ridge, with the air full of what he called—and Cud was a great mimic, I'll admit—red-hot plowshares, trace chains, and flying cookstoves with the fire not put out good, and the charge was going splendidly until the man next to our hero asked him for a chaw of terbaccy.

At this point the hero began to waver a little on his feet, and said how when he turned to the fellow, right that second one of them flyen cookstoves just swiped the fellow's head off, casual in passing. The body was still marching, and the words asking fer a chaw still hanging in the air, but the mouth them words come out of jist warn't thar no more, and the hero got, as he put it, a strong disinclination fer flyen cookstoves and dropped his gun and started down the hill, and when he hit bottom he was going so fast he said he couldn't of stopped even if he had wanted, which he shore-God didn't, so he just waved to Gin'l Lee in a friendly way to keep him informed, and his legs kept right on a-pumpen till along 'bout middle Tennessee he realized he was out of breath and got married and settled down, and if I warn't the first man up Cemetery Ridge, he said, I was shore-God the first one off it, and I thank you kindly, it was shore as good dinner as ever I et that you ladies done laid out fer me.

Which narrative, I, as a veteran, thought was a little more like it.

But sometimes the taletelling gave out, and the night drifted aimlessly and amiably on in an atmosphere of drowsy, slightly boozy, shadowy, and unspecifiable sensuality, and the logs redly crumbled on the hearth and the ice melted down into the late highball, and Rozelle sat on the floor and leaned her head against Lawford's knee, and he played with her hair, and her head fell back and her eyes squinted almost closed like a kitten's. Meanwhile, some last couple might be dancing to the sourceless music in a yawning parody of romantic rapture, or Amy Dabbitt got some man—or even two of them—to strip to the waist and lie prone on one of the polar-bear rugs while she gave the magic massage.

Amy Dabbitt was a dark, slight, lissome girl with an intense, neurotic face, not beautiful certainly but provocative in a tubercular Aubrey Beardslean way, and she began the magic massage by gently treading, with her bare feet, the region of the postulant's kidneys. That stage accomplished, she would get on her knees, straddling the small of your back, and let herself drop back to sit on your rump, and then, leaning forward, slightly rising and falling, would, with long, thin, phthisically astute fingers, now sharply probing, now brushing light as a baby's breath, work your spine, all the way down from the back of your skull, down almost to the very spot where you were feeling the heat of her crotch coming through to your buttocks as she slowly moved back and forth in her devoted occupation.

The first time I ever saw the magic massage I was dancing, at a late hour, with Rozelle, and Amy had two subjects flat on the polar-bear rug, taking turns with them, their eyes shut, out cold it seemed. Such a sight being news to me and to Claxford County, I naturally kept staring as I danced.

"Yes," Rozelle whispered to me, "that's the way she builds up her hots."

"Theirs, too, I expect," I said.

"She did it to Lawford once, and he was sure whickering before he got them all cleared out of the house. I thought he was going to tear my clothes off."

"When does the orgy start?" I asked.

"Listen," Rozelle said severely, and definitely meant what she said, even if she was smiling, "we run a good, clean establishment. No orgies. Not even polite copulation between consenting adults. We are strictly legal and strictly private, that's house rules. But if you hone for orgy, there's one house in Nashville—respectable to the point of death in other regards, too—where you can get it. Just a tight little respectable circle of WASP vestrymen and Junior League matrons. Amy is in on it. But make a date with Amy and you've got a one-man orgy. I'll even provide the polar-bear rug for the preliminary hassle. But further than that—no."

By this time we had danced fairly close to the current transaction on the polar-bear rug, and before I knew it, Rozelle was saying, "Hey, Amy—the old bum has kinks all down his back"—and was jerking me toward the rug, saying to me, "Get that shirt off!"

"But—" I began.

"But nothing," Rozelle asserted.

Amy had risen.

"You see," Rozelle said, "you've led this lady on. Now be a gentleman and get that shirt off."

Amy began to help me unbutton the shirt, just like a Roman pro.

So when I describe the method and effect of the magic massage I speak with some authority. But I never got but one massage from Amy, and never any follow-up treatment.

It was Maria McInnis I drifted into having dates with, the daughter of the red-faced, white-haired banker, and, according to Rozelle's official rating, the smartest girl in Tennessee. Whenever, in the first few weeks, I saw her, she was with some nondescriptly eligible young man, and it was she and some such who, on the next Sunday after the Carrington party, took me out to exercise the Cudworth stock. Then, one Saturday, when Maria was spending the night at the Carringtons', they asked me if I would drive her back to town on Sunday afternoon; and Maria gave me a highball and cold supper, which we ate, with a strained, desultory conversation, in the big, old-fashioned, copper-gleaming kitchen of the McInnis house, with silence heavy when conversation failed, and a sense of the weight of all the darkness brooding in the great, silent Sunday hollow of the house above us, ready to encroach down the wide stairs, or flood slowly up from the cellarage.

Soon people began assuming that I could produce Maria on request. Or that she could produce me.

I didn't particularly mind. In her quiet, dark-eyed way, she was good-looking. Certainly she was intelligent. She could even be quite humorous, in a sly but never acid fashion. I was to learn that she was also capable of a companionable silence. And she did not demand that I talk. In fact, she seemed to demand nothing of me, nor of life.

Maria had, in her non-expectation, a sort of selflessness which was manifested in a sympathetic concern for the ups and downs of the lives around her. She was a performer of small, thoughtful services, a listener to troubles. She never mentioned herself, and because of this very refusal of self, she was, in a way that I could not quite understand, institutionalized in her little world. People always had to have her around. They all loved Maria, they said. They all depended on Maria—though for precisely what, it was not clear. And even now, if I look back on that time to think of people I knew then, I have the picture in my head of a group talking and laughing, with Maria slightly to one side, her eyes, always darkly bright as a bird's in shadow, and as attentive as a bird's, shifting from face to face, in humility and calm possessiveness, to follow the flow of thought or humor or badinage. Those people seemed to regard Maria as precious in an undefined talismanic way, a communal possession. Her presence appeared to authorize them, bless them, give them a sense of their own identities, certify their little concerns as of worth.

She was, clearly, different from all the people around her, but the peculiar thing was that she was so much of them. She had every virtue and every grace to be expected in the daughter of a rich Nashville banker of good family; she danced well, rode well, played tennis well, dressed well, had lovely female manners. But in a secret way she was studious, a great reader, now and then doing special work in the Graduate School in psychology and philosophy (topics that she never mentioned); and several days a week she was a volunteer worker in one of the hospitals in the city. She was, as her friends put it, "serious" —as though this was some mysterious ailment not to be discussed further.

Then, one day, the most mysterious and most obvious thing about Maria dawned on my cloudy consciousness. Here she, with her quiet good looks, intelligence, kindness, and other sterling qualities—not to mention the wealth that she, as the only child of Daniel Hamish McInnis, would inherit—was unmarried and, to put it brutally, getting long in the tooth. Well, I didn't want to marry her. And she, who, apparently, did not expect anything of the world, did not expect me to want to marry her any more than she wanted to marry me. So I could float gently, contentedly, bodilessly, in the vacuum of my non-desiring and of her non-expectation.

Then, on my cloudy consciousness, one more thing, as mysterious and as obvious, dawned. I remembered how, down the dingy halls of Dugton High, escorted by the entourage of whickering boys, Rozelle Hardcastle had always moved with another girl, arms entwined, heads bowed together in a whispery communion. So now, as they moved through the world of Nashville, Maria was the best friend of Rose Carrington. She was always there.

The fall wore on. I worked into the late hours, alone in my little house by the woods. I went to the ritual dinners. I went to the Carringtons'. I went to the Thanksgiving football game—with a group that, of course, included Maria—and afterwards to a supper and square dance at the barn, with country fiddlers for music and Cud Cudworth, an expert in all such folksy matters, calling the figures. I rode decorously and inexpertly, in my new corduroy pants and old Government Issue shoes, at the Cudworths', mounted on their gentlest nag, and sat with them in their handsome old brick farmhouse, where a new saddle might be found abandoned on beat-up Chippendale and a bottle of horse liniment be found on the bar, and once Cud, late at night, simply walked out and, fifteen minutes later, led a filly back into the sitting room to exhibit her beauties to his guests. There I began, too, to suffer envy at the simple completeness of their life, their obvious and unashamed satisfaction with each other, their energy, with Cud putting in a twelve-hour day and Sally as ready as he to mount a tractor for fall plowing or deliver a calf, their total absorption in the world of their creation. But, with some bitterness I suppose, I would ask myself what their world meant: a charade of the past.

And now, too, to punctuate my week, there was the Dante afternoon, on Friday, at Mrs. Jones-Talbot's house.

It was Lawford, again, who had negotiated this. His aunt, he said, had been in one of the women's colleges at Oxford, studying Romance languages, and she had, for a time, lived in Italy. She wanted to return, Cud said, to a serious reading of Dante, and would I help her and a friend, a widow named Mrs. Beacham, another intellectual Nashville lady. By this time, I had some acquaintance with Mrs. Jones-Talbot, and liked her. Also, I knew that she was very rich, and I had those debts in Chicago, with their grim symbolic weight, and Lawford, quite subtly, made it clear that price was not a consideration. I made it clear that the price depended upon Mrs. Jones-Talbot.

So every Friday afternoon we discoursed, as occasion demanded, on points of syntax, niceties of translation, the history of Florence, the Guelphs and the Ghibellines, the theology of Aquinas, and theories of allegory. Bit by bit, as the reading most pleasantly proceeded, I learned, from Rozelle of course, something of the history of my pupil, Aunt Dee-Dee—now fiftyish, with a level, commanding, blue-gray glance, a face of great clarity of modeling, hair still black but slashed by a streak of white on the left side, drawn back tight to a bun, a figure brisk, clean-waisted, and erect, with the head up high and alert.

As a girl, she had been, as Rozelle put it, "too restless for Nashville"—the phrase echoing, no doubt, what the female contemporaries of Mrs. Jones-Talbot still said of her; so she had gone off to Radcliffe College, and thence to Oxford, not to come back to Tennessee for some twenty-five years, just after World War II. Immediately after Oxford she had married an Englishman, somewhat older than she, a Jones-Talbot who later, on the death of his older brother in the war, would have become Lord Toddsmere except for his political ambitions, and seat in the House of Commons.

Back then he had been, paradoxically, a waxing force in the Labor Party, with strong Marxist leanings, and again paradoxically (I began to gather that Jones-Talbot had loved paradoxes, the flashier the better) an ostentatiously devout Catholic convert, with his young American wife probably another paradox. But she was, strangely enough, to leave him and his paradoxically fashionable weekends in great country houses, for an Italian slightly younger than she, and of straitened circumstances and limited life expectancy. To account for the last fact, there were sound reasons to believe that the young lover (Jones-Talbot was too good a Catholic to consider a divorce) would wind up in an alley with slugs from a Beretta in his back, or in a cellar, with the slugs in the back of his head, the slugs, in either case, having been fired by one of Mussolini's secret police.

Originally, Mrs. Jones-Talbot had explained the Dante sessions to me by saying that she just couldn't subsist on a diet of horse talk and Nashville gossip, that she needed something to get the scum off her mind; but one day, in late November or early December, a day of foul weather when her fellow pupil didn't make it, Mrs. Jones-Talbot, looking up from the page, asked me if I, in my time with the Partisans, had ever encountered a young man named Sergio Gaspari.

When I said no, I hadn't, she let her gaze drop again to the page.

After a moment she looked up again, fixing her level, blue-gray glance on me, and in a most detached way, said: "This canto—it was one of those he loved best."

Again she looked down at the page, then again at me, saying: "The first year of the war, before Italy entered, we were hiding out in Switzerland, in the village of Sparezza—they had made one attempt to assassinate him—and while we were snowed in, he'd read Dante aloud to me. In late afternoons. In the evening. He had a strong, beautifully expressive voice. The *Commedia*—he could get both the musicality and that brazen clangor."

I observed that there were some beautifully expressive metrical effects in the passage before her. That was all I could think of to say. Then I added: "Why don't you read it aloud and try to point them a little more?"

She obeyed, in her clear, faintly British voice, but with a good Italian accent, and looked at me as though for criticism. When I made no remark, she, very matter-of-factly, as though merely continuing a line of thought that had not even been interrupted, said: "In the fall after Italy did get into the war—in 1940—he simply left. One morning just wasn't there. Just a note saying he had to go and couldn't bear to tell me goodbye, if he tried that he might not be able to go. Please to take our love-making of the night before as his goodbye."

She stopped, her face showing nothing; then resumed: "He would send word, he said, when he could. I did have several messages. Then I didn't get any more."

Then: "But I had to go. I couldn't just sit and do nothing."

Abruptly, she picked up the book, saying briskly, in a new voice: "Oh, by the way, there was a question here, and . . ."

I tried to answer the question, and we went on.

At the end she served tea to me, as usual by the fireside in the antiseptically modern living room, which, however, accepted the few elegant pieces of old furniture and, to my untutored eye at least, seemed to set them off. I rose to go. All at once she said: "I'm sorry I let my tongue run away with me. It was just—"

She stopped.

"What was wrong with that?" I blunderingly managed to utter.

"Well, nothing," she said, thoughtfully. Then, with a slight stiffening of the shoulders and lift of the head: "Yes, if you can't learn to appreciate things, you don't deserve what you do get in life. Appreciation—it's all you can ever keep, anyway."

Then, with a sudden, bright, crisp social tone, like a wet sponge across a slate, leaving it shiny clean: "What foul weather! You'll be drenched."

.   .   .

I did get drenched, getting to the car even; and creeping along in the blinding gusts of rain, on the asphalt slick with fallen leaves, I remembered what she had done after she left Switzerland. She had, according to Rozelle, joined one of the British women's auxiliary organizations (having, of course, a British passport) and had wound up driving a camion in Egypt.

Then I realized what the Dante sessions were: a ritual of appreciation.

.   .   .

There is a trait that, I realized during my stay in Nashville, Southern girls all share. Of course, I am here generalizing from an insufficient number of samples, as the logic handbook puts it, for even if it be granted that the girls of Heaven Hope, Dugton, and Blackwell College were Southern in anything more than a geographical sense, I knew none of them (white or black—the black better, but only in the dimension of carnal knowledge) well enough to justify the generalization; and as far as Nashville is concerned, I knew only the members of the little circle in which I was fortunate enough to move, plus a few girls I put my arm around and swayed with at the dances.

But the generalization, based on however restricted a number of samples, is that the Southern girl has the talent, which she ordinarily exercises only to keep it in trim, of making you feel, in the first few minutes of acquaintance, that you and she have some deeply significant, if unspecifiable, background in common, some body of experience to which even the most casual remark represents a secret allusion, some germ of intimacy that, in the very next instant, may stir and burgeon. This art of the mystic promise—which can be as subtle as the shrouded glance or fleeting moth-wing smile or as crude as wide-eyed flattery—must be enjoyed purely as an art, as an illusion, as a complex poetry of the soul and the gonads. But with the willing suspension of disbelief, life is thus the richer; even if you are fed, and know it, on a meat of shadows.

It was, of course, in relation to Rozelle, that this fundamental insight first dawned upon me, and the occasion was by the fireside in the more intimate north end of the barn, the first time I ever sat alone with her. I had been asked to drop in for a "family supper" after my Friday session with Mrs. Jones-Talbot, presumably to spare me the preparation of a lonely meal at "the coop," as my house was called; but when I arrived at the barn, about 5:45, Rose told me that Lawford had just telephoned that he would be late, that his New York dealer, who was in town a day early, would not be able to come out with him until well after 6:30.

So I found myself by the flames of the little fire, in the north end, where most of the pictures and sculptures were, sunk in a big tiger-skin easy chair, a highball in hand, with Rozelle on a dark blue leather hassock, at a distance across the hearth, which on this side was elevated, the marble surface set on a jutting base of the limestone of the big chimney structure. She was far away over there, wearing light blue corduroy slacks—aquamarine is the word for the color, I suppose —and a black blouse like a T-shirt, with the black, even at that distance, accenting the shell-white of her throat and the shell-flush of her face, and with the flicker of flames and the discreetly subdued lighting of the room doing what seemed appropriate to bring out the gold-to-bronze tones of her hair. Her feet were bare except for the merely token sandals held in place by minimal black thongs anchored between the big toe and the second. The toenails were colored in aquamarine to match the slacks, and all at once you realized that the feet, because of this fact, were not bare, but naked.

She was, as I have said, far away over there across the hearth, sitting on the hassock, legs crossed, right knee over left, leaning decisively forward at the waist, forearms crossed on the right knee, face lifted as though yearning across the unplumbed, salt, estranging distance. "We are all so glad you are here," she was saying.

I murmured something.

"Lawford," she said, "it's meant so much to him. He keeps saying so. You know, in spite of everything, Nashville is a little limited, and Lawford does need lots of intellectual stimulation—some variety . . ." She paused. "But you—you'd have a lot to offer, anywhere. To lots of people," she added. "Aunt Dee, the Cudworths, the—"

"The Cudworths," I echoed, "they're great," and felt a little flush of pleasure in remembering them.

"And to me," she was saying.

I looked across at her, at the face leaning forward to annul the distance, with the glimmering accent of firelight on the right cheek and on the hair that curled dewily off the temple. Then I noticed that, on the right foot—a foot high-arched, shining in the firelight like polished marble but faintly flushed with the warmth of flesh—the token sandal hung loose by the thin black thong, and that the big toe of that foot was slowly crooking up and down to make the sandal wiggle ever so gently, in a perfect rhythm. I have said earlier that Rozelle had the gift of stillness, and as I now watched, bemused in the motion of the sandal, I sensed the absolute immobility of all the rest of her being, sure that even the heartbeat was muted.

I found that I myself was not breathing at all.

I jerked my gaze from that little hypnotic focus of motion that the sandal was, and sought her face. Her eyes were fixed across at me, her face smooth in perfect calmness and patience, as though she could keep on waiting, in serene confidence that, in the end, my gaze would meet her own.

And now that my gaze had, in fact, found her own, her voice continued: "Yes, to me, too—for our talks have meant a lot. You see, I can talk to you. Differently, I mean . . ."

As her voice continued, another voice, in some cold corner of my mind, was severely questioning: *What talks?*

For we had had none. Nothing more than a moment now and then, dancing, or sitting together in some rump-session after a party. And as her voice went on, I became aware—how coldly, too—that all the air of shared experience, the sense of intimacy, of secret understanding for which words would be superfluous—of, even, complicity, however innocent and marginal—was an illusion. I reminded myself, coldly, that even back in Dugton I had spoken with Rozelle Hardcastle on only two occasions, briefly and without pleasure.

Thus I became aware of the technique of the mystic promise, and, consulting my memory, made my generalization and filed it away for future corroboration. But meanwhile I was staring at the foot tinted by firelight—warmed by it, too, no doubt, and it would be warm to the touch—and at the small, undemanding but persistent rhythm of the dangling sandal. And Rozelle's voice was going on: "Oh, I don't mean I'm not happy in Nashville. And that dear, dear Maria!—I couldn't live without her. And Lawford is darling to me, and if anybody is really what you might call old Nashville, it's a Carrington, but you know . . ."

Her voice trailed off.

"I don't guess I do—" I finally said, then paused, looking up from the rhythm of the sandal. "Whatever it is, I don't know."

"I guess a man wouldn't," she replied, thoughtfully. "But a girl, coming into a place like this, she's alone. With other women, I mean. A husband—even a Carrington—can't help much. I can't even talk about it to Lawford, he laughs at me. Woman stuff, he says. But with you, you see, it's different. You're . . ."

Again, the voice trailed off.

For a moment I refused to help her. "Outside," I offered, finally. And by way of a question, added: "Dugton?"

Looking across the distance, she said nothing. Then: "Oh, no."

But the sandal, I noticed, had missed a beat.

I saw it resume.

"No," she repeated, "not especially, that is. It's just that a girl's on her own. You have to watch for things, know things. You—you're a man—you don't know what some women can be like."

"No," I agreed.

The sandal had missed another beat. But it began again, and with a quick brightening of the eyes, she seemed about to giggle, and then was saying: "But sometimes it's sort of fun. The things you do pick up. Like the time I fixed that Mrs. Blandon. For keeps."

"What's that?" I asked.

"Back in the 1920's," she said, controlling the giggle, "when girls around here began to do things in parked cars out at the old Belle Meade Country Club that their mothers wouldn't ever have dreamed of just thinking about. Well, one night back then, with her date in a car parked way off to one side of the lot, a certain debutante was performing fellatio—that's the word, isn't it?"

"It's the word if that is what she was doing," I said.

"Oh, you're such a smarty-pants!" she retorted. "Well," she began again, "this debutante got so carried away with her work that she bit, and he squawked, and a couple of people came running, got her date to a doctor, and her, with hysterics, home to Mummy-Dear.

"The lid got kept on the story pretty well—as far as names and addresses were concerned. But the story itself was just too good to keep and it has kept on popping up around Nashville, and details creep in, and, you know, after all those years, I just put two and two together and I figured out who got so carried away. She's of Aunt Dee's generation and is crazy jealous of her, and when I first came to Nashville she was sort of mean to me."

At this point, Rozelle really giggled out loud.

"I fixed her," she finally managed to get out. "One time—two or three other ladies listening—I just said to her how I had heard she was the most sensational Charleston dancer ever in Nashville. She preened herself a little and said, 'Now, hush that flattery.' But I said, as sweet as can be, 'Oh, yes, and they all say you really caused the biggest sensation ever at the Belle Meade Club'—with just a little special emphasis on 'sensation.'

"You know, she was just speechless, and I just stood there smiling while she got red and gulped for air. She didn't know how much I knew, but she sure knew what she knew, and she's not taking any chances about me."

Rozelle's eyes wandered from me, and fixed on the fire. A section of gray ash fell off the log to the hearth, to expose the rose glow of incandescent coal. The big toe of the right foot continued its motion, and the firelight glinted on the aquamarine toenail as the sandal moved in its delicate, precise rhythm.

All at once Rozelle turned back to me, eyes bright as mischief and another giggle building up. "You know," she said, "Lawford has a good friend at the University—he's been out here a couple of times this fall. The man with those thick bifocals. Well, he's writing a history of Nashville. So Lawford asked him about Lawford's own family skeleton, about one of his great grandfathers. Not Carrington

—God, no—but in the Carrington connection. This skeleton made a fortune in the Civil War dealing with the Yankee army when they took Nashville, and was the secret partner in the finest fancy house for Yankee officers in the whole town, where it seems just about every other house was in the same business. It was true, Dr. Burbank—that's his name—said, and so Lawford, at a dinner party, trots out the story. Lawford's got old General Carrington and a flock of governors and senators in the family, and he just thought it was fine to have a whorehouse operator, too, to highlight the picture.

"Lawford told the tale, how his great-grandfather the General was broke on Confederate bonds, and after the war his son recouped the family fortune with a dowry from whoremongering for Yankee brass, but Lawford went on to claim, as straight-faced as could be, that the whoremongering great-grandfather was really a Confederate patriot, too, for he wouldn't have a girl in the house who wasn't certifiably loaded with VD, and thus put a whole Yankee division out of active service for lack of officers. All this with documentation and acknowledgment to Hal Burbank."

She couldn't contain the giggle, but when it was finished, said: "Lawford, too—*he* sure created a sensation."

I must have been blank or been watching the hypnotic sandal, for she explained: "Not the Carrington part of the story. Not that there aren't some other people in town stemming off the whorehouse money who think they're pretty toney. No, the real sensation was that everybody at the table learned that right here in town somebody is digging away, night and day, and is going to publish everything. There's a time bomb ticking away and nobody can do anything about it except wait for the bang. Nobody can even bribe Hal Burbank off with flattery and dinners and parties—not that they haven't tried. He just keeps on staying away from such things, and peering through those inch-thick bifocals like a wise old rabbi—he's Jewish, you know, and he's married to a plump little pretty Jewish wife with identical bifocals, you remember her, don't you, out here? Anyway, all Hal cares about is his plump little wife and his yellow old documents and the truth. So the bomb ticks right on and I can't wait for the bang."

Then she was looking into the fire, and the slow, shadowy, inward expression drifted across her face. But, after a moment, she lifted her head, and her eyes brightened.

"You know," she said, "Hal is a wonderful person and smart as all get-out, but he's got no sense of humor and a single-track mind. If you ask him how his work is going, he'll tell you and it takes six hours. Which is fine for me. I ask him a question and I've got my private seminar on Nashville, and I put in a few questions like a serious-minded little student, to sort of guide him, and boy! do I really have a head full of useful information.

"Nashville," she said, musingly, and for a full minute watched the little flames on the hearth. Still musingly, not looking at me, she said: "Lawford talks sometimes about moving to New York. You know, to get into the main swing of things." She kept on looking into the fire. Finally, not shifting her gaze, in a voice with an edge to it, like teeth biting off thread, she said: "But he won't."

Then: "Not ever."

She lifted her head. "You see," she said, as though trying to be careful with an explanation to me, "he's part of everything here and everything is part of him. He has a place where he belongs."

I considered what she had said, and with my eyes still on the sandal, asked: "Do you ever go back to Dugton?"

The sandal stopped.

"Why do you ask that?"

"Dugton is the rock from which we—you and me both—were riven," I pronounced. "So the question seems natural."

She was studying me. "And the answer is no," she finally said, "I never go back."

"Why?" I asked.

"I was an orphan," she said. "You know that. Well, my aunt—my mother's sister, who raised me—she and my uncle, they're both dead now." For a moment, her eyes turned to the fire, her face hardening. Then back to me: "And that fact suits me down to the ground." And she added: "And six feet under."

"Why?"

"Can't you imagine!"

"About her I might guess," I said.

155

"Well, guess."

"She tried to use you. Illicitly, shall we say?"

"Don't you want to guess about him?"

"I thought he was nice to you," I said. "He let you use his flashy automobile, didn't he?"

"Why do you have to bring that up?" she said, and rose suddenly from the hassock, and stood very erect, coldly regarding me. With both hands, in a slow motion, almost like a firm, calculating, controlling caress, she smoothed the aquamarine corduroy down her hips and thighs. The slacks were, I noticed, beautifully fitted.

"Why do you hate him?" I insisted.

"He let her do what she did."

She began to pace back and forth in the space across from me. I was still in the tiger-skin easy chair, watching her, but she seemed to have forgotten my presence. She had kicked off the sandals, and I watched the bare feet with the aquamarine nails move, under the slight flutter of the aquamarine corduroy, across the gray-and-rose geometrical design of the great rug, and over the burnt sienna of the waxed brick, before returning to the fireplace, where the abandoned sandals lay, to resume their track again. Now and then the feet would stop, for she would pause to finger a piece of sculpture, or at the fireplace would touch the stonework or one of the watercolors. She stopped by the sculpture of the thrown-back female head, a forefinger lightly laid on the straining throat. All at once, she was looking across at me.

"Maybe one place," she said, "is no different from any other, anyway."

I was just about to say that if such was the case, I had squandered a lot of time traveling. But at that moment, the special tinkle of the phone from the house came. She turned from it to me to say that Lawford and the dealer had arrived, and she had to go and install the guest in his room, but for me to wait here, they'd have drinks here. On the way out, she turned: "Oh—I got so wrapped up talking I didn't tell you that a whole new batch of Lawford's stuff is back from the foundry, and all set up. Over there." She pointed to the other side of the room, behind where I had been sitting. "Look at it. It's lovely."

She went out, and I heard the outside door, at the other end of the barn, close. I stood in the middle of the great space, in the new silence, with the peculiar sense of curiosity, expectation, and guilt that sometimes comes when you find yourself completely alone in a house—one not your own. There is the closet door to open, the drawer to investigate, the books to touch, the letter on the desk to read, the small object —a silver paper-knife or a cheap ashtray—to purloin. You will, of course, do none of these things, but the air is heavy with possibility, like perfume, and you hear your heart beating in the hollowness of your chest. It is as though you half-expect to turn around and find a woman there, innocently naked, hair loose, face illumined by tenderness and desire, one hand with a warning finger laid to the lips.

For a fleeting instant I stood in the middle of the floor, my feet on the rose-and-gray geometry of the deep-piled rug, and heard my heart beating. It was, for that instant, like being powerlessly trapped in an indecipherable dream. Then, all at once, I had a recollection of the dim afternoon silence of the house on Jonquil Street, back in Dugton, Alabama, when I would come home from school—the afternoon silence and maybe a single ray of light coming from under a pulled-down window shade and dust motes drifting in it.

I turned to the new pieces of sculpture. There were six, each mounted on a black boxlike structure, all in a silvery metal of dull patina, all of the same subject: a pair of female arms. A plate of the same metal was attached to the nearest black stand. It read: BALLET: A SUITE.

Each pair of arms, not quite life-size, was supported in the air by a square-rod metal bracket, somewhat in the shape of a tuning fork, one prong to each arm, set in a base of the silvery metal; but the metal of the base and bracket was roughly cast and much darker than the arms, like silver going black. The forks were not symmetrical, the prongs sometimes of different lengths, or twisted from the central stem, so that a pair of arms might seem to spring from an invisible body in some fluid and natural posture. In each case, the main stem of the bracket rose, too, at a different angle from the base, to suggest the primary angle at which the body might be envisaged.

The arms, and hands, too, I should add, spectrally suggested—not crudely, quite subtly, in fact—the ballet of love.

I examined the works. Then I looked across to the black door in the white wall that cut off the artist's actual work space. I moved toward the door, then stood before it. I imagined that there was a couch in there. Some of the poses would demand a couch.

.   .   .

After we four had eaten the "family supper," not in the barn but back at the house, Lawford and the dealer returned to the barn to talk business, and I lingered with Rozelle only long enough for a second coffee. Then I pleaded the pressure of work, and took my leave.

Work there was, but more immediately my unanalyzed need was to be alone. Sitting at my desk, not working, I returned to Rozelle's last remark to me before Lawford's arrival had not only cut short my answer, but had also fallen across the unscrutinized impulse to show her a letter that, at that very moment, I had in my pocket.

The letter clearly documented the notion that, for some people at least, one place is not always like another:

> Dear Jed, I didn have no news or nothing to say would not wait so did not write you right off. Am glad you like Nashville, Tennessee, even if they aint no good reason, but I wish it was further off like a thousand miles from Dugton, for coming back to Tennessee it looks like you are back tracked which is what you ought not to do, like I told you to git out of Dugton and keep headed out. Nashville I bet my bottom dollar is like Montgomry, Ala. and them places full of high mucky mucks dont hold no time for you no more then you for them. Keep moving you dont belong in Dugton, Nashville neither. No news here. Mr. Simms is a good man and him and me we git along. He suffers some back trouble off and on and my teeth aint too good some time. If you think on marrying again wait till you git shed of Nashville.
>
> Yore loving MOTHER
Elvira (Mrs. Perk) Simms
>
> P.S.   I reckin I love you but dont reckin that is no call to be seeing you in Dugton. How much they pay you in Nashville, the paper didn say, to teach about love in the Middle Age? They ought to let me teach them or are you gitting old afore yore time, ha ha. Gitting fat and puffy,

ha ha. Gitting butt sprung? Breath short? Anybody broke yore nose lately?

I studied the letter, trying to imagine what my mother looked like now. Then I laid it on my desk, to one side. I decided it was just as well I hadn't shown it to Rozelle, after all.

CHAPTER VII

In early December, after a long spell of lowering sky and sodden earth, with the daylight shading into dark with never a sign of color over the western hills, the weather turned suddenly frosty-bright, and Mrs. Jones-Talbot, who was working, she told me, every daylight hour training a couple of three-year-olds, invited me to come over on a Sunday afternoon with the Carringtons.

In the last few weeks I had entered upon a strange period. I felt that I had somehow lost my vote in the council that determined the fate of Jed Tewksbury, that I was simply waiting outside great closed walnut doors of the room in which the decision would be made. But a decision about what, I did not know. All I could do was wait, alone in an enormous bureaucratic anteroom, waiting for the dark doors, with heavy, chased brass fittings, to swing soundlessly open and a voice to summon me.

It had become a period of oscillation between apathy and restlessness. In the apathy I would sit staring timelessly out the window at the bare, black boughs outlined against the sponge-gray sky from which not enough light came to give any glint to the wetness of the black boughs; or would stare at the page on which the black marks, as I suddenly discovered, made no sense; or in midmorning, fully clad, would lie on an unmade bed, my arms crossed under my head, and study the plaster of the ceiling. The condition was not unpleasant. It must be, I thought, like the calm irony of age, after the death of ambition and desire: the last wisdom or the last blankness. More than once the postscript of my mother's letter crossed my mind: *Gitting fat and puffy, ha ha. Gitting butt sprung?*

Maybe this was the first hint of age.

But restlessness might unexpectedly seize me. In the middle of the afternoon, on one of my free days, I would discover the urgent need for some book, and drive in the rain to the university library to get it, and there would start an aimless but intense conversation with some near-stranger encountered at the loan desk, and then would walk, in the rain, across the campus with my savior—or victim—unwilling to face the moment when I would have to get into the car and drive home. An almost pathological gregariousness—that was one of the symptoms. A number of times I had been on the verge of telephoning Amy Dabbitt to ask for a date—and the one-man orgy—but always stopped. Once, after I had actually dialed, I stood with the phone in my hand, hearing her somewhat husky, lingering voice as it kept saying, "Hello—hello—who is it—who is it?" I listened avidly, beginning to get a hard-on, uttering no word, but aware of the sound of my ragged breathing; while she must have become aware, too, for in a most dulcet tone, she said, "Shit on you, darling," and slammed her phone up.

In any case, it was the aimless, angry restlessness that, on a clear Sunday afternoon, had placed me on one of the white benches at the edge of the great sweeping meadow back of Mrs. Jones-Talbot's stables. Over to my right were two riding rings, defined by the usual white board fence. In front of me and to the left, but far off across the splendid turf, now enameled bright as spring, were the fixed jumps—the brush jump, the snake fence, the chicken coop and the water, as I learned to call them. The water was natural, there being an active little branch across the meadow, irregularly set with clumps of willows. Beyond all, westward, the hills sleepily humped, dark in the distance with leafless woods.

Directly in front of me was a section of rail fence, with the bar set at about three and a half feet, and at it Mrs. Jones-Talbot was setting a three-year-old. Critically watching her, his back to me, was a Negro man, small, somewhat stooped, getting grizzled, wearing blue jeans and old chukka boots, and a red flannel shirt. Finally, after one of the jumps, Mrs. Jones-Talbot rode to him, dismounted, and engaged him in earnest conversation.

"That," said Rozelle, who, in jodhpurs, sat beside me on the bench, "is Uncle Tad. He's the trainer."

I nodded.

"Let's go watch the others," she suggested.

"Aren't you going to ride any more?" I asked. I hoped she would. If she did, I could simply sit here, alone, in the sun, watching, and not watching, people moving about their concerns, which were none of mine. My restlessness was gone, the apathy had returned.

Rozelle said that she had twisted her knee yesterday, here, helping Aunt Dee. So we went across the meadow to the fixed jumps, where Maria, her father, and Lawford were taking turns at the fences. There was a bench there, too, just above the middle hedge but not close enough to distract a horse on the approach. Mr. McInnis had just taken the jump.

"He's short on style," Rozelle said, "but he's got all the guts in the world."

"You talk like you know something about it," I said.

"I do," she replied. "Something, anyway."

"Not Dugton," I said.

"No—Florida," she said. "Butler—my husband there—he kept horses. He didn't get his money till he was along in life, but he tried to make up for lost time. In every way." She fell silent. Then: "He never got style, but he—he did have guts, I'll say that for him."

Again she fell silent.

"Weren't you afraid?" I said.

She looked at me, a slow, steady look, not quite in question.

"When you started jumping, I mean," I said.

"Like death," she said. "But, you know," she said, "I just told myself it was something I'd do if it killed me. I never got a really bad fall. Just a leg." She drew back into herself.

Then: "It's funny, you know, I got so I'd look forward to that second of being really, really scared—that second when it's too late, you can't change your mind, you're in the air, or about to be. It got to be like dope or something. I couldn't wait for the take-off and flight and swoop—and being scared, that was part of it."

She was looking off across the meadow, to the hills dark with the leafless woods, under the brilliant sky.

"You know," she said, still not looking at me, "I'd find myself dreaming of that at night—that feeling. When the animal gathers himself, like a cat, and you're afraid—but then you're up!"

I said nothing. We sat side by side, in silence, not looking at one another. Then I heard her voice: "Look!"

I looked upfield, where the others were.

"Maria's next," she said. And added: "She's got style. She's really schooled."

Maria hadn't yet started.

"Guts, too," Rozelle was saying. "You know, when she gets to a jump, you can just tell. She's got more guts than anybody. She's always afraid, but she does it anyhow."

"How do you know?"

"Her face," Rozelle said. "I've watched, and all of a sudden her lips go straight and tight, and her face, it goes blank as a mask. You know what I think?"

"No."

"I think she's got some trick of just blanking out, that her body goes right on and does what it does, slick as can be, all that style, but she switches on the blankness and doesn't come out till the horse has recovered stride. Now, look—look—" and she held the binoculars out to me.

Maria was coming on, and through the binoculars—guiltily, even pruriently—I watched the face. All at once, I felt terribly sad for her, as though she were riding right into what she knew was waiting for her, and I couldn't cry out to make her stop.

Then it happened to her face, the mouth like a neat, colorless cicatrix across flesh, the face white and chalky and inanimate as it leaned forward, and she, with beautiful precision, lifted in the saddle, and horse and rider were one in the air.

I let the hand with the binoculars down to rest on my knee.

"Did you see it?" the woman by my side asked, in a voice suddenly low, as in complicity, as though she were asking for a secret.

"No," I said, still watching the mounted figure of the young woman wearing blue jeans, a red turtleneck sweater, and one of those casque-shaped hard black hats used for riding, for skull protection, I suppose. On the far side from us, she was passing upfield, her mount at a walk, outlined against the swell of land beyond and the westward hills. The turtleneck was very bright against the darkness of the hills. She looked very much alone.

Rozelle, I sensed, was watching me. I turned to her.

"Are you making time with her?" she asked, as though she had known that I would turn and had been merely waiting.

"You talk like you're in the matchmaking business and want a progress report," I said.

"Sure," she said, and laughed. "We're all matchmakers, women are. People used to say it was just women closing ranks in the war of the sexes. But I'll tell you a secret, it's just plain, old-fashioned—what do you call it?—voyeurism, or something like that. In the old days women were stuck—and a lot of them still are—with just poor old tired hubby, but if they can work up a wedding they all get as excited as if everyone of them had a private peephole on the bride getting the business."

"You make it sound rather dirty," I said.

"Nope," she said, "it's just that to a mind as pure as yours every-thing looks dirty, darling. And don't get me wrong, either. Personally speaking, Lawford Carrington is definitely not old and tired, and I love him to distraction. But, you know—anyway, a lady may sort of have her—"

"Her what?" I demanded.

"Generous concern," she said, triumphantly, and was grinning at me, her face mischievous as she continued: "Now about that sweet thing Maria—have you kissed her yet?"

"None of your business, my dear."

She straightened up on the bench, drawing back from me. "Oh!"

she cried, stricken. "Haven't you even tried?"

"None of your business."

"Oh, yes indeed," she exclaimed, "it is my business! Here I work my hands to the bone, trying to marry you off to this wonderful girl —rich, too, and as full of not yet unbunged love as a hive is of honey —and you say it's none of my business! How ridiculous can a man get?"

"Or woman, either?" I said.

She pondered a moment, then brightened: "Well," she said, "if you're so difficult, I'll just have to try another tack. I'm going to be very indirect and take you off guard. Just as casual as can be, I'm going to ask you if she has told you yet about her mother."

"I ought to say that that's none of your business, either. But since I'm taken off guard, I'll say no."

"Well," she said, preening herself, "now I know all I need to know."

"I don't know if it's your business to know anything, but just what is it you think you know?"

She leaned at me, glittering. "You see," she said, "you're hooked! Now it's you trying to find out something. But I'll be nice and tell you, now I know that you haven't gone any further than a nice, refined good-night kiss. I know you haven't even tried to generate any heat —to even get her lips open—"

She lifted a hand in rebuke. "You're about to interrupt," she said, sternly, "but don't. No, maybe you did try a couple of times, but she just pulled her face aside and maybe pressed it against your lapel and then, like she'd been stuck with a pin, jerked up straight."

"How the hell do you think you know a damned thing?"

"Because, silly, she hasn't told you about her mother."

"But, damn it," I said, "what about her mother?"

"That," she said, with a great show of severity, "is what she will tell you. In her good time. But—" She fell thoughtful for a moment. "But there's one thing I will tell you. When you did try to push Maria a little bit, your blood wasn't up. You weren't ripe on the bough, yourself. For one thing for sure, Jed Tewksbury—"

She stopped.

"Yes?" I said.

"It's my guess," she said, "that when your blood does get up, you aren't easily deterred. And so, for the present, it's just as well it isn't up. What I mean is, Maria now thinks you're just too wonderfully intuitive and considerate and deep and strong—no, don't start arguing, I can tell—and she's going through a lot of turmoil right now, trying to work herself up to tell you what she is going to tell you, and when she does, she will be across the Great Divide."

Between me and the rise of land and the dark heave of hills beyond the great meadow, nothing now moved. I looked upfield and saw there, far off yonder, the positive splash of red that was the girl sitting on the black mare, close to Lawford's mount, both motionless in the brilliant light.

"You aren't even listening to what I say," Rozelle said.

"Oh, sure," I said.

"Well," she said, "it's not that she's ever yet crossed the Great Divide. Up till now. But then, she's just been around with these Nashville boys. She's never before met the mysterious and deeply intuitive Jed Tewksbury from Dugton, and I know she's in a turmoil now. About sending you that invitation. By the way, did you get it?"

"That dance? Yes."

"For a second," she said, "I thought she might have welched on it. Lost her nerve." She paused. "Are you going?"

"The last time a girl asked me to a dance—a real dance," I said, "things didn't work out too well."

"Aren't you ever going to let me off the meat hook?" she asked, smiling ever so sweetly. Then turning serious: "But this is Maria. And I think you ought to go."

"Why should I fool around with things like that?"

"To broaden your horizons," she said.

"I haven't got the clothes," I said. "A tuxedo, and all that."

"Well," she said, "buy it. You could even rent it, but you'll be needing it again, you'll be invited this Christmas to a dozen things. Besides—" and she looked me over assessingly, from head to foot, "a rented one wouldn't really fit you. With those shoulders, and—"

Just then, Lawford and Maria, side by side, swept down on us and over the brush jump, then, last, over the water, and we watched them walk their horses upfield, along the western border of the meadow.

"They look good together," Rozelle said.

And, when I did not answer: "Not that a minute ago I meant anything against Nashville boys. Lawford's one." And, after a pause: "Besides, though, he's got a lot more, too. A great big plus, for anywhere." She studied the pair of figures across the meadow. "But he wouldn't have ever done it for her. Too much off the same bolt of goods. Too much alike—like everybody else around—to see what's different."

She looked at me, her eyes somewhat narrowed in a cool, assessing way. "But you," she said, "are different. And Maria knows it."

"You just have everything taped up, haven't you?" I said.

"Maybe not everything," she said, suddenly smiling—grinning, rather—in a gamine-ish camaraderie, "but—"

She pointed upfield. "Look!" she commanded.

I looked.

There was Mrs. Jones-Talbot in the act of mounting a tall gray animal that kept jerking his head and trying to dance, while the small, grizzled Negro man in the red flannel shirt hung on to the bridle. Then she had swung up, and the animal half reared, then curvetted.

"Now you'll see something," Rozelle said.

"What?"

"That's Winter Weather," she said, "one of Aunt Dee's studs. Not for babes and sucklings. But not as bad as Dark Power."

"Dark Power?"

"Her prize," Rozelle said. "Nasrullah blood in him. A fortune a throw for his gizlum." Then: "Look down yonder at Aunt Dee and Winter Weather. How she's handling him!"

She turned to me. "I'm pretty fair," she said, "but I'd as soon cuddle a rattlesnake to my bosom as set foot in a stirrup attached to that brute. Not many folks around here would. Lawford rides him, he's good and got nerve. Uncle Tad."

"The trainer?"

"Yes. And, of course, Aunt Dee. Look!"

I looked.

Mrs. Jones-Talbot was setting the gray horse to the first fence, far away up there. Then they were over, and were cantering in a great circle, returning on the jump.

"She'll probably do that a couple of times more," Rozelle said, "then uncork him for the whole run."

She was right. Returning on the fourth circle, Mrs. Jones-Talbot pushed straight on for the brush jump, was over, and in the instant, as Rozelle, leaning forward, said, "Look, look!" the big gray horse lifted over the snake fence at us. He seemed to float weightlessly, effortlessly, as though drawn up by a secret power in the clamped knees of the rider, whose thighs were in the air over the saddle, horse and rider moving, it seemed, in a dreamlike retardation, with the rider's face forward-thrusting and glisten-eyed, with lips slightly parted in a smile of expectant excitement, but with the face somehow calm and pure—all clearly defined, for one instant, against the blue sky.

Then, with the pounding glint of hoof-stroke and burst of turf-spray, the horse was past, on the approach to the chicken coop and the water.

Again, watching the beauty of timing and fluid force and dreamlike retardation of flight, you felt that, as the last hoof broke contact with earth, both horse and rider had imperially floated into a dimension beyond gravity, time, and contingency.

Then they were gone.

"Whew!" Rozelle exclaimed, letting out her breath. "Now, wasn't that something?"

"Yes," I said, even if, in my ignorance, I could scarcely have seen what she saw.

"You know," she said, in that clear generosity of feeling that could sometimes burst from her, "she's a wonder, Aunt Dee is!" She was watching the rider, now across from us, walking the tall gray stallion slowly upfield. "I don't mean just jumping," she said, her eyes on the receding rider. "It's that she's so—so—"

She was studying the distant figure. "So completely *in* whatever she does. She gives herself to it. All the way—so open. It's sort of—"

The rider was out of sight now, beyond the chicken coop, and cut off from us. Rozelle turned to me.

"Sort of innocent," she said, and waited as for confirmation.

"Isn't that it?" she demanded, finally.

168

I thought of the rider's face at the apogee of the upward flight, outlined against the sky. "Yes," I said.

We sat there silent for a time. Mrs. Jones-Talbot was again in view, far off, upfield. Rozelle was again watching her.

"If I had to choose somebody I could be like," she said, meditatively, "I think it would be her."

She continued to hold her eyes upfield. Abruptly, she stood up.

I had seen her rise and stand there, looking into the distance. I had suddenly caught myself wondering what it was about her mother that Maria might tell me. Then wondering why Rozelle would not tell me. Wondering why nobody else, even if they talked so much about Maria, had ever hinted that there was something to tell. Wondering why everybody in Nashville was waiting for Maria to tell me something. Wondering if they all, like Rozelle, thought it was Maria who had to do the telling.

And thinking, all at once, that I'd be damned if I would pry and spy around, let her tell me in her own time, whatever the hell there was to tell, and who cared—God knows, it was nothing to me—and in that instant, feeling a flicker of the same sadness, a flicker of the same pity, almost tenderness, as when I had seen, that very afternoon, on her approach to the jump, the white mask of blankness come over her face and the mouth tighten like a whitely healed cicatrix.

But now there was Rozelle standing there, saying something. "Oh," I said, "I'm sorry, what did you say?"

"You old dummy," she said, grinning, "don't you ever listen to anything I say?" And immediately: "I said Aunt Dee was the person I'd most like to be like."

"I heard that," I objected. "But what did you say just now?"

"That everybody, I guess, is just stuck with what he is, anyway."

.   .   .

Once on a June afternoon, when I had hitchhiked back from Blackwell College to visit my mother before I began my summer job, I was coming down Jonquil Street and saw four or five little boys, about nine to eleven, sitting on the cracked cement sidewalk, where a maple made a little island of shade, playing some game with cards. I stopped and looked down at them. They were using a tattered old deck—maybe remnants of two or three old decks, for I seem to remember some duplications among the cards—and each little boy had a fistful of cards that he studied with ferocious attention. In front of each, on the cracked cement, was a little heap of Coca-Cola bottle tops.

One little boy put out a bottle top, and said: "I bet a dollar."

The betting went back and forth, to dizzying heights, until one little boy said, "Ready!" They all laid down their hands, face up. "I got more pictures!" one shouted. And then another, "Naw, I got more pictures!" and scrambled for the central heap of tops.

"What you playing?" I asked.

All the little dirty faces, getting to be boy-faces but all still having the same babyish wide-eyed gaze, were lifted toward me, the faces floating in the slow dapple and flicker of sun sifting through the maple.

"Poker," one of the little boys replied, with large authority, and spat into the gutter.

"Mister," said another, not to be outdone, "doan you know nuthen? It's poker."

I said no, I didn't know nuthen, and passed on down the street in the summer heat, in the silence that was broken only—sadly, sadly —by a rooster, far off, crowing in somebody's backyard, and now, writing this down, and at the same time remembering that Sunday afternoon in Mrs. Jones-Talbot's meadow, I feel like one of the little boys playing poker on the hot, cracked cement of Jonquil Street. Even if I do know the rules of poker and know the values of cards in that game, I do not know the rules or the values of cards in the game I am now playing. All I know is that I have a lot of pictures in my head and I merely count them up. I do not know that some blank-looking card with a simple design may be worth more than any picture, that sometimes, even, a card with a lowly 2 or 3 on it may sweep the board. It may be wild.

I put down the "picture" of that Sunday afternoon in the meadow, with the jumpers rising into the blue air, then flying, flowing, over the bars or hedges, all in the silence of dream, and I am not sure that now I know any better than then what the picture meant. Or means.

———

170

In my game now, I know even less than the little boys in theirs. All I know is that it is more like solitaire than poker, that, in fact, as it is suddenly clear to me, this is a final sort of solitaire. I lay down another "picture" and stare numbly at it.

On the card I have just turned over is the picture of a scene of that same Sunday night, after the jumping in Mrs. Jones-Talbot's meadow. We all have come out to the Cudworths' for dinner. We—some score in all—are sitting around the enormous, somewhat battered old rosewood table, sitting on whatever our bottoms had seemed to find, rosewood chairs, presumably relics of an original set, old kitchen chairs, stools, God knows what, and our faces shine in the light from candles stuck in a massy old silver candelabra, a couple of brandy bottles with the labels long since overwhelmed in dripping tallow, an old champagne jereboam, and a little crock jug. All the faces, smiling and bright, seem, in that moment, to float in a tide of happiness, and I, with a strange, uncertain awe, feel the tide lapping at me, too. I feel like a child who has wandered out knee-deep into the sea and feels the sand going fluid and slipping underfoot, and the little slap and tug of the wavelets, and sees, out where it is deep, the other people, the big people who can swim, and they are laughing and splashing and calling for you to come on out, they'll take care of you.

Cud Cudworth, at the head of the table, is standing, a wineglass in his hand, saying something, and everybody is laughing at him, but I am feeling the wash of happiness around the table, feeling it tug dangerously at me. I am not listening to what Cud is saying, but, suddenly, I am. This is an engagement party, he is saying. He and Sally, he says, have been trying out matrimony, and it's not so bad, and now they are going to get engaged.

They are going to be, he says, heavily engaged. In walking the floor and singing hymns all night to soothe the colic, in fixing the formula, in changing diapers. For Sally is, he announces with a dramatic sob in his voice, the small beads of sweat on his weathered, round red face and balding pate agleam in the candlelight, "knocked up."

With that, he lifts his glass, light glittering red in the wine, and pronounces: *"Vive la République! Vive le mystère de la nature! Vive la réproduction! Vive* the delirium of the Life Force! *Vive la* Sally!"

171

There is a tremendous amiable hubbub, with some wine spilled rather than drunk, a gabble of toasts, sometimes amiably obscene, and in the midst of the general corruption of manners and decline of decorum, Maria has slipped from her chair by me and reappears leaning over the mother-to-be, arms around her shoulders, kissing her on the cheek, saying, between kisses, "Oh, I'm so happy! So happy!"

I am watching them, and then, the kissing done, I see the two heads, the two faces cheek to cheek—the dark head and the red, the dark hair soberly glinting in the light of candles, the red giving off a sparkling sheen, the dark eyes deeply bright, the fox-brown eyes, the tawny brown of an oak leaf in October with dew on it in the morning sun, both faces alive in the candlelight, but shining, too, with an inward incandescence communally shared.

Across the table, I see Rozelle, her gaze deeply—and, I think sadly —fixed upon the two faces; but I cannot read what that gaze means.

Then, Maria having come back to her chair, Sally is looking toward Cud, who, still standing, has launched again forth, declaring that it is all, on second thought, very little cause for rejoicing. It's all, he declares, a low female form of malingering, demanding who the hell now is going to ride the tractor to do the spring plowing.

Until Sally interrupts, addressing him in the tone of high melo-drama:

> *"You have displaced the mirth, broke the good meeting,*
> *With most admired disorder!"*

And adding: "Besides you talk too much."

"Who the hell you think you are?" Cud demands, in outrage. "Lady Macbeth?"

"Ssh!" Sally admonishes the company, finger to lips, then continu-ing in the same high style:

> *"I pray you speak not, he grows worse and worse.*
> *Question enrages him."*

"Right!" declares Cud. "I'm manic!"

.   .   .

172

And another card with its picture:

Cud is at the bar, at one end of the living room, glass in hand, talking to me, saying: ". . . and when I went up there to Yankeeland, to the Yale Law School, I was out for blood, and when I got in a swell firm like MacFarlane, Kimball and Kershaw, I was going to grind their bones to make my bread. I was fighting hungry, and I was doing fine. Living it up, too, but I wasn't getting caught out in any company that Old Man MacFarlane wouldn't approve.

"I had me a nice little apartment—all decor-ed up—and a king-size bed and two bathrooms off the bedroom—and I even talked myself into falling in love with a lovely young cunt that even Old Man MacFarlane would have regarded as eligible—since he didn't know all I knew about her. Then I won a really big case—one I was running because they figured it was a dead duck.

"You know, I woke up the morning after I won that case and just stared at the ceiling. I didn't have any hangover, either. Then I got out of bed, careful not to wake my little socialite—almost-fiancée—pretty as a picture, she was, too, lying there, in spite of being all tousled and tuckered, not to mention fuckered, and with a slight tendency to breathe through the mouth. I kissed her reverently, and slipped my pants on and tiptoed out and went down to Wall Street and went right into the old man's lair."

"You mean Mr. MacFarlane?" I said.

"Yep, him," Cud said, "and his eyes cold as blue ice with the sun on it and his eyebrows bristling out like a thorn hedge loaded with hoarfrost, and I got my courage up to say, 'Sir, you have been a father to me, you have wiped my nose and kicked my ass, but I'm a damned ingrate, and I've got to go.'

"For a full minute he studied me, with a look like bad news, a Democratic Administration, a falling barometer, and wind in the angry airt, as the Scots say, then opened his lips to show the most awe-inspiring set of dentures on Wall Street. 'Am I to understand,' he said, with the characteristic clack of those tombstone-shaped and marble-white falsies, 'that you think you can blackmail a promotion in this firm?'

" 'No, sir,' I said to him.

" 'Your efforts,' he said to me, 'are not only unethical, they are superfluous, you have already been promoted. Junior, however.'

"I couldn't get a word out. I swear I had tears in my eyes. Then Old Man Mac said: 'So that's not good enough for you?'

"I stammered out that it was too good, but I just had to go. But—" At this point Cud squinted down into his glass, his head inclined toward me enough for me to catch the glint of reflection from the wall fixture behind him, on the slick, sunburned skin of his bald foreskull.

Then he lifted his head, and said, very earnestly: "It was one hell of a near thing. I damned nigh stayed."

He again looked studiously down into his glass. "But I didn't stay," he declared, looking up from the mystic glass. "I walked out of the Old Man's office, and in that very split instant I felt real. Only once before in my life had I felt that—and boy, do I remember! It was D-Night drop over Normandy and I was in the First Airborne, and *wow!* it was me, the next to go, and I gave one great fart like a bugle blast and I was out, and under me the night sky was full of floating bed sheets like God-a-Mighty had inadvertently kicked over the laundry basket of the whole goddamned Heavenly Hotel, and I was counting for the pull on the rip cord and I felt real. They had been honing us to mania and murder, and I felt real."

He set his glass on the bar, holding his hands out before him, prone, with the fingers spread and slightly cupped downward as though to grasp something. "Now I wake up in the morning," he said, "and I've got something to do. To lay hand to, literally. I can look around me and see things, I can touch things. I feel real."

He inspected his hands, turning them over slowly. They were big, muscular hands, redly weathered, the nails square and thick, a scarcely healed scar marking the back of one. He dropped them, and looked sheepishly at me.

"I know nothing I'm doing is important," he said. "Sure, I'm just a waste product of history. Maybe nothing I'm doing is even real, after all. But I was born right here, in this old house, and I look out the window and know what I'm seeing, and I know some people I like to be with, and I like what I do all day long, and maybe that's all that realness is, anyway, and when Sally pops that little squawking blob of protoplasm out, I'll be feeling so real I'll yell, but right now I bet

I'm just a leetle bit drunk and talking balls to a heavy thinker like you."

I felt a sudden embarrassment, then it spread out, slowly, into my being, like a stain in a glass of water, into a more diffuse, more undefinable malaise. "Hell," I said, "I'm not a thinker, I'm a college professor."

He was grinning at me, not drunk, just friendly, with his strong-looking near-bald skull cocked to one side, one eye squinting quizzically at me, and I found myself liking the guy as well as I had ever liked anybody, any friend; but in a burst of cold clarity, as though somebody had knocked out a dirty windowpane to show the dazzle of winter sunlight beyond, I asked myself, *What friends?*

And now, looking back on that moment, and on the years before that moment, I cannot name one. Not at Dugton High, not even among the teammates, the nearest thing being Mel with his whiskey and little black gals, nor at Blackwell College, nor at Chicago, for Dr. Stahlmann was not a friend—an uncle, a father, an affectionate guardian, a benefactor, but not a friend—nor in the Partisans, for my ties to Giacomo and Gianluigi and the others, though profound, were not the ties of friendship.

To return to the scene at the Cudworth bar, just as that icy-bright realization burst upon me, I saw again, in my mind's eye, how Maria, when Sally's pregnancy was announced, had risen and gone to her and leaned to kiss her cheek, with her own face glimmering in the candlelight with the shared joy. In that recollection, my heart leaped up, even as I heard, in a kind of mystic synchronization, Cud saying, "Hey, you know, there's a really nice farm coming up for sale right here, overlapping me on a corner. Right price, any terms desired. Part of an estate being wound up. You're a Southerner, why not come home like me, settle down?" Then, after a pause: "Gosh, it'd be great to have you all—"

He stopped on the phrase, looked foolish, took a quick gulp of his whiskey, and said: "There goes my old likker-loose blab-mouth again. But hell, we'd love it. Mix farming and professoring."

"Hell," I said, floundering, dodging the issue, "I haven't got any money."

"Now, look here," he said, switching to a businesslike tone, "the place will carry itself. I swear it. I'll rent a hundred acres from you at the going price—I need more pasture and grain, too. This thing can be worked out."

"But—" I began, not going on, the word lost in a vague sadness, like distance.

"But nothing," he said briskly. "We'll take a look in a day or two. I've got to go over to see the caretaker about coming here as a tenant for me. Now, the house, it's good, you could move in tomorrow, fix it up along the way. It won't hurt to look."

I said no, it wouldn't hurt to look.

. . .

And another card:

I am standing in the middle of the floor in the drawing room of the McInnis house, I have come to take Maria to the Christmas Cotillion, and the butler has led me here to wait for Maria to come down. We are to have a drink here before going to the club. I am in black tie, for the first time in my life. I even own the dinner clothes I stand in. I stand in front of the fire, waiting. I try not to look into the great mirror above the marble mantel-shelf.

Maria is entering, flushed, eyes gleaming, pleased with herself, but stops, exclaiming: "Oh, how gorgeous!" Coming close to me to receive a ritual kiss, she pats one of the silken lapels, saying, "My, my, how handsome!"

I catch a glimpse of the young couple in the big mirror over the mantel, the large man in his black, the slight woman in white with a bouffant skirt—I think that is the word—slashed in crimson, her dark head slightly bowed as she pats the lapel, murmuring, and I say: "It's just like an advertisement for Hart, Schaffner, and Marx."

Maria looks up and catches the image in the mirror and studies it critically. "No," she objects. "Not at all alike—the man in the ad, he's handsome all right, but this man, he's not only handsome—look how distinguished he is, and oh, what dignity!"

And we both laugh, looking into the mirror, and somewhere, deep in my inner darkness, a voice, softly, soothingly, repeats the very words she has uttered.

I slip my arm around her and kiss her again, but not enthusiastically enough to disturb cosmetics or coiffure. With my arm still lightly around her, we admire the effect in the mirror. The eyes of the young woman in the mirror, catching the play of flame from the hearth below, are shining.

.   .   .

I turn over another card:

Cud and I are standing in the dim emptiness of a farmhouse, while a man in overalls is busy opening shutters.

The man is a tenant and caretaker on this farm, but he has given notice, and Cud is here to talk with him about coming to his place, for the man is said to know horses. I am here, as a prospective buyer, to look at the farm. We, having walked over the place, are being shown the house. As the shutters of the tall windows open, one by one, the November sunlight floods in to make the big room even emptier and the oak floor, worn and somewhat dented by more than a century of use, seem even dingier.

But Cud is saying: "A nice place. Look at that molded ceiling. Real handsome, and good sound plaster even now." He continues his scrutiny. Then: "More style than our place." Standing in the middle of the floor, he jumps and lets his not inconsiderable weight come down hard. "Not a vibration," he says.

I mumble agreement, and we go into the dining room.

"Look at that ceiling again," Cud says. "And the fireplace."

I am thinking of a big table there, and people around it. Then, all at once, what I am seeing is the table in the Cudworth dining room on the night when he announced Sally's pregnancy, and the gleam of candlelight on the two girlish faces, cheek to cheek, smiling.

"Yeah," I say, "it's great."

As I stand there, I become aware that the man in the patched and faded overalls, the tenant of the farm, is covertly watching me. He is a man in his fifties, once robust and handsome, but now stooped and with muscles thinning on the big bones, and long, ragged mustaches, once black but now gray-streaked, and the gray stained yellow with tobacco juice, and under the shadow of the low-pulled brim of the old worn-out black felt hat, the eyes, bloodshot and defeated, glare in outrage at me. He reminds me, in that moment, of the pictures by

177

Brady, and other such photographers, of Confederate prisoners captured in late, disastrous battles of the war. As he spies at me from under the shadow of the low-pulled brim, he is, I see, secretly chewing at the long, ragged mustaches.

In the boxed-in air of the room, I catch the smell of whiskey.

And then I find myself abruptly turning to Cud, and the words burst out, as though in anger, hatred, and, strangely, relief: "Yeah, the place is great, but I told you, I haven't got any money!"

The jaw of the man in overalls has stopped that slow motion of chewing the mustaches. The lips have drawn back in a grin, like a panting dog's, but the bloodshot eyes do not glare at me now in outrage. In a hard glitter, like joy.

Cud is saying: "Hey, come off that. I told you, it's a cinch. Like I said, I'll . . ."

I am not listening.

That is the picture. But I should add that as we rode away down the lane, our mounts side by side between the leafless hedges of bodock, I looked back once. There, through a gap in the bodock, I saw the house, high on the bluff above the creek, set among big oaks and tulip trees, the brick mellow with age, the white shutters sharply defined, the slate roof glinting like gun metal in the sunlight that, still bright, poured over all the land.

As I lifted rein, Cud broke the silence. "Damn it," he said, "I just can't take him. Good hand with stock, knows horses, but God damn it, he drinks. In the afternoon, and you could smell it like a distillery." He turned accusingly at me: "You could smell it, couldn't you?"

"Yes," I said.

"He had a farm once, his own," Cud said, after a little. "Not much of a place, but something. He lost it." He fell silent. Then: "Drink, I bet."

"The poor bastard," I said.

I was thinking that this man was about the age my own father would have been. This man, too, had once had fine, black mustaches.

.   .   .

There are pictures that, now with the years, come blurred, but some even in the beginning were blurred, the way cards are if you firmly grasp one end of a deck and with the thumb of the other hand bend them back and let them, one by one, snap straight. You catch a flash of color, of outline, on one, but before it is clearly defined, another has snapped across it, and so on to the end. It was that way with the whole period of the Christmas vacation, that year.

I, who had been to but one regular dance in my life, the Senior Prom of Dugton High, and that for only three minutes, now went to five in less than two weeks, and began to feel quite at home in my black-tie rig, and had to buy two more shirts, the laundry being slow. In that time everything seemed to blur with everything else. After a dance, the next day, I would find it still going on somewhere in the back of my head. Or I'd be waiting for the next one. I'd be working and suddenly find myself sunk in a kind of blankness of waiting and wouldn't even know how long I had been like that. But what I was waiting for was a blankness, too, a hypnosis, a dream, with the new face looking up at you, the new smile, the new scent in your nostrils, a new voice saying, "Oh, my, how lovely Maria looks tonight," and your own voice saying, "Why, that's exactly what she said about you," and the smile, the voice, the scent, the fleeting pressure of a hand—all strands to weave the gossamer of illusion, delicious and fraudulent, that you and the enchantress are bound in mystic intimacy. And all the while the flood of music sustains you, powerless in the flow of time, in its sensual communion, not only with the body you feel flexing and flowing under your hand, but with all the other bodies all around you that shift and sway.

And always, at some moment in the evening, it would be Rozelle's face looking up into mine as the music bore us along, her face alive with mischief or drooping back in a pose of swooning rapture, her voice saying: "Why, bless my soul!—what a dancer the Old Bum has turned into, you slay me, you do. You're slaying them all, they never knew what life was like till that handsome, ruthless brute took their teeny-weeny little waist between his big old thumb and forefinger and turned those mean old dark smoldering eyes down on 'em!"

To which I would reply: "Hey, just feed me that stuff with a spoon —don't use a trowel, you'll choke me."

But once, having settled characteristically into the dancer's arms— the dancer being me—Rozelle looked up and said: "You didn't dance this way at the Senior Prom. I do think I am entitled to know how you learned. Since you wouldn't let me teach you."

"You always want to know everything," I said.

She nodded, leaning her head gently back to look directly into my face.

"All right," I said. "I got my start with the patriotic girls of the USO who offered their fair white bodies to the grip of a redneck while he trampled their feet to hamburger. I got the finishing touches from Roman whores or simply young Roman females who needed a square meal."

"Ugh," she said.

"Don't ask me if you don't want the truth," I said. "You are the only person I always tell the truth to." Then adding: "It must be my tribute to Dugton."

Then our dance was over. Then the dance itself—like all the other dances—would be over, just when you felt it had really begun, when you had really crossed some line, had learned some ritual secret. Then, at 3:30 in the morning, or later, approaching down the lane, you see the white blur of your house, then, as the car lights strike, you see it suddenly leap into stark definition against the blackness of the woods; and you feel overwhelmed with sadness, guilt, loss, and emptiness, a feeling unspecifiable but most resembling the moment after some episode of boyhood masturbation.

You feel like crying out in the emptiness of the house to demand what—what in God's name—is reality.

But a good night's sleep will fix up everything. It always has.

.   .   .

Those first five dances were all alike. The sixth, a New Year's Eve party given by the Carringtons, was different not only from the Christmas dances, but also from any parties they had given earlier—in my time, anyway. It was different from the earlier parties, first, in being more mixed. There were a number of people I had never seen before, including some older people, university (distinguished) and town (wellborn and probably well off), and a Hindu, turban, caste mark and all, whom Amy Dabbitt, it developed, had brought. ("Oh, she's got a guru or swami or something," Rozelle said, "always latching on to something, Christian Science, psychoanalysis, cold baths, medieval Catholicism, organic foods. Now it's the Wisdom of the East, including all the beautiful positions, I bet.")

To accommodate the mob, all the furniture had been moved out of the north end of the barn and the trestle tables set up on the west wall for a bar and buffet. The Steinway was down in the space in the jungle where the tables had been, and a five-piece jazz band, all-black, was there for the music. (An import from New Orleans, somebody whispered to me, in awe.)

The most marked difference from my other dances was, however, an atmosphere. It was not only that this was in a house, not in a club, for here, tonight, I found strangers, too. But strangers here did not seem strangers in this world of unselfconscious gaiety and willingness to live in the innocent flow of experience in which to ask for nothing was to receive all. Even the swami, for whom a chair had been brought (he did not dance or drink alcohol), seemed to participate in the joyful process as he held court, with several young women leaning above him or seated on cushions at his feet; for, as he sipped his orange juice, his deep, dark, limpid gaze might be thought to bless all those frail mortals caught up in the ritual of hope and renewal.

I may have had a little more to drink than usual, but for me a deeper and more arcane chemistry than the absorption of alcohol into my bloodstream must have been in train. In any case, a man's friendly grin or clasp of hand in greeting, a woman's smile of recognition or sway of body or droop of the eyelids—even the most fleeting event— seemed a significant state in the unfolding of a mysterious promise. Then, at midnight, a deafening peal of bells broke out (an amplified recording that Lawford had timed), and we all lifted the champagne and drank and plunged into a flurry of promiscuous kissing (and what might be regarded as my nonpromiscuous kissing of Maria, the first real kiss I had ever had there, surprised at the depth and warmth of her lips), and then we scurried to get rid of glasses so that we might take hands in a general circle and sing "Should auld acquaintance be forgot and auld lang syne."

So, on one side clutching the hand of a middle-aged woman in glasses, whose name he didn't even know, and on the other side the hand of Amy Dabbitt, who had even managed to drag her lordly swami into our circle to hold her other hand, in the midst of new acquaintances, not old, Jed Tewksbury lustily raised his voice to blend with all the other voices in praise of fulfillment to be found in the cherished flow of time; and his heart was, to his surprise, swollen with sweetness. He really did not know what to make of the fact.

.   .   .

By 1 A.M. the musicians were packing their instruments, and some guests, chiefly the older set, were slipping unobtrusively away. A few minutes later Lawford blew his fox horn, and, gracefully mounting a chair, announced in his commanding voice that all art lovers were invited to attend a little unveiling in the studio end, after which a light collation would be served at the buffet. Even, he said, to non–art lovers.

"What's he unveiling?" I asked Rozelle.

"I don't have the foggiest notion," she said.

"He hasn't even told you?" Maria asked.

"Oh, it's a great mystery," Rozelle said, smiling.

So we trooped into the north end, to find the swami seated regally in the big tiger-skin chair by the hearth, in the midst of an earnest discourse with a substantially increased group of auditors, including even two or three men, all very attentive. Several guests had been prowling among the pieces of sculpture, chiefly those of the "Ballet." When Maria joined the swami's audience, I idly wandered over, with some of the other art lovers, to join the group already clustered around "Number 5."

On "Number 5" the tuning-fork-shaped support leaned somewhat forward from the base, conforming, as it were, to the line of the spine of the unrepresented female—unrepresented, that is, except for the silvery arms. The right arm, elbow bent, reached down and forward, with the thumb and forefinger closing as though about to grasp a stalk, the lower fingers curling slightly inward. The left arm reached out somewhat higher, the palm turned slightly down and the fingers cupped a little, the whole effect being that of a gesture of surprise and delight.

Now, in the middle of the circle defined by the forefinger and thumb of the silvery right hand of "Number 5," a splendid banana reared.

From the faces of the audience—ranging in expression from maidenly blush to masculine leer—it was obvious that no further exegesis was required to relate art to life. Indeed, the other "Numbers" of the "Ballet" had all leaped, by contagion, into more precise significance.

Just as I had surveyed the scene, Lawford called me to come help him, but even as I turned away, Mrs. Jones-Talbot, with a smile all around, both condescending and disciplinary, stepped forward, saying, "Tut, tut, my pets," and removed the offending object and went, quite calmly, still smiling, to replace it where it belonged, in a great bowl of fruit from which some wag had extracted it.

I helped Lawford trundle out from his workroom one of the black, boxlike stands on which pieces were exhibited, this one heavy for its size, the shape of the object on it not even suggested by the folds of a white cloth, almost as big as a sheet, that shrouded it. Rozelle stood there waiting, holding not only her glass of champagne but, dutifully, the highball that Lawford had left with her. Behind her, in a semicircle, backs to the fireplace, the others waited.

Rozelle handed Lawford his glass. Suddenly, I realized that, though he had shown no sign of drink, his face had become tense and brittle, and I remembered that his hands had quivered a little, back in the workroom, when he had pulled taut the cloth shrouding the object. His eyes were darting from face to face.

Almost rudely, not a word, he thrust his glass at me, and stepped forward. I saw him fix his eyes on Rozelle's face. He seized the ring attached to the middle of the cloth, lifted it as high as possible, and with his gaze still on Rozelle's face, snatched the cloth free, and flung it carelessly behind him in my direction. I caught it. Then my eyes fixed on the object.

It was a man's head, in bronze, the head of an aging man, perhaps an old one, the big round skull almost bald, the head thrown back, eyes wide with outrage, the mouth straining open in a soundless scream, open to the painful fullest so that, in fact, in that dark recess, you could see the tortured lift of the tongue.

"Oh!" Rozelle uttered, in a breathy exhalation, and in the long moment while she stared at the object, which was facing her, and while Lawford stared at her, there wasn't a sound.

All at once, she stepped forward, set her champagne on the black stand beside the screaming head, and exclaiming, "Oh, Lawford, it's wonderful!" ran to him, lifted her hands to seize his head and draw it down to her, and kissed him; and standing close there, seeing the sudden and positive in-suck of her cheeks—seeing, literally, only the right cheek, but knowing more vividly than by vision how the other would be sucked in, too—I knew the open rounding of her mouth at the instant she made contact with his lips, and knew the soft-strong, wet, plunging, twining thrust of her tongue into his very throat.

Then, refusing what I saw, rejecting it, I snatched my eyes away. I found that Mrs. Jones-Talbot, standing beyond her nephew and Rozelle, was regarding me with what I can only describe as a cold and clinical air. I was sure I was flushing.

By that time, however, Mrs. Jones-Talbot was talking animatedly to an older man at her side, and the general congratulatory babble had broken forth.

.　　.　　.

When we began to drift back into the south end, fresh logs had been laid on the hearth, chairs had been replaced, hassocks had mysteriously appeared, and large leather cushions of various colors were cast about, here and there, and the bar and buffet had been handsomely refurnished.

People ate. Some went away. I did not see Rozelle at such moments of leave-taking, but Lawford was there, giving a lady a last New Year's kiss, laying a hand of warm friendship on a man's shoulder. This again and again. Then he was moving among the remaining guests, making them feel that he could not bear to see them go, listening to each, his head slightly inclined in a characteristic pose of devoted attention, his smile flickering with the flow of voice he attended to, as though his face were the electric bulb of some scientific apparatus of measurement, easy and graceful in his height, and charmingly selfless.

People were making themselves comfortable. Conversation, idle and punctuated by laughter, had begun. The sourceless music, turned down soft, had begun, too, and several valiant couples, including Maria and Cud, were dancing. I stood watching the dancers, not really seeing them, thinking of the moment when, as Rozelle kissed her husband, I had surprised Mrs. Jones-Talbot's eyes on me.

I was now standing alone, or thought I was. But I became aware of someone by my side, one of the guests whom I had not met, a youngish man, elegantly turned out, smiling, arrogant, and fresh-faced. He caught my eye. "She's a swell dancer," he said, nodding toward Maria. "Built, too," he added. Then, turning his slick, composed face full on me, his glance sweeping me from head to foot, he said, in a mixture of incredulity and condescending approval, "Well, you know how to pick 'em."

He lowered his right hand a little, turning the forearm from the elbow, bringing the hand more fully into my range of vision, making a slight circular motion with the thumb against the tips of the fore- and second fingers, offering the sight to me slyly, as though it were obscene. I didn't get what he was up to. I lifted my face, stupidly, to him. He smiled faintly, knowingly, connivingly at me, barely moving the corners of his cleanly carved lips. Then I heard what he, raising the hand and the softly rotating thumb a little more fully into my sight, was saying.

"Got the moola, too," he was saying, softly, like a secret.

For a second I didn't react, didn't really understand. Then I fought down the impulse to slug him, and turned sharply away.

I moved down the alley in the middle of the jungle, toward the south end where on one side was a kitchen and on the other, the washrooms. I entered there, a place half as big as a hotel's, it seemed, glittering white after the dimness of the jungle. Nobody was there. I stood at one of the three urinals, relieving myself, refusing, for the moment, to think.

I moved to the basin, looking down at my hands in the water.

I dried my hands, looked at myself in the mirror. My face clearly needed washing. My black tie, not too expertly tied at best, was coming unknotted, and sagging dispiritedly to one side. My shirt was now scarcely a starch-enameled white, being worn for the second time. My general appearance suggested that I had recently slept in a dust bin.

I began doing what I could to put things right, beginning with the face. I dried the face. I continued the project of rehabilitation. Then, as I surveyed the not entirely satisfying results, I thought how Maria, when I had come to take her to the Christmas Cotillion, had, with murmurs of admiration, patted my lapel, and how, with my arm about her, we had smiled at the lovely young couple in the big mirror above the marble mantel in the McInnis drawing room; and now, as in a vision, she was beside me in the washroom mirror, and behind us and around us were all those men in correct black and glittering white, and the women with light on their bare shoulders, and all the eyes—even the eyes of Cud, for he was there, too—regarded us, regarded me, slyly, knowingly, connivingly, and a hand of each of the mystic spectators, held just at waist level, made, as though in secret, for my eyes alone, the obscene rotating motion of the thumb across the tips of the first two fingers, and I heard the whisper, "Moola, moola."

It all came in a flash, then, in a flash, was gone. But I stood there, again hearing the voice of Cud Cudworth, there in the empty farmhouse on the bluff, saying, "You could swing this place easy. I told you, it's a cinch."

And then I saw again, in my mind now, the face of the stooped, aging man in patched overalls, with eyes bloodshot, defeated, and outraged, spying on me from the shadow of the pulled-down old black felt hat.

As I stood there, I thought I was on the verge of being throttled. I simply could not breathe. I jerked the tie almost loose, and ran my fingers through my hair, letting it make what mess it would. Then I left the washroom, passed through the jungle, and made directly for the bar.

Nobody was dancing now. The company had dwindled further. Everybody left was now sitting. One of the men was just finishing a tale of some sort, the point of which escaped me. But everybody was laughing fit to kill. I stood there looking down on them all. I had just taken the last of several deep drags on splendid, aged sour mash when Cud called across the distance of the hearth: "Hey, Jed, I bet you know some juicy old Alabama stories."

"Nope," I said, and tried to grin.

"Stand and deliver!" Cud called. "You've never even told one. Do you expect me to entertain you all the time?"

There was a polite general burst of exhortation.

I looked down on all those people, their faces turned toward me.

I did not know who the hell they were. I saw the face of Maria, in the distance across the hearth. I took another drag of the sour mash. Then, stooping to set my glass on the hearth, I rose and, in the nasal accent of hill Alabama, I said, stagily: "Wal, reckin they's one I could tell ye."

"Quiet!" Lawford commanded, and lifted a hand for general attention.

" 'Bout Pap, how he got kilt," I said.

So I told them.

. . .

I told them all the way through, with gestures, acting it out with as much realism as would leave a shred of decency—on to the moment when Ma r'ared up and th'owed that-air cal-vry sword in the crick, and I showed 'em how she done it.

That seemed to be a natural stopping place, so I stopped there, winding up in a wildly exaggerated dialect: "So Ma jest set back down in her split-bottom cheer, thar in the wagin, behind me and the nigger, and she said: 'Drive on.' "

I stood there in the ensuing silence, caught a glimpse of Maria's face, with an expression of peculiar intensity, then turned and walked back to the bar and took refreshment. Behind me, I heard Cud calling out: "Great—just great! I knew you had it in you."

There was some clapping and murmuring behind me.

When I came back, and stood there a moment at the edge of things, I noticed that Maria had gone. As I looked for a cushion, one of the men, a regular in the rump-sessions, asked: "Now where did you pick up that tale, Jed? Alabama?"

"Alabama, yes," I replied. "But it's not a tale."

"It's a beaut of a tale," he said.

"It may be a beaut," I said, "but it's not a tale. It is straight autobiography."

"Hey, come off that," the man said.

I firmly and clearly asserted that it was indeed autobiography, adding that it was a matter of public record in Claxford County, Alabama. "And further," I asserted, "the deponent saith not."

· · ·

Having slept till midafternoon of January 1, I got myself into some
sort of order to go to the crossroads store for a few supplies—an
old-fashioned country store where a dodderer, under the single fly-
specked bulb, was always there, at any hour, to sell you something.
It was well after dark when, that evening, I got back to my house.
Carrying a sack of groceries, I entered by the back door, kicked the
new snow off my feet, turned on the kitchen lights, and stowed the
groceries away. Not turning on the hall light, I proceeded the few
steps to the bedroom door, opened it, and entered.

I heard a slight sound, and froze, trying to locate it.

"Don't turn the light on," the voice, not much more than a hoarse
whisper, said.

CHAPTER VIII

On January 2 I tried all morning to anesthetize myself with term papers (which should have been graded during the Christmas holidays), but around the margin of that blankness of being there was the flicker of an unacknowledged awareness that nothing would ever be the same.

Finally, I rose and went to the kitchen with the firm intention of making myself a Swiss cheese sandwich, but once there, I found myself observing, quite dispassionately, my hands as they poured two ounces of bourbon into a tumbler and added water and ice. Then, doubly against my principles, I drank a midday and solitary highball. That done, I forced myself to make and eat a sandwich.

I stood in the middle of the kitchen, and sunlight, intensified by the whiteness of new snow over the land, poured in by the big south window. I scrupulously observed how sharply that light defined the cracks in the old linoleum. With equal scrupulosity, I looked about me at the objects in the kitchen. I had lived here, in this house, some three months now, and now, as I stood there, I realized that the room, and the landscape beyond the room, were very strange to me.

I knew that I myself was very strange to me. I thrust forth a hand to regard it. I did not, in the deepest sense, know whose hand it was. I stood in the middle of timelessness, lit by the brilliance of snow, and carefully drew in each breath slow and deep, trying to live in this new medium, in which there was no past and no future, only the strange present that existed only breath by breath.

But, suddenly, I did know that the past and the future did exist, and I must live in them, too. For from the old weight-clock in the hall came the tinny whir and *bong* announcing that it was one o'clock. The mail would have come.

I seized on this reason to get out of the house. I thought how if I kept walking forever into the brightness and distance of the world, nothing would have happened.

I got to the mailbox, took out the mail, did not look at it. I stood in the brilliant abstraction of the world. Then, without decision, I found myself slowly returning to the house. But as I approached the end of the lane, I stopped again. Swimming before me in that brightness, I observed what was there—just a commonplace little frame house, a story and a half high, white but in need of paint, standing in a place of white snow, backed by the darkness of cedar woods.

I turned and looked at the distance in the perfect circle around me. Far away, beyond my sight and knowing, were people doing what they had to do. But I knew that I would turn and go toward the house.

The faint crunching of my feet on the crisp new snow, as I passed through the brilliance, was like the sound of unidentified steps in darkness, the steps of an unseen, and unseeable companion.

I entered the house, the bedroom, laid the mail on the table near the window, drew the curtain against the daylight—being unaware of that last act until it had been accomplished. I switched on the reading lamp on the table and began sorting the mail—the newspaper, some advertisements, one letter. The writing on the envelope seemed vaguely familiar, but without pausing to speculate, I opened it and began to read:

Dear Jed:

I hope—I pray—that you did not misunderstand why I so abruptly disappeared tonight when you had finished telling the story. So many things swept over me, dear Jed—dear Jed, for that is how I feel about you right now as I sit here in my room in Rose's and Lawford's house, and hear the sounds of the party still going on in the barn.

I was saying—yes, how I had to be by myself to try to make sense of all the things that swept over me as I listened to you telling the story. For one thing, I felt that I knew—I was sure that I *really* knew—why you were telling it, and I felt all at once that I knew you in a way I never had before. Now I suddenly saw how solidly you are yourself. Just yourself—like a rock sticking up out of water and the water just sloshing around its base, and it was this idea of how solidly you are yourself in the middle of the world and things just slosh against you, that made me feel that perhaps I could be enough of myself to tell you something that . . .

I lifted my eyes from the letter, from the black, precise, almost too precise, too painfully etched calligraphy. My hand still held the sheet there under the rays of the reading lamp, but my eyes were fixed on the heavy dark blue curtains a little beyond the table, that just now, on some unformulated impulse, I had drawn to cut this room off from the daylight world.

I thought: *Now she is going to tell me.*

I had been staring at the dark blue fabric that, with a light-proof lining, cut off the afternoon, but now, with the letter in my hand, I turned to face the room. Beyond the circle defined by the tight shade of the lamp, the room was shadowy.

When, late yesterday, not even twenty hours ago, I had entered this room, the early winter dark had already fallen, and then the only light was coming from the hall behind me. For an instant I had stood there reaching for the wall switch just inside the door. Then the voice, low and stifled as though a hand were laid on the throat it came through, had said: "Don't turn the light on."

.   .   .

For that instant—yesterday—as I stood there, I had not known whose voice it was. But I did not turn on the light. I remember, even

191

now, every sensation I experienced as I stood there, how my heart was making a slow thump in what seemed the enormous vacancy of my chest, how I swallowed a big lump in my throat that felt coarse and sharp like a chunk of stale corn bread, how I strained to adjust my eyes to the darkness beyond the weak shaft of light from the hall at my back. I remember how, out of the dimness, the huddled dark figure on the foot of my bed, which had no footboard and was covered with an old army blanket, slowly assumed shape and identity.

I moved forward, but stopped some three paces short of the bed.

She was huddled there, still in her coat, a dark fur of some kind, feet still in fur-topped boots, some snow still clinging to the fur tops, lying on her left side with knees drawn up tight and elbows over the breasts and hands over the face, altogether in the position of somebody who, being assaulted by a gang, tries to protect the vital parts. I stood stock-still, looking down at her, not saying a word.

To this day I do not know the reason why I did not, or could not, utter a word—whether because a thousand different words struggled for utterance, or because there was, literally, no word to say to the inevitable event. But as I stood there, she slowly raised her head, twisted to force her shoulder up a little, with her hair falling in disorder over one side of her face. In the dimness I could tell that the face was chalk-pale. I could see the lips move a little.

Then the words, thin and dry, did come out, and if Rozelle Hard-castle had not uttered precisely the words that did come, nothing would ever have happened.

If she had said nothing. If she had said anything else. If she had done anything else. If, even, she had suddenly risen before me with nakedness gleaming white in the dimness. If she had laid hand to my sex.

Even under such circumstances, nothing would have happened.

But, lifting her face, with the disordered hair falling across one side, she said what she did say.

"You knew—" she said, and stopped.

"Knew what?" I demanded.

With her free hand she pushed the hair back from her face, staring at me across the distance.

"Knew that I'd have to come," she said.

Which I had not known, but, on the instant, knew that, without knowing, I had known it. And in that knowledge, I felt, too, that some massive concurrence of forces had been working, all my life, in darkness, to bring me to this spot and instant. All sense of my own force, even of identity, seemed to flee from me. But, even as I stood there, a peculiar thing happened. In my powerlessness, it seemed that I was becoming identified with the very powers that had drained me of power. I knew, in other words, what hero, saint, Marxist, criminal, artist, and madman must know: identity with fate.

Even if I was, God knows, none of those things.

Though my eyes would have been fixed on her, I must even have forgotten that Rozelle Hardcastle was there. In fact, I remember the shock with which I rediscovered her identity, a shock more profound than at the first, literal discovery. She had now pushed herself further up, almost to a sitting position there on the foot of the bed, on the old army blanket, and in that dimness, her eyes, open wide at me, caught some glint of reflection from the light at the doorway.

"Oh, it was awful!" she began. "It—"

"I don't want to hear anything about it," I said. "Whatever it was."

Out of the dimness, the light was making a glint in the wide eyes.

Then I heard my own voice, harsh and tight-throated.

"You know why you came here," the voice was saying, "don't you?"

Not taking her gaze from me, she moved to let her feet find the floor, then in a slow, awkward motion straightened up and stood there. Awkwardly, her hands fumbled at the top button that held the fur across her breast. She was still staring when the hands sank to locate the next button.

.   .   .

That had been on January 1. Now, the next day, as I turned my eyes from the very spot, now empty, where she had stood, with her hands on that button, I found again the new letter lying under the lamp, the second sheet now exposed. So I thought of Maria McInnis, sitting late at night in a bedroom, hearing the distant

193

sounds of a party that, in her way, she had sought to be absorbed into, picking up a pen to tell me what she thought she had to tell me.

How her mother was in a mental hospital and had been there for many years. How her father had tried to protect her, but boarding school and protracted visits with relatives had not saved her from having to become aware of that world of delusory hates and fears. How, in spite of all medical assurances and of her father's profound love and self-sacrifice, and the confidence of dear friends, she had grown up with the sense that she, too, was doomed to be drawn, sooner or later, into that world. How, though her mother had long since ceased to respond to her or anyone else, she felt the compulsion to go every week, and sit with her, feeling somehow that this was some sort of magic to save herself, or at least guarantee that someone would remember her when she came to be locked up.

How her own doctor had forbidden those visits, but how she herself fell very ill. No, not in her head. Just plain ill, with fever and terrible insomnia. How for years she could not take trips, except for a few days. She had to see her mother. Yes, she had been happy in the happiness of her friends and even had a kind of happiness of her own —but, oh, if she could just be sensible and see the truth.

That was what the letter said.

And then:

> Things, as I said, came flooding over me last night, when you were telling the story. Now as I sit here, I feel, in a slow dawning way like watching the sun rise after a night of bad dreams. I am going away for a while. I really can do it, I know! It may be for a long time, weeks, months, for I must be very sure and very careful. But oh, dear Jed— maybe—maybe—
>
> And I owe it all to you.
>
> Oh, thank you, Jed!—dear Jed!
>
> Maria.

I read it slowly, numbly, as though I had to spell out the words, knowing, however, that the numbness would not last, no matter how much I wanted it to.

It did not last, for I made the mistake of closing my eyes, and then I saw Maria's face when, at the Cudworth dinner, she had leaned over Sally Cudworth's shoulder, embracing her, and had pressed her cheek against Sally's, and her own face had gleamed, not only in the light of candles, but with an inner joy that appropriated Sally's joy as her own.

And with that I heard the words *too late, too late,* as clear as from an external voice behind me, and I was remembering, like a movement glimpsed out of the tail of the eye or the single flicker, in the woods, of a leaf behind which some unidentified creature has disappeared, the moment when, at the New Year's Eve party, in the midst of the happy racket and the midnight burst of the recorded pealing of bells, I had, for the first time, really kissed Maria McInnis, kissed her, that is, to sense in the touch of the lips a warmth and depth of body.

Then, as I stood with the paper clutched tight in my hand, that recollection was gone, and the numbness had come back.

So I could open my eyes. I saw that at the bottom of the last sheet, well below the signature, there was the word *Over.* On the reverse side was a postscript:

> Do not answer this letter. I want to be by myself. To see if I have a self. I'll let you know when I get back.

But a little farther down, written in obvious haste and agitation, not at all like the too precisely controlled calligraphy above, I saw:

> It was three o'clock when Rose came to my room, still in her party clothes, but no shoes, and in a frightful state. She lay across my bed and kept crying in a dry silent way that made you think she would choke. She wouldn't talk, all I could do was hold her hand and wait. She finally went to sleep, across the bed. I put a blanket over her. It is now past four-thirty and snow is falling. How can I ever go away and leave her in trouble! God, what will happen?

.   .   .

I knew one thing that had happened. It had happened yesterday, in this room, with the only light the shaft admitted by the open door to the hall. Now, sitting by the table, I let my head sink forward till

---

195

my forehead was pressed against the sheets of paper at the edge of the table, and what had happened was now happening again in my head.

In that dim room, on that bed, from which the covers had been jerked back, balanced on my right knee, naked, the knee thrust down to dent the sheet into the mattress and the left foot forward and flat and the knee bent at right angles to steady me, I looked down at the body of Rozelle Hardcastle Carrington. It lay supine before me, the left leg to the right of my down-thrust knee, the right leg extending into the space between that knee and my upright left lower leg, by which I held my balance. The left arm of that naked body before me was extended above the head inert and loose, the palm emptily upward, as the arm had trailed when I had laid hold on the body and drawn it toward me into its present position. The head was thrown back a little, as it too had fallen in that process, and the right forearm was crooked across the eyes. All—the arm trailing upward, the dropped-back head, the blindfolded eyes—suggested not merely passivity, but rather some vast, fatalistic indifference toward whatever might happen to that nakedly defenseless body, a repudiation, even, of that body.

I leaned forward and very deliberately slipped a hand under each buttock, and even now I remember my surprise at realizing the contrast to the substance of the body now visible before me, to all earlier impressions of slim and fluent grace—my surprise, that is, at the sense, beneath rondure and softness, of a resistant, challenging animal weightiness.

I lifted the buttocks well clear of the bed, and drew them toward me, aware how, in what crazily seemed to be distance, the arm above the thrown-back head limply trailed down the sheet, how, in that dragging, the head, with the forearm across the eyes, seemed to fall further back, more indifferent than ever to what might happen to that trivial body.

I brought the buttocks higher, closer, slowly splitting them, set them firmly astride my down-thrust right thigh, halfway between knee and crotch. It was an action that, though totally unpremeditated, was performed as though with deliberate slowness, passionlessly, and at the moment of contact what I was numbly aware of was simply an impersonal wetness.

Then, all at once, there was the stabbing sensation at the spot. It was a stab of heat and a stab of cold, of both but somehow undifferentiated and interfused, a very oxymoron come alive to stab through skin, flesh, and muscle of my thigh to the very bone.

Bemused in that sensation, I held the body pressed against my thigh, then, suddenly, pushed it from me, and looked down. First at that spot on my leg where the stab was and where dampness gleamed, then at what I supported in my hands, the thighs that, slowly and whitely, had fallen further apart to present, in the midst of the lush yet brambly-looking pubic corona of damp-curling, bronze-gold hair, the orchidaceous swell of the waiting sex. Staring down at it, what I was aware of was not the poetry of the yearning, anonymous wound with the faint gleam of light caught there to give some hint of the roseate inwardness, but for the first time in my life, of the true, archetypal ass, the unbolted breech so simplistically and brutally designed for its blankly abstract function and the plunge into depersonalized, and depersonalizing, darkness.

I raised my eyes. How far away and irrelevant seemed that face yonder with the forearm across to cut off sight, and beyond that the other arm trailing and, farther in that distance, the supine, empty hand. The remote and contemptuous indifference of the shielded eyes to what I held in my hands, and had stared down at, evoked in me, like a burst of light, a wild sense of liberation into meaninglessness, the certainty that it could not matter what went on in that beautiful, back-thrown head, what thoughts, feelings, memories, or aspirations might lie behind those shuttered eyes.

Or behind my own unshuttered ones.

What were such things?

Froth on a dark wave.

But there had been no dark wave, to tell the truth. The actions I had performed were, as I have said, passionless.

Everything might have been only the blank enactment of what was inevitable but was, in its inevitability, meaningless. Then, as I knelt there, shivering in the sense of unreality, the right leg of the body I held in my hands drew upward in a slow jackknife motion, and as my left knee slipped down to the bed so that now I was fully kneeling, it began to extend itself to the side, to my left side. Having reached its length, with naked toes seeming tight together and pointing like a dancer's, the lowering leg, very slowly, moved toward me, and around me, bending in a dreamy, sickle-like motion of embracement.

Meanwhile, the forearm still covered the eyes and the face seemed calm as sleep. That motion of embracement seemed totally unrelated to what life might be behind the calm face I saw there. The motion, however, continued, as slow and impersonal as though of a frond, or of a great elongated white petal, moving in slumbrous tropism in jungle shadow. Then I felt the heel touch me, every so slightly, just at the left kidney.

The skin of the heel must have had some small, dry scaliness, and it was that imperfection that, when the heel made, in its pressure, the slightest rubbing, demanding movement against my flesh, brought actuality, in that instant, to focus.

. . .

That was what had happened the day before, and what now, as I leaned forward with my brow pressed against the sheets of paper at the edge of the table, was happening again behind my closed eyelids. Then it ceased to happen, and there remained only a distant, slow sadness that, from moment to moment, I had to remind myself had any meaning at all.

I remained thus, in memory, until I heard the click of the back door being bolted. I rose, quickly turned the three sheets of paper over and laid a book on them, and then, standing there, felt the first premonitory, tumescent stir at my crotch. Now was now.

That creature now waking down there, in the darkness of the crotch, led, it seemed, a life of its own that had nothing to do with whatever had set Jediah Tewksbury in a chair in a room where curtains were drawn against a bright January afternoon, with his forehead leaning downward to press against written-on sheets of paper laid on a table.

. . .

What was to happen this afternoon—the clutch, struggle, and spasm—had happened before, but now wordlessly, with no delay, enacted as though in a vacuum of time and with the barren simplicity of a natural law—like gravity.

Afterwards, the principals of the enactment lay in silence, apart, not even reaching out to touch. Even then, when the bodies had just fallen apart—not merely now in the perspective of years—it seemed —seems—as though I was merely a consciousness suspended in the dimness of the room to look down on the bodies abandoned there like swimmers who have made it through difficult surf and lie sprawled, each locked in the privacy of his exhaustion.

And now as that old image—and old feeling—comes to mind, am I asking if that nightmare image of history is what all the books—this book, too—are written to avoid seeing?

.   .   .

How long we lay that way I can't be sure, but at last I got out of bed, feeling the sweat all over me gone prickly on my skin, padded on naked feet to the table, picked up the three sheets of paper on which the writing was, and moved back toward the bed. Rozelle—for she was now Rozelle, not Rose, never Rose again to me—had rolled to her side, and in the dimness her eyes were wide and fixed on what I held in my hand.

I thrust the sheets at her. Her right arm came out from under the covers and, beautiful and white in the dimness, stretched toward the sheets of paper, while her gaze was searching my face.

I turned on the reading light at the headboard, then recovered two pillows from the foot of the bed—noticing that one, clearly the one that had been used to prop the archetypal ass—had a lavish wet stain. I turned the stained side down, and said: "You better pull up so you can read."

She thrust herself up against the headboard.

"Lean forward," I said, "I'll fix you some pillows."

She obeyed, with the covers coming across some inches below her breasts.

"They're great," I said, "but you'll catch cold, all wet the way you are."

"I like being wet with you," she said, and smiled a brief smile that, it was clear, she was trying to make me believe in. But her hand, clutching the papers, trembled a little.

"Be that as it may," I said, "you better cover up."

Again she obeyed, and I thrust myself under the covers, not in contact, lying on my side, supporting my head on a hand, the better to watch her face as she read. For a time I saw nothing on the face, but when she shifted to the third sheet of the letter, I saw that her hand shook.

Then she had finished.

Still holding the letter, she was staring beyond it, across the room. I could see only her profile, but on my side a large tear was slowly brimming over from the lower eyelid. I saw it go, very slowly, all the way down, diminishing on the chin. Then another was coming down the same now-wet track. This one actually made it all the way to the edge of the jawbone, and disappeared.

"I want to die," Rozelle said, in a thin, distant voice, not looking at me.

"What were you crying about?" I said. Then, correcting myself: "Not now—New Year's Eve, that night up in her room."

"Oh, that!" she exclaimed. "That's not the point! It's Maria. Whatever will become of her now?"

"That," I said, "is precisely what I prefer right now not to think about."

"It wasn't what I planned—what I hoped," she declared. She turned suddenly at me, saying, "Oh, I swear it wasn't!"

Then, before I could decide what it was I might or might not believe about whatever it was she had planned or hoped, she was crying out: "Everything—oh, everything I do goes wrong! All my life! I can't help it."

She turned directly to me, as though desperately anxious to know the answer. "Can I help what happens?"

Her hand reached out to lay hold on me, but somehow didn't quite make it, and fell to the cover. "Can I help who I am?" she cried out, her gaze fixed on me in appeal.

"What the hell are you talking about?" I said.

"And you?" she demanded, pushing herself up, leaning at me. "Can you help who you are? All I know is, you're all I've got. Don't you see how I'm all alone here? Maria's gone now—I could believe in her, she was good—I at least had her—but there's nobody here now I can—"

"I thought you liked Nashville so goddamned much," I said.

"I shouldn't ever have come here," she said, not to me, in a different tone, bitterness turned inward, sinking back against the headboard. "Not ever. I shouldn't have ever done a single thing I've done in my life, for I wound up here, and—" she paused "—and alone."

She was breathing slow and heavy. "Maybe I kidded myself awhile," she said, not to me. "But not now. I know the truth now, and I'm all by myself." She slid down off the pillows, and lay looking up at the shadowy ceiling. "I am all alone," she said, in that thin, distant voice. "Except—" she said, and waited.

Then: "—for you."

I said nothing.

"And you—" she added, in an even more shadowy whisper, "—you're alone, too."

We lay there, not moving. After a little, in a voice so wispy it might have been nothing but a thought, I heard her: "For you—you've always been alone, too."

The clock in the hall struck.

"Is that clock right?" she queried sharply.

I said it was.

"Four o'clock," she said. Then, quite calmly, in a brisk, factual daytime voice: "And I've got to be out of this bed and out that door in not more than twenty minutes. I've got to dress and get to town for a dinner party and—"

She stopped, reached out for my hand and thrust it against herself. "You can feel it," she said, still quite factual in her tone. But then, as she pressed the hand against herself, moving it back and forth ever so slightly, the voice changed, sinking to a rhythmic whisper: "You can feel it, you can feel how I've got to have you, now, now before I go, now, so I can just forget, forget even just that long, so all I'll have to know is just you, you inside. You—"

"All right," I said, in a voice like throaty rage.

.   .   .

———
201

Maria had left Nashville. She had left on January 1, the very afternoon when Rozelle had first come to my house at the edge of the
woods. She had told nobody goodbye except her father.

Not even Rozelle, though it was Rozelle, according to her own later
account to me, who had made her go, who gave her the decisive push.
When Rozelle woke up on New Year's morning, still in her party
dress, barefoot and tear-stained, stretched across the foot of Maria's
bed, she found Maria, now in street clothes, sitting by the window
watching the dawn come over the newly white countryside.

Maria came and kissed her and asked how she was. Intuition made
Rozelle realize, she said to me later, that something big was up. Maria
had been planning to stay over a day or two, and here she was dressed
to leave and with her bag, though open, clearly packed, with a toilet
kit on top. "But you're staying!" Rozelle cried out.

"I'll stay if you—if you truly need me," Maria said.

The upshot was that Rozelle wormed the news out that something
—what, she didn't find out—had happened, something to make Maria
feel she had to go—could go. So Rozelle insisted that she didn't need
Maria at all, that her own disorder and tearfulness, when she had
rushed to Maria's room after the party, was nothing, just a little
ordinary family spat with Lawford, and it had seemed important
simply because she was so exhausted from the party, and if she hadn't
had the curse to boot, she and Lawford would have made it up in ten
minutes in the good old-fashioned way, and then gone sound to sleep
in each other's arms. To clinch matters she talked cold turkey to
Maria, as she put it, telling her if she didn't go now, get up that minute
and go, she would never make it.

"That's what I told her," Rozelle said, "and it worked. It worked
faster than I'd guessed possible—she grabbed her car before I even
saw her at breakfast, and was gone. To hunt up her father, tell him,
and get some money, no doubt, the banks being closed on New Year's.
But she didn't even let her father go to the airport, and didn't even
tell me goodbye—just a note mailed from the airport, saying all love
and goodbye and not to try to write her."

And as Rozelle was saying that, I imagined Maria standing in the
Nashville airport, wearing a severe dark coat and dark hat, an unobtrusively expensive piece of luggage at her feet, her face masklike as

when she approached the jump. She was standing there alone.

This narrative came to me weeks after the event, when Rozelle, one late winter afternoon, half-propped against the headboard of my bed, the sheet just high enough to cover the nipples of her breasts, one strand of hair still sticking wetly to her cheek, and the faintly sweet, wheaty odor of our sexuality in the dim air, apparently out of a deep compulsion, began to talk. When she had finished, I said nothing. She was looking at me in a sad, assessing way. "You don't think I'm telling the truth," she said, finally.

"I'm not thinking anything," I said.

"I wouldn't blame you for thinking I'm not," she said. "It looks a little like I talked her into getting out of town and raced right over here, pulling my clothes off on the way."

"I'm not thinking anything," I said.

"It wasn't that way," she said. "Maria didn't even mention your name. She just said she was going to try to leave for a while, to see if she could. She must have said that to me a hundred times before, how if she could only bring herself to do it. Said it to me long before she ever laid eyes on you. But you—you don't even know what it's all about, and—"

"You forget, I've read the letter."

"I wish to God I'd never read it," she burst out.

Then, after a little: "I thought it would be nice for both of you. I thought you all would look good together. Would make out just fine. Would be good for each other. And when she talked about going away, I thought things just weren't working out, that something had happened between you to the bad. That very night. So she had to run, couldn't bear it here." Then: "You've got to believe that."

When I didn't say anything, she suddenly leaned at me, staring. "I've got to believe that, too," she said. "Oh, I've got to."

There was nothing to say to that.

"You see, I thought—" she began again, and stopped. "Oh, I don't know what I thought!" she wailed. "I didn't think anything. Just everything was the way it was, and there I was, just like I didn't even know how I got here, huddled up in my coat, on the foot of this very bed."

She dropped herself back against the pillows.

She lay there awhile, then said something so low I couldn't catch it.

"What?"

"If she hadn't gone—" she was saying in almost a whisper, as though to herself, not to me, "if she hadn't, I'd never have come here. I wouldn't be here now."

She lay there and I could hear her breathing. I was trying not to think about what she had said.

Then she was saying something else, but even lower.

"What'd you say?" I asked.

"Fuck me," she said, in almost a whisper. "For God's sake, quick. That's what I said."

. . .

When, that afternoon, I had said to Rozelle that I wasn't thinking anything, it was not a way of saying that I did not think she was telling the truth. When I said that I wasn't thinking anything, I was telling the absolute truth. I did not think anything for the simple reason that I thought—to be paradoxical—that nothing you could think would make things any different. If I had felt distress, it had never arisen from any wish that things had been different. I could not, in fact, have now even conceived of things as different. The past, the future, all values, vengeances, costs and pangs of conscience lay far beyond, and irrelevant to, the shadowy sanctuary of the timelessness where I had my refuge; and weeks before, when, in the middle of the night after the arrival of the letter from Maria and Rozelle's second visit, I had risen and barefoot walked the cold house, it was not any image of Maria that I saw glimmering in the dark.

Indeed, there had been then no image before my eyes nor thought in my head. What I had waked from was, I gradually realized, a confused dream that involved neither Rozelle nor Maria. It was of a grave on a prairie at night, with snow falling, and around it many people. I knew that they all were people I had known in childhood or later, though I could not for the life of me remember a name, and even people I had seen only fleetingly on the street or in a bus station at night in a strange town, perhaps even an Italian town in the war, and they all stood silently weeping while the snow fell on their bare heads.

But I could not weep. The people were asking me sympathetically, imploringly, why I could not weep. It was, in the dream, an anguish that I could not weep, and I was trying to tell them that I wanted to but could not. My lips were moving, but with the strange numbness of flesh after the dentist has shot in the procaine, and no sound would come, no matter how hard I tried. In the strain of trying to speak, I woke up.

Then, standing barefoot by a window in the dark house, seeing the literal night snow falling here in Tennessee, and fumbling into the dream, I suddenly felt my eyes go damp. Even as I stood there, the memory of the dream merged with that of Maria's face, at the Cudworth table, shining in candlelight and with generous joy as she embraced Sally. But in the very instant when my heart stirred, I knew, with a hard clarity, the inevitability of things, and knew that I would not have wished them different from what they now were.

I could not wish that Agnes Andresen was alive. I could not wish that Maria McInnis had not fled. I could not wish that Rozelle Hardcastle had not come to my bed. What I might have wished different—not existent—was only the shadowy hopes and sad ironies that were the context of the inevitable present. But I knew, with a bright, sharp hardening of the heart, that I would repudiate, deny, cut off root and branch that context.

On her next visit, Rozelle, lying by my side in the after-coupling silence, suddenly said: "Maria—what will she do?"

I sat up, and looked down at her. "Do you want her back?" I asked.

"It's all so terrible," she said.

"Terrible—yes," I said, "but do you, right this minute, want her back in Nashville, Tennessee?"

She covered her face with her hands. I leaned over, took her by the wrists, and drew the hands from her face. "You know what you said?"

"What?"

"That we are what we are. You remember that?"

"Yes."

"Well, remember, then, that right now, here in this room, on this bed, naked, this is what we are."

I spoke the words, if I now remember correctly, with a cold flash of logic and a kind of ironic detachment, as though what was happening had nothing to do with me—instead of everything to do with me. Rozelle rolled away from me, and lay there a long time making a muffled sound, with a pillow pressed against her face. I thought she was weeping.

But she wasn't. She took the pillow away, and she was laughing in a kind of strangled way, and through her laughter saying how the joke was on her, for being what she was.

"I don't see anything so damned funny," I said.

"Oh, I'm so ashamed!" she cried out. "But that's part of the joke, too!"

"What?"

"I've been wanting to tell you—I want you to know everything, I really do—but I was so ashamed."

"What?"

"All right," she said, and sat up in bed, not looking at me now, staring off across the room. "When," she began, very factually, "I opened the newspaper and found you had come to Nashville, I was scared. I was in a panic, for a full minute. What you might say about me. I don't mean anything awful—just Dugton and all—maybe my father—maybe Chester Burton—"

"So you took me into camp," I said.

"Yes, and here you are, right in bed with me and me loving you till my heart will break, and the joke is on me." She began to laugh again, in that strangled way.

I waited, then said: "You had taken Maria into camp at the beginning. You'd seen her possible value. Is that right?"

"Yes, God help me," she said. "I was so lonesome and lost. And then—then I began to love her—you couldn't help but love her."

She began to laugh again. "And that joke's on me, too!"

But then the strangled sound did turn into crying.

.   .   .

There is a natural history of love affairs, as of trees, men, and revolutions, and there are clearly defined stages. The motto of Stage

I of any love affair, licit or illicit, is *carpe diem*—or *carpe noctem,* as the case may be. Seize the day—or night—for the moment is all, no past and no future. In this stage, lovers may, and often do, tell each other their personal history, but this act is essentially not an affirmation of, but a denial of, the past: the past, with all its errors, follies, despairs, and fleeting triumphs, is precisely what love will, in its redemptive act, expunge. Lovers may, too, make plans for the future, but the planning serves, primarily, as a justification for the next moment of the blind clutch, much as, theologically speaking, the creation of an immortal soul for the Glory of God is taken to disinfect the filth of animal coupling. And even the vow of faithfulness, henceforth and forever, is only a way of saying that the act of the clutch —the clutch with this particular beloved—is all. The vow merely rolls the future up into one ball—and crams it into the hot, wet, dark aperture of the timelessness.

Stage II has its motto: *in contemptu mundi.* As Stage I denies Time, so Stage II, which intimately issues from, and fulfills, Stage I, denies Space. The lovers are not of this world. Each is the other's hermitage, and the world falls away, and in the drive toward orgasm—which, we are instructed by the poet, may later seem but a poor, bewildered minute—the world is well lost. As suggested by the plaster casts at Pompeii of men who died even in some obsessive private concern, no doubt more than one citizen of the doomed city, who, as he entered upon the long dark slide toward bliss, didn't even miss a beat as the ashes fell.

For Stage I, at least, Jediah Tewksbury and Rozelle Hardcastle Carrington were absolutely archetypal. For them, the motto was, quite literally, *carpe diem.* There was no *noctem* about it, and as for Stage II, it is the daytime assignation that most positively affirms the contempt of the world.

For night is the natural contrast to the day and its worldly business, and when, after what is called the act of darkness, the lovers fall asleep, they know that they will wake, with the alarm clock, to the day, and to Time. Even illicit love, if nocturnally practiced, has something of the licit about it. You have to remind yourself that this isn't just another, if rather more titillating, domestic scene.

So, for Stage II, the afternoons of Jediah and Rozelle were, in their illicitness, in as total contempt of the world and its business as they were of past and future. It is true that Rozelle, on the first afternoon at my house, pushing herself up from the huddle on the old army blanket on the foot of my bed, had exclaimed, "Oh, it was awful! It—" But, in some instinctive repudiation of all time and the world, I had not let Rozelle finish the sentence. And I had held off all subsequent knowledge of what it might be that had been so awful; so the moment that, when I found Rozelle on the foot of my bed in the darkened room, had mysteriously detached itself from Time.

Later, after a number of encounters, it did begin to dawn on me that what Rozelle had called so awful could not have been the business about Maria, which had not been introduced until the next day, when, after our grappling, I had shown the letter to Rozelle. So now I did begin to question her about the awful thing—whatever it was—that, after the party, had driven Rozelle, shoeless and weeping, to Maria's room. But now it was she who refused to admit any context of the world to penetrate into our room, in which curtains were drawn against the light of day. She would evade my question, or give some transparently false or incomplete answer, saying, for instance, that Lawford was worried about his work and took it out on her. Or, at other times, at my questioning, she would merely burst out: "Oh, what does it matter, we have each other, don't we?" Or simply seizing me, she might take refuge in the contact of our bodies. Once she even wept.

There was a point beyond which I, instinctively, never pushed her. The questioning was, I might say, a ritual, and how well, now looking back, I realize that it was merely ritual—that I uttered the questions merely to extenuate myself in some shadowy way, to give myself a polemical and moral standing, for I could now fall back on the alibi (to be offered myself if need arose) that I had really tried to find out the truth. But now I know perfectly well that the truth was the last thing I wanted to find out.

Whatever the truth might be, it would certainly be the thing most likely to fracture the thin shell of the enclosed world of the timelessness in which, in the curtained room, I could plunge into the contextless darkness of passion—the moment in which Jediah Tewksbury could abolish the self that had once stood under the chinaberry tree in Claxford County, Alabama, had sat late at night with an open book and had not known why, had yearned for something and had not known what, had buried a wife on a prairie where snow now lay, and had fled in guilt, and, seeing the smiling face of Maria in the Cudworth candlelight, had had, briefly, the dream that he might enter the dream in which these people around him, in Nashville, Tennessee, seemed to live.

For certainly those shadowy afternoons were not only a flight from any temptation of entering that present communal dream inhabited by Cudworth and all the rest; the shadowy afternoons were lived with the undertone of angry self-contempt and of sardonic relief that now I did not ever have to play with the pretense or the self-delusion of joining Nashville, or any other goddamned place, of being Southern, or any other goddamned thing, that now I'd never have to stand, while music played and people danced, and have some slick-faced bastard in a two-hundred-dollar dinner jacket, with real kitty-cat-asshole buttonholes worked for the sleeve buttons, grin at me, in congratulation and condescension, and rub thumb across fingertips and whisper "moola," that now no colleagues at any university would ever lean their heads together and whisper, in envy or contempt, that Jed Tewksbury, the stuck-up bastard, sure knew how to play his cards, that now I'd never have to wake in the night and wonder if the body beside me—which might have been that of Maria McInnis—was really what I wanted to screw, or not.

Now I was free to be only what I was in the moment in which I was.

. . .

But the world survives all contempt, even that of lovers. It is like a smell on the night wind, it is breathed like air, it seeps into a room like smoke under a door or through the keyhole, it rises like water silently creeping up the cellar stairs. And so we have Stage III, and even as the world returns, the lover recognizes more sharply than ever its lineaments. Repudiation, by its very nature, leads to definition. Furthermore, the conflict with the world, raised to a new level and intensity, leads to a conflict between lovers: i.e., Stage IV. Each lover, we may say, becomes a part of the world that the other confronts, and inevitably, as in all cases, the first conflict of wills between Rozelle and me concerned the relation to the world outside our closed orbit.

A week or so after our affair had begun, she told me that they— the Carringtons—were having a small dinner party for a poet who was to read at the University, just a few other guests, whom I especially liked, Rozelle said, and that I really must be there. I said no, I was through with parties at the house of Lawford Carrington, that I was certainly not what is called a Southern Gentleman, or any other kind, and that I laid no claim to a delicate sense of honor, but I'd be uncomfortable in my own redneck way drinking his likker and eating his grub while making time with his wife. To which she replied that more than one Southern Gentleman she knew, with names on request, quite regularly put knees under the same table with a host whose wife he had that very afternoon screwed breathless, and that as far as being an S.G. or not, I wouldn't ever be making any more time with Lawford Carrington's wife if I didn't show up.

At this point there must have been a rush of angry blood to my head, for she looked at me and said no, oh no, she hadn't meant what it sounded like, that she couldn't live without me, but that if I suddenly dropped out of the Carrington circle, gossip would break out like a flu epidemic, and then, oh then, what could we do! Especially, she said, because Maria's unprecedented decamping had already put me in the limelight of speculative gossip. "Listen," Rozelle wound up, "I know Nashville and I know how things like this work, and you've got to trust me."

So I sat with my knees under my cuckold's table, swallowed the discomfort that, among the more gently nurtured, might have passed for a sense of honor, and washed same down with sluices of alcohol ranging from black label sour mash, through a generous Médoc, on to a noble brandy, and in general managed to have a pretty good time talking to the ladies, wondering why the swami was there (until I was told that he was himself a poet, who, though writing only in Hindi, could refer learnedly to certain works of the guest of honor), and watching the guest of honor drink himself into a condition approximating the blind staggers of a mule whose manners have just been rectified by a hickory fence rail laid across his skull.

At the most superficial layer of my consciousness, I had almost forgotten that life had greatly changed since I was last in this house, but when, in the hurly-burly of getting the drunk poet afoot and of organizing the general departure, Rozelle and I were, for an instant, together in the cloakroom off the hall, she seized my organ, gave it a friendly little twitch, and, looking at what must have been my white and horrified face, deliciously giggled. It wasn't the last time she was to scare me to death.

The other guests already on their way, the head of the English Department and his wife were settled into the back seat of Lawford's car, one to each side of the poet to prop him upright in transit, Lawford took the wheel, Rozelle slipped over beside him, and I got in, and we were off. As the car sped along, we on the front seat were quiet, listening to the desperate attempts of the, literally, supporting cast on the back seat to make conversation with the principal performer. He, however, seemed to be in deep communion with his internal goings-on, and made no response except a few memorable hiccups. After a decent interval, they simply gave up the conversation, and for some miles silence reigned.

But as soon as we had come into the lighted streets of the city, the poet burst into a vatic volubility, strongly reminiscent of Hebrew prophets, William Blake, Walt Whitman, and Victor Hugo in his attacks of more promiscuous blather. It was to be, in fact, this protracted seizure that saw him through his hour's strut and fret upon the stage, where, drenched with sweat, tie carefully unknotted, and hair over the eyes, he read his compositions with an impassioned eloquence which they scarcely deserved but which evoked great applause.

That, however, is getting ahead of the game. As we bowled along, I, cocooned in the silence of the front seat and the faint anesthesia of alcohol, sank into myself, aware only, when on a left curve, how centrifugal force favored me by the pressure of Rozelle's body against me in lax surrender. Once or twice, in such an episode, I stole a glance at the fine profile of Lawford Carrington, faintly illuminated in the light from the dashboard. He might have been a chauffeur hired for the occasion.

Then I even forgot his presence. The anonymous driver was a

non-person. Except as an appurtenance of the machine, he did not exist, and I slowly began to realize that in all the months since my arrival he had been simply that: an appurtenance of the expensive machine of the Carrington household. The graceful manners, the engaging modesty, the white-toothed smile, the careful attention to the opinions, tastes, comforts, and vanities of guests, the elegant bohemianism of huaraches, espadrilles, and Turkish slippers, of red silk shirts open low to exhibit the not-too-proletarian hair on his chest, of denim and suede jackets, of white duck pants and turquoise-encrusted belts, of commanding grace in the saddle and powerful strokes in the Olympic-size pool, of well-modulated anecdotes, of the schooled finish of his sculpture—all, I suddenly decided that night, as we whipped past the lights of approaching cars, were nothing but a façade, a mirage, a *trompe d'oeil.* There was no Lawford Carrington. And if he did not exist, how could a man in my position feel any guilty discomfort?

So, as far as guilty discomfort was concerned, it was to become easier and easier to go to the parties at the Carrington house; and oddly enough, I began to like Lawford more. He could not help being what he was—or not being what he was not. I discovered, even, that I could like the world around him better than before. I could enjoy it differently and more fully. Every conversation, every piece of gossip, every anecdote or reminiscence, every observation on art, politics, or human nature seemed now to be diminished in a distance of irony and pathos.

In this world I discovered a new responsiveness to the people about me, a new ease and a new warmth, and I might catch a new timbre in my own voice, deeper and more open, a new pleasure in the existence of the creatures around me. For, as a corollary of that diminishment of the world, I recognized, for the first time, the essential gallantry of the creatures in that world as they strove and suffered in total ignorance of the precariousness of the illusions by which they existed at all. And sometimes my heart was touched by a strange generosity or a fleeting tenderness, like a moth wing that brushes the cheek in the dusk.

Sometimes, however, everything might, of a sudden, go blank—at a party, for instance—and there would be nothing there except the figure of Rozelle lying back in a chair in one of her postures of lassitude or seeming weakness that might fall across the characteristic flow of vitality, the sense of some yearning to be released.

From what? I would ask myself.

And like a slow bell, deep inside me, the answer would toll: *From oneself.*

For that was the only answer, it seemed, to my own great surprise, that I had to give to such a question, and with that answer, I always felt the need to lay her head on my shoulder and assure her of something.

But of what?

I did not know. All I knew was that it would be of something different from whatever assurance she found in my shadowy room of the curtains drawn against day.

At such times when I saw her at a party and felt that impulse, I would inevitably remember the afternoon in the hall of the Dugton High School when she had asked me to that date with her, how in the end it had been not beauty or charm or perfume, but the way a hand tentatively reaching out to me had lost courage and faltered in the air, the way it turned and hung empty in the air and I saw the pale blue veins there of the inner wrist.

And once, seeing such a moment of sad lassitude take her in the middle of a gay party, I felt a great swelling of the heart; and I found myself saying, almost out loud, *I love her, I love her.*

This to my great surprise, as I seemed to hover on the threshold of a new dimension of being.

Or I might see her leaning in a devoted attitude toward some elderly lady who was holding forth at interminable length, or dancing with some decrepit hulk whose face now glowed with spurious youth, or nodding in deep understanding to some serious confidence being unveiled by a callow college boy with a hint of acne yet blooming on his cheek. What was she doing with such fools, I would bitterly demand, and even in demanding an answer, I would sense—or tell myself I sensed—this sympathy, this kindness, as a reflex of her own mysterious yearning.

213

But there is no use pretending that anything, least of all the human soul, is simple, and once, sitting in a group by the fireside in the studio end of the barn, I watched her kick off her sandals and prop her feet on the marble hearthstone, and aware of other eyes on those feet pink in the firelight, I was in a rage, thinking of the secret and delicately acrobatic uses to which they had been put that very afternoon—as though they were other hands that might reach, seek, find, feel, tickle, and caress. It might be thirty-six hours, or more, before I could see her again. I might make my painful calculations, and then rise and leave the room where the people were trapped in their fatuities, and go and stand outdoors, under the dark sky.

Nobody had ever told me that anything could be like this.

CHAPTER IX

Needless to say, in those weeks my professional duties were becoming more and more a shadowy routine for me. I went to my classes, answered questions, greeted smiling faces on the campus, but nothing seemed significant. I might, indeed, bless these people in the pathos of their gallant unreality, but that was all. I found myself admitting, however, that the weekly afternoons at Mrs. Jones-Talbot's house, to guide her and Mrs. Beacham in the Dante reading, was somewhat different. Those middle-aged ladies worked so hard at the self-imposed task, they found such a gratuitous pleasure in the mounting rhythms of a phrase or the stab of an image, that I found myself trying to respond and accept the world as they saw it. I might, on such occasions, even feel a sense of loss or a pang of envy, at first aimless and irrational; and then I would realize that the emotion sprang from the fact that these two women still possessed, innocently and effort-lessly, a joy that I had lost.

Then I would withdraw within my own world. What was all that fiction, that fancy folderol, in contrast to the truth I knew?

Even in the period at Chicago, when I was nursing my unavowed sexual grievance against my wife, I had clung to the reality of my routine—the class bell, the muted shuffle of feet, the neat stack of papers on my desk. I had fingered every such item as a sick seminarian might desperately finger his rosary in the dark night of the soul. Later, as my wife lay dying hideously, I had counted my beads and, more-over, had sat at my desk at one midnight and watched, with a peculiar excitement, my hand write, on a blank sheet of paper, the title "Dante and the Metaphysics of Death."

Now, however, the notes in which I had been groping toward a new book were stuck away in a drawer of the table in my bedroom, and once or twice, as I lay in the afternoon bed, in post-coital silence, Rozelle at my side, I looked across at that table, with a twinge of ironic contempt for the self that had found pleasure and hope in scribbling those pages now locked in that darkness of the drawer. And more than once, in my weekly seminar on Love, Sacred and Profane, in the Middle Ages, as I heard my voice discussing the code of courtly love, I thought, with a scarcely suppressed irony, how all that postur-ing, that *courtoisie* and *foedelité,* that famous lyricism and bloated elegance, those lies and gabblings, those complex rhymes, were noth-ing but bright scum and lacy froth on the dark stream.

More specifically, this reminds me of the dismally dripping after-noon in early March when, after I had been discussing certain key passages in that historically important but inconsequential confection the *chante fable* of *Aucassin et Nicolette,* I read aloud, to make some point (what I now forget), the passage where the noble youth seeks his beloved Nicolette in the dark forest wherein, after her escape by the knotted sheets from the window of the prison tower, she wanders. I came to the *chant,* one of the interspersed verse sections, in which appears the line:

De s'amie o le gent cors.

I began to explain that the word *gent,* meaning charming or graceful, does not now exist in French, and the word *gentil* is different in Latin derivation and meaning; and continued by saying that we may think of the phrase *o le gent cors* as translated by *au corps charmant.*

What I am getting at is this: right in the midst of my dreary but necessary little pedantries, even as I uttered the phrase *au corps charmant,* I suddenly saw, not in the dark medieval forest, but in the curtained room in my house by the woods, the *corps charmant* of my *amie* bare and glimmering, and lifted, for the first time, forked in my hands.

Sitting there at a seminar table, on a gray afternoon of sodden skies, I saw it with such vividness that the dreary world disappeared, and in that instant I felt on my upper right leg, halfway up from the knee, the wetness, the hot-cold, oxymoronic stab to the very bone—this as vividly as in its first reality. My eyes blurred, a dizziness took me. I felt the stir and bulge at the crotch and, grateful for the protection of the table, shifted in my chair and sneaked a hand down to loosen my clothing.

My voice, I was aware, had stopped in mid-sentence. The eyes of the eight graduate students were fixed on me. I clenched my teeth for a moment and took a deep breath to gain control of myself, then feigned a great fit of coughing. When I resumed, I could not even remember what the point of my discussion had been, but stumbled on.

That event, I should add, marked the first appearance of what I have come to call, quite ungrammatically, and with no ecclesiastical justification, my stigmata—that plural form being the most usual and sanctified at least by familiarity. After the seminar I cut questions short and hurried away. At home, between the garage and the house, I stopped and stood in the drizzling darkness, breathing slow and heavy. I was discovering something, but I did not know what. I shut my eyes, and now I remember thinking, as I did so, that if my eyes were shut nothing would be real. Then thinking, with a sudden terror, that even if I were dead my body would keep on remembering, in its own way, everything that had ever happened to me. Maybe I—whatever the *I* was—was nothing but a dream the body was having.

In the house, I went to the bathroom, unbuckled my belt, dropped my trousers, and stared at the spot on my right leg. Nothing, of course, was there. "Christ!" I said out loud. What a fool I was. I had gone straight there as blankly as though under hypnosis. So I had my sacred spot that I felt but never saw.

When Descartes stared with open eyes upon the world, he could not know, really know, that it existed, and when he shut his eyes he could not be sure that he existed. Until he struck upon the brilliant formulation which is the basis of our modernity: *cogito ergo sum.* Well, I was to go one step beyond him to a more radical formulation upon which a new era may be founded. Even though I laid no claim to thinking, I still had an argument for my existence: *debatuo ergo sum.* I fuck, therefore I am.

This was, in a way, an argument, too, for the existence of at least one item in the external world: Rozelle. It was as though my own *was-ness,* in the pressures and slidings of flesh, had rubbed off on her. But this did not tell me much beyond the mere fact—the mere facts, external facts—of that existence called Rozelle. Of the internal fact, what did I know?

There were, however, various kinds of external facts. There was the Rozelle of poetic murmurs, slow brooding caresses of feathery fingertips, sweetly sacrificial flesh offered almost somnambulistically with a whispery sigh, like pain in a dream, and half-shut eyes that, at one point, always went tight shut and then, at the climax, blazed unseeingly open as the first throaty little cry was uttered.

There was the Rozelle who might act like a single-minded backcountry slut, slack-jawed and slack-cunted, full of cheerful indecencies, juicy giggles, and gut-grunts, who, as devoid of finesse as of poetry, would hoist knees and plant feet flat on the mattress with what hung between as free-swinging as the canvas seat of a sling chair if you thought of the two front suspension points as the lady's knees. And here I remember how Rozelle's face, in this phase of her being, really did look different, the face really gone slightly slack and the lips with a suggestion of bruised puffiness, and a glistening trace of saliva in one corner of the mouth after she had wiped her tongue across the lips. And in this phase, if you put your arm around her, the flesh—I swear it—really did feel slacker on the bone. She could draw you, unresisting, into the deep, rich slime of being.

But to take another phase, or avatar, there was the Rozelle who had an almost clinical detachment in her researches into the capacities of the body of her collaborator for sensation. For example, when I was lying on my back, she might push my near arm up and snuggle confidingly at my side, like a chick under a mother-bird's wing, and begin, slowly, to nuzzle me in the armpit, blowing gently into the damp hair there, stopping now and then and lifting her face to demand: "How does it make you feel? Tell me exactly."

Sometimes, however, my testimony was of no concern whatsoever, for her investigations could become purely objective. Almost inch by inch she would scrutinize, examine, study the hulk that was Jediah Tewksbury, totally absorbed, it seemed, in that occupation. "What are you doing?" I might ask, and she'd say, "Nothing that concerns you," or, "Hush, can't you see I'm busy?"

But once when I asked that foolish question, she turned the amethystine gaze fully upon me and said: "All right, I'll tell you. I'm trying to memorize you, every little bitsy-bit, so when I'm dead and can't see you I'll have something to think about."

And with that she fell to kissing me on the face, no particular place, just where a kiss happened to land, randomly, like a child.

Five minutes later, when I had sunk back, she was lying prone, at right angles to me, breasts pressing against me, head hanging a little over the bulge of my chest where the heart would be, face twisted toward me but almost concealed by hair flung forward, the left hand lightly over my mouth and chin, the little and third fingers thrust into my mouth and gently moving against the inside of the lower teeth or exploring, ever so delicately, the softness of tissue under the tongue, the right hand, beyond my vision but, as I was well aware, cradling my genitals. We lay that way a long time.

Except for the minimal stir of breath or the infinitesimal explorations being conducted by the fingers of the left hand, she was absolutely motionless. The bathroom door had been left slightly ajar, with the light on there, and I could see the coppery glinting of the tumbled hair that half hid her face.

After a while, from under the tumble of hair, I heard the whisper: "Bite my fingers."

I did.

"Harder," the whisper commanded.

I obeyed.

"Harder."

I bit as hard as I dared.

219

The whisper came again, but I couldn't make it out. I pulled the hand away from my mouth, and held it. "What did you say?" I asked.

"Just that I want to die," the whisper said. "Like this. Now. Then there wouldn't ever be anything else."

I jerked myself up, dumping her down so that she lay across my lap, her face bare, the eyes looking up at me. "Don't talk like a damned fool," I said, feeling, to my own surprise, a blank anger at her, an anger at myself, too.

Looking up at me from a great distance, she finally said, again in that whisper, but in a perfectly matter-of-fact, detached way: "Or maybe I just want to die."

"God damn it—" I began.

But I didn't know what I had started to say.

She pulled herself off my lap, and with what seemed a sudden, sharp, angular awkwardness, rose there by the bed, and what I vividly remember now is the inexplicably cranky awkwardness, as though she had, in an instant, in contrast to her usual fluidity and grace of movement, gone old and arthritic.

"I've got to go," she said, in a harsh, impersonal voice, standing there by the side of the bed.

"Come back here," I ordered with a tone that must have clearly revealed a false heartiness, and patted the bed beside me.

She looked at me for a slow instant, in an assessing sad way, then shook her head and moved toward the bathroom.

I lay back down and pulled the sheet up to my chin. I was lying like that when she came out, her heels quick and competent on the floor, seized her coat, and on the way to the hall door, head scarcely turning, flung me a perfunctory goodbye kiss, and was gone.

Outside it was now dark. But I did not get up. I saw her now in my mind's eye, how awkward and creaky in her nakedness she had looked as she jerked herself off the bed and said, "I've got to go."

Go where? I demanded in my head.

I thought of how she had said she wanted to die, and I lay there in the tumbled bed, trying to untangle that fact along with all the rest.

Suddenly, I understood one reason why she came to the shadowy room! I understood that the orgasm was like the "black hole" of the physicists—a devouring negativity into which all the nags and positives of life may simply disappear like dirty water when the plug is pulled at the bottom of the sink. It was the death in life-beyond-Time without which life-in-Time might not be endurable, or even possible.

And so she had said: "I've got to go."

But where?

There is only one place to go. Back into the world of nags and half-measures, to the world where she lived, hour after hour, day and night, far from this shadowy room and Old Broke-Nose.

Well, today she had chosen, without warning, to run away from Jediah Tewksbury. Had, simply, fled.

But suppose—and the thought struck me like a chill—I had not patted that sheet, with whatever degree of falsity she had detected, as an invitation to plunge again into blackness, but had simply reached out a hand to her. Suppose she had then come quietly to lie by my side and take what human comfort might be found in that quietness.

It is hard to analyze certain experiences, and I see now that I have been incomplete. Before the chill struck, another feeling had overcome me, the simple need for the human quietness that we might have found had she come to my side and wordlessly lain there. But then the chill did strike—or at least this is now my interpretation—for the thought of that quietness would have implied a future, and that would mean the fracturing of the steely encapsulating present into which I had managed to lock myself with a dream named Rozelle Hardcastle Carrington.

So now jealousy was born. I heard the click of the latch of my back door as Rozelle departed, and all was changed. In the past, hearing that sound, I had felt that Rozelle was passing into some limbo to move, while beyond my sight, spooklike among spooks, to reassume the form of the dream only when, naked and damp-lipped, she had again laid herself down on my afternoon bed. But can a dream speak of wanting to die? Furthermore, dreams, in their absoluteness, have no past and no future, no context. Who can be jealous of a dream?

But now she was no dream. She was real and was going into a real world; and after the click of the latch as she left me, my imagination slavishly pursued her. Into her car (parked discreetly behind the cedars) or into the darkening woodland walk (the preferred method of return when she had time, for it might give, at need, the perfect alibi

---

—"Oh, I'm so sorry I'm late, I was just taking a walk, it was so lovely and sad in the drizzle"). Into her house. Into her bed. To the moment when—as I knew in the x-ray clarity of my new vision that thrust through time, distance, blanket, and sheet—a hand, in that world of reality, would be laid on her thigh.

.   .   .

I thought of all the hours before I could see her again. Then, when all those hours had passed and she had again come, after a prompt, mechanical and peculiarly short coupling, after we had fallen apart to lie in the period of silence, I said, in a detached, indifferent tone, looking at the dim ceiling: "How are you and Lawford making out on sex these days?"

"What do you mean?"

"I mean, how much is he fucking you?"

She hesitated a moment. "You might have been a little more— tactful, or something. In the way you put the question."

"There have been occasions," I rejoined, "when I have not been struck by excessive refinement in your vocabulary."

She rose on an elbow and looked at me. "Listen, my darling, my dearest," she said sweetly, "when you are fucking me, I think that's the nicest word in the world. But it didn't sound nice just a second ago."

"All right, how often do Lawford and you make love?"

"Love—" she said, and stopped. "There was a time I was in love with him. At least, I couldn't do without him," she said. "Then something happened."

"What?"

"You," she said. "Suddenly, you were there."

"That's exactly why the question is in order," I said. "How often do you and Mr. Lawford Carrington indulge in sexual congress?"

"What's come over you," she demanded, studying me. Then, when I didn't answer: "Listen, funny dear Old Broke-Nose, I live in the same house with him, I sleep in the same bed with him, and even if things aren't what they used to be, I can't help all that, can I, and he's healthy, and I'm pretty sure he's not whacking it out with some of those little coeds that are always swooning after him, or some tarty little Nashville deb who just loves art and who's got hot pants for him, and so sometimes things do happen."

"And you like it," I heard my voice stating dispassionately, objectively.

"No," she said. "I definitely do not promote it. But if he is already after it under his own steam, I've got to keep the peace, and it only takes ten or fifteen minutes and it's over—oh, I can hurry things up —and it doesn't mean a thing."

I lay there, hearing the blood beat in my head.

"I know what you're thinking," she finally said. Then: "Jesus, don't be such a baby. If he gets at it, I'm bound to react in some way. But I tell you, it's purely mechanical."

I didn't say anything.

"All right," she said, after a little, "why don't you go ahead and ask me? If I come with him."

"All right," I said, "do you?"

"I do pretty well in that department, as you ought to know," she said, "and the answer is, I come with him sometimes, and then it's over and I don't give a damn. It's about like sneezing. And since we're on the subject, I'd have you clearly understand that it's not like that with you."

I knew that she was looking directly at me, but I kept my gaze on the ceiling.

"And if you're such a baby as to want comparisons," she resumed, "I'll just ask you what was the first thing I ever said to you. That is, the first thing the first time we ever started to make love—and you, you beast, notice that I said making love, not something else—which was like the first time for anything for me, for I swear my real life didn't begin till that minute. Do you remember what I said?"

I remembered it, all right. That first time, on the afternoon of January I, after I had entered her body, and entered upon the life I now lived, she, after the first, long exploratory silence of the first realization, had said, *Jed.* Then *Jed.* Then, after another long silence, in a voice blended of a throaty breathiness, she had been saying, *It's you—you I love.* Then, in the timing of her breath, in the rhythm now being discovered: *You—you—you—*

Now she repeated: "Do you remember what I said?"

223

So now I said: "Yes."

"Well," she said, "don't ever forget it."

I lay there and did not know what I was feeling, anger or shame or what, with the blood beating in my head.

"Not ever, you funny Old Broke-Nose darling," she was whispering.

I found myself standing up by the bed, naked, in the middle of the floor.

I was saying: "Well, if you love me so much, there's one thing you can do."

Again she was leaning on an elbow, studying at me. "What do you mean?" she finally asked.

"Just one simple thing," I declared, in sudden, dizzy elation at the dazzle of truth inside me. "Just get your clothes on, go home, pack a suitcase, and when Lawford Carrington comes in the front door, tell him he is through. *Finito*. He has had it!"

"Jesus," she said, pushing herself up, twisting over, propping herself up with both arms straight, breasts hanging down with their rounded weight, face thrust upward toward me, white and round-eyed. "Jesus," she repeated, "you don't know what you are saying."

"Get a plane to Nevada, get a divorce. And as for me," I said, "I'll be moved out of this house by noon tomorrow. To a hotel."

She had drawn back a little, elbows of the supporting arms now bent somewhat, head at a wary angle as though I might step forward and strike, eyes wide and appalled. "You're crazy," she was saying. "Perfectly crazy!"

CHAPTER X

It was now past the middle of March, and spring very late, for, in spite of some sudden streak of green in a pasture or the lonely golding of a willow at the creekside, the season seemed stuck at dead center. And though I never specified as much to myself, that was the sense of what my life had become. Jealousy had, indeed, brought the concept of time into my curtained room—and of space to boot, other-where as of other-when. But soon after the moment when Rozelle had shrunk from me as from a blow, saying that I was crazy, perfectly crazy, time, if only for a little, again seemed to lose its reality.

I can't imagine what the upshot would have been if Rozelle and I had been allowed to play out that scene in which I commanded that she get a divorce. In any case, the clock in the hall struck, and with that hollow, tinny sound it seemed as though invisible threads had jerked a puppet-Rozelle off the bed. And, with that expression of round-eyed, glittering appallment still on her face and the word *crazy* still hanging in the air, almost like the verbal balloon in a comic strip anchored by a thread to the lips of a speaker, the naked puppet was jerked inexpertly here and there, to grab discarded clothing and jounce into the bathroom. Even the words accompanying the jouncy movements—"Jesus, it's five o'clock—I'm due in town—" seemed not to be uttered by the puppet-Rozelle but to come from a ventriloquist somewhere in the upper shadows.

I had been standing naked in the middle of the floor—and uttering words fraught with the authority of passion, and the woman on the bed, stark naked, too, had been in the act of exposing a mysterious inner nakedness of self that I had never suspected. But with that first tinny *bong,* a force beyond passion and appallment—the voice not merely of the world but of Time itself, by which the world lives—had interrupted our postures and rhetoric, and the puppet-Rozelle had been snatched off; and, even as I watched, I was struck by the cold thought, like a gust of air on sweaty flesh, that the puppet-Me might be suddenly snatched off, too, on some errand I could know nothing of—each of us like a grasshopper that, impaled on a boy's fishhook, is swung out, twitching, kicking, spitting, and gesticulating, over the dark water.

That aborted encounter occurred on a Thursday. The schedule that circumstances dictated for Rozelle and me was, with academic precision, Monday, Wednesday, and Thursday afternoons, those being the afternoons Lawford dedicated, from two to five-thirty, to his advanced studio class, with Tuesday out for me because of my seminar and Friday committed to Mrs. Jones-Talbot. So now, from the tinny *bong* of the clock at five on Thursday until two on Monday afternoon stretched ninety-three hours, a most desolate heath to be traversed. Or rather, that period constituted a cosmic void, a stage with no spectators, on which I had to endure the perpetual reenactment of the unfulfilled scene, with all its angers, morbid curiosities, and despairs. And this perpetual reenactment was like nothing so much as an expansion of the state consequent on the blocking of an orgasm. Though the nature of the orgasm to which the scene between Rozelle and me drove, I could not know.

Thursday night I tried to read, but could not, went to bed but could not sleep, got up, dressed, walked the house, then went outside and walked the now moon-flecked woods' path toward the Carrington house, and stood to stare at it. Now the slate roof was the blue of night sky, or night water, the walls bone-white in moonlight, the whole structure solid and somnolent, stuffed with a century and a half of unrecorded history, with the lives of people I had never heard the names of.

Standing in the blackness of the woods' edge, I looked across the calm, moonlit space toward the house. It was, I remember thinking, a little like the Burton house, way off in Claxford County, Alabama, which, as a boy, sitting by my father, while the wagon, at the slow pace of the span of mules, ground the pike-gravel, I had once seen. I had sat examining it, wondering what it would be like inside, wondering what it would feel like to go inside, wondering what kind of people God permitted to go inside such a house. And then my father, seeing my eyes fixed on the house up its rise, had said: "Ole Man Burton—his house."

Then he had spat, the long golden stream of ambeer—tobacco juice, that is—lancing precisely out to spatter on the off-rump of the near mule, shining on the coarse hair. My father had then jerked his old black felt more firmly down on his forehead and from that ambush had glared out—wordless mile after mile, up the white dazzle of the pike.

Now, bemused by that sleep-locked house in Tennessee, I thought how natural it would be if Rozelle Hardcastle—never to be Carrington—were, at that very moment, lying in an upper room in Alabama, beside a man named Burton. Even in that image there was no pang of loss or jealousy, it all seemed so natural, so much a part of the law of things. If, in that fantasy, I felt anything at all, it was simply the stoic resignation a man must feel—*does* feel, I should say now—at the approach of age, in remembering, with the law of things, with the inevitableness of things, the old phrase *lacrimae rerum*.

As I stared across the moonlit space, there may even have been a tinge of regret that Rozelle Hardcastle was not now lying in that other house, far away. In that case, I would not have to be here now, in the dark of the woods' edge, staring.

But here I was, and in a flash all was different. Rozelle Hardcastle was, in truth, in that house yonder, by the side of J. Lawford Carrington in a room I could not even visualize, but, in pain and anger, now strained to visualize in order to realize more fully the pain and anger, straining most of all to see her as she lay asleep.

All at once, I realized that I had never seen her asleep.

How does a dream sleep? But she was no longer a dream, she was real. Jealousy had made her real.

I did not know what position she would lie in. Would she be sprawled face down, elbows out and crooked upward, hands above the head, the head in that broken arc made by the arms, one cheek thrust deep into the pillow, loose locks of hair forward over the face? Or would she lie on her back, one bare arm flung out to show the molding of the inner elbow—where, perhaps, in the moonlight, the blue artery would be visible—the throat, in the tension of the backward drooping head, defenselessly exposed? Or would she lie on one side, with knees drawn tight up like a child, the right hand in a gently curled half-fist, just touching the chin, the lips slightly parted, as though she had in sleep, in a reflex of long-forgotten infancy, lifted the thumb toward her mouth?

No, I had never seen her asleep. And the thought rang in my head like a most desolate *cri de coeur.* It was as though I had had nothing of her. What had I had of her? Only what I had had, and that seemed, in that instant, nothing at all. It was as though there could be no possession, not even blind and timeless pleasure, unless confirmed by the sight of a sleeping face.

So, I found myself trying to imagine what her face, asleep, would be like when she was old.

I could imagine nothing of such a face, and knew that, years later, looking back, I would know that I had had nothing.

.   .   .

There had been nothing to do but go back to my own house, where, toward day, I fell asleep. When I awoke, I knew instinctively that I had missed my morning class. I felt the dead weight of the occupation-less day. Then I remembered, with relief, that it was Friday. I had to go to the Dante reading.

By two-thirty, I was steering my wreck of a car off the highway and over the cattle-guard between the massive old stone gateposts, preten-tious in this new age, that marked the entrance to the old Carrington property, and moving up the drive across the rolling meadow set with great oaks left over from the old forest time, the oaks now late in coming to leaf. Off to the right, in the distance, a few horses were grazing. A quarter of a mile in, rounding the shoulder of a slope, I could see the house that for four years now had enriched the idle gossip of Nashville, and for six months had been a little floating island on which, out of the heaving blankness of my existence, I could encounter, with whatever condescension or incredulity, my old self and the old concerns I had once, long back, thought important.

There, at the end of the winding drive, on the most commanding swell of the land, was the old structure. The old Carrington house—something approaching a manor it must have been—had once stood there, a red brick structure with the Neoclassical portico of movies and novels and, no doubt, the crinolines and goatees and, too, the dyspeptic disposition that made for a high sense of honor. Through wars and panics and the rise of rednecks, by means of revenue from the whorehouse for Yankee brass and general business acumen of a most un-Confederate sort, political influence and lucky marriages, the Carringtons had managed to hold on to the place, and in the Coolidge Boom it had been still breathing its last enchantments. Indeed, according to Rozelle, it had been breathing them even more effectively than ever, with new paint and new paddocks; for Nicholas Carrington (the older brother of Mrs. Jones-Talbot and the father of Lawford) had been then riding high, sportsman, socialite, and financier, and well knew the value of the Old South as a façade for the New Order, especially when he was dealing with money from Chicago.

Well, in 1930, the Carrington house had been burned to the ground, and common gossip had it that Nicholas badly needed the insurance money—this even before the first indictment against him and the morning, a little later, when his heart went on a permanent sit-down strike.

But by 1946, Mrs. Jones-Talbot, who found herself "hog-rich," as Rozelle put it, and had unexpectedly appeared in Nashville, after all the years, bought back the old Carrington farm and imported a fancy architect to build her a new house, which she referred to as her "allegorical whimsy," on the ruin of the old.

There the new house stood, or rather perched, a flat, asymmetrical box, astonishingly modern, all glass, and the kind of steel that rusts to a rich reddish brown and holds that finish—set athwart one end of the burned-out ruin, hanging in the lee of the end wall and a great stubbed-off chimney, but cantilevered sharply out from the old ruin on both sides. At right angles to the glass and steel box, on the filled-in foundations of the ruin, was a rigorously formal garden, all raked white gravel and low-clipped box hedge, on which the main entrance of the new house gave and to which the guest ascended by the old granite slabs that had once constituted the steps to the august portico. On the far side and at the right end, the little formal garden was backed by shrubs and perennials of a scrupulously untended look, interrupted here and there by evergreens that looked like the Italian cypress, all set against the old brick walls that had been irregularly and discreetly broken down and were now laced with ivy.

I paused in the garden and looked westward beyond the shrubs and the wall of the ruin. In that vista the land fell away a little to the stables, training field, the little stream and the pastures, and beyond lifted again toward the wooded hills in the distance. It was all very quiet, very orderly, from the rigor of the house and the sharp geometries of the little garden to the far hills, where order faded calmly into the elegiac color of distance.

Then, in a flash, all I felt was disgust, and anger. It was, I recognized, the same reaction I was now sure to have, sooner or later, at any party at the Carrington house, and even, at one moment or another, when I went out to the Cudworth place. What falsity, what self-deception, what lies, I would inwardly exclaim, thinking, in a flash, of some mean side street of Nashville by which I had passed in the winter twilight, with the lights just coming on in the houses, or of the section around the black college where, on a couple of occasions, I had visited seminars.

But was that real, either—real for me? I now, in recollection, demanded that of myself, and as I asked the question, I felt caught in a great wave of despair, of lostness.

"Hey," the voice called cheerfully, "school bell!"

And I turned to see Mrs. Jones-Talbot in her doorway, book in hand, smiling.

Mrs. Beacham was already there (she often came out to take lunch with her old friend before our session), so we fell to work. Toward four o'clock, Mrs. Beacham announced that she had to run, so she gave Mrs. Jones-Talbot a peck on the cheek, tossed me a smile and wave of the hand, and was gone.

The little fire that had been set to knock off the unseasonable chill had died, and the fireplace was a black geometrical hole in the expanse of white wall, on which now the dominating Seurat to one side, and the two smaller Ben Nicolsons on the other, seemed flat and trivial. The floor of big ceramic tiles, of a pale gray with a subdued design in blue, with a dull gleam now from the window at the east end, seemed to stretch away for a great and unnatural distance, as though viewed through reversed binoculars.

For a time neither my pupil nor I said anything. Her hands palm-down, tanned, well-tended, nails tinted a dull rose but rather square-cut, with one broken to the quick, were laid calmly on the exposed pages of her book. The hands were, perhaps, a trifle large for a woman of her build, and though the general impression was feminine enough, I noticed, now for the first time, how under the tan skin of the rounded wrists the muscles defined by the long manège of a mount drew together at the wrist joints and flowed subtly into the hand.

Breaking our silence, Mrs. Jones-Talbot shivered a little, rather theatrically, and said, "It's cold in here, it's blackberry winter with a vengeance, and this box of a room always looks cold without a fire." She got up, laid a few sticks on the ashes, and stuck a lighter under them. "Dark, too," she said. "What kind of a spring is this?" She turned on a lamp behind our table.

"Shall we go ahead a way?" she asked briskly.

I nodded, and she began to read.

We had come into the passage in Canto VI of the *Purgatorio* where Dante and his guide Virgil see the noble figure of the poet Sordello on the track ahead, and the leonine figure interrupts the first word of Virgil, crying out to the fellow-son of Mantua, whom he recognizes, that he is Sordello of the same *terra*.

"Read it again," I suggested, "for the fuller rhythm."
She obeyed, winding up with the cry of Sordello:

> *"O, Mantova, io son Sordello*
> *Della tua terra!"*

She looked up. Meditatively, she repeated the word *terra*. "There'd be no way to translate it," she said.

I said I reckoned not.

"Not land," she said. "Not earth, soil, place, home, fatherland. Not *patria.*"

"Jesus, no," I said. "Not *patria.*" Then: "Unless, you just mean everything together, all the things you've said. The things that made you what you are and that must be lived by you because you are you."

"But there's no such word."

"Not in English, anyway," I said.

She, as I should have realized, had fallen into her own thoughts. But I had fallen into mine, too, and in a moment I heard, with a mild surprise, my own voice saying, "When I was with the Partisans—" I stopped.

"What?" she demanded.

"Oh, nothing," I said.

"What?" she demanded.

"Just, I used to talk a lot to the men," I said. "To the officers, too, for that matter. To feel things out. There were quite a few peasants in the gang—and one day I was sitting with one little dried-up, over-age fellow—name of Guglielmino—on a rock, sort of probing things out. Suddenly, he stopped me. '*La politica,*' he said to some remark of mine, spitting; and spat that really thin, sharp, needle-like way of an Italian peasant that makes even a one-gallus Confederate sharecropper sitting on the steps of the crossroads store look like a blundering amateur."

"I know," she said, and laughed.

" 'Politics,' Guglielmino said, with infinite distaste. Then: '*La mia politica—*' and here he leaned over and raked up a handful of dirt and gravel, and opened his hand to exhibit it to me. And he wound up the sentence: '*—è la mia terra!*'

232

"I was big enough fool, and full enough of the indoctrination *merde* or American sentimentality, to think he might mean Italy. You know, the *la patria* stuff, patriotism, and so I said, sort of like a question, 'Italy?'

"He looked at me as though I were certifiably nuts. He shook his head sadly, as though there were no help for the case, and said very gravely, *'No, la mia terra.'* He closed his hand over the dirt and gravel, his dirt, his *terra,* his whatever it was, and shook the clenched hand at me to show possession—or the being possessed, identity or whatever you want to call it. *'La mia,'* he added."

I paused, trying to remember. Then: "He was from that desert-like country near Siena, and that is one hell of a patch of country to have to call *la mia terra.*"

"But," Mrs. Jones-Talbot put in, "it doesn't seem to matter what kind of *terra* it is, just so it is *la mia.*"

"Yeah," I said, and laughed. "That is, if you are built that way."

Mrs. Jones-Talbot, I felt, hadn't been listening to me. Then she said: "Sergio—he came from a beautiful country. Tuscany, not far from San Casciano. Machiavelli's country. His mother had an old place there. But I'm sure it wouldn't have mattered to him, beautiful or not. He had that real, that deep, instinctive piety." And added: "For *la sua terra,* I mean."

She looked down at the open book. I thought she was about to resume reading. But the hands remained, palm-down, on the pages.

"It was odd," she said, finally. "That piety for place and all the blood-experience that has gone into it over the years. But also—and this is what is odd—his passion for an idea. For an abstraction. He was—dear, sweet boy—you know, I was almost three years older—so old-fashioned."

"Old-fashioned?"

"Oh, you know," she said. *"La libertà*—things like that. In the old-fashioned way. Poor boy—he might have been the fanatic young *Garibaldino*—all fresh face and flashing eyes."

She looked at me. "Don't misunderstand me," she said earnestly, studying my face to see if I had got her meaning. "I don't mean he ever orated, or got fiery. If he referred to *la libertà* or *la giustizia* or something, it was as natural as referring to the weather or the state of the wine crop."

Then, brightening with an idea, she exclaimed: "How stupid of me! To think it was odd—I mean that piety about *la terra* and the passion for the big ideas. Why, the piety—it was just like—like oil to feed the flame. Just the same thing in the end!"

She rose abruptly from her chair, infused by the energy of her discovery. She went to the fireplace, threw a stick on, then drew the bellpull that hung at the right, a strip of brocade that ended in a massy gold tassel. "It's fake," she said, noticing my eyes on the pull. "Not the pull, that's real, just the fact that it works an electric buzzer back in the kitchen. I thought we'd have some tea."

When the tea had been poured, she said: "You know, I interrupted you. With my gabble. You were talking about Guglielmino and his *terra.*"

"Oh, nothing," I said. "But *il nonno*—that's what they called him —Gramps was sure one brave little dried-up, over-age booger." I paused. "A lot of 'em were. Over-age or not." Then: "I was always trying to figure out what made 'em tick."

After a while, for I had fallen silent, she said: "I've heard tell you didn't do so badly."

"Me—" I said. "I did what guys like me do. I didn't do well and I didn't do badly. In my state of anesthesia, I did what I did—that is, what I had been programmed to do. But my crew of brigands— they were different. Nobody had programmed them for anything. Listen, and I'll tell you—" and out of a blind impulse I was telling her. My voice was telling her the tale of the Nazi lieutenant, the SS officer that I, in contravention of the rules of chivalry and of the Geneva Convention, had shot, very precisely, under the left ear. I found myself trying to enumerate every single detail that flooded my imagination, and my nervous system.

I came to the footnote on this episode when, back on the hill above the farm, with a piece of white sheeting over my head for camouflage and binoculars at my eyes, peering over a boulder, I gave the order, *"Adesso!"* and the brigand with me pushed the plunger of the detonator and our little underground hideaway, with present occupants, very abruptly and untidily lifted skyward.

I took a well-earned drag of my tea. The event, which had been for those few minutes vivid to me, became, again, unreal—no, untrue. "That's all," I said, lamely, as though apologizing for the lie. I set my cup down: "I forgot to tell you that after I had pulled the trigger on my personal victim and given the next man over to the tender mercies of Gianluigi—all this well before the end—I went out and vomited. Under the stars, I should add."

"Well, you might," she said sympathetically.

After a moment, I said: "I reckon there was more to it than that."

"What do you mean?"

"You see," I found myself saying to her, in a tone of patient explanation, "we had to get that information. Our little war was not very civilized."

"Yes."

"But also," I was saying, "I reckon I did it because I had to get some kind of respect from my wolf-eyed pals. And because—"

She waited, studying me. "Because of what?" she finally asked, in a cool, conversational tone.

"Because I hated him," I said.

Then, under her steady eyes: "Because I envied him."

I waited.

"So that's it," she said, half question, half answer.

"I reckon so," I said. "At least, it was so the second I pulled the trigger."

She got up and moved a few paces. "You didn't have to be jealous of him," she decided. "That Nazi—he was just programmed, as you put it."

"He was programmed in a hell of a lot different way from me," I said. "He was programmed not just to do, but to be."

"Well," she declared, in what seemed to be suppressed violence, "Sergio—he wasn't programmed. He was what he was. All the way through, to the very center."

She stepped sharply to the table, picked up the open book. "You know what," she said, "that night before he left—you remember I told you how he left?"

I nodded.

"Well," she said, her voice dispassionate, "he used to read to me, as I told you. Do you know what canto he read?"

I shook my head.

"This one," she said. Then, holding the book in her hand, but not looking at the page, began: "*O, Mantovano . . .*"

On to the end, pouring out the disgust of Dante—and, no doubt, Sergio—who found his *terra* become a whorehouse and a sty.

She closed the superfluous book, and laid it on the table.

"If the world hadn't been so filthy—" she said.

She began again, "If things had worked out, I would have gone to live with him in *sua terra.*"

She stood there, one hand still touching the book on the table. All at once, in a painful surprise, I observed how old she looked—a middle-size woman in a dark gray, unornamented dress, erect enough but with graying hair and a face that, at the moment, in that light, was gray and drawn. I looked down at the hand on the book. For all the tan, the muscularity, the tinted nails, it was an old hand.

"So I came here," she was saying, "to my *terra.* And—"

She flung her gaze about the room. Then continued: "—and built this goddamned beautiful, expensive, trivial, stupid house."

She shrugged. "And now I have to live in it."

She moved across to the fireplace, picked up a stick, and, standing with it forgotten in her hand, turned back to me. "At least," she said, in an easy, conversational tone, "I hope all they did was put a pistol to his head."

"Oh, I'm sorry," I burst out, "I'm sorry, I—"

She lifted a hand to stop me.

"You didn't make the world," she said, tossing the stick into the coals, and reached for the bellpull.

"I hope you may be generous enough to have a drink," she said, "with a very foolish old lady who's just thrown a tantrum and spoiled a perfectly good Dante lesson."

.   .   .

So had passed the first twenty-five of the ninety-three hours between my assignation with Rozelle on Thursday afternoon and the next that I might anticipate; and the remaining sixty-eight were worse.

I had left the Jones-Talbot house, about six o'clock, in a mysteriously sodden mood that, by the time I had reached my own kitchen and was spooning a can of corned beef hash into a skillet, was becoming a depression of damned near clinical proportions. I knew well enough what it was all about. That is, I knew as soon as I let myself know. I was jealous of something they had had—Sergio Whatever-His-Name-Was and the young woman Mrs. Jones-Talbot had once been. That, clearly, was the reason.

No, it was clearly not the reason. Whatever the real reason was, this was merely what it had reached out and seized to wear for a mask. Meanwhile the real reason, unknown, grinned at me through it as I sat, under a nakedly blazing bulb, and ate the flannel-tasting greasy pap, not overwarm, on which a fried egg yellowly bled to death.

Oh, I well knew all the remedies for such acedia. Read a hard book. Correct a student paper. Memorize a poem. Vow to begin the study of a new language. Get out of the house and for hours walk the night streets of a city, or a country road, dusty or muddy, moonlit or drizzly dark. But none of these remedies was now appropriate. The trouble was, I wanted to sit right where I was.

So I sat there, regarding the undevoured mass on my plate, and picked the scab of past pleasures as though they had been wounds. And they were.

For instance:

Your hands, she had said, *they're so strong and big. When they lay hold of a girl she sure knows it. They're the strongest I ever—*

And she hesitated.

She had, clearly, been about to say *felt*—the strongest she had ever *felt*—and I was already grinning in idiotic vanity, thinking how Old Broke-Nose's hand could cradle a football for the pass, or a buttock. But she had hesitated, and in that instant, I remembered, quite coldly, how she, in some casual connection, had once said: *You know how strong a sculptor's hands are, working in clay all day, or stone or—*

And remembering that, I knew what had made her hesitate, and the grin of vanity went cold and stiff on my face, like plaster drying for a death mask.

I did not grin in idiotic delight at anything that came into my mind.

237

If in one phase of our affair, when I had seized the day and had had no concern except with Rozelle the dream—none beyond the moment when our bodies swung into conjunction—I had been able to remember with pleasure such moments. But now there was no pleasure in the past pleasures. Nor could I repudiate the past. I was devoured by it. I had fallen into it, was submerged in it, and like the unfortunate traveler fallen overboard in the Amazon, I was being eaten alive by the innumerable and insatiable piranha that swim below the surface of the stream.

To be accurate, it was the past that obsessed me. She belonged to it. She did not belong to me. As for my own past, I knew it all too well. It was nothing, a blankness, and it was the reality of the jealous pain at her past that, somehow, was the sanctuary I could flee to, to escape the unreality of my own.

But, all at once, I shoved my chair back. I was remembering that, coming back from the Dante lesson, I had been too glum and preoccupied to pick up the mail. Well, that was something to do. I could go and get the mail, all the way to the highway, in the dark.

A half-hour later I reentered the kitchen. I held a newspaper and three letters in my hand. The top letter was addressed in the scraggly, strong handwriting of my mother.

I dropped the other items to the chair by the table and held my mother's letter in both hands. I turned it over, and stared stupidly at that side, too; then over again to fix my eyes on my own name written in that hand, far off, in Dugton, Alabama. It was the past.

The envelope held me with superstitious bemusement. It was as though the past, for all my repudiation of it, had pursued me here. It was as though, over space and out of time, it had been summoned here for a purpose.

I laid the envelope, unopened, on the table, by the plate that was still half full of yellow-streaked hash. I would read it.

But not yet.

.   .   .

Much later that night, in bed, drifting at long last toward sleep, I thought again of the letter that lay on the table, unopened, and in the last instant before consciousness blurred completely out, a truth seemed to dawn on me. The letter was from Dugton, Alabama. Both Rozelle and I were from, and of, Dugton.

The letter meant that we were together, after all.

. . .

Or did it mean that?

For when, the next morning, I opened it, I found among certain idle items of Dugton, this:

Aint things funny, so they aint no way of knowing the truth of nothing except by looking right hard at it. Take my Perk. Nothing special, you might say. Strong but gitting old and losing his shape. (Me too.) He never was good looking fer moving picturs. Not like yore blood-Pappy, he was one looker! And Perk, he never done nothing special, sure never made no money and had no luck, but loves to do a little job as well as he can and loves his tool box. Dont wash and shave enough maybe unlest I make him. And aint got good sense; fer he calls me a "looker," who never was no "looker," but knowed my own mind and looked at folks as straight as God would let me, allowing fer some mistakes, like yore Pappy. Even tried to look straight in the looking glass and see one dam fool.

Here I laid the letter down, and waited a full minute before I could pick it up.

But back to Perk. We been married a long time, and the luck was mine. I dont know ner care what he looks like to nobody else in the world, but just he comes in the door and I see in big gold letters printed all over him one big word like one of them neon advertisements. It just says GOODNESS—like fer coffee or something. And it is the last thing he knows, him feeling so bad sometimes fer all his stumbling and falling. Just born to goodness and never knowed it. But me, I seen it right away. Now aint that funny?

At this point I did not know how funny anything was. So I laid the letter down again.

When I had pulled myself together enough to pick up another sheet, I was lucky enough to discover that my mother, in whom the rhetorical principles of unity and coherence had not been properly inculcated at the Heaven's Hope schoolhouse, had completely switched the subject to one which, I am sure, she had been holding back for her snapper. She even put it in a separate paragraph.

Chester Burton had been divorced by his toney wife of New York City, Long Island, and Nassau, and was, in fact, back on the family seat (read *farm*), in Claxford County, to get his ma, according to my informant, to give him a sugar-tit.

So Dugton had claimed her own.

My mother added:

> I always knowed he did not look like he had right smart juice. And I reckin Miss Pritty-Pants (you-know-who) is doing better the way she is, whoever she is doing it with, even if them Burtons did kick up dirt in her face.

With grim amusement—since I had never found it good to mention to my Mother that "Miss Pritty-Pants" was in Nashville, much less in Old Broke-Nose's afternoon bed—I acknowledged that she might be doing better in some departments than if, in the logic of things of Dugton, she had taken up with Chester Burton.

But I did not know how much comfort that was to me right then. It was still a long time until Monday. I prayed to God to lead my steps aright, as the hymn of my childhood put it, but knowing myself and my gonads, I had little faith that He would.

Anyway, I had to brace myself for Monday.

.   .   .

For nothing—it turned out. The dramatic topic of our parting on the previous Thursday simply did not now exist. Rozelle came in as glowing and bright-eyed as from the morning shower, all innocent gaiety and bubbling with a secret which she refused to divulge until I had done what she called my duty by her.

"You know," she said, once the duty was done, "Lawford flies off to New York, early Wednesday. For his show."

I had forgotten the date, but nodded.

"Well," she continued, "I'm going to get sick. I've got a bad bug —flu or something—coming on."

She pulled a long face and her shoulders sagged, but I had scarcely uttered a faint grunt of commiseration (and surprise, it may be admitted, after her recent display of energy), before she gave a grin, and said: "Dumbbell!"

Then, by way of explanation: "You see, I'll be droopy tomorrow, and by night it'll be pretty bad. Stomach flu, that's what it will be, plus chills and diarrhea. I simply won't be able to go. I'll just have to miss the opening," she said.

She paused, and with glittering childlike glee, exclaimed: "Dumbbell!"

Then with histrionic grief: "But maybe little *hims* is not dumb. Maybe *hims* just pretends to be dumb. Maybe *hims* just doesn't want to spend a whole night with poor little me."

So that was it. And was the way it was going to be, as I well knew, even though remembering, with a cold, clinical surprise, how when Rozelle, immediately after our little adulterous adventure had been initiated, insisted that I come to the party at the Carrington house for the visiting poet, I had declared that, if only in my redneck way, I'd be uncomfortable drinking the likker and eating the grub of my freshly cuckolded host. Now it never occurred to me to gag at the thought of posting to the cuckold's own freshly laundered sheets for the business.

But when, at nine-thirty, two nights later, I instinctively hesitated at the edge of the woods and looked across the cloud-darkened pasture to the farmhouse where light shone dimly from a single window, it was not passion, nor lust for adventure, nor taste for intrigue that lured me on. It was, rather, the sense of a process to be completed, a doom to be fulfilled.

No, there was another factor, too. I had the need to look upon the face of Rozelle Hardcastle as she slept.

When, after preliminary barking, the big brute of a German shepherd greeted me as a friend, I approached the house and stood on the granite slab at the side door of the ell, and drew forth from my jacket pocket the key, cold to the touch, which Rozelle had provided.

I fumbled my way to the bottom of the back stairs, then stood immobile, breathing the odors of a strange house. If in light, on a legitimate errand, with people, or even alone, you enter a strange house (and this ell was totally strange to me), odors are overwhelmed by a flood of sensations, perceptions, and concerns, but in darkness and silence, odors become the dominant data, and so, withdrawing my hand from contact with the banister, I stood there, swaddled in the blind isolation of my being, and breathed the mysterious air, and when I expelled that air from my lungs I felt as though, with each expiration, some inevitable part of my identity, my very *anima,* was being drawn out and absorbed into the undifferentiated blankness of the world in which I stood.

But now a faint light showed at the top of the stairs, apparently the light from a partly opened door down the hall, and, an instant later, not louder than a whisper, I heard my name.

"Yes," I answered, and realizing that the word I had uttered was, too, not more than a whisper, I was mounting the stairs.

At the head of the stairs, the hand, pale in the dimness, fluttered out to take mine, and in silence, not a word, not an embrace, I was led toward that shaft of light that marked a doorway down the hall.

Rozelle entered ahead of me, slipping through the aperture that had been left minimal as though from caution, and once inside, hand on the knob, let me have the extra inches I needed for passage. Once I was in, she softly closed the door, and I wasn't sure that I hadn't heard a bolt thrown. Then she was leaning with her back against the door, both hands behind her, presumably still on the knob, but the face lifting toward me, as I stood a couple of paces away, was sweet, the eyes wide in hope, in trusting appeal, in candor, in humble question, their color and gleam muted in the dim light from a lamp on a little table by the big fourposter set head-end to the wall beyond the door.

I did not move toward her. There may have been something new and portentous in the purity of her gaze, something that cast all my impulses and emotions, my very nature, into a new distance, into a perspective sweet and sad but sharpening all outlines like late light coming over water, like time or age.

It was, too, as though I was seeing her for the first time—or rather,

242

as though we were alone for the first time. I was, all at once, aware that the robe or peignoir or dressing gown or whatever it was that she wore, of some soft, light gray fabric sprigged in blue to catch a reflection of her eyes, looked like something of a century back, high-waisted with skirt flowing to the floor, the little touch of lace at throat and at wrists. It was the sort of robe some woman, so long ago, might have worn in this very room, at night, as she lifted that same gaze of hopeful innocence and humble question to a man standing on the very spot where I now stood.

I started to say something, and got as far as to utter her name. At that she brought her right hand up, and laid a finger to my lips. "Hush," she whispered, took me by the hand, and led me around the foot of the fourposter, across the considerable length of the room—very considerable for a bedroom—to a wing chair, upholstered in a dust-blue velvet, that stood by the hearth. A tiny fire smoldered on the bricks.

"Take off your coat," she said.

I obeyed, and as I stood holding it, she reached up to unknot my askew old black knit tie. She took both objects and dropped them on a chaise longue, also dust-blue, at the other side of the hearth.

"Sit down," she said.

I sat down.

"I'm going to sit in your lap," she said. "That's something I've always wanted to do. Just curl up on your lap and have you hold me."

She stepped out of her slippers, which I had not even seen under the flowing skirt, looking suddenly smaller and defenseless, and proceeded to do exactly what she had always wanted to do, and I did what she had always wanted to have done to her. I held her quietly on my lap.

Again I started to say something, but again she put a finger to my lips. "Not now," she whispered. "Just let's be."

After a time she slid off my lap and, barefoot, laid a couple of little sticks on the fire, saying she was glad it was so unseasonably cool so we could have a little fire, just a blaze, she'd always wanted to sit in my lap by the fire. She slipped beyond the chaise longue and came back with an ice bucket. As I started up, she said, "Don't budge, I'm a pretty good barmaid," and proceeded to prove same, and after the authoritative *pop* of the cork, poured two glasses and set them on a taboret by our chair.

Again she curled up on my lap, and, somewhat awkwardly, we each took a sip, and set the glasses on the taboret. Her head was at my left shoulder, my left arm around her, my right hand supporting her crooked-up knees. My face was against her hair. We stirred only when I had to reach out for one of the glasses, which we would then share.

The glasses, however, were long dry, and the blaze down to a few coals, when the telephone rang.

I felt her body jerk in the split second before she slipped down and ran for the little table at the bedside, where the phone was.

"Yes," she was saying, "yes, I accept the charges."

Her right hand had now moved out to draw back the old-fashioned counterpane on the bed, even as she was saying, "Yes, yes, and how did it go?"

I noticed that there was no term of endearment.

Then: "Oh, wonderful! Oh, I'm so glad!"

Then, as she paused, listening, I found myself trying to assess her words, or rather, her tone, the degree of sincerity with which they came. Meanwhile, her free hand, I noticed, was opening the bed, drawing down the blanket, exposing the sheets, which, in the light from the bedside lamp, shone fresh, crisp, and white, awaiting, I was suddenly aware, dishevelment and stain.

Even as the voice, now and then punctuating some flow of information from the other end of the wire, kept saying, "I'm so glad" and "Oh, I wish I had been there," the free hand was untying the belt of the robe, was drawing it back to slip from the shoulder—this with a kind of slow, sinuous, fluid, weakly shrugging motion, innocently provocative. Then, as the flow of information continued unstanchable over the wire, the instrument was switched to her other hand, and the robe fell free from the left shoulder to the floor. She was wearing a white sleeveless nightgown, of a flowing cut. She was saying, "Yes . . . yes . . . yes."

She was sitting on the edge of the bed now, was leaning back, drawing up her knees, and with the free hand was modestly controlling the white flow of the gown as she inserted herself between the sheets.

I was wondering what the man at the other end of the line was making of those breathy, joyful words, *Yes . . . yes . . . yes.*

She had put her hand on the mouthpiece.

"Jed!" she called me, in a hoarse whisper, patting the space beside her where the sheet was now pulled down.

Then into the phone: "Oh, I'm so sorry! I missed something."

She saw that I had made no move. She again covered the mouthpiece, turning to me. "Jed!" she begged. "I've got to have you here —by me."

Then into the mouthpiece: "I had to cough. You don't want me to blow out your eardrum, do you? . . . Oh, yes, I'm better. No, not flu —tummy . . . Yes, I'm coming . . . Four o'clock plane . . . Yes, tell me more, I'm dying to hear . . . No, don't meet me."

By this time I was standing in the middle of the floor, stark naked. I looked at the pair of old flannel slacks across the blue velvet chair, at the crumpled underwear on the seat, at the unpolished G.I. shoes, one flat on its side, tongue gaping out, dropped at random on the creamy carpet. Everything—particularly the shoe on its side, with the mud-crusted heel—looked very funny.

Stealthily I got into bed. Not near Rozelle, lying on my back, looking up at the ceiling.

"Yes, yes," the voice was saying, "you mean the whole Ballet Suite?"

I felt the hand on my belly, groping.

Now and then the voice spoke. I kept feeling myself at the other end of the wire, hearing the words, but not hearing them in ignorance.

In knowledge.

I was seized by the wild impulse to push myself up and reach across and grab the telephone from the hand that held it, and say into it: "Hey, Lawford, ole fella! Guess who!"

And I broke into the next thing to literal giggles, pleased as punch.

Well, that would settle something.

But the voice at my side that had been speaking, had suddenly stopped.

245

I heard the click of the instrument being racked up, and felt the slight shift of weight on the mattress as the speaker sank back down. Not looking, I knew that she, too, was lying on her back, staring at the ceiling. The hand that had, earlier, groped over my belly, now motionlessly held what it had groped for.

"You did splendidly," I said.

"If that is what is called irony," the voice beside me said, "I don't appreciate it."

"Frankly," I said, "I don't know what it is."

The hand that groped for what it now held, dropped it, and Rozelle rolled over, pushing herself up, and with her hair hanging loose from the side-tilted head, some strands falling across the face, the face shadowed since the light was beyond but the wide eyes glinting even in shadow, was demanding, "What would you have me do? I was the one taking the rap—and what else could I do?"

The words kept on pouring out. "It's a trap—we're in a trap—and I have to do what I can, and whatever I do, it's all for you—because I've got to have you—" She paused. "I just had to have you here tonight," she went on, "—for the first time, like this, I couldn't wait longer, and oh, I wanted everything to be sweet and calm and slow and gentle—"

She was weeping now.

"And oh, be sweet to me!" she cried out. "Or I'll die."

With that she buried the wet face against my naked chest.

So I was as sweet and gentle as I could be, as she had asked me to be and as I really now felt like being—and calm and slow, too, and what came after those things seemed so naturally and gradually to grow out of them that it seemed part of them, too.

That is, until what finally happened.

Without going into the logistics, geometry, and clinicism of the event—which, I assure the reader, are all quite reasonable—even as I knew that she was approaching her moment, she seized my right hand, which had been manipulating her left breast, and put it, palm down, curling across her throat, her own hand, the left, of course, over mine to make it close tighter. What happened immediately thereafter, in the struggle and blur of what the poet, as I have remarked before, has called the poor, bewildered minute, is not quite clear in my mind,

246

but now she—*in extremis,* one might say—was trying to make my fingers clutch the throat, and I, then plunging over the verge, too, was struggling, not only against the tense pressure of the fingers of the would-be victim's own hand, but against the suddenly evoked darkling impulse in myself which seemed an aspect of the apocalyptic goings-on in my vitals.

Then we had fallen apart. To lie with no contact, as though each had made some private discovery that had to be regarded in silence and the darkness of inner isolation. But after a time, she propped herself on a wadded-up pillow, eyes fixed across the blankness of the room.

"He was manic," she said.

"What?" I asked, hearing the words, but in my inner darkness recognizing no context for them.

"My husband," she said.

I had never before heard her call him that: *my husband.*

She resumed: "He was perfectly manic. He couldn't stop talking. Everything was so goddamned wonderful. Yes, and thank God it was, and I hope it will be, for that makes it an awful lot easier on me— oh, you don't know what he's like when he gets one of his black fits on."

"I'm not sure I want to know," I said, not being quite sure what I meant.

"But he's manic tonight. Really wrapped up in himself. Couldn't even remember that I was sick, couldn't even ask how—" She turned on me, for the first time, saying: "Oh, I know you think that fact sort of ironical or something, but—"

"I didn't say a word," I said.

"Well, sure it's ironical, and I know it's a lie I'm sick." She was again staring off across the room. "But if I were dying on the floor, it would be the same way. Just that manic flow, all about that goddamned opening. Oh, I know, the women swarm all over him, he's so goddamned strong and handsome and swings that profile around higher than anybody's head like a light on a lighthouse on the horizon, on a dark night, and they all get damp in the crotch just looking at him—oh, yes, there was a time when I used to, too."

Not turning to me, she said: "Get me a glass of that wine, please."

247

I went across to the bucket and poured a glass.

"It's flat," I said.

"Give it to me anyway," she said. "Please."

She drank it, her gaze still across the room. Naked, I crouched on the hearth, blowing up the coals, peculiarly aware of my nakedness, feeling my testicles and flabby member swing free above the bricks as I crouched there, feeling the itchy drying of sweat on my skin, and the slight chill at my back, away from the wispy little flame.

"Is there any more?" the voice inquired.

"No," I said, eyes fixed on the flame.

"If you'll go in the second door there," she was saying, and I turned to see her point to one of the two doors at the other end of the room, "that's his dressing room. You'll see a little icebox in there, and almost sure, some more. Maybe a split, unless you want a whole bottle opened."

Then, as I moved toward the door: "You see—my husband, he likes to have a little champagne handy."

I came out with a split and began picking at the foil.

"If you want," she was saying, "you could find some sticks in there."

"The fire's all right," I said.

"*Sticks*—" she said. "You know—marijuana. In the first cabinet, the bigger one, in a blue box. My husband"—she was using the word again, with just a slight emphasis on it—"sometimes likes to have a little stick handy. You know, after a hard day. Sometimes a little champagne. Sometimes a stick. The best quality of both, of course."

I was pouring the wine, thinking of J. Lawford Carrington, of Mr. Nashville himself, basking by his fireside after a hard day, clad in crimson pajamas, by Countess Mara or something fancy, and a really truly antique mandarin robe draped on breadth of shoulders, Turkish slippers on feet, a Scots tam on head or maybe a genuine tenth-century B.C. Mycenaean helmet (if wealth can buy such a thing), glass or stick in exquisite but strong fingers, taking his ease, building his strength up for a tussle.

I carried the wine to Rozelle. With her hand on the glass, looking up at me, she said: "Then after his highest-quality champagne, or his highest-quality Acapulco Gold stick, whichever, then, of course, me next. For me—I am of the highest quality, too, don't you know? I mean, since I belong to him, I must be the highest quality of ass."

After a sip, she said: "*Quod erat demonstrandum*—as we used to grandly put it in Dugton High."

"Does he want you to smoke with him?" I asked.

"Yes," she said, "and I do it. And he makes me drink champagne with him, too, and admire the very high quality. Anything, to keep the peace, that is my motto."

Then: "It will be easier to keep the peace for a while now. Since things go well in New York. The Ballet Suite is sold already. To some balding swinger, to have all over his posh, wheeler-dealer apartment. Jesus, you can just see it." She hesitated, took a sip. "Well, that's all it's fit for," she said, studying the bubbles in her glass, golden in the light.

"You posed for those things, didn't you?" I heard my voice asking, in enormous casualness, as I attentively began to pour my own wine.

"Yes," she was saying, and I looked up to meet her gaze, as she continued, "and the next thing you'll be so damned casually and cunningly trying to find out is, did I ever have real honest-to-goodness intercourse with him."

I started to say something, something like *Well, did you?* but was saved from that fatuity.

"Well, I did," she was asserting, "and I thought it was great."

Then, as anger throttled whatever I was about to say—whatever it was—she added: "But let it be well noted that the verb *to think* appears here in the past tense—i.e., *thought.*"

"Well," I declared, "if that is the case, and you hate him so god-damned—"

"Look!" she cried out. "You've made me spill all over me! All that *yak-yak-yakking* and—"

"Here—" I began, and took a step toward her, bottle in hand.

"Oh, I don't want it, I don't know why I ever took it," she said, leaning to set the glass on the bedside table. And turning back to me: "All I want is for us to stop our *yakking*—we mustn't ever *yak* at each other—just be together and forget and—"

She had wriggled the wet gown over her head, leaning forward to pull it over, then with one hand flinging it to the foot of the bed and with the other simultaneously jerking the cover over her new naked-ness as she fell back.

She lay there with the covers to her chin, saying: "I just want to forget everything." Then: "Except you, Jed—oh, Jed!"

With that, she rolled over to bury her face in the pillow, face down, the covers huddled at her shoulders, nothing showing but the loose hair, gold-streaked in the dim light.

I stood in the middle of the floor, bare feet ankle-deep in the cream-colored carpet, naked as a shaved baboon, the dying coals behind me, and clutching the bottle in one hand, with the other lifted the champagne glass to my lips, to methodically drain it. That done, I looked at the split. There was no use bothering to pour what was left. I set the bottle to my lips and drained that. I set the glass and bottle on the mantel shelf, moved toward the bed.

Things were as they were.

CHAPTER XI

When I laid hand to the back door of my house, the sun was just rising over the woods. The moment I entered, a great weariness hit me like a blow. I knew that there were things that I knew, but suddenly I did not know what they were. It was as though my mind had closed like a fist on the things I no longer knew and would not open that fist to let me see. Meanwhile, somehow arriving at the bedroom, the non-mind Me was managing to kick off shoes and strip to underwear before falling into the unmade bed. Somehow the non-mind Me did manage, too, to set the alarm for nine, to make a ten o'clock class, the undergraduate class in types of tragedy.

When the alarm rang, I had no awareness of time intervening between the winding and the racket. I let it ring on, promising myself to be up in just a minute, asking myself what the hell I was supposed to talk about this morning, then imagining myself going into class and announcing: "Dear Little Pets, my Little Lambs, I cannot say what the hell type our tragedy is this morning, for I have forgotten, but I bring you, nevertheless, a profound, though distasteful, message, and I quote from Edgar in the great heath scene in the storm in which King Lear receives his revelation: *Let not the creaking of shoes nor the rustling of silks betray thy poor heart to woman . . . and defy the foul fiend.* "

And then I was weeping and imploring them, my Little Pets, my Lambs, not to believe what I had just said, what Edgar had said, for Edgar had blasphemed, for I had blasphemed, for if the heart is not betrayed, then what is life worth—oh, what—

At this point the alarm went off, only it was not the alarm, it was the telephone, and I was being snatched not from my witty imagination but from a real dream, to pad, barefoot, in broad day, for it was long and disastrously past nine o'clock, to the telephone. And even as I moved across the floor, I knew that it was Thursday, that Rozelle Hardcastle would not be here, would be far away, above the world, and the blankness of the day to come almost overwhelmed me.

It was Sally Cudworth on the phone. Cud, she said, was going to be off for the afternoon and this weather was so beautiful, wouldn't I come out and help exercise the stock and have a quiet little family supper, and keep tabs on how disgustingly and blissfully big she was getting around the tummy. They hadn't seen me in a coon's age, she added.

No, they hadn't.

And I knew why, for the last time I had been there, a month before, when he and I were exercising the stock, Cud had—oh, so innocently —again ridden over toward the neighboring place, and had commented on how fine the old house looked on its knoll beyond the creek, and had said that it wasn't sold yet, and he'd be damned if he understood why, especially since the price had again been cut. Then later, when he and I were back by the bar doing some private collaborative work on the bourbon problem, he had, again, said: "The price—it's a steal now. And financing it would be no real problem, I just know." Then: "Don't think I'm pushing you."

Then: "But, by God, I am. Simply because Sally and I, we can't think of anybody we'd rather have for neighbors."

And he thrust his strong-fleshed, weathered, round face toward me, an even more earnest and devout expression on it, and little beads of sweat glistening, as always when he drank, on the strong bald skull, and asserted: "I just know everything is going to be all right; I just know it in my bones, and you believe it, pal."

"Your bones," my own voice was, at some middle distance, calmly and distinctly saying, "don't know a goddamned thing, and—" this as I carefully watched the china-blue eyes of my auditor go round with surprise and the flesh at the corners of his mouth twitch back in distress "—if you refer to Maria McInnis, I suggest that you drop the subject. Permanently."

With that I turned sharply—glass in hand, however—and, with savage glee at the thought that his goddamned bones certainly did not know who Old Broke-Nose was slipping the meat to, and wouldn't those bones be surprised, stalked into the other room, and, joining a little group, mostly female, assembled about the swami, began to contemplate, with a mixture of savage glee and savage self-contempt, the phthisic charms of the Dabbitt creature, who, crouching on a hassock at the knee of the Wise One, was hanging on his every word.

The swami was just in the act of reading aloud, in the original Hindi, of course, one of his own poems, and when he had finished the original text, he gave an English translation, in verse, too. After the coos of awe and rapture were over, he began another original composition and drove through to the bitter end. At this point his gaze found me. "Ah, dear Professor," he said, "you can tell our friends how much is lost in any translation, how the vital pulse of language is diminished, and this newer composition I must, I humbly apologize, render somewhat freely and pray to offer a more adequate translation in the future."

But now he plunged in, with an effect much like a mélange of R. Tagore, Lawrence Hope, E. B. Browning and Felicia Hemans, not to forget considerable allusion to some handbook of the exotic positions practiced in his native land. Having quickly had enough of such rich fare, I rose as quietly as possible and began to thread my way through female forms seated on cushions, meanwhile murmuring my apologies, and I swear to God that, as my eyes momentarily engaged those of the swami, he almost winked—or maybe did wink—and gave some sort of complex smile that seemed to be full of ironical dimensions involving, among other things, camaraderie, amiable contempt and brotherly knowingness—as though he were just trying to indicate that if I didn't mess with his racket, he wouldn't mess with mine.

Well, plenty of people had seemed to think that I had a racket going, but they weren't yet up-to-date, thank God!

Now, as I heard Sally Cudworth's voice coming over the wire, warm and teasing even in its distance, I felt a gush of relief, of happiness as at forgiveness. For I, who had never had a friend, a real friend, would rather have had Cud Cudworth for a friend than anybody I had ever seen—Sally and Cud for friends, for they belonged together indissolubly—what a fool I had been not to understand the wicked stupidity of what I had done.

Sure—at their place I had felt, now and then, a sense of unreality in their world, but now, even as I held the telephone, the awareness struck me that I had clung to that notion of the unreality of their world simply because I could not face the painful reality of their joy. The joy sprang from their willed and full embracement of the process of their life in time, and I, God help me, was in flight from Time. I could not stand the reproach of the sight they provided.

What I have stated here was not, as I heard Sally's voice, strung out analytically in my mind, like wet laundry on a line. Rather, it was a kind of hot, churning magma of feeling as I hung on to the telephone, and I was babbling yes, yes, I'd come, I'd love to come. And as I hung up the instrument, I had the fantasy of talking to Cud, of being able to tell him everything, that very afternoon, a vision of some relief and blessed wisdom thus to be gained. Hell, what was a friend for?

As I turned from the telephone, I had a sudden burst of energy—it now being far too late to make class. I took a cold shower. I prepared and ate a hearty breakfast—enough to stay me until Sally's absolutely splendid little quiet family supper. I washed my teeth vigorously, and sat down at my desk and resolutely drew forth a folder of notes (ignoring the dust and slightly curled corners) and began to inspect them. I took delight in the way my mind seized on facts, shuffled them into new and interesting configurations that looked like truth.

I inspected my watch. It was not yet eleven. I had two good hours of work before I had to leave for the Cudworth farm.

But the telephone rang.

"I'm at the airport, darling," the voice was saying, "and I just couldn't leave without calling—oh, I prayed you'd oversleep, I just had to tell you how blessèd and sweet it was, just to sit on your lap, to curl up in your arms—"

"Listen," I said.

"Oh, darling, I can't stand it. Here it is Thursday and no wonderful Old Broke-Nose—"

"Listen," I said peremptorily, "I love you. But things can't go on this way—are you listening?"

"Yes," the voice said.

"Well, listen hard. You've got to do a lot of hard thinking on this trip—are you listening?"

"I'm going to die on this trip," the voice said.

"You are not going to die, but—"

"I think I'm going to cry," the voice said.

"Well, cry or not, you had better—"

"Oh, it's my plane they are calling," the voice said.

The phone was dead.

I stood there and remembered how I had, indeed, seen her face as she slept.

That morning, toward 4:30 A.M., I had slipped from the bed, dressed by the romantically dim light that had not been turned off all night long, and had tiptoed, in the G.I. shoes, on that expensive and soundless cream-colored carpet, to the door. Before I set hand to the knob I drew the key from my pocket and left it, by the empty champagne glass, under the direct rays of the bedside lamp. Then I looked down at the face.

She lay on her right side, facing toward the door, the face profiled against the pillow, the face smoothly chiseled and calm. The eyelids closed calmly, hieratically, over the large deep-set eyes. The lips were slightly parted, and I thought of the sweetness of breath that would, ever so lightly, be passing in and out.

Finally I opened the door, with great caution, and slipped out. Something would be lost if she awoke.

.   .   .

255

On Thursday afternoon I went to the Cudworths' and floated happily awash in the tide of their happiness, their ease, their purposefulness. But I didn't have that friendly talk with Cud that had seemed so imminent and inevitable in the moment of my insane fantasy when I had held the telephone in my hand that very morning.

On Friday I had a Dante session with Mrs. Jones-Talbot and her friend, then went into town for a cafeteria dinner and a movie, alone.

On Saturday morning I woke up thinking of the ultimatum I had given Rozelle on the telephone, and felt a burst of energy and freedom. I would put my life in order. After breakfast I saw the notes on my desk and sat down, and as I sat there the first stirrings of an old excitement began. I was thinking that perhaps—perhaps—

Whatever it was, what fleeting glimpse of an idea—like the flicker of white of a fish-belly in dark water—I was superstitious about putting it into words. I got up and walked the room, trying to make my mind blank. I was trying to make the idea seize me.

It was hanging in the air, just out of my range of vision. I did not want to think it. Not yet.

Then I was thinking that I might—*might*—do a study, in the Provençal and Italian poets before Dante, of the relation of the concept of Love to that of Time. I jotted down a couple of notes to myself—questions, speculations, references—and, shifting the sheet before me, saw a passage I had copied down long back, from Arnaut Daniel, that prince of troubadours—his plea that God would grant, if it so pleased Him, that he and his lady might have at last their agreed-on love-meeting:

> *Voilla, sil platz, qu'ieu e midonz jassam*
> *En la chambra on amdui nos mandem*
> *Uns rics convens don tan gran joi atendi,*
> *Quel seu bel cors baisan rizen descobra*
> *E quel remir contral lum de la lampa.*

There, too, were all the old scribblings, full of erasures and cancellations that I had once made in trying to catch some little flicker in English, even without the rhymes, of the magic of the passage:

> *That I and my lady may together lie*
> *In the chamber agreed on for our rich rendering,*
> *On which great joy I now attend, and that,*
> *Amidst kissings and smilings, I may unsheathe and gaze on*
> *Her most fair body, in the light of the lamp, bare.*

But the last line was canceled, and a revision put in below it:

> *That unblemished body, in the light of the lamp, bare.*

With increasing distaste, I read the translation, then, aloud, began to repeat the words of Arnaut. I got up from the desk and, numbly as a somnambulist, moved back toward the bedroom and stood in the middle of that dim disorder. I regarded the tangled bed, the dirty shirt in a corner, a book face down on the floor, the curtains not yet opened to day, and said out loud:

> *E quel remir contral lum de la lampa.*

There was the very lamp, on the table beyond the bed, even now dimly illuminating the false night of this room of the drawn curtains, where the *bel cors* of unblemished nakedness had first lain exposed to my sight, as now to my painful imagination.

For with the vividness of the image in my head had come an overpowering sense of deprivation. It was as though this would be the last sight I would ever have of it, that it had already been withdrawn from me. I flung myself athwart the tangle of the bed.

I don't know how long I lay there, clutching the bedclothes in both hands, but somewhere along the way, in the sense of loss, I was groping toward some tenderness—I suppose that is the word for it— for Rozelle Hardcastle that I had never known before. Or at least toward some intuition of her being, and some pity.

. . .

Six days passed and no word. I had sworn not to exist during whatever period of absence there would be. Or rather, to put a part —the essential part—of myself into the deep freeze of science fiction, to be revived later, better than new, when the time came to resume life. Meanwhile, I fulfilled my academic routine and when at home sat at the desk and shuffled my notes, like a devout player of solitaire marooned on a desert island with only one pack of cards and those wearing thin and colorless. What pale pleasure I did take was not, I may add, in groping toward truth, whatever the hell truth may be conceived to be, but in listening to the purr of well-oiled mechanism in my head.

Let truth grope toward me.

On Thursday morning, a couple of minutes after I had cut off the alarm, drawn my pants on, and downed the first cup of coffee, but before I had shaved, I heard the knocking at the back door. There she was, and not looking her best.

She threw herself into my arms, grasping herself to me in an infantile fashion. I murmured something, drew her in, kicked the door shut, and offered her coffee, to which offer she shook her head, saying for me to sit down and hold her in my arms. This I did, in a straight-backed kitchen chair.

To summarize:

In New York, her "husband" had, at first, been "manic." He seemed to be on some sort of high, especially at a dinner party the dealer gave on Saturday night, with a lot of flashy people, and especially high with the Sunday edition of the *Daily News,* in which a gossip column said that a certain unnamed art "lover" had purchased a whole set of "provocata" from the current show at the Dalforth Galleries by the Tennessee sculptor and socialite Lawford Carrington. She thrust a crumpled clipping at me—a paragraph entitled "Come Up and See My Ballet Sometime," and two little inset photographs, on one side a candid shot of the sculptor-socialite himself and on the other a shot of the item of the Suite which, at the New Year's Eve party, had been central to the banana episode.

Sunday hadn't been so bad, Rozelle said, though bad enough, for no paper had yet mentioned the show. On Monday the *Times* carried a brief note appended to an omnibus review regretting that an artist who had at one time shown promise should not only prostitute his considerable technical endowment, but reject so utterly his relationship to his own age. On reading this, her husband had ordered her to pack, had checked out of the Waldorf, and when arranged in a cab, had, to her great surprise, given as destination, not LaGuardia, but a definitely unfashionable hotel on the West Side, where, she continued, he had registered as James Carington. The *James,* of course, was a part of his name—J. Lawford Carrington—but she wondered if the loss of the *r* in the family name was a slip, or some mystic gesture toward concealment. At the hotel her husband ordered meals —vile, she said—sent to the suite, along with, she added, half the cellar and bar stock. He passed from aggrieved silence to ironical loquacity, thence to the accusation, elaborately developed over an afternoon, that her lack of faith in him, and her failure to appreciate his devotion, had subtly undermined his art; then, by the route of sentimental pleas for understanding and forgiveness, he proceeded to bald and rather perverse sexuality.

On Wednesday, by an afternoon plane, they slunk home to Nashville. On the plane a stewardess provided a new *New Yorker,* and Rozelle watched Lawford skim its pages, then pause to read. His face went from red to white, with jaws rigidly clamped. He rose from his seat and, taking the magazine with him, went to the lavatory. After a long time he came back, without the magazine.

He began to proclaim, in great animation, a new idea he had for his work, an idea that would combine the modern rigor of form with a sense of the warm depth of life—a wonderful revolutionary idea, which, however, he did not seem to be able to formulate. After a time he took her hand and, in silence, clasped it in a most lover-like fashion all the way to middle Tennessee.

No sooner were they at their house, and had eaten scrambled eggs (which she had prepared in the now servantless kitchen), than he, with the aid of an ancient bottle, which he proclaimed the prince of brandies, launched on a philosophic monologue, equally compounded of self-pity and stoic dignity. The theme was that he had sacrificed fashionable success in his art for love—such was his tragedy—and in support of this thesis he adduced the *New York Times,* which had made passing reference to his earlier awareness of technical problems confronting the modern sculptor, and the *New Yorker,* a ripped-out page of which he produced and flung at her, and which she now flung down on my kitchen table, beside my empty coffee cup.

I hastily scanned the comment—here, as in the *Times,* merely a slaughterous footnote to an omnibus review, in which the most telling phrase was "slick low-jinks from the art world of Tennessee." There was no reference to an earlier talent or integrity forfeited for any jinks, high or low. There was, however, one piece in the show snatched from the general bonfire—the head of the screaming man, which, the reviewer declared, though old-fashioned and imitative of Rodin, and perhaps drawing its impulse from Munch, exhibited a certain raw power.

"What's that got to do with it all," I demanded, "that head?" She huddled in my lap, my left arm around her, my right hand holding the clipping out to look at it. "Nothing," she repeated, "it's all crazy. Just hold me."

I tightened my left arm in its embrace, and after a little the narrative was resumed.

Well into the bottle of the prince of brandies, her husband had begun to insist that she join him. When she accepted a glass, but merely pretended to drink, he grew more and more accusatory. To placate him, she downed several glasses. At some point, monologue continuing, he switched to Scotch and soda, and she, at gunpoint, followed suit. Without missing a beat, the scene was shifted to the bedroom. She took refuge in her bathroom, hoping that when she emerged the alcohol would have done its work.

It had not, and when she tried to beg off from sex, there followed accusation, recrimination, and finally manhandling and simple assault. The assault began promisingly enough, from a strictly anatomical point of view. But something fizzled. The assaulter—to the surprise, it must be noted, of the assaultee—just wasn't up to his victory. This fact brought on another storm of accusation, followed by tears, avowals of love, threats of what would be forthcoming if he were spurned and abandoned—all this culminating in the overdue oblivion.

The principal in the action, wearing the top section of burgundy-colored, raw silk, monogramed pajamas, lay bare-ass across the foot of the noble fourposter in the big bedroom, the bedroom with the cream-colored, ankle-deep carpet. The scene is not the fruit of my imagination, for the only detail not volunteered by Rozelle, I had asked for.

"What color were the pajamas?" I had asked.

"Burgundy, I guess you'd call it," she said. Then: "What do you want to know for?"

"It just seems it's something I ought to know," I said, "to complete the picture."

This bit of dialogue occurred after I had, for the third time in the course of the narrative, got the clinging narrator off my lap and left her in the chair while I went to get more coffee. Twice I had gone back, set my cup on the table, and taken the not-always-coherent narrator back on my lap. But this time I continued to stand by the stove, imagining the scene in the bedroom I remembered so well.

Then I turned to look at Rozelle. She sat in the chair but was leaning forward to lay her head, in profile, on the table, hair loose, arms spread forward. Her eyes were closed.

"That New Year's Eve party—" I began, not looking at her now, but out the kitchen window, at a woodshed, a carefully rustic split-rail back fence, and a green pasture where white-face cattle grazed. "Do you remember it?" I continued.

"Yes," the weak voice said.

"That night, was it the first time you ever had one of those rows with him?"

After a moment: "The first big one, I reckon."

I turned and noticed that the eyes weren't open. "About what, that night?" I asked.

"Oh—things," the weak voice said. "One thing or another." Then: "I'm so tired."

"That sculptured head," I said, "that yelling head he showed that night—that had something to do with it?"

"I reckon so," the voice said.

"He sure made a big production of showing it."

"I'm tired," the voice said.

"He had his eyes on you the whole time. The show was for you."

The voice said nothing.

"Then you went and stuck your tongue down his throat."

Again, no answer.

"I could tell," I said.

Rozelle Hardcastle raised her head toward me across the kitchen, in which the hard light of morning made every object sharp-lined and clear. The eyes were red-rimmed and the morning light was not kind.

"It was nothing to you," she said. "Then."

"But what was it about?"

"I was trying to keep peace," she said, bitterly. "I was trying to keep the lid on."

"Where did the head come in?"

"Listen," she said. "Butler—you must have guessed it was him—was anything but upper-class. A ward-heeler, a shanty-Irish Chicago politician who got rich as Jesus H. Croesus and got him a college-girl wife not half his age, to show what a man he was—and he was—and J. Lawford Carrington was not going to let me forget I had married for money—and maybe I had—and that he had lifted me—Lawford, I mean—up from my fallen condition, and does that answer your question—and, oh God, haven't we got something else to talk about right now?"

"Yes," I said, from my distance. "You are going to do what I say. You are going to go home, pack one suitcase, pick up your jewel case, for I presume you have one, and get out of town, destination unknown. As for you and me, I trust that we can legalize things in short order."

She was now staring at me with wide, glittering eyes.

"And," I added, "I'll resign here, shake the dust off my feet, and hunt a job for next year."

I felt, all at once, free, reborn, redeemed. Life, all at once, seemed to be simple and bright. Every blade of grass in the far stretch of pasture shone individually in the sun.

CHAPTER XII

That moment when I heard my voice coldly laying out the program, and when I saw, out of her distress and dishevelment, Rozelle's eyes suddenly come agleam with life—that moment can, now and then, return to me with its full sense of elevated and icy triumph. And remembering her face across the distance of that kitchen table, I have sometimes wondered if, over the years, that moment ever returns to her with its full reality. For then the vision of freedom and fulfillment in love seemed not a promise, but a thing already accomplished.

For that one moment, outside the texture of actuality, outside of Time, we seemed, paradoxically, to be living in the meaningfulness of time.

"Yes, yes!" Rozelle cried out.

"And I'll hunt me another job," I was saying, feeling another surge of release.

Then I realized that the eyes were fixed on me with another kind of look, a look of confusion, of alarm: "No," she said, in a sort of throaty whisper, shaking her head, the lips framing the word in a strange, mechanical motion, as though they had just learned to frame it.

"Listen," I said, with a violence that simply burst out of me, "I've had a bellyful of this place—hell, I don't want to ever see it again, and I shouldn't think you'd want to, either."

She was still looking at me in that way.

"You don't mean to say you want to come back here."

"No," she said, "God, no!"

"Well," I said. "I can't predict where we'll go. We'll just have to wait and see where I can get a job. And one more thing. We'll live, except for your personal little luxuries, or an occasional spree, on the scale of my salary. Is that clear?"

She was motionless now, and staring at me, with a peculiar depthless blankness, like an upland pool, on an absolutely windless day, staring up at a lead-gray sky.

Then she said: "I've got to go! I've got to be there when he wakes up. I've got to—"

"You've got to get that bag packed," I said, and moved around the table toward her. "If you mean business."

"All right," she said, in a placatory tone, even as she seemed about to retreat before me.

I grasped her firmly by the upper arm. "This is serious," I said. "You use the word *love*. And I use it. I'm not too damned sure I know what the word means, but I'm damned sure it doesn't mean me hanging around in this shanty waiting for you to take a half-hour off for a quickie. I'm not cut out to be your stud in a pen. Do you get me?"

She nodded, still looking at me with that depthless blankness, even as I felt a slight pull against my grasp.

"Phone me," I commanded. "As soon as you get a chance."

"If I get a chance," she said hurriedly, her face a little averted.

"Make a chance," I said. "I'll wait in, all afternoon, all evening. And the call I'd like to have would be from you at the airport."

"I'll have to see," she said, and again I felt the pull against my grasp.

"Get one thing clear," I said, tightening my grip. "I might just take it into my fool head to come right over to the Carrington house and make an awful stink. Especially if there are guests present."

I released the grip, and even as she stepped back a little, her right hand reached out to rub her left arm, the upper arm, as though I had hurt her there.

"Remember," I said, resurrecting my most theatrical Dugton accent that had once wowed 'em in the Chicago Graduate School, "I mought come ri-et over to that-air J. Lawford's big ole white house, and—"

"No," she cut in breathlessly, "no, it'll be all right," and with this she had flung herself against me, flattening herself, left arm around my body, right raised in an embrace to draw my face down to her.

I let myself be drawn down to kiss her. It was, for both, a dry-lipped, mechanical, cold operation, but suddenly, tightening the embrace on my neck, she tongued me.

In my instant of surprise and confusion, she pulled away from me, and was out the kitchen door.

I stepped out the door and stood on the back stoop, watching her as she ran across the yard, not turning to the gate to the pasture, the shortest way back, but toward the right, to the stile to the woods' path, where she would have cover from all that openness. She ran with a full, free stride that somehow absorbed without canceling the fluent side-sway and arc of female motion. Back in the early fall I had seen her, in tennis shorts, on the Carrington courts, and the first time I had been favored by the spectacle of the brown-legged sickle-sweep and swaying intercalation of motions, that pivot, sway, swing, torsion and tiptoe, that interabsorption of speed and femaleness—well, that moment had damned near jarred the gold out of my back teeth. I now stood on the back stoop and watched her run, not once looking back, to the stile, mount it, leap down beyond, and disappear among cedars, still running.

As she disappeared, I became aware that, watching, I had been standing there with the spread fingers of my left hand over my mouth —the gesture of a retarded child. I became aware that in the back of my mind had been lurking the image of Rozelle Hardcastle, at the

New Year's Eve party, geological eons ago, at the instant of the unveiling of the sculptured head, when she had embraced her husband and given him the treatment.

To keep the lid on, she had later explained to me.

I withdrew my fingers from my mouth. I stood there staring down at them.

.   .   .

I set to work at my desk. I had resolved to focus all my strength on the scribbled notes before me, or on the blank page on which I hoped I would, now and again, be scribbling. After three hours I heard the clock strike two, and felt a leap of the heart and a twitch at the groin. Then, with an ironical twist of the mind, and of the face, I realized that the joke was on Old Broke-Nose. This might be Thursday, and this might be the sacred hour of 2 P.M., but today no little girl from Dugton would come switching through the kitchen door wearing a dewy smile on damp-gleaming lips and toting that nonpareil Alabama pussy, which was, no doubt, damp-gleaming in the darkness of its appropriate anatomical location.

But the joke on Old Broke-Nose wasn't very funny, at least not to him, and the morally snobbish pleasure in self-irony did not prevail, and there was nothing left to do but open a can of tomato soup and try not to look angle-wise out the kitchen window toward the stile where the path debouched from the woods, and where now the sunlit whiteness of blossoming dogwood fringed the darkness of cedars.

When the telephone rang, I held my breath and moved with immense dignity toward it, telling myself all the while to take it easy, then soberly holding the instrument in my hand a solid second before speaking into it. All my control turned out, however, to be superfluous. It was merely Mrs. Jones-Talbot saying she was dismally sorry and sorely dejected but she had to miss our session the next day, a Friday, she had been called by pressing business up in Kentucky, and would I forgive her. I forgave her.

Meanwhile, there was this particular afternoon to get through with, so I manfully hunched at my desk. At six o'clock, I took a half-hour off. By ten, when no call had come, I got up and began to pace about the house, and as I paced, the house seemed to get tighter and tighter around me, to be contracting like some peculiarly ingenious and diabolical medieval device of torture. With relief I suddenly remembered that I hadn't answered my mother's last letter. To answer it seemed, again suddenly, very important.

I took penstaff in hand and wrote. I acknowledged with appreciation the latest chapter of what I had long since termed in my mind the "matter of Dugton." I said that I agreed with my mother's estimate of Chester Burton, and that no doubt Miss "Pritty-Pants" was better off where she was—and piously added, "wherever that was." But as I wrote that down, I wondered uncomfortably how I'd ever clear things up with my mother when "Miss Pritty-Pants" packed that suitcase and we started to legalize our bliss. Well, there was no use worrying one's gray-haired mother now, I decided. But, disingenuously, I did begin to lay a little groundwork. I said that she, my mother, was, I had to admit, right about Nashville, Tennessee, as being too close to Alabama, and I was seriously considering hunting a job elsewhere.

Somewhere out of the South, I went on—maybe in South Africa, ha ha!—or south Chicago, but not in *the* South. Nothing wrong with Nashville, I said, that a thousand miles wouldn't cure, if I was at the other end of the thousand miles. Or a good earthquake, either, if I was where I could read about it in the newspaper the next morning. Writing this down to make her laugh, it being the sort of thing I knew she would laugh at and read aloud to Perk Simms. Writing it down, too, to please her by admitting my mistake in coming here in the first place. To soften her up for the big shock. When it came.

With this, I began to wonder what Nashville was really like, for, in that moment, I realized that I didn't have the remotest notion. What did I know? Quite coldly, I asked myself what my life here would have been—what Nashville would have seemed—if Rozelle had never laid eyes on Lawford Carrington, who was Mr. Nashville Himself. I would not have known Maria McInnis. Nor Cud Cudworth, who declared himself to be a by-product of history, or a waste-product. Nor Mrs. Jones-Talbot, with her horses, and perfect

Italian accent, and the house she called her allegorical whimsy. Nor anybody else I did know.

Nor would I have known, Biblically speaking, Rozelle Hardcastle herself.

I tried to think how things might have been. I would have worked late at night in my hotel room or little apartment. I would have had a new article nearly done by this time. (On what? I wondered.) I would have begun taking some female graduate student out to the movies, or maybe a junior lady professor. I would have begun to have a friend in the department. A *real friend,* I amended, of the sort I had never had. We would have swapped ideas. Eventually, I would have told him about my childhood. Then later about Agnes and how she lay in South Dakota. I would have begun to take an interest in my students. In some boy from the mountains who would twist his big hands together as though tearing something apart, saying just give him a little time, Professor, and he'd get it, he could learn anything, give him time to get a grip on it, and the big hands would work and twist. Or some girl from a cotton farm in Mississippi, with a plain face and gray yearning abstract eyes that would flash when she caught the rhythm of a line.

I might have stayed on in Nashville, five years or so. Till my next book, and the offer of a better salary, less teaching, at some fancier place with a big research library, a step up. (From what, to what, I asked myself. Why?)

No, I might have stayed here, have married the lady professor, or a nice scrubbed-looking technician in the Medical School, have had a couple of children, become gradually a fixture here, with a lengthening bibliography, a sound name in the trade, a name that, if not one to conjure with, was enough to make me locally great, balding and getting a paunch, and maybe beginning to drink too much.

When my meditations had reached this point, I marched into the kitchen and poured a drink. I hadn't really been thinking about Nashville, I decided. I knew I hadn't. What was I really thinking about? I stood there, drinking my drink, by the electric icebox. The box hummed like a pain in the head. It hummed like the question: *What am I thinking about?*

In my mind, then, I said it: *I am thinking about me.*

Then I said it: *I am thinking about me—if there were no Rozelle Hardcastle.*

But there was one, and she lay yonder in that white farmhouse beyond the woods, beyond the meadow, and I had to struggle to prevent myself from going out of the kitchen into the dark, and over the stile and down the woods' path to stand—as many nights before, I had stood—in the shadow of trees and stare across the open, unprotected space toward the house where she lay.

.   .   .

The next morning, toward noon, the call came. She said she couldn't talk then, the voice quick and muffled. For me to come out through the woods—no, by the longest way, the back woods, and she'd meet me there as soon as possible, to come about halfway and wait.

The phone went dead at the other end.

By three I had entered the other woods, west of my house, and begun the long circle around. It was overcast and drizzling now, with a falling temperature, more of the same lousy, late spring, and as I walked the soft, soundless path, huddled up in my old black slicker, I could hear the drops of water on small new leaves, these woods being deciduous. About halfway I spied a sort of glen to one side, backed by a humped-up, lichened outcropping of limestone, masked by a growth of cedars. I stopped in the path, and waited.

Ten minutes later Rozelle appeared around the bend of the path, saw me and began running toward me. She ran right into my arms, not holding her face up to be kissed, just clinging to my body, pressing her face sidewise against the slick black rubber of my chest, breathing hard. I pushed her off a little, and loosened the black slicker so at least she didn't have to press her face against that. Her face was now pressing against my old flannel shirt.

I can't say how long we stood thus. I was hearing nothing but her gradually subsiding breath and drops on the leaves. There wasn't even a distant crow-call. I finally said for her to tell me, tell me what was happening. She said no, not yet, no, for me just to love her; a minute later, standing there, she slipped a hand up to unbutton my shirt (the top button being already open, or rather lost), and thrust her face, her mouth actually, against my chest. She moved her mouth a little to one side, where the swell began, and set her teeth in, almost enough to hurt.

She wouldn't go to my house. There wasn't time, she said. We went off the path, into the cedar-masked glen, and there, at the end of the open space, with her body propped against the big bole of a leaning beech, in a cold, quick, strained way, with the drizzle beginning to turn into rain, we drove on through to the end of the operation. She had forethoughtedly not worn any impedimenta.

So she, with her raincoat still on, even if the rain hat fell off, and me in the black slicker, the black-rubber rain hat not falling off but generating excessive sweat in my unventilated hair—we did it cold, quick, and untender, and then I quickly got back to my question, what the hell was happening.

Her husband was sick-abed. The doctor had come twice. It looked like pancreatitis, he said—though Rozelle said it was nothing but a sham, a way of feeling sorry for himself, or at the best just psychosomatic. He wouldn't go to the hospital. Hell no, he wanted to have her by his bed, so she had to listen to him talk all the damned time, he claimed to have new ideas for his work, how they should move to New York or Rome, quit teaching, it was so stultifying—though, she added, he'd never have the nerve to go anywhere. Never get out of this womb, this goddamned daydream in which he was Mr. Nashville and Leonardo da Vinci in one package. But he was now being so sweet —if only he wouldn't pull that sweetness that she already knew too goddamned much about!

At this point I asked if the suitcase had been packed, and she finally managed to say no, how could she under the circumstances. At which I demanded what circumstances, the bastard wasn't going to die, was he? She suddenly burst out, with a savagery that surprised me, that she wished he would die, then seemed overwhelmed by what she had said, saying no, no, not that, but I ought to try to understand and not make things harder.

With nothing settled, the conversation wound up on the ground, for the bleached-gold beech leaves of last season gave a thick and unbroken, if wet, carpet that would leave no mud-mark or stain on the back of her gaberdine, and the black slicker, unlatched but still on its owner, outstretched like the wings of a monstrous black bat, wounded and fallen, heaved and flapped, stirring the carpet of bleached-gold old beech leaves in its pain, while the rain fell.

.   .   .

This scene occurred on Friday, and in substance was repeated thrice in the following week, twice in the little glen and once in my curtained room, for Rozelle had by this time managed to work up the alibi of some urgent shopping. Each meeting was brief, for Lawford was still abed, and at our meetings the same old conversation, though with increasing intensity, was replayed. As for the love-making, it was becoming a rather marginal feature of the assignations, obsessive but marginal and—to adapt Thomas Hobbes's description of life—nasty, brutish, and short. It was both an interruption of, and a flight from, the scarcely specified struggle between us.

I am sure, looking back, that we were blaming the not totally satisfying nature of our trysts on the lack of civilized comforts in our glen, and I am sure that, in the occasion at my house, we both had expected to recapture something of the old magic. But there, things were, in a way, worse. And the intensity of the conversation was worse, too. I finally and flatly declared to Rozelle that I thought she was, at the best, kidding herself, that she had no intention of packing that suitcase. This brought shock and tears and the accusation of lack of trust.

"What the hell are you waiting for," I demanded. "You don't owe him anything. In a week he'd have something lined up for his health's sake, and—"

"Oh, there's always some little art-loving debutante tart breathing heavy around him," she said, with what struck me, even in my preoccupation, as an irrational bitterness.

"Sure," I said, "and why should you care? And if he's not really rich, he's got plenty of money, and—"

"No, he hasn't," she said.

"Hasn't what?"

"Got plenty of money."

271

"Well, somebody has," I said, "the way it gets spent, and if it's yours in such quantity, and you feel you have to buy him off, give him some and get shed of him."

Here she again gave me that blank look. And I declared, with the sudden excitement of a vision, that I thought she was afraid of J. Lawford Carrington. "No, no," she protested with great excitement, "not that!" She added that I didn't understand.

So there we were, with tears, and sharp fingers pushing me away, and the accusation that I had never loved her, and my blurting out that if this was love, then to hell with it, and to cinch matters, the highly identifiable snappy little white Mercedes sports car was zipping down the lane toward the highway with no hand out to wave goodbye.

Then, standing by my open garage door, behind which the highly identifiable little white crate had been concealed during our love-making, there was me staring down the lane, wondering what love was, if this was it.

.   .   .

The next day was Friday, on which, as I had told Rozelle, I was to resume the Dante lessons. That afternoon, shortly after two, I mounted the old granite steps to the geometrical garden of my pupil's architectural whimsy, and for a moment paused to look westward over a land lying lyrically beautiful, I had to grant, in the wash of a perfect spring day that was only some four weeks behind schedule.

When I was admitted, I found my pupil and two guests at what was apparently postprandial coffee, a man and a woman, the man of thin-shanked, tight-muscled, sun-burned, and balding middle age, wearing old flannels and an even older shooting jacket, with leather piping and, at the right shoulder, leather reinforcement, the woman much younger and looking like an advertisement for the well-heeled country life, with eye shadow and plenty of it. After introductions, they quickly finished their coffee and withdrew, but before we settled down to work, Mrs. Jones-Talbot explained that my other pupil, Mrs. Beacham, would not be coming today, and that, alas, a little later there would be an interruption, some farm business laid out for the morning had had to be postponed, *force majeure,* but she wanted to get every scrap of the lessons possible, and she hoped I would not take things amiss.

Toward three-thirty a black lad, in castoff horsy clothes, came to announce that they had things ready down at the lot. Rising, Mrs. Jones-Talbot asked him to tell Uncle Tad she'd be right down. Then to me: "I don't know how long things will be, but maybe not very long. If everything goes well, Dark Power will be covering that mare in short order." The mare, she added, belonged to the people I had just met, the Hollingsworths, from down in Maury County. He knew horses, she said, but "nothing else." And: "Certainly not women." And I could well see that Mrs. Hollingsworth was certainly not my pupil's cut of woman, my pupil in checked blue gingham, some kind of a kerchief tied around her head, bare brown feet stuck in beat-up sneakers, and no eye shadow.

Meanwhile, my pupil was saying that of her three studs, the one today was the best. Nasrullah blood in him, she said. She asked me did I know much about horses. I said I knew something about mules.

At which she laughed in a friendly way, and I gave an ironical inner twist of mind at my private joke.

With Thoroughbreds, she was saying, breeding was always natural. "Natural," she said, "if you want to call it that. It's certainly not natural like out west where a stallion just runs with a herd and nature takes its course. With Thoroughbreds there's a lot of pomp and circumstance, as you'll see. But at least it's not like the artificial—or half-artificial—insemination for harness animals."

We were approaching the space in front of the first barn, where a group was already assembled.

Anyway, Mrs. Jones-Talbot was saying, it was a pretty complicated business. And, she concluded, rather awe-inspiring.

In the area ahead of us, in the middle of a group of people standing well back, I could see a man holding the lead of a sleek, sun-bright, nervous roan animal, and another man, some ten feet away, held that of a little colt, roan too. That man kept fondling the head of the colt.

"What's that colt doing there?" I asked.

"That foal," she said, "belongs to the mare that's going to be bred. They brought mother and child up yesterday—in that red van yonder

—up from Maury County. You see, you separate a mare from her little foal and she goes crazy. This foal is just three weeks old."

"Three weeks," I echoed, in what was supposed to be polite astonishment, and she said, "Yes, gestation is eleven months and the ideal time for birth is March or April."

We had come up to the group around the mare. The old black man —Uncle Tad—stood there in his red flannel shirt, old tweed cap, old jodhpurs, exuding an air of quiet authority. There was, too, a young college-student type, chino pants stuck in boots, and a young girl in dungarees and blue shirt with sunglasses (horse-crazy like him, and part-time from the university). Then a middle-aged man in a disreputable black cardigan (Mrs. Jones-Talbot's manager, it developed), and a couple of black stable hands. Then, off at a distance, the owners of the mare. All this, not to mention five or six assorted dogs and as many cats, all gravely watching the proceedings.

"Hello," Mrs. Jones-Talbot said cheerily. "All set?"

"Yes'm," Uncle Tad said.

The college boy, standing a little to one side, gathered the mare's tail into a neat, glistening red swatch, and Uncle Tad produced something that looked like a broad Ace bandage and, from root outward, began, with scrupulous accuracy, to bind up the tail.

"That," Mrs. Jones-Talbot explained, "is to keep any tail hairs from getting caught in the process. Cuts, infection." Then, saying, "Let's go over to see the corespondent-to-be," she led the way to a little shedlike building in which were four stalls, with gates of steel netting giving on the open space.

Some twenty-five yards away, in a paddock, a glossy black horse that had been grazing lifted his head toward us, then suddenly whinnied, tossed mane, and began madly racing and curvetting about the enclosure. "It seems he knows what's in order," Mrs. Jones-Talbot said. Then toward the black horse in the midst of his cavorting: "You'll just have to wait, young fellow, your time's coming." Then back to me: "Right now, it's the track, not family life for him, and we have good hopes for him. Last year he won the Youthful—that's a stakes race in New York."

Only two of the four stalls in the little shed were occupied. "There's the big boy," Mrs. Jones-Talbot said, and there, after the bright sun,

I saw the shadowy shape of the big boy, a big black horse with a white star on the forehead, the big eyes in a wide imperious gleam from the dimness. "He's blood royal," she said, indicating a frame of printed sheets affixed beside the stall door, "and there's the Almanach de Gotha to prove same."

I looked at it, the printed sheet, under glass, in a most cursory fashion, for nothing meant anything to me. The big black fellow with the white star, whose ancestry was thus attested to, gave a great snort and pawed once. His owner reached over the gate and ran a hand from the star down the long thrust of bone, down to the flaring nostrils. "Just hang on, fellow," she said, "it won't be long now."

And to me: "Let's go. I reckon they're teasing her now."

"Teasing?" I said in question.

"Yes, that's the term for it in the trade," she said. "Just a little preliminary, you might say, to prepare the mare's mind. But the gentleman in the case, he is only a stand-in. It's not for him, poor fellow."

The group that had been in the open space was gone now. We went on into the first barn, where in the shadow, in decorous silence, the group, human beings, dogs, cats, little foal and all, were disposed in a wide semicircle. The mare was facing a stall, her head thrust in over the gate, and inside there was the head of the teaser, nuzzling the mare, then twitching and jerking from side to side. The mare's bound tail had lifted.

"She's a-blinken," Uncle Tad said.

Then I saw what he meant. The tail of the mare being lifted, the aperture about which all the ritual centered, was indeed blinking, with a flash of inner flesh-red visible at every blink. *Blinking*—there was no other word for it.

"All right, Uncle Tad," Mrs. Jones-Talbot said, and led the way back into sunshine, followed by him, by the mare (led by the boy), by the foal (now in charge of the girl), by the rest of us, including a few additional cats just acquired.

Uncle Tad went to the stall where the big black waited; he entered, snapped a lead line to the halter, and led him into the open. After him, with great dignity, looking neither to right nor left, a billy goat stalked out, some five paces behind the stud.

"Hello, Natty," Mrs. Jones-Talbot addressed the dignitary, then turning to me, said: "That's Natty Bumppo. He is Dark Power's guide, philosopher, and friend." Natty had, meanwhile, taken a lordly position, well detached from dogs and cats, as well as human beings, and regarded the whole affair with a critical air.

"He's beautiful," Mrs. Jones-Talbot was saying to me, nodding toward the black. "He has the nearest to perfect conformation I've ever seen, and he passes it on. His get all have his head, and his shoulder especially, and that real soundness of limb. And look at that short back—" and she pointed.

"You seem to know all about horses," I said.

"Nobody knows all," she said, "but I do know more about horses than about Dante."

"You know a lot about Dante," I said.

"Not like horses," she said. "And I ought to know something about them, I've been at it since the age of three. My father, he knew as near all as anybody ever, and he always had me with him."

Uncle Tad was doing something to the stud's dong.

"It's a ring around it," Mrs. Jones-Talbot explained, seeing me eye the process. "To keep from losing sperm—spilling it on the ground, as the Bible phrases it. It's pretty valuable, you see."

I laughed.

"Oh, I mean it, quite literally," she said. "That's the way he earns his keep."

The ring was off now. Uncle Tad took the lead line from a helper and led the stud back of the mare. The girl held the foal some ten feet ahead of the mare, in full sight. There was perfect silence, human beings, dogs, cats, goat. The stud was whiffing at the mare. Then, at an angle of some thirty-five degrees, and slightly to one side, the stallion thrust his head out as far as possible, head and neck making a straight line, straining toward the sky, and the bright sunlight poured down. The great instrument of the stallion was emerging, assuming its portentous shape.

Again the whiffing, and again that strained, ear-flattening, aspiring straight line of neck and head angled toward the sky. Suddenly all was ready, and the beast, with more of a deep-chested snort than a whicker, had risen, front hooves pawing the air as though to climb that empty bright blueness. There was the big black dong, rigid and looking like a baseball bat, big as an old Louisville Slugger, with the grip-end set toward the business, true as a compass. Then, with one touch of guidance from Uncle Tad, the stallion, for the home thrust, now fell forward to cover the mare, a foreleg to each side, just back of the mare's shoulders, the forelegs moving with a short, curling-back, tense pawing motion.

After a little, Uncle Tad said: "That's it."

He gave a slight tug to the lead line, and the stud disengaged himself, and, on the instant, the group began to mill around, conversation broke out, and dogs and cats drifted away on their private affairs, while the girl, setting a yellow plastic bucket on the ground, sponged off the now less impressive member of the main performer who had just favored the roan mare with the fabulous seed of Nasrullah. Uncle Tad reestablished the preventive ring. That done, the goat led the way back into the royal stall.

The Hollingsworths had turned toward what was, as God predictably willed, a bright-red new Cadillac coupe, and my pupil was moving toward me, across the now vacant area. I looked westward across the beautiful stretch of training field and meadow, through the bright air, to the far-off hills.

"All right," the voice said briskly, near me, and I turned.

"Now," she said, "for another juicy little chunk of Dante."

There was, over all, that strange, timeless farm silence that comes in the middle of the afternoon, the kind of summer silence that may be broken only by the thin, tinny crowing of a rooster, at a great distance.

We moved up the rise toward the house, Mrs. Jones-Talbot's face with the expression she must have habitually worn in solitude.

"Well," I remarked after a moment, "it was, as you said, rather awe-inspiring."

"Oh, yes," she answered mechanically.

I looked down and saw the trim feet in the not-new blue sneakers move in their precise tread, each foot set perfectly straight in the small

277

gravel. Some dirt, I noticed, had got smeared on the tan of the bare left ankle. The ankle toward me.

"One of the Sforzas—" I began, then stopped, feeling pedantic and foolish.

As though from a bored politeness, she said: "Oh, yes—the Sforzas." Then, seeming to remember her politeness: "What about them?"

"Oh, nothing," I said, "just something that happened to cross my mind."

After a moment: "Well, what?"

"One of them, I forget which—the old ruffian himself, Francesco or Galeazzo or Il Moro—" I said. "Anyway, one of them, to entertain his lords and ladies on balconies of the palace, would have a number of ready mares turned into the courtyard, and then stallions released to them. Torches flaring from the balconies. Wine being served. Music, of course." I paused. "Or it might not have been a Sforza at all. Just some other Renaissance type."

She laughed, but in a cut-off way that did not encourage conversation.

So we went on up the rise.

In the house, she moved toward the little table, where the two books lay open. Then she stopped, looking across the distance at the books with what suddenly seemed to be an air of distaste. As I stood there, puzzled, she lifted toward me a cloudy, uncertain, inward-nagging, almost resentful gaze, totally different from her natural clarity.

She had been wearing a kerchief or bandanna or some such cloth to bind her hair, and now she drew it off—snatched it off, really—and tossed her hair loose in a quick, irritable motion. She flung the kerchief toward a chair, and when it fell wide, I made a movement to pick it up.

"Oh, leave it alone!" she burst out.

When I proceeded to pick it up and lay it on the chair, she did not even notice the act, much less acknowledge it.

"You know," she said abruptly, "I've just thought of something I've got to do. If you'd forgive me for breaking off the—"

She stopped.

278

"Sure," I said.

She stood there for a long moment, still not looking at me. Then she swung toward me. "What a liar I am!" she cried out angrily.

I must have been standing gap-jawed at this outburst.

"At least, God damn it," she resumed, somewhat more controlled, "I don't have to lie to myself. I'm too old for that."

She was looking me full in the face now—eight or nine feet from me—with the directness that was her way, nothing cloudy or uncertain or self-nagging now in the blue-gray eyes.

I felt a sudden dryness in my throat. I looked down, and saw the smudge of dirt on the brown skin of the left ankle. I noticed how the lace of that sneaker had been broken, then knotted together.

"You know," she was saying in a very even, very detached, voice that, to me, seemed to come from an immense distance—or to be coming from nowhere at all, to be originating in my own head—"for whatever interest it may be to you, I suppose I feel like those ladies of Sforza's court were supposed to be feeling when the Duke put on one of his torchlight shows down in the courtyard."

I found that I had made a movement of surprise—scarcely a movement, some automatic shift of stance. Then, aware of that, I froze myself.

"What a fool I am!" she was saying. "And me an old horse-breeder, too." She gave a quick, ironical little laugh, and a smile, then, one that seemed to have girlish innocence and sincerity in it.

"And nobody," she said, "is more surprised than I am, at what a fool I am." And turned away toward the corner of the room where the discreet stairs were. There she paused, a hand on the railing, and turned toward me. I had not moved.

"You're an awful nice fellow," she said, with something of that smile, ironical though friendly and sincere, yet on her face, "but don't feel you owe me any politeness—Jesus, not that. For I intend to just go up and jump into a pair of jodhpurs and go run a horse to a lather and come back and take a cold shower and down a lonely bourbon and eat a hearty dinner—if Lucille ever gets back to fix me one—and tumble into bed and sink into a middle-aged lady's blameless sleep."

With that, she was disappearing briskly up the stairs, the sneakers making no sound. She had, in fact, disappeared before my G.I. shoes began to traverse the pale gray-blue ceramic tiles toward the foot of the stairs.

I didn't believe a word of what was happening. It was happening, and I was thinking, at that very instant, that nothing—mysteriously nothing—would have happened if I had not seen that smudge of dirt on the tan left ankle that thrust so trimly down into the beat-up old sneaker.

.   .   .

In the little hall at the head of the stairs, light fell through the open doorway. Within, I could see her, back to the door, by one of the wide, low windows that gave on the west. I had entered and was standing there—sheepishly, no doubt—before she turned. She gave that smile, more friendly now than ironical, though still cool, a perfectly natural smile. Out of the tail of my eye, I observed that the gray covers of the big, very low platform bed, backed against the inner wall to face the panorama of the west, had been neatly laid back. I stood there wondering if she had done that before she heard my tread on the stair. Or had a maid done it? In a crazy jerky way, like a June bug on a thread, I wondered if she could always tell how things would come out.

"In a minute," she was saying, in a perfectly natural tone, and opened a door to what, I gathered from the glimpse as she entered, was a dressing room.

The door closed, and I stood there paralyzed in my sense of unreality, and trapped, too, in the crazy notion that she could foretell everything. I was not even noticing what the big room was like, aware only of size, light, and air, in a kind of unclutteredness. Then I began to undress, slowly arranging my garments, carefully folded, on a chair. From the dressing room I could hear the faint sound of water. Gingerly, as though I might break something, even myself, I got into bed, very careful to not rumple things. Once in bed, because of the lowness of the window sills, I could still see the sweep of greening land and spring sky, across which gleaming white cumulus timelessly lazed.

I heard the faint click of the dressing room door. Mrs. Jones-Talbot stood there, very trim and erect, wearing a long dark gray raw silk robe—or what looked like that—with dark red piping and sash, the sash tight about the neat waist. Her gray-streaked hair had been brushed now, no longer in the disorder left when she had snatched off the kerchief and flung it, so inaccurately, at the chair.

She looked toward the open windows and beyond, and at first I thought she was going to draw the curtains. Then, somehow, I knew with perfect certainty that this was not something she would do. She merely looked out the windows, as into distance, then, in the full light of afternoon, seemed to take a deep, slow breath, moved toward the hall door and, with a quiet businesslike air, threw the latch and approached the bed. With the same air, she threw a little switch by the telephone. For a split second, she stood there looking down at the bed, including me as though I were part of the bed, holding the robe tight about her (this to no disadvantage of her figure), her hands at the knot of the red sash.

I saw the fingers making small secret motions at the knot, as though they were trying to do something on the sly, without her knowledge. Then, quite deliberately and resolutely, the fingers untied the knot. The robe, however, was not allowed to slide off and down. Rather, in a sidewise swaying motion, she seemed to slip out of it, the robe still in her hands, still between her body and the bed, so there was scarcely more than a flash of the paleness of flesh I had unconsciously thought would be tan, and the provocative fusion of female awkwardness and gracility as the body was inserted between the sheets.

She lay close to her edge of the bed, fingers holding the hem of the sheet to her chin. "Oh, dear, oh, dear," she said, in a small voice, somewhat whimsical, somewhat comic, "what a silly old goose of a fool!"

She lay quiet for a moment, then, in an even smaller voice, but one that was not the slightest bit whimsical or comic, she said: "Oh, please be nice to me."

.   .   .

Well after four-thirty, toward five, really, I was sitting alone in the big living room, with the late light pouring in through a western window, waiting. She had asked me to wait for her downstairs, saying she wasn't one for post-mortems but didn't I think a friendly cup of

---

281

tea would be in order. Lucille was off this afternoon, she said, and disappeared kitchenward, leaving me in my strangely therapeutic post-coital languor and a dim, incredulous blankness.

As brisk, fresh, smiling and detached as ever, she was suddenly there, was pouring the tea, was holding out a cup to the large, brown broken-nailed hand that mysteriously was my own. "Two sugars?" she asked. "That's right, isn't it?" It was right, and I took a sip of scalding draft to restore my sense of reality.

"As I was saying earlier," she casually remarked, taking a sip of her own tea, "I'm not one for post-mortems, though I must say that this little unexpected and, I may add, unique caper will demand some private ones from yours truly. But what I was about to say is that I am one for appreciating to the best of my ability what is worth appreciating in life." She fell into her thoughts. Then: "You know— no, you wouldn't yet have had time enough to learn—that the faculty of appreciation, it's about the only thing that endures to the end."

There didn't seem to be much to reply.

"I was just saying that, appreciation aside, you now look upon a middle-aged lady who's just got herself into a most awful pickle. Through, I should in candor add, every fault of her own."

As I looked at her in some confusion, she said, quite calmly: "You see, I am deeply attached to a certain fine gentleman, of appropriate years. You might say, indeed, that I am in love with him—as he, I flatter myself, is with me. So I, being the sort of simple-minded and single-hearted dame I trust I still am, have stuck myself with a problem. I'm in a pickle with myself and with the gentleman to boot. I've got to 'fess up—but first I've got to figure out the true inner nature of the confession that is in order. By the way, you need some more tea."

So I did.

The tea being provided, the clear, not-quite-British, not-quite-Tennessee voice resumed: "But this isn't your problem, and I devoutly hope that you have no problem, my dear boy. What I am about to say, and—" and here she sipped her tea with a sudden distant and assessing, if not unfriendly look at me over the cup rim, the glance in sharp focus from the tan and shadowy face, her head being backed by the westering light—"I might never have said it—if things had not fallen out the very agreeable but—pickly—way they have."

She had recourse to her tea, then, with the slightest impression of bracing herself, said:

"I am preparing to be impertinent. What I say is said because you are clearly a young man with a splendid future—and, I hazard, a splendid integrity—and I'd hate to see things spoiled. Even for the good old classic—no, I mean romantic—reason. You know Rose Carrington, of course, and—"

I made some automatic stir in my chair.

"—no, don't be alarmed" she was saying. "I am fairly observant, and in this case I have had special opportunities and reasons for exercising my talent. But I'm not a gossip. Speaking of gossip, you have no doubt heard of my brother Nicholas Carrington, who died, back in the Depression, penniless and with a stack of indictments hanging over him. Not, as some gossip still has it, from an overdose of pills. He would have been more likely to use a twelve-gauge. But it was simply a well-timed thrombosis.

"In any case, young Lawford grew up under a shadow. You might say, in a wilderness of shadows. Even at Exeter and Yale and summer camps far from Nashville, and then in the Yale Art School. By a lucky accident I still had my share of the inheritance from Pappa, and I could try to keep him outside the hard facts of life. You see, I was mad about Nicholas, my handsome and charming brother, who was always so wonderful to me, back in the years before things got too thick for me here and I ran away to Radcliffe and Oxford. And Lawford—he was so much like Nicholas.

"Maybe I was wrong. But he was so handsome and charming and like my brother, and at the Yale Art School he was such a star—and nothing could seem wrong, and I loved him like a son—"

She stopped.

"I didn't mean to get so autobiographical," she began again. "It was just that I had to come home to start over. And there was Lawford, the boy I had been praying for as well as paying for, out of my love for my fool brother.

"And Lawford *was* charming! Charmed you to the bone until you saw something else. That it is a tool, a weapon, too.

"Well, I spoiled him. We began to quarrel. He thought he had me.

283

I did think he had talent, he did have talent, and the thing I can't abide is to see people squander talent on vanity. Anyway, if he didn't have talent, he had enormous facility.

"I wanted to get him out of here. To some place where he'd have to match himself and his goddamned vanity against the best— against some uncharming stunted scrofulous wretch of a genius. But oh no! he wanted the easy thing. To be a big shot here—sleep with the debutantes and go off cruising on the Gulf on some damned boat my money paid for. He does know the sea, though, I'll say that for him. Anyway, I finally told him I was going to give him a fixed and not fantastic allowance and a modest annuity in my will, and that was all.

"Then he thought he'd fox me. Turned up married with all sorts of vows to settle down. So I did give him the farm for a wedding present. As for the wife, well, I can't say I greatly took to the way she did over the barn—new already, a rich man's toy in the booming Twenties, but a real barn then, stone, not a Tennessee type. Anyway, she was sweet and in love, in an almost pathological way—her eyes would devour him. But she was so anxious to please, so appealing, so anxious to learn. And spunky. The way she'd go at a jump, I loved it. And the way she'd look you in the eye.

"But there was a sort of wariness. Of suspicion, of calculation, fear even. Like when you surprise a doe, and she stands for an instant with the hind legs slightly bent, and maybe trembling, and one front foot lifted just a little and bent so the tip edge of the hoof just barely clears ground.

"But she did seem good for Lawford. His stuff, though, it got awful. And awful-er. Maybe he was having a delicious tussle in the boudoir, but his advertising of it struck me as a trifle tasteless. Oh God, the *art nouveau* of some new type of *maison de tolérance.* But you've seen it. Only one good thing in years—that screaming head. And that not really good—just expert. What I'm getting at is—you remember the night he showed it at the party?"

I nodded.

"I didn't know what to make of it—not the object—just the fuss and feathers he had made over it. And—or am I dreaming?—the way he was looking at her face all the time. Did you see it?"

"I saw what I saw," I said.

"Perhaps it was all nothing," she said. Then: "No, it was an assault, a threat, something done against her."

I sat there thinking, not looking at Mrs. Jones-Talbot, simply feeling very lonely as though I were surrounded by an infinite space of pale ceramic tile dimly gleaming in late night. I was thinking back on the morning visit to my kitchen when, after I had given my command that she pack up the suitcase, Rozelle had so unexpectedly kissed me goodbye—in a single cold, dry kiss to wind up the kissless morning —and then suddenly had driven her tongue deep in, cold and agile —before she fled across the backyard, to the stile and the shadow of cedars.

"Listen," Mrs. Jones-Talbot was saying, "it's been a slow, growing something. And I don't know exactly what. And there are lies somewhere. He told me long ago that he met her in New York at a party —and gave the date, July, 1946. Then later on, by accident, I heard her tell somebody they had met on Long Island, and the time she specified was in September, 1946. Well, I knew Lawford was in Florida, off on a boat, in September. I had a letter from him. And the bills. Then—"

She stopped.

"At this point," she said, rising, "I am going to give myself some much-needed Dutch courage."

She disappeared pantryward.

"No," she said, returning, "not Dutch courage, just plain old black-label Tennessee courage."

And so poured two drinks.

"A little later," she said, having braced herself, "some months after the marriage, Lawford told me about the husband's death. How she was learning to sail and was at the wheel—this in the Gulf—but a sudden gust hit, and a jibe she should have prevented, and a sweep of the boom knocked the husband off the cabin trunk, where he'd been lying. She did manage to throw him a preserver, but the boat was out of control and she was hysterical and had to watch him drown or die of a heart attack. His body was never recovered."

She set her empty glass down and studied it.

"Maybe," she said, "it's just that things go badly with them. More and more, some desperate little tension getting bigger. Damn it, I'm sure I'm right there!"

She rose, began to pace about. She was not now wearing the checked gingham of the horse lot and the old sneakers. It was the gray knit dress I remembered from the last lesson—when we had read the Sordello passage. She stopped and looked directly at me.

"It's all none of my business," she said, "but I'm making it my business. If you're not in any way involved, put all this down to my evil old mind. But do think it over. There's some logic that would lead the poor, sweet little creature—and I *do* like her, I do find her very appealing—to turn to you. You're from the same little town in Alabama, aren't you?"

"Dugton, Alabama," I asserted, "where my mother works in a cannery."

"And you were friends," she said, ignoring my remark, a fact for which I, in a sudden access of shame, thanked God.

"Not friends. Acquaintances," I said. "She was the Queen of Dugton High, and I—I was what I was."

She looked at me in her level-eyed way—an assessing and accepting way, it might be described—and said: "It is because of what you were —and are—that I'm being so impertinent. But oh, I have so greatly enjoyed the Dante lessons, you've quite scoured my mind and opened my imagination again. How I regret that there'll be no more lessons! For I don't suppose there should be."

I stood up. "I've enjoyed them, too," I said, then found myself going on: "It always meant something to me to come here. To see how you loved the Dante—working at it. I guess it was the best thing around here for me. I'm grateful."

I hadn't meant to say what I said. I hadn't even thought it before. I stood there in embarrassment, feeling my feet big and my wrists getting longer.

"Anyway," I declared, "I guess—maybe, anyway—I'll be leaving Nashville." Then added: "I haven't told anybody yet. Not even at the University. That I'm thinking about it."

"Forgive me for saying so," she said, "but it might not be a bad idea."

She was regarding me in her cool way. "Jed," she said, and I realized with a shock that she had never called me by that name before, not even that afternoon.

"Jed," she said, "your middle-aged, admiring, and grateful pupil would appreciate it if you would come right here and kiss her good-bye."

As I stared at her, remembering the recent past, and all the past, she lifted the right forefinger to touch her cheek.

"Right here!" she commanded, and took the finger away, and gave me, not one of her smiles, but a grin that made me see, with a shock like a jab to the bread basket mixed with a sweet elegiac pain, what she must have so high-spiritedly and shiningly looked like at the age of fifteen or sixteen—or later, much later, even now—if you were lucky enough to be around when the grin came. So she grinned, and lifted the now-unfended cheek, at a slight angle to allow for my height.

I crossed the intervening space, and kissed the cheek as directed—or rather, gave it a sort of embarrassed, chap-lipped peck.

I stumbled back from the kiss, and she put her hand out. "Goodbye, Jed," she said. "I'll always be looking for the great news of you. And I'll always tell myself how proud I was to know you."

"Goodbye," I managed to get out. And plunged on: "I can't tell you how—"

"Hush!" she said, setting a monitory finger to her lips, then removing it to say: "Maybe it would be nicer if you didn't even try."

She was again giving that grin as I turned away.

I was at the door, hand on knob, when she spoke.

"Listen," she said, "didn't I read in the paper that you're going to Florida next week—to Stafford University, isn't it? Don't they call it a 'Salute to Youth'—you being so young?"

I nodded.

"Well, you'll be giving lots of addresses over the years," she said, not moving. "Have a good time."

I mumbled something and went out and climbed into my wreck of a car. I honest to God don't remember how I got out on the highway and on to my house. I remember going into its emptiness, though.

CHAPTER XIII

As the plane heeled on the long descending curve, I caught the first flash of white beaches backed by vitriolic green of trees, and as we looped lower and landward, the same beaches now backed by an infinity of glittering Atlantic and sun-blaze, and there was Florida, like a post card or a tourist's 8mm movie. That is, just the way it was supposed to be.

I had left Nashville in a spring running weeks behind schedule, and now, a calculable matter of minutes later, as I emerged from the interior of the plane, a fully inflamed summer hit me like a karate chop. Then, as I came out of blinding sun into the blindness of shadow in the airport, I blinked at the smiling and predictable, but hallucinatory faces that seemed to float in the air, the faces being those of the welcoming committee of Phi Beta Kappa, a mixed bag of dotards and downy chins, and I found myself grasping for one hand after another, managing to communicate the idea that yes, it had been a fine flight, yes, it was my very first trip to Florida, yes, I liked what I saw, I sure did.

And I was to see more.

In that world of glitter and blur, purple vistas and arcades of shadow so green it was black, nothing seemed quite real. Not all that millions of dollars' worth of glassy, classy, angular and thrusty architecture that a fabulous Mr. Carlos Stafford had lavished on the landscape to create Stafford University. Not the uncountable number of pairs of blue eyes that seemed almost white in the non-ideographic faces of sun-baked but juicy-looking flesh. Not all the hair, male and female, bleached the color of an oat field in harvest time. Not all the nigh-bare, Gauguin-colored bodies flung unaccountably and uncountably about on white sand. Not all the incunabula in the Treasure Room of the Emily Stafford Library. Not the array of delicately swaying masts lined up at the dock, waiting for roll to be called for Sailing II or Sailing XII or something. Not the sound of my own voice when, looking down on rows of politely non-entranced faces, more old than young, except for the impending crop of Phi Betes, I heard, with stunned incredulity, the idiocy I was uttering. The only reality I was, in fact, sure of was the clink of ice in the glass when, finally, all duty done and passion spent, I sat in the Faculty Club, my well-earned nightcap in hand, in the company of local eminence and wisdom, and made grunts that I hoped would pass for conversation.

I had, in sum, three nightcaps—even though the third was tendered me with a marked lack of enthusiasm. Enthusiasm or not, I continued to sit, and wondered all the while if I would ever be as old as the men I now sat with. With the third nightcap down, I thought I might risk going to bed.

It turned out to be a bad risk. At 3 A.M. I was still staring at the ceiling. At 3:30 I was sitting, in pajamas and barefoot, at a desk, leaning under a lamp to stare at a letter.

The letter had reached me by messenger—Uncle Tad, it was—scarcely after dawn that very morning, before I left for the airport in Nashville. I must have read it twenty times on the plane. Now I was reading it again.

———

Dear Mr. Tewksbury—or rather, Jed:

I write this at the risk of being slapped down for not minding my own business, but I accept the risk. If, on your arrival in Florida, you will immediately telephone the number below and ask for Mr. Al Dickson, who will be expecting to hear from you, he will be able to give you certain background material you may find useful in making, shall I hazard, decisions. I do not know Mr. Dickson, but I am assured on the best authority that he is very reliable and scrupulously honest.

You will, by the way, assume no obligations of any sort by making the telephone call or by accepting any information.

Very sincerely yours,

your admiring and grateful pupil,

Rebecca (Dee-Dee) Carrington Jones-Talbot

P.S.   The name of firm is Information, Inc.

Every one of the twenty times on the plane that I had read the letter, I had had the initial impulse to slap down my admiring and grateful pupil, as she suggested, and now, reading the letter in the middle of the night, I had the same initial impulse. Now, as each time on the plane, the initial anger dissolved into a fear of loss, a fear that became focused on the loss of the *corps charmant;* and each time as the fear came to focus in the image, I was aware, automatically, of the thrilling oxymoronic "stigmata" on the right thigh. But each time, reading the letter during the flight, I had known, in stoical despair, that I would, in the end, make the call.

For that very morning on arrival, even as the phone booth had been surrounded by the dawdling covey of Phi Beta Kappas, I had actually made the call. So, in the middle of the night, I knew that this very morning, after a barbarously early breakfast, I would be taking another plane, to Fort Lauderdale, to confront, as per arrangement, Mr. Al Dickson, of Information, Inc.

I got up from the desk and stood barefoot in the middle of the floor of the luxurious Stafford University guest suite. Standing there, heavily breathing the conditioned air of that expensive cubicle, I became aware of the image that now—when? one second, five seconds, ten seconds ago?—had replaced the earlier image in my mind.

The new image was that of another face, the black hair, with the white streak on the left side, loose on a pillow, the head back a little and the commanding gaze gone gleamingly abstract into some distance beyond the ceiling, lips parted, somewhat tensely drawn back at the corners. It was the same face I had seen that bright December afternoon, as she, in what had seemed a dreamlike retardation, lifted Winter Weather over the jump, her face thrust forward into the wind, with an expression, in spite of the excitement, somehow calm and pure. And the face, as now seen, in recollection, was calm and pure, even if there was the rhythmic gasp for breath between the parted lips and even if the rhythm was not now set by the pound of hooves on turf, but by the controlled, synchronic struggle of two naked and intertwined bodies, the rhythm accelerating as for the apogee of the upward thrust against the brilliance of sky.

Then I was again remembering how Rozelle, that same bright December afternoon, watching the face of the rider as the gray mount was lifted over the jump, had turned to me and, in a sudden candor of admiration, burst out that she—the woman lifting the gray mount into the sky—was the person in all the world she would most want to be like, she was so innocent, so complete. Yes, those were the words Rozelle had used of that woman, in that moment: *innocent, complete.*

And this recollection did nothing to simplify my own feelings as I stood in the middle of that floor, long before a May dawn in Florida.

I sat down again in the chair by the little desk and contemplated the smudge of white on the dark floor that was the letter, and I felt a sense of despair as I knew that this morning I would fly to Fort Lauderdale to the telephoned appointment I had made yesterday.

.   .   .

Before leaving Fort Lauderdale, two days later, I knew that there was one very impractical mission I had to accomplish before returning to Nashville. I got a cab out to Bougainvillaea Drive, found the number, and told the cab to wait a block away. The number was in wrought-iron figures set in a great gatepost, the post really being a more massive part of the orange-colored fake adobe of the high wall, capped with red tile, that ran around what Mr. Butler would certainly, with some justification in acreage and dollars per square foot, have called his estate.

Bougainvillaea did, as a matter of fact, spill lavishly over the long wall, here and there. Between the gateposts was a pair of heavy wrought-iron gates, each supported by rollers on a semicircular steel track set in the drive, the gates now closed tight. But between the curlicues, leaves, and scrolls of iron, I could see would be termed the gracious curve of white-shell drive and the gracious sweep of lawn—to adopt the language of the realtor—that looked like nothing so much as the top of the expensive billiard table that Mr. Butler must have had in his game room. Revolving sprinklers misted the slant of late afternoon light. Beyond, I could see the house, very big and clumsy in the Spanish-mission-cum-Hollywood style popular among the rich in the 1920's, in that same orange-colored fake adobe, with juts of dark brown timbers. Along the walls of the structure—the mansion, really—blooms from shrubs or in deep beds screamed with eye-splitting stridency. A silver Rolls waited on the white drive before the deeply shadowed entrance.

I had never been in such a house—that type, I mean. But actually something very funny was happening to me as I stood there. It was as though I'd never been in any house where rich people lived, as though I'd never been in the Carrington place or Mrs. Jones-Talbot's, or even the old Castle of Otranto. I was just standing at a closed gate, staring in, and as I stood there, staring between the curlicues and scrolls of iron, I was trying to imagine what the interior would be like. Something in a movie, perhaps, deep and cool and shadowy, sunlight only filtering through leaves and jalousies, with tile floors, lots of deep divans and cushions and hassocks, the sound of a fountain dripping somewhere.

Inside that house the bridegroom of Pritty-Pants, old Butler, had kept the rough side of life at arm's length, he had really wanted to be toney, and regular, and I was imagining the inside of that house at night, with the guests in elegant clothes, and old Butler's college-girl bride by his side looking the most elegant of all, but all sitting in dimness, with the glimmer of men's starched white shirt-fronts and of female shoulders, while somewhere the fountain prinked and the whir of the projector was faintly audible as it projected one of the blue movies with which Mr. Butler was accustomed to divert his little court.

So I stood there, and an awful sadness and pitifulness came over me, I didn't know why. Then I knew, for I realized that all the time, staring through the closed gate, I'd been trying to relive what Rozelle Hardcastle, at a time in her life when she'd never been in such a rich house, must have felt as she stood on this very spot, looking in and trying to imagine what it would be like to be inside.

Now tears came to my eyes.

For I was asking myself—or rather, knew myself full of the unphrased question—what everything would have been like now if, long back, on a June night, to the muffled music of the Dugton High Senior Prom going on in the gym, I had not merely given Rozelle the single ritual kiss she had so piteously, and calculatingly, asked for, but had clutched her to me, across the distance of Chrysler seat-leather and the impediment of the gearshift, and all the as yet undivulged accidents of time.

But things were the way they were.

.   .   .

Things being the way they were, I arrived at Berry Field, at Nashville, just after dusk, got my car out of the parking lot, drove to my house at the edge of the woods, and waited all evening for a telephone call that never came.

The next day I had to be out at the University all day, but in the morning I waited as long as possible before leaving. At the University the second day, in the afternoon, my office phone did ring. It was a strange voice, asking if Professor Tewksbury was in. I said it was me, and the voice immediately changed, saying, "Jed."

Then again: "Oh, Jed."

I clutched the instrument hard enough to crack it, and history was, for the moment, wiped out. I finally managed to say: "When?"

"Not till Monday," the voice said. Then, in a whisper: "Oh God."

Monday afternoon was my undergraduate examination. But I could manage for that, I quickly decided. I said yes.

"I've been desperate, trying every chance to get you," the voice said.

I said I was sorry.

"You were gone so long," the voice said. "Oh, why were you gone so long?"

I felt the nausea grip my guts, and I was gripping the phone, while a student, a young man in a chair facing my desk, was pretending not to be listening. I said, in a matter-of-fact, impersonal tone, "You see, I'm busy now, I'll tell you when I see you."

"Oh God," the voice said, weak and far away, and I heard the little click of the instrument's being cradled.

I sat there, still gripping the telephone, not racking it, merely staring at it. This until I became aware of the student's eyes on my face. I replaced the phone.

"As for the recommendation," I said to him, "the answer is yes. And a strong one."

Yes, people had to live. They all had to live. That boy, he had to live, had to go to graduate school. All over the world people were trying to live.

To get through the day. Through the night.

Well, I thought, looking at the stuffed brief case on my desk as the student closed the door behind him, at least I had the term papers from my seminar to read. They would get me through till Monday. The papers and, I suddenly remembered, the other things I had to do.

So I returned to the task of sorting things out of my desk drawers. After that I did a lot of telephoning. The Florida number kept on being busy. Then it did not answer, and I'd have to wait, no doubt, till business hours on Monday morning.

I almost forgot to fill out the form for the boy, but I saw it in time. Well, people had to live, didn't they?

.   .   .

Driving back from the University at noon Monday, I had in mind to waylay her in the kitchen, to set her in a kitchen chair and talk across the kitchen table the whole time, in the unblinking light of God's own sun. But my timing was bad. Fifteen minutes before the expected hour, I was in the garage, my hand lifting to close the trunk of a U-Drive-It car, when I heard the slam of the screen door of the kitchen.

By the time I got back to the kitchen, there was nobody there, and I remember, in every distinct detail, the little start of excitement, followed by a pang of shame and guilt, and then the quick flick of self-justification as I reflected that it wasn't my fault, I hadn't made her come early—this as I bolted the kitchen door and turned to move with swift and silent stride on to the spot where I knew she would be.

She was standing there, wearing a blue summer dress, with some sort of white piping on it, looking very fresh and girlish and out of place in the dim disorder of the room, which was, today, even more disordered than usual. Just inside the door, I stopped. She didn't move or say a word, simply looked at me, with eyes wider than usual, even brighter than usual in this dimness, gazing across space with an expression of sadness sweet and unnerving. Then she said, in almost a whisper: "Jed."

Then: "Oh, Jed."

Just as the voice had said on the telephone, and I, trying not to remember anything, aware only of the irrational pumping of my heart, moved slowly toward her. I stopped and stood before her.

Then, as on that afternoon a thousand years back, in the late afternoon light of June, standing on the black-oiled boards of the vacant hall of Dugton High, that afternoon when Rozelle Hardcastle, the true and blushful Princesse Lointaine, had asked me to go to the Senior Prom with her—what I am saying is that now, in the shadowy room in Tennessee, I again saw the face lifted toward me in the same sad, humble, fatalistic innocence and the hand again drift slowly out in the dim air, to revolve on the rounded wrist and expose, at last, the palm, slightly cupped in its pitiful emptiness.

I now stood numb, absolutely catatonic, in this doomful tangle of time. I was waiting for something to to happen. Something did happen, and the last thing I could have possibly predicted. She let the suppliant hand sink, and all at once, as she dropped to her knees on the floor, she reached out to seize my hand—my left one—to press it against her face, kissing it in a soft, shy way, saying between kisses that she knew she could not live without me.

I felt, too, the wetness on my hand, not on the part she had kissed, and knew why the eyes, even in the shadowiness, had been so definitely shiny.

That was what had happened, and it was quite adequate for the occasion.

Afterwards, though overwhelmed by what had happened and

newly convinced that the clasping of bodies was the only thing in the world that could matter, I also had the sense of entrapment, of power-lessness, as though my deepest mind would always be most casually read and my most cunning gambit blunted with contemptuous ease.

But by whom?

By that girl who now lay by my side?

Or was she, in her every word and motion, merely enacting an iron script long since drawn, as powerless as I?

All this, even as, lying by my side, again holding my hand, she was saying: "I kept calling and calling—whenever I got a chance, that is —but there wasn't ever an answer."

"I got back Thursday night," I said.

Then, after a long wait, she said: "What made you stay away so long?"

"I had to."

"But why? Why?" Then: "I thought I'd die."

I fixed my eyes firmly on a defect in the plaster job of the ceiling. "When did you first meet J. Lawford Carrington?"

In the silence I had plenty of time to study the defect in the ceiling. I had the sense that her eyes were fixed there, too.

Finally, she said: "Oh, let's see—it was at a party in New York— or was it Long Island? I'd gone up east—after it—after everything— had happened. To get away, and—"

My voice—from which phenomenon, in that moment, I felt perfect detachment—cut in, admirably cool and objective: "By February 21, 1946, you knew him well enough to go out for an afternoon in his chartered power cruiser. Perhaps, of course, for the first time. The cruiser was named *The Gannet*. If you remember."

The information had, that very morning, been made available. The call to Florida had gone through.

And now I had said it.

The hand holding mine tightened on it. Then it, my hand, was flung aside.

"Don't you understand anything!" she cried out.

"As for the answer to that," I said, "I simply don't know."

"Oh, I wanted to have you know everything, to tell you everything. Don't you even try to understand?" she was demanding. "How things

296

had gotten the way they were with Butler, and—"

"Whatever made you marry him?" I said, eyes on the ceiling.

"If you'd only known what it was like at home. My aunt, how she kept hacking at me, saying in her awful tenpenny–nail-biting, self-pitying sort of way, how she had been the ugly one—oh, she thanked God for being the ugly sister—and my mother, the pretty one, but what good had that done her in her boy-craziness, falling in love with that awful boy—that boy who couldn't get any job but a brake-man—"

Her breath gave out.

Then resuming, cold and calm now: "Oh, she'd lick any Burton's spit, and you know what happened. And she blamed me, she said she bet I'd opened my knees to that—that Chester, Jesus Christ!—and he didn't respect me any more, that was why he had thrown me over. Then the University. I hated that, all those pimply little smart-alecs and those sweat-popping athletes all chomping Juicy Fruit chewing gum with their big white teeth. Oh, yes, I even tried to fall in love— oh yes, I lost my maidenhead. One good pop and it was gone. On the third floor of a frat house while you could hear the lousy dance band below and the laughing that all seemed to be at you."

Then: "And the son of a bitch—I found he was bragging about it."

She stopped again, but not from lack of breath this time, for I stole a look at her, and, her hair hanging down from a side-slanted head, a desolate inward expression on her face, she seemed to have totally forgotten my presence.

"Then Chester Burton got married, and my aunt, she . . ."

So, in the end, she had run away to Florida. Maybe she was on the make. But by God, she said, she hoped she'd find somebody she could be really fond of in some way. She lived cheap, but she hung round nice places, and she usually had her sketch pad or paint box and easel, and would set it up. So she would be in the grounds of a great hotel. Or on the beach. People always notice an artist. For she was a good enough artist, she said, twisting her face, to pass for an artist. In Florida.

In the end, with her money running out, she had, actually, stood outside the gates on Bougainvillaea Drive. At that time, on one side, there was no other estate, so she'd just walked past a realtor's sign and past the palms and brush and tangle of vine, to the beach, and it was low tide and so she'd crossed to the Butler side, not even knowing the name of whoever it might be, and set up her easel, and the third day somebody saw her, but it was old Butler himself who came down to order off the intruder, and found the college girl in her simple smock, with feet bare, the loafers kicked off, and probably a smudge of blue paint on her nose, no doubt, and encountered the amethystine gaze head on, full of appeal and apology—and oh, she was so sorry—but the view here was perfect, couldn't he just let her finish?

She had shown the picture to him, shyly, and explained to him what it was she was trying to catch. She even used some technical language, and the well-set-up, prime-of-life, sun-tanned character, in British walking shorts, with clipped graying mustache and no doubt discreetly dyed hair and belly sucked in—no doubt he nodded gravely as she spoke.

A month or so later they were married. She had, according to her aunt's formula, kept her knees together. Maybe she had had to weep a little, maybe begged him, telling him she wasn't that kind; maybe she had histrionically seemed to have to struggle against her own inclination and preference, then suddenly pushed herself away. This last is, of course, my improvisation.

Anyway, old Butler had a college-girl bride.

She had liked him, she said, really liked him. He was good-looking. He was considerate, and wanted to make her happy. And she was so sick of those boys. "You know," she said, "he was a man, you know what I mean, and—"

"I think I know what you mean," I said, with detachment.

"—and sort of fatherly—well, protective, sort of. And, you know —well, I'd never had anybody like a father around me—to take care of you—my uncle, he just did what my aunt said. And it was sort of nice, feeling somebody valued you, somebody who was strong, and knew things—Oh, can't you understand what it is to be alone in the world? To belong to nobody."

Then, as on that December afternoon at the Jones-Talbot place, she said how Butler hadn't got his money till middle age, and was always trying to make up for lost time, and to learn to do everything right, and always had a dictionary by his bed. He wasn't just satisfied to own race horses and win; he had to be a hell of a fancy rider, too, and he had an instructor, right there on the place. He was always taking care to be young—exercises and health foods, and a masseur coming out every morning.

But even if he was kind and fatherly with her, he just had to be one of the boys, too, to wipe out all the lost years, and so it was always younger people that he had around the place, and showed off to. She meant guests to the place, socially speaking. Other types, Butler only saw in what he called his office, in a wing with a separate door. Rozelle caught only glimpses of them.

The younger gang were toney. Or maybe *fancy* was the word she used. One fellow had been to Princeton—"like Chester Burton," she said, "and he never let you forget it." One of the men was English, and had been in the army over there, and played polo. Another was sort of a Hollywood type, had produced a picture, and was always just getting ready to do another.

"Oh, I thought it was all grand," she said, "thought this was the real thing, the real world. For what did I know? Just Dugton and Tuscaloosa, where the University was, and the movies—and all this looked like the movies, people all dressed up, and the quietest servants around always handing you something. Except—"

The word stopped her.

"Except when?" I finally said. I could hear her breathing in a slow, painful way.

"Except," she said, "when—when he had the movies."

I waited, listening to the way her breath came. Finally, I said: "You mean the blue movies?"

"I loathed them!" she burst out. Then: "There were never any servants around then."

But things were very decorous, according to her. After a movie, the lights would come up somewhat, people would have a drink together, which they'd fix for themselves, no servants being about, and they'd chat, and maybe somebody might tell a not too off-color joke, really clever, and then people would drift off to walk on the grounds or go to their rooms—they even seemed superior to the movies, as though they had merely stumbled casually on them. As though they belonged to another world. It was all very decorous.

Even the night when somebody, after a movie, said they ought to try a round of "Fanny Hill," and out of the dimness, the lights not being up yet, somebody—the Englishman—called out, "What about it, Butler, old scout?"

"I was sitting right there," Rozelle said, "and Butler, he was holding my hand—that's all he ever did at a movie, though some did other things on the sly—and his hand sort of tightened. Then I saw his forehead crinkle sharp and vertical just above the nose, between the eyes, the way it did when he got mad but controlled it."

But then the Englishman called out, "Come on, Butty, you're a true-blue sport!"

That was what did it, Rozelle said, that business of being a sport. Butler swallowed hard, and said okay, and somebody called out, "Bravo, good old Butty!"

Rozelle wasn't quite sure what the game was going to be, but the book was one the girls had passed around in her sorority house back in Tuscaloosa, sometimes cuddling up together for reading parties, and she had a pretty good guess, and guessed right. Cards—bridge cards, just the number of those to play—were divided into two little stacks, one for women, one for men, Ace of Spades and Queen of Hearts being the pay cards. A man announced himself and showed his ace, and then, shyly, one of the women rose, despairingly shook her head, made a cute little *moue*—or what from Rozelle's description must have been such—and wailed, "Oh dear, oh dear, whatever will my mother say?"

And everybody burst out laughing.

The man came and gallantly kissed her hand. The lights were barely up at all. There was only one round that night. That night whoever had laid out the stacks had made each stack one short of the head count. The cards were not offered to Butler and his college-girl bride.

At this point in the narrative I cut in.

"But time marches on," I said, guessing, "and the night the draw was offered to Butler finally came, and I bet he didn't refuse. I bet he remembered that 'Bravo, good old Butty,' and carefully not looking at your face, drew. Is that right?"

After a moment the voice at my side said, "Yes. And I thought I'd die when he took it. Then there was the hand holding out cards at me."

"And Butler wouldn't look at you, would he?"

"No," the voice said.

"Did you draw?"

"Oh, what could I do?" the voice almost wailed. "It was so horrible. Butler pretending not even to be there. All those eyes staring at me. And, too, there was my ignorance, my not knowing how people—outside of Dugton, I mean—how people out in the world really lived." And after a pause: "I've finally admitted that to myself, just scared of being a country hick come to town, or something."

"So you took it?"

"It just sort of happened," the voice said.

"But," it said, "nothing—I mean nothing really—happened."

"You mean Bravo-Old Butty had been playing Russian roulette, and he won?"

"He may have won the game," the voice said, "but he lost me. Right there."

And he lost the game, too, later. A couple of months and two or three games later, his luck ran out, the Queen of Hearts did get drawn, and Rozelle—she thought, hell, she might as well go through with it, it already having happened a dozen times in her mind, and one night, late at night, after a game, when Butler was now sleeping the sleep of the just, having drawn the Ace of Spades, she slipped out and went down to the drawing room, now dark, where the movies were always held, and where waited the big, low divan on which the Queen of Hearts always wound up getting the business, unless somebody had something very exotic in mind, and she lay down there, and with heart pounding like crazy, arranged herself in every detail, even untying the knot of the yellow satin ribbon belt to her yellow silk sleeveless nightgown, and getting ready to remember for always how ice-cold her fingers had felt in doing it. She even lifted her arms to embrace the nameless and spectral lover, and squinched her eyes shut tight and tried to imagine how if you can shut your eyes tight enough and can draw deep enough inside yourself, you might just feel nothing and nothing would matter.

She remembered, too, how once earlier a real nice-looking, well-mannered young woman, not flashy-fashionable in her dress and married to a man sitting right there, a real sort of gentleman-type, had drawn the Queen of Hearts and gone through everything like a breeze over blue grass, just superior to it.

With all this preparation, Rozelle, when she finally got tagged, thought she could manage. But, almost undressed—the Ace of Spades now only in his black silk monogramed boxer shorts (somehow that detail stuck in her head), gallantly doing the undressing—she got panicked, quite literally and etymologically, with shame and disgust, and automatically started to resist the undresser, but everybody thought it was an act, and a couple of people applauded—decorously, of course. And then she really did, in her deepest, self-deriding self, say, oh, to hell with it.

Afterwards Butler had a black dog on his back. He told her she hadn't had to make such a damned show out of it.

But there were no more blue movies. And certainly no more "Fanny Hill." The barn door, however, had been shut too late. The mare was long since gone, spiritually speaking. And before long, more literally speaking. For J. Lawford had appeared on the scene. Not at the house. When she was out painting, which she had taken up again. "I wasn't any good," she said, "but it was a way to be alone. To pretend I was somebody else."

The black dog stayed on Butler's back. Things got grimmer and grimmer. And there was Lawford. "He was so sweet," she said, "he could really be so sweet, back then."

"In June," I announced to the ceiling, "in June, 1946, one evening, Lawford's chartered cabin cruiser foundered. This was some twenty miles down the coast, and he saved himself by swimming ten or eleven miles in."

There wasn't a sound.

"It was the night of June 16," I continued, "the day that Butler died."

Then, after a time, in a strange, calm way, the voice beside me said: "That was the day."

And after a time, in the same tone, added: "But it was not like you think."

302

"I don't think anything," I said.

"Oh, he was a fool to come!" the voice said, not calm now.

"Who?"

"Lawford," the voice said. "He knew it was the place we went."

"We who?"

"Butler and me. To that little isolated island, a cove on the west side. Where he'd exercise on the beach, do handstands and show off, then we'd swim. Naked. But when we got there that afternoon, there he was."

"Lawford?"

His boat was at the end of the cove, she said, and he came over to them in his dinghy. He had grease on him, so he couldn't shake hands when he introduced himself to Butler—and to her, too. He must have thought that was a great joke, she said. He reported that he had engine trouble, but he could fix it, being an old PT-boat man in the Navy. If only some damned fool hadn't taken some kind of spanner he needed, and did Butler have one.

Butler, Rozelle said, was leaping at the interruption. Sure, he'd have the spanner, but he began talking boats in general, then his own in particular. "He was so goddamned proud of everything he had," she said, "including me, I guess, even if he was sore at me. And he just had to show me off a little, the way he said 'my wife,' when he introduced me, and watched Lawford's face for surprise or admiration or something. So we went out in his million-dollar yawl to show off. I was at the wheel so he could be showing every little thing, all his fancy equipment—his fathometer, his luff meter, and radio telephone, and all that crap."

Finally, Butler got bored, and was lying on top of the cabin trunk. Lawford was starboard about midships—I think that was the way she put it—slouching a little against the leeward life lines. Butler was on his back, a hand over his eyes against the sun, for a time making a pretense of conversation.

Coming back in, on a fresh northwest breeze about eighteen to twenty knots, they had hardened up, as she put it, to a close reach to loop the island counterclockwise, it now lying north of them. As they came under the lee of the island, a strong, freak gust hit them, and the boat—it was a big boat, mind you, some forty-five feet or more

—heeled over on its beam ends—what she called a knockdown—and she instinctively put the helm down to bring her up into the wind, and the acceleration, Rozelle said, or her own confusion, carried them right through the eye of the wind, and this simply back-winded the huge genoa jib.

The boat was now falling off fast on the other tack, so Rozelle let go of the wheel, and dove for the cleat that anchored the genoa. She did free it, but for some funny reason it jammed in the snatch block. So the boat kept on turning till it was stern to the wind, with the big boom again sweeping back across the trunk, but this time like God's own scythe. And Butler was what got scythed down, coming out of his doze and floundering around.

"I heard the noise," she said, "and looked up as the sheet I had been struggling with came free. Butler was down by Lawford now, where he had been knocked, staggering and holding his head, just staggering overboard. He was overboard before the yell came. And Lawford was standing there, with one arm sort of in the air, not too far for you to be sure he hadn't made a grab at him. He just stood there frozen now, with a funny, blank look on his face. He didn't even try to throw a life preserver, just staring like he was paralyzed.

She yelled at him to throw a life preserver, there being one atop the cabin trunk, then suddenly she looked up to see about four feet of the boom broken, and whipping and dragging sail back and forth in the cockpit. Anyway, she jumped out on the fantail to dodge the thing and was trying to throw a life preserver. "But," she said, "there he was —Butler—falling behind, maybe not trying to swim, with his mouth wide open, like screaming—like that—that goddamned statue— screaming, even if I didn't hear a thing. Then the whole ocean seemed to be running into his mouth.

"I looked at Lawford—this all in a matter of seconds, you know —and he lifted his eyes to me. I cried out, it just popped out of me: 'Why didn't you grab him!'

" 'But I tried—I tried,' he said, out of that glazed, strange hypnotic trance he seemed in.

" 'Why didn't you throw a preserver?' I yelled, and he said it wouldn't have done any good, Butler could swim and he hadn't even tried, it must have been a heart attack.

"Lawford suddenly seemed to come out of that trance, and I thought he was crazy when he all of a sudden grabbed the life preserver and threw it wildly, off to one side, yelling at me, 'Throw a preserver!'

"But Butler had fallen so far behind now he wasn't visible half the time, and I yelled: 'He's gone!'

" 'Don't be a fool!' Lawford yelled at me. 'Throw it anyway!'

"Then he was down on the fantail with me, and had a preserver loose and had thrown it. He gripped me by the upper arm, looking after the useless life preserver, saying, 'God damn, don't you see, it'll look better this way.' Then: 'Thank God, the boom busted. That will look good.' "

So they crouched there on the fantail, him clutching her arm till it hurt, she said, and telling her that if anybody ever knew he had been on Butler's boat when the accident occurred, it would look bad, for if an investigation got going their affair might come out, and they'd both be lucky to stay out of jail. Even if it was an accident.

His eyes were fixed sternward now, where nothing showed on the water except a life preserver, far off. He was saying in a low voice, as though to himself: "For that's the way it was—an accident."

Suddenly, he was gone, but almost immediately back to announce that he had thrown the radio-telephone out of order in a way that couldn't incriminate anybody, adding, again, that he hadn't been in the PT boats for nothing—oh, he was proud of that! Now he was going back in his dinghy to the island and his boat, and told her, for God's sake, not to start the foghorn or fire off her alarm pistol till he was over the horizon, and if anybody came along, she'd just have a fit of hysterics. Meanwhile, better just lose the pistol.

"But your engine—" she began, and he said: "Hell, I've got a spanner laid away. But lose that pistol. Now!"

At that, she said, he seized her and began kissing her, and she thought for a second or two he was going to drag her into the cockpit and go at her, with the broken boom-end dragging over them. But he didn't. He cast her from him, saying, "Remember—remember what it's like!"

Then he was in the dinghy, ordering her to cast off.

It all worked out fine. The only inconvenience was that Lawford, having decided upon scuttling as a way of establishing an alibi (an alibi that would depend on some luck—but he had it), and being stuck with the idea of swimming in, was stuck, too, for verisimilitude, with the necessity of abandoning his kit and traveler's checks and other such oddments of living aboard. So, in the deep of night, just before dawn (he made it as late as possible, doing some loitering, once he got near shore, to throw the time of the foundering as far back as possible), he made the beach, cold, hungry, about naked, and penniless, and put on a good show of exhaustion.

He had his tale all prepared. He had, he told reporters, done a bit of cruising that day, up and down, and a little fishing, and then, rather late, had been taking a half-snooze on deck, with a highball, but he must have been tireder than he thought, for the half-snooze became a real snooze, long enough to allow, it seemed, for a head-clip to have popped off the through-hull fittings and gently opened the boat to the whole Gulf of Mexico without making him miss one snore. It must have been that way, for when he did wake up, the foundering had gone on so long he had no chance to save anything, especially, since to cap it all, the goddamned dinghy got stuck.

But to cut back a moment, I asked her if she, had she been in Lawford's place, would have grabbed Butler to save him. "Of course, you beast!" she cried out. "And Lawford—maybe he tried to, too!"

"Maybe he did," I said, soberly.

Then she said, in a slow, bemused way: "After I got picked up, after dark, and was put in a hospital, I woke up crying for Butler. I cried a time, then I went to sleep again. And at dawn I woke up remembering that there wouldn't ever be any more Butler. It was the strangest feeling.

"I didn't cry now. I just felt numb, like everything had happened long ago. I felt cold, to my very toes, like ice. Then I was asleep again, and somehow, in my sleep, I knew I was smiling. When I woke up, I could feel how there had been a smile on my face. And that made me feel awful. I tried to cry, but I couldn't. And later—"

She paused for a long time. Then: "Everything was a tangle of dreams. Sometimes I would wake up at night and think it was all only a dream. Sometimes I'd wake up and not know who I was, just for a few seconds that seemed forever."

She paused again. Then: "Later, after we were married, I'd wake up at night and grab Lawford's hand. I'd have that to hold on to, I'd tell myself."

.   .   .

After a while, she said, "It's awful, not knowing."

"What?"

"What really happened."

I lay there a minute, then said: "Listen, why was he there in the first place? Lawford, I mean?"

"Because he's a damned fool," the voice said. "He'd get some kind of a kick out of turning up, looking at Butler and knowing that he knew what Butler didn't know, talking in a kind of double sense, and watching my face—just feeling like God. Oh, I didn't think so at the time—all I did was think he *was* God."

"Even when you yelled at him about not grabbing Butler?"

"That was just a second," she declared, "just popping out of me. It was like it wasn't even my voice. I didn't think anything, really, I was so wild about him, just to be with him."

"Well," I said, "maybe Lawford just had no chance to grab. Or the guy may have had a heart attack."

"Oh, I've told myself those things a thousand times. All night long, sometimes. But when he began to get mean to me—then, in spite of everything, I began to see it."

"See what?"

"I began to see how he just stood there, hypnotized, like watching a dream come true. Like he was God watching Creation. And later on—"

I waited until she pulled herself together, and resumed. "Until," she finally said, "everything began to go wrong. He'd blame me for everything. Then, when he wasn't blaming me, he'd be crazy on sex. Then things began to go wrong there, too. Then that terrible night—"

Very quietly, I interrupted: "New Year's Eve."

She began to nod, mechanically.

At last she said it. "He said it was my fault," she said. "Said I was a good enough sailor to keep a boat on tack if I wanted to, and maybe I was just waiting for a gust—I must have known how they came off that island. And I said if he was such a hell of a swimmer, Yale and all, why didn't he go overboard, if it was a heart attack? Wasn't he man enough for that? Then he blamed me for ruining his sculpture, for long before the show he knew it was bad, all the mixing up of sex and the rest. Anyway, I burst into tears and ran, barefoot, to Maria's room, my last glimpse being of him picking up a bottle."

I jumped off the bed. "Listen," I said, "I'm leaving this place. Pack your suitcase, and no later than day after tomorrow you be at the West Mark Hotel, in New York, which you never heard of, it being far West Side, with pale green corrosive copper stains around the drain in the not very clean tub, and all at my price level. I'll be there all day tomorrow, that night, until six the next day. Then I'll be gone. With no forwarding address."

"I've been trying," she said, "and you don't give me any credit."

"The hell you have."

"I've even been praying he might die, and I don't mind saying so. Or fall in love—whatever he means by that."

I managed a smile.

"Oh yes, I've been trying to buy a divorce," she said. "But he thinks he's got it all anyway, so why take a measly half-million or such. So he talks about love, how he loves me. The real thing is he can't bear to think there's some woman he can't mesmerize. He says if I leave him, he'll do something drastic. He says he'll confess he was on Butler's boat."

"Little good that'll do him," I said. "And a husband can't testify against his—"

"Oh, but that's not the point, it would ruin me anyway. You see, I was a fool. I played fair with him, I was so crazy about him I told him all about me, before we married—everything, even the 'Fanny Hill' business—and now, do you know what he says?"

"I can bet—" I began.

But she cut in. "He says plenty of people are alive who'd know all about it, and he'd spotted some of them. How would I like to hear about it in a courtroom—or see it in a gossip column?"

"To hell with him and his threats," I said, and swung my right fist into my left palm. "Just up and leave—any kind of a divorce, or none. And I'll go where I can get a job and then we—"

"He'll ruin you," she said.

"Ruin me," I said, and burst out laughing. "If ever he—"

She was shaking her head. "Do you know what he says—the worst?"

As I gaped at her, she went on. "He says that no matter how rich I am, I know I'm just Dugton, and I want to be respectable, to have position, more than anything in the world, and not be trash—*trash*, that's what he said—and I'll never be anything but trash again—even if rich trash—if I leave him, he'll see to that!"

I saw the tears welling from her eyes.

"Am I only that?" she was demanding.

"No," I said.

"I don't mean trash," she said. "I mean—I mean the kind of person who just wants—position?"

"No," I said. "And to prove it, you are going to be at the West Mark Hotel."

I watched her face, and saw it falling back on some inward pain. I saw her hands lift, fingers spread to touch her head, on each side, at eye level, and then pull downward. She was in an inner darkness, fumbling along a dark wall.

I was now sitting on the edge of the bed, and I rose abruptly.

"Well," I said, "that cooks it."

But she was heaving herself toward me, across the bed, reaching out for my hand, managing to seize it. "Listen!" she exclaimed. "Listen —I don't give a damn about anything but you. And it's all so easy, and we just didn't see it! We'll just go to Europe—you like to be there —and nothing matters there, nobody knows us—and we'll live there, just ourselves, the way we want to—I've got money there, in Switzerland, lots of it—Butler, he always kept a lot there, and my lawyer knows how to send more—nobody'll know where we are—just you and me—for always—"

She was tugging at my hand. I stared down into her face. She was, indeed, very beautiful. And only an arm's length away. But as I stared down into the face, all at once I was not hearing the words. It was as though I were looking at somebody across a great distance, and I saw the mouth moving and straining, the mouth shouting at me, but there was a strong wind between, and it snatched the words away.

Then I was hearing: "—your kind of work—you can do it any-where, I can buy all the books you need, we can travel where you need to be—I—"

I sat back down on the edge of the bed, and I saw the flash of relief on her face; then I detached my hand from her grasp.

"I want to tell you something," I said.

She looked at me, and drew back.

"Lie down," I said.

She lay down, quietly and carefully, propped on an elbow to face me. I lay down, too, where I had been before, and again focused my gaze on the defect in the plaster above me.

"In the year 216 B.C.—" I began.

But she broke in: "What's that got to do with us—that long back?"

"Everything," I said. Then, continuing in my most pedagogic tone: "In that year, at the Battle of Cannae, Hannibal and his Carthagin-ians—"

"Wasn't that where they picked up a bushel of gold rings the Roman knights wore?"

"The record is very unclear on the whole business," I said. "As for the rings, some historians go as high as seven bushels. But that does not bear on my point. Livy says that after the disaster, the Romans consulted the Sibylline Books to see how to purge the city of the pollution that had angered the gods, and the Book of Fate demanded extraordinary sacrifices. Now, the Romans were not accustomed to human sacrifice, except when a strayed Vestal Virgin got buried alive, but this time was pretty special. In a stone chamber—constructed under the cattle market—the Forum Boarium, to be exact—they—"

"I don't want to hear about it," she said.

"—they entombed," I continued, "two Gauls, man and woman—"

"I don't want to hear, I told you," she said.

"Oh yes, you do, it's interesting," I said. "Let's just try to imagine what happened. Down there in the chamber. The last sound is lost. There is total darkness. The man is crouching in a corner, stunned by his fate. Finally he realizes that somewhere in the dark the woman is weeping—a woman, shall we say, whom he had never seen before that day. She is moving around, groping in the dark, and weeping, finds him, crouches against him for comfort. After a little, a wild sexuality hits him—a flight from actuality. He lays hand on the woman, and so, on the stone, bruising themselves, they couple in frenzy. They fall apart, then when strength returns, fear returns. And so on, to exhaustion."

I waited for her to say something. But she did not.

"And then," I said, "as he hears her breath heavy from exhaustion, the idea comes over him that she is breathing his air. There is only so much air. He tries to seize her, but, struck by the same thought, she eludes him. So, in the dark, as quietly as possible, the tiniest scraping on stone, breath bated, the stalking continues—for how long? Eventually, he gets her.

"But now, to his surprise, the sexuality—the need for blind escape —hits him again. And once his hands are on her, she gets the contagion. And so, hammer and tongs, hell take the hindmost, there they go. But it's different this time. You see, as soon as he makes it, not even taking time to get himself clear, he gets her arms pinioned with one of his own—oh yes, it would be quite possible—and with his free hand begins to throttle her."

I could hear her breathing.

"So he's left there with the body," I finally said, "which is not now using his air. But then what? Let's try some guesses. After a while his strength, and his fear, come back. What then? Does he try to use the body?

"Or maybe it was different, maybe she killed him. With a long pin, in the last embrace. Right in the jugular. Then she is in the pickle, you might say, and even worse off. What does she do?"

I waited for an answer that did not come.

"Anyway," I went on, "if the air holds out long enough for the survivor, there is the question of hunger. If we explore that topic—"
I stopped. "You are getting the point," I demanded, "aren't you?"

The answer did not come.

"Well," I said, "I'll tell you. Whatever happened, you and Mr. Nashville have got yourselves down a deep, dark, airless hole. I am perfectly willing to assume—believe—that you are both innocent, nice people, and all that—but it is a deep, dark hole, since neither of you trusts the other."

There was the same silence, then the slight stir at a little distance from my side.

"You see," I said, "if I—we—did what you propose, we'd also be down a deep, dark hole disguised as a luxury hotel or a villa on the Aegean, and no doubt eventually I'd be off in a corner of the deep, dark hole called the bar, drinking on your money."

"God," the voice at my side said. Then: "You don't trust me."

"I trust you," I said. "I even trust myself. It's simply that I don't trust a certain situation."

I lay there quite a while with my eyes closed. I kept saying to myself that I was going to get up. But I did not.

It happened. I heard the cautious stir at my side, then felt the feathery touch at my crotch.

.   .   .

The U-Drive-It car in the garage was already packed, and my brief case, raincoat, and old gray felt hat on the front seat. On Saturday I had sold my old wreck, just driving into a dealer's lot and asking what he would give and sticking the check into my pocket. The storage people had come out this very morning, Monday, for I had left the door open by prearrangement, to pick up the crates of books and papers, and would hold them for later instructions. My assistant, who was administering my last examination for me that afternoon, would be at the airport with the papers. In my pocket I had two stamped letters to mail: one to the head of my department, a courteous and appreciative but unexplained resignation; the second to Mr. Nashville himself, enclosing a check as a thirty-day notice and informing him that my weekly cleaning woman was already paid to leave the house in good order.

So all was under control, and I drove through the city bathed in the calm and healing light of a late spring sunset, and past the campus where I had more or less earned my bread, out to Berry Field, turned in the rented car, and received the examination papers from my faithful assistant, and mounted the American Air Lines plane to New York.

312

It was logical, I suppose, that, once settled into my seat, with the green hills of Tennessee falling away into oblivion, I should be overcome by self-contempt. If only I had not got into the talking jag on the Livy business—which I had certainly not intended, it had just popped into my head at the moment.

But I had time now to realize that I had made an unscholarly error of fact in recounting the entombment episode. A brace of Greeks, I suddenly remembered, had been put in with the brace of Gauls, and it flashed across my mind that I had unconsciously deleted the extra pair because their presence would have blurred the perfect parabolic point of my narrative.

Even then, as I sat there in the plane, the trivial shame over an academic inaccuracy was a mask for a deeper shame.

Ah, if only, having once done with the Livy business and the poor Gauls, I had risen from the bed, said goodbye, and cleanly gone. No, I had lain there, not admitting to myself my foreknowledge of—and hope for—the hand that had reached out, and the necrophilic performance to follow—necrophilic because Rozelle Hardcastle Carrington was, as of the instant, dead to me, even if the *corps charmant* could execute certain appropriate movements, the way the leg of the dead frog jerks when you put the electric current through it.

And now I saw her as I had left her. The last automatic business concluded, she had rolled over, very impersonally, face down, sheet down to the buttocks, and buried her head in a pillow, both arms joining above her head to crumple the pillow inward. So, coming from the bathroom after my hasty cleaning, I stood in the middle of the floor and made one last survey of the perfectly formed *corps charmant* yonder on the bed.

Looking westward across the great continent toward sunset, I knew that I had better get up and go back to the lavatory. Which I did.

Once ensconced there, with the door latched, I sat on top of the lid of a closed can, and put my hands over my face, and let the tears come as long as there were any.

What finally stopped them was, I hazard, the fact that, being a historian of literature and a lover of the beautiful word even out of my field of specialization, I unconsciously summoned up an apt poetry quotation, the one from "Crazy Jane Talks to the Bishop," in which

313

Yeats marvels that Love should pitch his mansion in the place of excrement.

Well, given the nature of my present hideaway and my precise location therein and my spiritual condition, the quotation was apt indeed.

It was also very funny—or seemed so to me. In any case, it tided me over the crisis, and I could wash my face in cold water and comb my hair, and return to my seat.

.   .   .

Once installed at the West Mark Hotel, I did not leave my room until the hour of the deadline. I even had my meals sent up. If a call came, I wanted to be on the spot. There was no joke to help tide me over this crisis of silence, but I did have the examination papers, my professional conscience, and a quart of black-label Tennessee whiskey. But I never had any ice sent up until my late lunchtime.

Book Three

CHAPTER XIV

I don't know how much longer I could have lived the life I had been living in Nashville, all the intensities, lies, self-divisions, dubieties, duplicities, and blind and variously devised plummetings into timeless sexuality. *Timeless*—that is the word, for when I escaped Nashville, it was an escape into time, into its routines and nags, which make life possible after all. Once in Paris, nobody could have been more blamelessly immersed in the routine and nags of time than I was. I slept on my penury-sagged and poverty-humped mattress, breakfasted on my day-old croissant and tepid chocolate, raced to the Bibliothèque Nationale, stinted myself for lunch, ate a companionless dinner in some hole-in-the-wall where unseasoned horsemeat would, in comparison with what I got, have looked like the *escalope de veau Vaudoise*, a *specialité* at Fouquet's, and went home to solitary if not always blameless slumbers. I washed my socks, underwear, and drip-dry shirts in tepid water in my basin. The chambermaid was appropriately scrofulous, ill-tempered, suffering from an advanced case of varicose veins, and notably deficient of Gallic wit. Furthermore, I never even met a female Fulbright sitting as lonely as acne at the Deux Magots.

My money was running out, and now, under the circumstances, I was not paying anything on my Chicago debts. Upon leaving Nashville, I had, of course, written to my dissertation-director and self-appointed protector at Chicago, reporting that I was entering on a long-range research-and-critical project related to my work on Dante and, having found research facilities at Nashville rather limited, had resigned. Even this late in the season, I wondered if he knew of any grant or fellowship for which I might be worthy. He did not, and so taking up another notch in my belt, I put a small ad out proclaiming myself prepared to teach French and English, and settled down to tough things out in Paris as I had once toughed them out in Chicago.

Then the break came. Dr. Sweetzer, who had claimed me as "his," did cable me that a half-time assistant professorship had opened up for the fall. So I bought my air ticket, converted one of my last traveler's checks into francs, and actually did go to Fouquet's, where arrogance, sheer bulk, a more than adequate French accent, a baleful stare, unkemptness so original that it might be taken for distinction, and two learned-looking volumes under my arm, overawed the pretenses of the Cerebus—even if I did get a rather obscure table. After the *escalope de veau Vaudoise* (my first and only experience with that dish and the source of my worldly reference a few moments past) and the wine the waiter recommended as appropriate, and with two splendid brandies to help digestion, I sauntered the quai-side of Paris until the hour to take my bus to Orly and the flight to the land I loved.

I knew Chicago better than any other place in the world, and I suppose I loved it. But when living in a place starts, then loving it plays second fiddle or flies out the window or hides in the lavatory for a good cry. Anyway, I was living in Chicago, working furiously at my courses, working at my own projects, trying to be pleasant and friendly with colleagues of my own age and rank (most of whom were married and had pregnant wives or wives full of talk about child care, already having produced squaw-fruit), and calling on Dr. Sweetzer every couple of weeks to go out for lunch or a man-to-man beer. In the light of all that Chicago had meant to me, I kept very busy indeed. I even went to the gymnasium three times a week, where I fenced, did weights, or ran a mile. I went to the gym not merely to keep my belly down, but to guarantee my sleep.

One night, unable to sleep, I rose, dressed, and sought out the street where still stood the Castle of Otranto. The street itself was sadly changed from what it had been that other fall, so long ago, when I had been accustomed to stalk the black-caped master of the Castle, trying to screw my courage up to the point of addressing him. The street itself had now been considerably widened for traffic, at the sad sacrifice of the lawns where an occasional iron deer or classic female form carved in rather soot-smeared marble had been accustomed to lurk among ginkgo trees, copper beeches, Norway maples, and hemlocks. Most of the trees were, of course, now gone, though a few specimens, lately planted in round apertures in the sidewalk, thinly struggled on, and in what was left of the lawn of the Castle of Otranto, the iron deer, along with the enormous maples, were gone, and the single hemlock, much mutilated, survived close to the structure, which was externally in dismal disrepair, and internally seemed to be chopped up into apartments, as a vacancy sign indicated.

I stood there a long time, bemused at the building, deeply engaged in the complex double-entry bookkeeping always set in train when the man confronts what had once been the habitat of the raw youth. Though the thoughts of youth are long, long thoughts, the thoughts of a man who has been that youth are longer still, and may often take all night.

More than one night, as the season advanced, I returned to that street, but I also wandered widely. I welcomed the coming on of fall, the stripping away of the last leaves from trees at the University and in what remained of the yards of the many now decaying streets, for the stripping away revealed the absolute and unnatural rigidities and angularities of the man-made world. I felt—or, looking back, I can now define what I felt—that I could survive only in such a world stripped naked to its rigidities and angularities.

But oddly enough, I also welcomed the early twilights, smoky and gravid, that scratched their sow-bellies over the roofs. In the night streets where fog smeared out the lights of approaching traffic, like a thumb smearing paint, I seemed to draw the fog around me like a dark woolly robe to protect me from all eyes. And one afternoon, as the first snow began to fall, I took a train up to the lake, and walked for hours along the shore, watching the sparse flakes ride in over the darkening water, out of the infiniteness of the north. Then, the light of the sky having died, the flakes were no longer sparse and did not now ride in on a reasonable wind, but hurtled, now white only as they approached the eyeball, out of dark air that was incessantly a handful of hurled knives. I felt the snow freeze on eyebrows and lashes, and, as I faced the boom of the lake waves on stone, toyed with the idea that I was some last man with nothing before him but the snow-blind lake and nothing behind but the tundra, and only one obligation, or doom—that of survival. I discovered that this was a kind of happiness.

It was late. I went back to the neighborhood of the University and stood in the attic room I rented in a disintegrating wreck on one of the side streets, and again felt the new happiness. It was a happiness based on a sense of pastlessness. If nothing has ever happened to you, then you can be happy. And tomorrow will be happy, too, for nothing has happened to you today, except, of course, the blank fact of your survival. You might, I supposed, say that this happiness springs from the discovery of the essence of selfhood: when before you the dark waters boom in with the driving, snow-laden wind, and behind you the tundra stretches, then selfhood is the moment of perception between pastlessness and futurelessness.

Be that philosophical observation profound or not, that night of the first snow, the night I returned from my walk by Lake Michigan, it was not until the euphoria had waned that I noticed on the floor an envelope, with a special-delivery mark, forwarded from my department, which must have been stuck under my door. I opened the envelope (on which there was no return address) to discover a clipping from the *Nashville Banner,* dated some weeks earlier, to the effect that Professor Jediah Tewksbury, the well-known young scholar who had abruptly resigned from the University there, was now on the faculty of the University of Chicago, after having spent a summer of study in Paris. The clipping, though neatly cut out by knife or scissors, clearly showed signs of having been crumpled in pocket or purse, but had been smoothed out at last and scotch-taped to a sheet of paper. At the bottom of the sheet was neatly typed: GUESS WHO!

I guessed the *who.* Then, even, the *why.* For longer ago than I could count, one afternoon on a tangled bed, in a shadowy room, just as Jediah Tewksbury came to the explosive end of his experience, a set of smallish, very sharp teeth, known to be pearly white, had closed on his shoulder even as he was involved in a consummatory embrace involving all the members of the biter; and after the disengagement, in answer to his blasphemous reproaches, the biter had said that she merely wanted to put her mark on him so, no matter whatever happened, he'd always remember what it was really like with her. Well, the mark of teeth, uninfected, had healed and disappeared. But here was the worn clipping. Sharper than pearly teeth.

He looked about the attic room and at the narrow iron cot, and dropped the clipping into a carton that served as a wastebasket, and went to bed and slept dreamlessly, as though no past had ever existed.

But it had. And a week or two later, again addressed to the department, a fancy envelope arrived, enclosing a card with a comic baby picture on it, a naked cherub clad in only sombrero and spurs, mounted on a bucking bronco, with beneath it the printed exhortation, "Ride 'Em, Cowboy!" Just below were the vital statistics concerning one James Cadwallader Cudworth: Born—September 25; Sex —male; Weight—7 pounds, 15 ounces; Hair—red. Scribbled on the card was the message that if Jed Tewksbury had been made a godfather to Jimmy Cudworth, it was not because the devout Episcopal parents of said Jimmy had any notion that said J. Tewksbury had any influence before the Throne of Grace or was fit to teach even a four-legged varmint anything, much less anything to a certain two-legged varmint who was a combination of Socrates, George Washington, Robert E. Lee, and Albert Einstein, but because the said J. Tewksbury could be held up as a constant cautionary example of general untidiness, faithlessness in friendship, idleness, an excessive taste for high-grade sour mash, and as a general bum. Then in Sally's hand:

Dear Old Bum:

I am so happy I'd forgive even your running away and not even writing a post card, much less not being our neighbor to help raise Jimmy right—all this if you'd just come to see us and let us show off our treasure to his honest-to-God godfather. And even if you don't pray for Jimmy (because of not knowing how to pray), I'm remembering you in my prayers. Oh, please be happy!

> Our love,
> Your happy Sally.

Since I was, by my recently discovered definition of the term, quite happy, there was no reason why I should stand hypnotized by the scribbled-over card and the illustration of the absurd cherub, or keep wondering why I hadn't at least the grace to write those decent people and tell them goodbye, and tell them, without too much abuse of language as I understood it, that, in fact, I loved them. And to this day, all these years later while I still love them, I wonder why, after I had finished staring at the card, and felt my heart swelling with their happiness, I did not write a single line, a single word. But even after I had determined to write, and had laid out paper and picked up pen, I had the sudden recollection of the moment at the "engagement party" given by the Cudworths to announce that Sally, after dallying in matrimony, was at last knocked up, how Maria McInnis had rushed around the big, battered, guest-crowded old rosewood table to kiss Sally, and how both heads, the dark-haired and the red-haired, had hung there, both faces suffused with communal joy in the candle-light.

With that recollection I laid down the pen, and so did not waste an evening writing about the spilt milk. What the hell was my life? I demanded of myself. Back to work, and let well enough alone, let sleeping dogs lie. Good principles.

But the trouble is that well enough will rarely permit itself to be let alone, and sleeping dogs wake up, and so, shortly after Christmas, when, with considerable pomp, jocularity and self-congratulation, Dr. Sweetzer informed me that my part-time assistant professorship had been regularized as a full-time, associate professorship, I had a letter from Mrs. Jones-Talbot, my first since that delivered by Uncle Tad concerning the mysterious telephone call to be made as soon as I arrived in Florida. This letter was brief, and except for amenities, made a single point: Maria McInnis, after almost a year of absence, had returned to Nashville. During the absence, Maria had written regularly to her father. She had hidden out in the wilds of

Boston University, as a graduate student in clinical psychology, and now, back in Nashville, was moving toward a doctorate. She had given up most of her social life in the city, my informant continued, adding what I had never suspected her of guessing, that Maria, it seemed, was no longer willing to play the role of "totem, luck piece, mascot, cripple-at-large, or pissing post for any stray dog inclined to void easy emotions."

For a long time after the letter, which I acknowledged by only a card of thanks, not a word from Nashville. And precious few from Dugton. My mother, in that first winter back in Chicago, did write one long letter, asking me to send a couple of snapshots:

> Now you done had the sense to get shet of Nashville, Tenn., and didn marry not even a school teacher there ner no high mucking-muck, and now got back to a real city a thousand miles from this-here Dugton, which I struggled and strove to git you out of and made you wear a clean white shirt to school even if it meant stay up late over the iron board, maybe you will condasend to send me a photo so I can know what you look like, not being able to tell from them black night shirts and that square hat black too in them newspaper pictures you sent from Florida. How much hair you lost? That why you wear that hat? A hat like that wouldn't go down on yore Pa's head. Yore Pa, he had more hair and stiffer on his head than any man ever. You may be too young to recollect but he used to set in a chair at night before them times come when he was never sober, him by the fire in sock-feet an I worked his head with a stiff brush as a curry comb to make it glossy and black and admired to do that. In them old days before you come along it would some time git him so worked up, you know how, and not to talk dirty but you are a growed man now, he would nigh not let me get myself ready for bed fer grabbing and pestering, me already doing the best I could to git to bed anyway, me then young and flesh-fond as air-y next one. Maybe this aint no way fer a Mother to talk much less write to a boy, but I am a old lady now, and you sure-God aint no boy unless you shrunk some after you left home. But like I was saying I hungers in my heart to see a good photo. I dont mean fer you to come back and let me look. I done worked too hard gitten shet of you. And I did not want you to see me old and ugly and one tooth gone in front. Gonna put back a artifisil one soon as I can pay cash.

Well, anyway, I had Dugton, and now I did not have to lie to my mother about Nashville being the stronghold of "Miss Pritty-Pants," since my adventures there had come to naught, and soon I sent a photo made specially for the purpose with my gut sucked in and my chin up, along with a check for a new tooth and a request for photo of same, once it was in place. A few weeks later I got a photo back. It was of a gray-haired woman with wonderful snapping black eyes —even in a portrait done by the Dugton Art Studio—and with mouth pulled back in a comic-strip, lip-splitting grin and forefinger dramatically pointing to a fine prominent brilliantly white incisor. Taking that picture must have been a unique experience for the boss-artist at the Dugton Art Studio. It also must have been the kind of experience my mother especially relished.

So with my definition of happiness, I moved on my way, lived like a monk, smilingly met my undergraduate classes and in my graduate seminar earned the reputation of being a Holy Terror, and worked hard to prove that a certain anonymous group of poems of the century, clearly influenced by Arnaut Daniel, were the work of one Manfredi di Siena.

The poems under discussion were, I would be the first to admit, worthless, and I even took a certain snobbish pleasure in making that admission; before long, I had the additional pleasure of seeing some meager references to these poems attributing them to Manfredi di Siena, even if the attribution was followed by a question mark in parenthesis. One of the poems, with an unquestioned attribution, even got into an anthology of medieval literature edited by a respectable scholar.

A full year passed in this wise. Then came the wedding announcement—enclosing a letter. The marriage was of Maria McInnis and one Jameson Beaufort, and the letter was from the bride. This announcement, the bride stated, was the first to be mailed, for she owed all her happiness to me. If she had not left Nashville, she would have died in her old rut. And if it had not been for me she would have come back too soon, as she was willing to admit now that she had been afraid of coming back and finding me not "not interested" in her. "Yes," she wrote, "I was in love with you, and in a different way I love you still, for in you I found certain strengths and qualities to

324

make me recognize them in another man whose love I was lucky enough to find."

The man she was in love with and had married was a psychiatrist, a very young professor at the University, a penniless lad who had earned his way through college, and had made his medical education on scholarships, and was now regarded as a brilliant researcher. His father had been, she said, a sharecropper (that is, I immediately noted, one step even lower in scale than my own progenitor), but the son had long since helped the father to buy a little farm of his own in west Tennessee, where she loved to go visiting with him. She and "Jamesie" had a place in the country near Nashville, which Jamesie farmed with "help"—by which I presumed she meant a sharecropper or tenant farmer. They kept a couple of nags there, and that was about all their social life—a little on weekends, they were so busy at library, hospital, and laboratory. "Oh, do come to see us!" she exclaimed. "You and Jamesie are born to be friends."

The place in the country bought by Dr. Beaufort to exercise his boyhood skills and inborn love of nature was the identical place which Cud Cudworth had tried to persuade me to "buy"—i.e., to buy with the backing of McInnis money. No doubt, a successful psychiatrist could get his own credit, but even so, since my eminent ex-colleague, of origins even more humble than my own, now had my girl and my farm and my friends, I wondered what he would make of the situation. I wondered, too, what he would make of the letter—if he ever saw it. Would he regard himself as victor over me, or the plate-licker of my leavings?

Also, knowing the facts, I was wondering what I made of them.

I even spent some time wondering all over again what would have happened if I had waited around for the girl. I remembered that single moment, the one kiss, at the New Year's Eve party, when I had, for the first time, sensed the deep, warm, dark inwardness of Maria McInnis. I wondered, too, if I, as husband of Maria McInnis, would have been able to take the Nashville I knew, in which, at the New Year's Eve party, the slick-faced bastard had rubbed thumb and forefinger suggestively together, and said, in his low, conniving voice, "Got the moola, too."

Or would she have come away with me to Chicago, where nothing, not even her moola, would have mattered? As I toyed with these possibilities, another was suddenly in my head: the possibility that I might have waited for Maria to come back and then married her, and then, out of some deep fatality in things, have entered upon a long and variously delightful, and delightfully guilty, intrigue with Rozelle Hardcastle Carrington, thus combining the best features of the world of Nashville.

I settled the whole line of speculation by sending the bride an excessively expensive and extremely conventional wedding present, for several days thereafter pursuing more grimly than ever my own very personal definition of happiness. I was, I decided, only what I was.

As I had once looked (and did still look) to the letters of my mother for the unfolding chapters of the "matter of Dugton," so even as I, month by month, pursued my personal definition of happiness, I awaited, consciously or unconsciously, the climax of the "matter of Nashville." For a long time fate toyed with me, withholding all hints. Then, huddled deep in the mass of the *Chicago Tribune,* I found the modest heading: NASHVILLE SOCIALITE VICTIM OF HEROIN. The brief account went on to declare that the circumstances of death of a J. Lawford Carrington were ambiguous, that a swami had been indicted for trafficking in dope, and that a Miss Amy Dabbitt was under medical care. The widow, who had voluntarily undergone extensive questioning, was reported to be clear of involvement of any sort.

A few days later arrived the letter from my mother, who, among many other Norn-like gloatings, affirmed: "It looks like gittin hitched to Miss Pritty-Pants just aint real healthy." And the next day arrived an envelope stuffed with Nashville clippings, with a letter from Mrs. David McInnis:

> Dear Jed:
>
> In the midst of sadness and confusion, I explain my new and long longed-for condition—and a very happy one, too, in spite of all the sad and sordid messes, news of which I enclose. David and I, whose marriage had been so long postponed until he—we—could be sure of Maria's condition (how splendid she is! and her husband!) were married as quietly as possible by a J.P. in the little town of Lebanon (near Nashville,

you may recall), and headed out for a honeymoon, only to return to this horror.

Am I sad? Of course I am—at all the human waste. Maybe I helped spoil Lawford after I got money—he was certainly spoiled and a coward to boot. I don't mean suicide—if such it was, as I think—but the hiding from reality and from his own talent (if he had it) in the pitiful role in Nashville. He and I had earlier had awful rows, but nothing like recently, when I made one last effort, and he took up with that girl, a slimy creature already shopworn as well as shoddy goods from the start, and I finally cut him definitively out of my will and told him so. I must say that Rose has borne all with dignity and self-control. I dined with her just this evening, and I must say, she has some very admirable qualities. Far better than my nephew deserved.

I write no more. I don't really have the heart to. But when David and I are next in Chicago (he comes there rather often on business), may we persuade you to dine with us? It would be a joy and an honor to see you.

Your admiring and grateful pupil,
Rebecca Carrington McInnis.

P.S.   Just to satisfy your legalistic male curiosity, I'll say that, though my English husband, being Catholic, would not give me a divorce, I just whisked off and got a good atheist one, as soon as I needed it. For reasons not interesting enough to go into—though the public press may have informed you—my husband, Catholic or not, was in no position to fight the case, or even, after some of his well-publicized low-life and love-life shenanigans, continue his political career.

.   .   .

Six months—all alike in their inner landscape—passed before the newly made Mrs. McInnis and her husband did appear in Chicago, and I joined them one evening at seven in their hotel suite. Over drinks and dinner, served in the suite, our conversation dealt with world affairs, the French-English-Israeli attack on the Suez and Eisenhower's intervention, the Presidential election of 1956 and the character of Stevenson (how long ago all that seems now! his name almost forgotten), and, inevitably, horses. When the table had been whisked away, and coffee and brandy produced, David McInnis took merely a quick coffee, shook my hand, and excused himself for a business conference.

He was no sooner out the door than Mrs. McInnis said: "See how sweet he is! Now many a nice husband would have told his wife he knew she had something to say to a guest, and would have said he would arrange a business meeting to get himself out of the way. Some might have just lied and gone on the town with a crony. But my point is this: my husband didn't say a word to me on the subject, he just let me overhear a telephone conversation about the meeting, and then apologized to me. Oh, isn't he transparent—dear David—in all his tactfulness! And he leaves wifey dear alone to—shall we say—chew the fat with her ex-partner in an adulterous, if brief, affair, for nobody was ever more really married than David and I for all those years."

There didn't seem to be anything for me to say, so I let the good brandy spread its glow slowly throughout my being and cast an aura over some recollections of the event to which she referred.

"As for the event," she was saying, "there was, of course, only one cure, and the cure was almost as painful as the disease. For there was the fear that the cure might not turn out to be a cure. The gentleman to whom my heart was pledged might simply have said he didn't want such a miserable, cheesy, and mite-ridden article in his emotional pantry. Well, do you know what he did?"

Now I did find something to say, and that was no.

"He laughed at me," she said. "The heartless beast—he laughed at me. Imagine a lady of a certain age, all girded for her tragic moment, suddenly getting the horse laugh. Never," she avowed, "never in my entire life, have I been so outraged and humiliated and embarrassed—" and her cheeks now really flushed with what must have been the old embarrassment, making her gray-blue eyes shine preternaturally.

She took a deep, wasteful gulp, not a sip, of the brandy, and added: "The wonderful, white-haired, smart-alec, old son of a bitch!"

And picked up again: "He kept on laughing just fit to kill—and I *was* about ready to kill him—for in spite of my conviction of sin, I had some womanly spirit left, and then—you know what he did?"

"No," I said again, rather enjoying the handsomely revived marks of her old discomfiture, she sitting up as straight as though mounted in a show ring, with her cheeks still flushed and eyes shining.

"Well," she said, "what he finally managed to get out through the fool laughing, was that he thanked God it was over and out of my system. In a strange way that made me madder than his laughing, talking to me with such condescension, and me a grown woman who had just confessed adultery—that and the twinkle in his hard old ice-blue Scots eyes, which sometimes get the color of the well-whetted claymore that used to give the English such dire conniptions. Then what he said—it just set me back too, it jolted me as much as if he had been ungentlemanly enough to poke me in the midriff.

"Anyway, I finally stood in the middle of the floor and demanded what he thought it was I had got out of my system. He kept on just sitting in an easy chair, cool as a cucumber, and then in his old uncorrupted and incorruptible Tennessee voice, said one word, this in a quite conversational tone. Just the word: 'Sergio.' "

She sat silent for a full minute or more, ignoring me with what seemed ponderous deliberation, gazing down into her snifter of brandy. She looked up at me, half in defiance, half in appeal, though against what, or for what, I could not tell.

"Well—" she began, and stopped.

"Well, what?"

"He just sat there in his easy chair," she said, "and not taking his eyes off me. I was standing there paralyzed. Then, not getting up, smiling a little, he stretched out his arms to me, the smile and the gesture both reminding me—now, at least, not then—of the way you make friends with a child, and I found myself taking one step toward him, pausing, then taking another, just the way a child does, trying out its own feelings. Then, not even believing the blissful fact, I was in his lap, my face huddling against his shoulder, while his voice, calm and distant, was saying how Sergio had been dead a long time but how something in me had refused to let the poor fellow die, saying that Sergio had earned his death if any man ever had, but I kept on cheating him out of it, saying that he had been truly honorable—and oh, I always love the way David will just naturally use such old-fashioned locutions, like *honorable,* or *blackguard,* or *the public thing,* or the *common weal,* things that nobody can use any more and not feel silly.

"Then David's voice was saying that Sergio had been a man whose devotion to me was just part of his honor and heroism, and that I had never realized that such a fellow is the most ready and ripe to die.

329

"All the while, I could feel his hand ever so lightly smoothing my hair, ever so gently, and the voice now saying, 'Just let go, my darling, my baby, and learn that the poor boy is dead. Don't you realize that what just happened and you have been telling me about as though it were something to be ashamed of—don't you realize that it had to happen if you were to be sure that he is really dead. Just realize that he has been dead all these years, even if you had to take this way of finding out, and now lie on my shoulder and cry all you want, for nobody ever deserved tears more than that fellow did. But don't you realize, too, that he was devoted enough to you to know that you would be brave enough to lead your own life afterwards?'

"That's what he said, and then stopped, and I wanted to cry, I was stifling from wanting to cry, and getting worse every time his hand touched my hair. But all at once, he seized me, a hand on each of my shoulders, and thrust me out to stare into my face, in his hard, probing, ice-blue way, then said, quite factually: 'And you might also try to realize that, for whatever it is worth and in the sad limits and metes God-a-Mighty has set for him, this fellow present right here is devoted to you, too.' "

Mrs. McInnis managed to locate her handkerchief, and dabbed at her eyes, and again took a sustaining gulp of the brandy, not a sip. She faced me then, and grinned, saying: "And this had a comic ending too—just like the pratfall his original laughing had been for me. Only the comic ending was not laughing now, it was crying. For as soon as he said that last thing to me, it was like snapping all your corset strings at once—in case anybody can remember what corset strings were—and I was bawling my fool head off like a calf, not like a tragedy queen, and then my head was back on David McInnis' shoulder, where it seemed to belong. Then, how long I don't know, I fell asleep, and, as David indecorously pointed out later, I was snoring away in comfort like a shoat with adenoids. David was also indecorous enough to point out later that that shoulder where I had done the snoring was nigh paralyzed for forty-eight hours thereafter."

After a time, half to herself, she said: "Poor, dear Sergio—my honorable Sergio, as David called him—well, I guess, I love him as much as ever. Maybe even more. But I love him in the way you love the dead."

Then: "And love the necessity for death, too, I suppose."

This seemed, at the moment, and even in retrospect, the appropriate end of a conversation, but ours did not end so tidily.

Mrs. McInnis disappeared into another room, and returned with a letter in her hand. "I don't exhibit this out of vanity," she said, "though anybody likes a compliment, but for its curious psychological interest."

The letter, from Rozelle, began by saying that the farm, automatically inherited from Lawford, was a gift from her to the University —the house, studio and art objects—to be called the J. Lawford Carrington Art Center. It continued that Nashville was not the sort of place where she, Rozelle, should ever have come. She was now leaving to find the right place—if it existed. But then she wrote: "In addition to my goodbye and my thanks for many kindnesses you may have thought I did not even notice or know about—" and at this point I remembered Rozelle's constant watchfulness and her catlike talent for seeing in the dark—"I want to say something that you may reject as impertinent. But it is as sincere as can be. Of all the people in the world, you are the one I'd most want to be like. I want you to know that fact, if even I am a very sad and long way off from realizing such a crazy dream."

Slowly, I folded the sheet and reinserted it in the envelope, and held it in my hand.

"Well," I said, suddenly feeling sad about the writer's distance from her crazy dream, "I can tell you one thing."

"What?" she asked.

"It *is* sincere," I said. "I know that. Do you remember that bright Sunday afternoon in December, the fall I came to Nashville, out at your place? Well, Rozelle and I were watching you doing the jumps, and right then she said that very same thing about you."

Mrs. McInnis laughed. "I'd never make the Olympic Equitation Team," she said. "Besides, she has style herself, and she has guts."

"She wasn't talking about that," I said. And added: "I'll maliciously torture you a little more. I'll tell you the exact words she used about you. She said *innocent* and *complete*"—and repeating the words, I recollected in a flash the connection in which I had last had those words in my mind, thinking not of Rozelle's description of the then Mrs. Jones-Talbot's face as she took the jump, but of that face as I had looked down on it with the hair spread on the pillow.

Mrs. McInnis was saying: "Poor girl—what will become of her?"

Suddenly, I was absorbed into a sense of guilt toward Rozelle, guilt however irrational, and a despairing bottom-dropping-out sense of loss.

Mrs. McInnis was saying that she had always liked Rose, as she called her, that she had spunk, the most essential and admirable equipment. Next she was wondering if, in the end, Rose had written at least a word of goodbye to Maria, she had been seeing Maria to the very end, always privately, never any more at parties.

She went on to say how beautifully things had worked out for Maria, then confessed that, in the beginning, she had pinned her hopes —not entirely unselfish hopes, she said, since her own relation to David was at stake—on me. For she had known that none of the little Nashville gang would ever serve the purpose.

What could I say except that I had been truly fond of Maria—and then she had gone away? Besides, I added, to close matters off, something that had never crossed my mind before, that I had probably been created to be a confirmed old bachelor.

She looked at me in a shrewd, critical way as if at a horse, then shook her head, saying sharply, "Don't be a fool!"

I sat with head lowered in shame for foolishness—or was it at the opening vista of blank years ahead? I did not know.

She asked me about my work, and I said that professionally I was doing very well and that I liked the process of teaching, but for work —and I underscored the word—I was carving cherrystones. Then I heard my voice: "It seems that I cannot find an idea charged with passion. I mean the kind of idea that touches life at the root."

I sat there appalled at what I had said. Had I had to find the truth this crazy accidental way?

Then I was saying: "But work—it fills up time. And I am not a solitary drinker."

"Well, if you are not," a voice boomed astonishingly forth, and Mr. McInnis was standing just inside the door, "I hope to God you won't make me one, for I am going to have a stout try right now. As soon as," he said, striding across the floor, "I have saluted the darling of my heart," and he proceeded to give the darling a real smacker of a kiss, on the upturned mouth.

He ordered up two highballs, the lady declining, and began to talk about an annual all-night poker game he sat in with cronies in Louisville, and from that back to the tale how, in 1811, a poker game was going on in a tavern in the same community, then little more than a frontier river town. A man had just filled a royal flush, and raise after raise was coming, up to him, the last raise a whopper. At that instant, the Great Earthquake—the New Madrid Earthquake—struck. Chimneys fell, and people ran into the street shouting the end of the world. The man with the royal flush just looked at his cards as though to make sure, and as the shouting in the street continued and got worse, calmly spread his cards out and laid them face up, remarking, "Well, gentlemen, it has been a beautiful world."

Mr. McInnis took a drink, then said: "That's the way I sometimes feel about the world, it is beautiful."

We finished our drinks. I shook hands with host and hostess, and thanked them very sincerely.

I left them standing side by side just inside the door, his arm around her erect shoulders, and as I closed the door behind me, I caught a last glimpse of the two faces, one large and florid under the thatch of white hair and the other strongly but delicately carved, with the commanding gray-blue gaze, moving into conjunction.

Thus endeth, apparently, the "matter of Nashville."

.   .   .

But this did not end the matter of Old Broke-Nose.

Before the year was out, he was married. Five years after that he was divorced.

CHAPTER XV

I am strongly tempted to say that my marriage initiated a new life. More accurately, I am inclined to regard it as an aspect of a process already in train.

I remember very well how, one evening when I was first in Nashville and living at the Old Hickory Arms Hotel—the evening after I had first been out to the Carrington place—I lay on the bed and stared up at the dark and promised myself to put my life in order. To shave every day, never to pick hangnails, to allocate $100 a month to pay my debts in Chicago, to get my clothes cleaned and pressed at regular intervals, to take regular exercise, to read newspapers and take an interest in politics and the modern world. And how, a year later, in Chicago—after Nashville and Rozelle—I had taken a similar and more complex set of vows, and high on the list had been to take my civic and political duties more seriously. Other people lived together in a great seething club or society or something, and found it a rewarding life. Why couldn't I?

So I had registered as a Democrat—a Chicago Democrat, no less
—a new experience, since I had never voted for anything in my life.
I had joined, too, a Neighborhood Defense Association, and by this
time I had climbed many a dark stair and pushed many a greasy door
buzzer in good causes. I had, too, sat longer and later on many a
committee, University and otherwise, and longer and later in my office
with some worthy dullard, trying, as twilight and fog gathered, to
spring some magic trigger of his mind or soul.

On my first return to Chicago, I had discovered the joy of standing
against the snow-blinded lake with the tundra at my back, but I found
now that I had need for another and deeper definition of joy. It was
as though news of the lives of people I had known, even the comic
photograph of my mother with her new tooth in place, or the last
glimpse of the David McInnises as the door closed on them, had made
me seek a new definition just as I had settled into the joy of my
romantic and stoical loneliness.

So here I was, you might say, trying to pull my weight in the boat,
to feel the joy of being part of the human project—to join, in short,
the human race. It seemed to me that I had been running all my life,
and now since I was back in Chicago, where, it seemed, I might be
destined to stay, I might as well do what you do when you stop
running and try to see what that feels like.

Matrimony seemed a natural extension of my new endeavor, and
a logical as well as pleasant step to procreation as a means of signing
on the dotted line as a full-fledged and serious-minded human being
who might, in the end, become a member in good standing of the
A.D.A. and the P.T.A. or even sit on a school board, with a finger
in the pie of the American future.

I do not mean to say that I ticked off and reviewed all these matters,
one by one, in my mind. But as a mark of approaching middle age,
they were there in the back of my mind—even as I was among the
last to rise at night to leave a carrel in the library, or my office, or when
I sat alone late in my little attic apartment or when I went, as I rarely
did now, to some faculty party (still in the younger set) and found
myself declining a gambit, or worse, accepting one and finding myself
doing the best I could to gratify a female, with whom I had scarcely
a speaking acquaintance, and who was now propped straddle-legged

against the wall of a broom closet, while the hose of a vacuum cleaner crawled round one of my legs like a young but vigorous python and occasionally I got my face embedded, not in the locks of my willing victim, but in a floor mop hung upside down—all this while the mop handle was trying to tap out in Morse code a play-by-play account of the sporting event in the broom closet, but all in vain against squeals of communal merriment or the rage of philosophical argument in the kitchen beyond.

Parties grew rarer and rarer for me, and hasty episodes in broom closets or back seats of cars rarer still, for I began to feel the dignity of my years and also, in my new personal vision of happiness, to regard such goings on as little more than therapeutic. What was gnawing away at that earlier and stoical vision of happiness was the yearning for the higher happiness of joining the human race, and, as I have said, it was this that led me on to civic obligations and matrimony, the last involving a very personable and successful lady photographer, both news and art, young but not too young, previously married only once and childless, and apparently beginning to feel the pangs of loneliness and a similar yearning for significance in life.

The lady I married was not only personable. She was, by many, including the present writer, regarded as quite beautiful, in a portentous, slightly feline way, or in the way of a smoldering wood fire beginning to glow when the lights are cut off. But what entrapped my imagination was not the beauty itself in its obvious quality. In one sense, it was clear that she had once been more beautiful. I am willing and able to grant that much, for she was none other than that Dauphine Finkel (now Phillips) in whose bed, in the bohemianly and expensively redecorated carriage house, I had spent so much time of pleasure and profit, in the early days in Chicago, who was the youngest and most advanced thinker of the Graduate School, had amassed the staggering string of A's, had volubly introduced me, her exotic Southern fascist and lyncher, to all the ideas that were going to redeem the world; and to whom, to the loss of her soft bed and self, violet-scented breath, and silken skin, I had been rude on the subject of the friendship of Stalin, her hero, and Hitler, lately the object of her detestation.

But when I first described her and now refer to the days of her voluble instruction and iron-clad convictions, I keep forgetting that this was not the whole woman. She had always been able to forget to say something instructive and curl up silently into my arms, and I, feeling her heart beat beneath the softness of a breast, could become fleetingly aware of a nameless truth deeper than any iron-clad opinion, a truth that we might learn to share.

Although, back in the early days, it turned out to be opinion, not truth, that ruled the day, and I did get thrown out of the bed in the exquisite little Bohemia, I had not entirely forgotten the moments of quietness and the sense of a nameless truth. But that earlier, fresher beauty, which I so clearly remembered had been, one might feel, a thing not yet in contact with life and experience, an impersonal creation of nature's happy blundering. Now, however, the beauty was distinctive in some sense of unfulfillment in the very beauty, an unfulfillment remote from certitudes and marked by a dark hungering. And nothing is more demanding to my soul (or had by this time become so) than the dark hungering for truth—dark eyes fixed into a metaphysical distance, lips slightly parted as if in thirst, a withdrawnness in the midst of the crowd.

This was precisely what the lady provided now when she and I went to concerts. Music meant little to me, but it meant everything to watch her face straining to enter into the truth of the truthless music. Striving, that is, to find the answer to all questions that life had proposed to her but left unanswered. There was, in fact, a strange and disturbing double appeal: on the one hand, the dark yearning eyes—like shadow that shone—and, on the other, and how contradictorily, the dusky scent she wore or, literally, was. So she could sit there, the eyes half-closed and set deep in their own shadow, all this while I secretly inhaled the scent of her being—an allegorical figure of Flesh Yearning for the Beyond of Flesh.

So, night after night, at concerts, or in small groups in her apartment, or, later, as I sat alone with her, a drink untasted in my hand, I watched that face yearning toward its truth. And as I watched the flow of music over the face, I knew that I was watching the flow of fate as it returned upon itself.

.   .   .

337

The marriage worked out very well, we respected each other's work and often made solicitous inquiries about it, she was pleasant, too, and much admired as exotic and "different" in the senior faculty circles that now claimed us, and having dug out of storage and enlarged the waistline of the dinner jacket originally purchased to wear to parties with Maria McInnis back in Nashville, I now wore it to parties that my wife got invited to outside of faculty circles, mostly artists, political-liberals, and the rich periphery of such worlds.

I had moved into my wife's commodious studio apartment, with a vast room like a museum, full of paintings and photographs of note, with plenty of subsidiary rooms, and there she—we—gave parties, too, and after them, with the last guest safely out, we grappled for each other in the dark and made the beast-with-two-backs before you could say Jack Robinson, had you been so inclined.

My wife, to surprise and consternation, turned up pregnant; but we gradually dismissed the consternation in favor of the joy of parenthood and (at least for me) that idea that thus one might move more directly into a sense of the general human destiny.

The period of pregnancy meant more and more quiet evenings together in which I could watch the flow of music over her literal face and the questioning and the yearning become more marked on the allegorical face.

And the little character, when he finally arrived, was the joy of my heart. I loved the nights when, after he was abed, my wife and I sat together and a less shadowy music, for a period anyway, flowed over her face. But—dare I be honest enough to say—I loved most the nights when, because of the pressure of my work, real or pretended, I was alone with him while my wife went out—to "keep fences built," as she put it. I could hold him on my lap to my heart's content. I could bathe him, and in the process investigate every little gleaming and flowery part of him. I could feed him, in the early time of bottle and later by the little curved-handled silver spoon from which his mother had once fed, enraptured to have a hand in the sacred process by which life went on, interrupting myself with such a flow and flood of nonsense that even now I blush to remember them—long improvised dialogues between father and son, in which he always got in the last and wittiest word, long quotations from Sophocles, the Old Testament, Shakespeare, Milton, or Edward Lear, often interrupted by Ephraim to improve my accent or correct a quotation, whiffs of balladry, grim or gay, old back-country square-note hymns from my childhood at Heaven's Hope Church, including such old favorites as

> *Mary had an only Son,*
> *The Jews and the Romans had him hung—*
> *Keep your hand on the plow, hold on!*

—this last item very odd for a man-child who, to my clinical interest and a grandmother's delight and according to the somewhat chic atheistic wish of the mother, had been circumcised on the eighth day with much pomp in the rich drawing room of said grandmother.

It had been determined by appeal to ancient law that if the mother was Jewish the son might be ceremonially circumcised, and so there we were, with me much on the sidelines though treated with biological respect, while the passing of the infant was made from hand to hand, from the grandmother, the *gvrterim,* to a male cousin of my wife, the *gvater,* to the most important of the trio of what might be called, in neutral language, sponsors or line-backers, to the *sandik,* always male, who supports the infant on his lap, while a clamp holds the pore little prick in place, and the scalpel does its work.

To return to my evenings with Ephraim: after he had been fed and burped, I would insert him into a garment which enclosed him entirely except for the face (and in some models, the hands) and tuck him away for bye-bye land in a large and very expensive antique crib in a large nursery next to the *camera matrimoniale.* My study was only two doors down the hall, and I could easily catch the least noise, from mouse-squeak to banshee-howl.

If after a suitable interval neither came, I would tiptoe down just to have a peek. But there was so much to peek at—the curve of cheek with its muted shadings of pink in the shadowy room, and the long black eyelashes against the pink, the exquisite articulation of a hand curved on blue flannel, tiny but with the promise of what power to seize and command, the outthrust of jaw now determining nothing, nothing, but someday to determine the destiny of humankind.

And then—sooner or later—my question: Had there been a time, before the panther-piss took hold, when Old Buck Tewksbury—then young Buck Tewksbury, with the biggest dong in Claxford County, and the glossiest head of black hair so stiff it needed a curry comb, and the yellowest pair of cowhide boots, and teeth the strongest and whitest under any black mustaches, and the lovingest little wife in the county, to boot—had there been a time when Young Buck crept at night into a darkened room and stood to look down at a black-haired male infant, in an improvised cradle, sucking, no doubt, at its thumb or a sugar-tit?

I could rarely abide the question. Most often I simply crept from the room. Once, I freely confess, when I did not creep from the room, but stood there with the question throbbing the blood-veins in my temples, I finally approached the expensive antique crib and leaned to kiss the upturned, rose-down cheek and let the tears just come.

Ordinarily, as I have said, I crept from the room with no such unmanly display of weakness and irrelevance, and buried that aspect of myself and of human experience in the rigor of whatever work I was doing. I would immerse myself in whatever work was at hand— its nature less and less compelling to me, but its mere existence the one thing that, more and more, I could flee to.

Flee to it, from what? From all the other activities to which I so programmatically dedicated myself? From the pleasure and satisfactions I sought? From the very fact that my work prospered—and prospered handsomely, too, and I could wear the ribbon of the Académie Française and had a shoebox of medals? From, even, fame?

My wife's work prospered, too, and I rejoiced. At the end of the fourth year of marriage her work was exhibited most importantly as a "one-man" show ("one man" still being an acceptable locution) and with great success. We celebrated that event with a little party at which Ephraim, now able to get about, was offered as a crowning exhibit. The next year there was a prize at San Francisco, and an even more prestigious one at Philadelphia. Two years later there was the show at the Museum in New York, where I accompanied her, and shortly thereafter the very handsome publication of the items there shown was enthusiastically received.

But there were separations, as when I went off to a conference or to lecture, or as I began to receive honorary degrees, or when she had an exhibit or a commission. It is true that she went with me to my first conference in Europe, and she did attend one of my degree ceremonies, but such joint trips could not often be worked out, even with her mother there in Chicago and anxious to have Ephraim. When we were at home—and that was often—things went on much as before, with both of us hard at work, each truly concerned with the other's occupation, both involved in decent social causes, both of us dutifully going out to parties (more and more, however, parties in her world), and coming home somewhat inflamed with expensive drink, to tumble into bed, indulge in a little foreplay (occasionally somewhat mechanical, excessively instructed, or somewhat frenetic), and make the famous beast.

Then one Sunday morning, after such a party, I came down a little late to breakfast, to find her pretending to read the Sunday paper, while the tears were dropping down by pints and quarts on the newsprint. Yet bleary from sleep, but on the whole feeling pretty good, still standing in the doorway, I asked if she had hurt herself. She lifted a tear-streaked face on which I saw the most shockingly desolate expression of my life, and declared that she couldn't stand it one second longer.

"Stand what?" I demanded, and with the obvious intention of offering a matutinal embrace, got halfway to her chair, before her face exhibited an even wilder desolation and the answer "Everything!" slew me in my tracks.

I suppose I was slain for the simple reason that out of my slightly alcohol-dimmed recollection of our activities upon getting home to bed, I had been inwardly congratulating myself on what a splendid (by recent standards, anyway) beast-with-two-backs we had indeed made. So with this shock to my ego—and thus slain—I stood there, and my corpse heard a voice saying how I might grab a bite and jump into some pants and track down Ephraim and take him to his grandmother's for Sunday, and come back so we could *"TALK"*—the word *talk* most sinister in quotations, all caps, and italics, as here indicated. I by-passed the bite, did jump into pants, tracked down Ephraim, and got him to his grandmother's splendid establishment, trying all the while not to listen to his prattle, trying, in fact, to persuade myself that he did not exist. How much simpler things would be if he did not exist!

341

Then, upon leaving him, I suddenly thought my heart would guiltily break, and I hugged him so hard that he yelled a real "Ouch!" and jerked away from me without a word.

On the way home in the taxi, I began to live over my old joyous evenings alone with him, and in the process discovered that there had been one feature which until this moment I had always edited out of recollection—a feature which, God knows, was not a criticism of my love for him. For a period, as I have mentioned, he wore what I assume was a standard night garment for infants, that sort of flannel bag I have mentioned, with arms and legs, with hand and feet attached and a headpiece that fitted over, and a zipper to make all into a comfy package.

But sometimes, as I regarded the stuffed package, the comfiness was not what I got. I got a panic of claustrophobia, a desperation of entrapment, a fear of not being able to breathe, as though I were thus bound up. So, jerking my tie loose (if I had one on) and snapping my collar button, I would stumble out of the nursery. In the unlit hall I might lean against the wall and gasp for deep lungfuls of air. If I had a coat or dressing gown on, I'd take it off before sitting back down to work—to the blessed oblivion of work. In a little I would, of course, feel like a fool and toss the episode away into some dark corner of the mind, where you throw old shoes, bills of past due accounts of all genre, out-worn lies that you yourself no longer believe in, old hopes, and dead cats.

But I was out of the cab, standing in the sunlight of a gentile Sabbath with latchkey in hand, ready to go into my own house to confront the desolate face and the "Everything" that waited to be talked about, even ready to insert the key—when one of the cats putatively dead in the waste-heap in the darkest corner of my mind uttered a distinct *meow*.

The nature of the *meow* being as follows: A few months after my more recent marriage, when I was in the midst of both my high-minded efforts to join the human race and the throes of my honeymoon bliss, then often unlubricated by an intake of social alcohol, I was giving one of the courses I had begun at Nashville—the course involving *Aucassin et Nicolette,* with the maiden lost in the dark forest —and again in one of the *chants* I came to the line, and again expatiated on the etymology of *gent,* remarking, as before, that in modern French the phrase might be rendered as *au corps charmant.* It was the same phrase that, late on a drizzly, wintry afternoon in Nashville, with the vision of Rozelle's stripped and surrendered body as first seen, had provoked, in the spot on my right thigh, the feel of the oxymoronic "stigmata"—and, in that classroom in Nashville, other significant symptoms. So, with the now highminded bridegroom, sitting years later in a classroom in Chicago, came the same old vision, fresher and more appealing than ever, with the same old undecipherable sensations coming on my thigh, the same old symptoms. But all this had, of course, been immediately and righteously consigned to the waste-heap in the dark corner dedicated to all dead pussy cats, until this ill-timed—or perfectly timed—*meow,* as I stood at my own front door.

Now, forgetting that on the afternoon of the class in Chicago, after having consigned the putatively dead pussy cat to the waste-heap, I had brought a very expensive bunch of roses home to my bride, and after dinner, well-flushed with social bourbon, Bordeaux, and brandy, had worked at the beast with two backs with unusual enthusiasm— now forgetting all that, I thrust the key into the lock and marched in soldierly fashion up to the discussion of "Everything."—Soldierly, because I was already aware in my heart that when "Everything" is what you have to talk about, you really have "Nothing," and when you have "Nothing" to talk about, the old gray goose, of the folk song, is really dead.

The lady of distinguished beauty and desolate face, who, incidentally, was my wife, really did have "Nothing" to talk about, and the "Nothing" had grown so terrible that, she confessed, once quite lately, on one of her New York trips, she had tried to create "Something," this by spending a weekend with a very charming and distinguished companion in an elegant hotel. As for the "Something" she sought, it might have been, indifferently, as she confessed, either an anguish of guilt and self-recrimination, or sexual bliss, preferably of a caliber to merit the name of love.

"But, oh!" she cried out to me, with some accent of accusation as though it were all my fault, "it was like—it was like—" and she struggled wildly for a metaphor grand enough for the truth of the occasion "—it was like trying to feel guilty for going to the toilet!"

"Yes, yes," I was murmuring sympathetically, patting her emotion-heaved shoulders while she dropped her face into her hands and wept.

"It was just," she was saying, "it was just an—*outlet!*"

For a moment, this being the period when Dr. Kinsey's lingo was still fashionable, at least among people pushing middle age, I thought she was, in her grief, making a gallant little joke, and laughed, but when the face was lifted to me, I immediately realized my mistake, and converted the sympathetic laughter into a coughing fit.

"Oh, we tried so hard," she exclaimed, "to do everything right. To make everything mean something. But nothing means anything!" she cried, and seized my hands and began to weep.

So in the end, the "Everything" she had to talk about turned out to be "Nothing," and rack my brain as I might, "Nothing" was the only synonym I, personally, could come up with for "Everything," and I suppose that the tone in which I have cast my recent account is a fair indication of the minimal degree of emotional involvement I then seemed to feel. It seemed that Ephraim had dissolved away like a dream. At least neither of us mentioned him.

Our divorce was very rational, very friendly, even shot through with mutual respect, with no alimony (she made much more money than I and was the only child of a very rich widow), and with only a token monthly sum due from me for child support (really a device arranged by lawyers to flatter my masculine ego), and a liberal arrangement for periods with Ephraim, who, as my wife kept insisting, was so proud of his *papa,* the word in an impeccable French accent.

.   .   .

But I was sometimes to wonder how proud he would have been of his *papa* if he could observe him on one of the occasions when, in his bathroom, he confronted a broken-nosed, time-ravaged, and tear-stained face, dabbed with shaving lather, that was saying, "But I loved her, I loved her—oh, what went wrong!"

Or had he seen me sitting on the edge of the tub, soap-smeared

razor drying in my hand while I wondered if I had ever loved anybody.

.   .   .

So the years passed. With somewhat shorter breath I continued my
little program at the gymnasium. Somnambulistically, I climbed dark
stairs and pushed greasy doorbells to get signatures on behalf of
worthy causes. I worked for justice for the black Americans, and
made speeches and went to Selma, Alabama. I did teach-ins against
the war in Southeast Asia.

In the primary of 1968 I worked hard for causes of virtue, even if
I did find some practitioners and prophets of virtue nauseatingly hard
to take—that is, I worked hard until disgust overcame me. Even so,
I cast my vote. I worked devotedly with my students, more than ever,
and even got an award for that. I published articles and books, and
got more and more honorary degrees, at home and abroad, for that.
I sat on committees and compiled reports, and got enemies for that.
For I found that lies more often stuck in the throat.

I saw my son even more than in the last period before the divorce.
He spent much time with his grandmother, for his mother, as her fame
grew, traveled more frequently. Ephraim seemed to find my attic
apartment (which had seemed my natural place to return to) a romantic contrast to the luxurious surroundings he was accustomed to. He
was bright at school, even brilliant, and liked to involve me in deep
arguments. We took hiking trips together, in New England, and the
Sierras, to collect his entomological specimens. I loved him and clung
to him.

As for ladies, I rocked along. After the divorce, I discovered that
the gentleman in such a case, unless poverty-stricken or direly
afflicted, tends to become the target of female curiosity and passion.
Indeed, when a divorce occurs in a closed circle like a university
faculty, a certain number of women, usually well-preserved specimens
in their early forties, who have been jogging along quite comfortably
in the matrimonial harness, catch a new scent on the air, become
restive and begin to snort and consider new possibilities, temporary
or permanent. But somehow with me, the only outlets I located, or

345

wanted, were temporary, and that was the way it seemed things would continue until someday they dwindled off.

Only once again did I approach matrimony, this to a quite beautiful, brown-eyed (with gold flecks in the iris) prance-y, and high-busted young graduate student, who, irrelevantly gifted with brains, had stumbled into graduate work, and who tended, as is sometimes the case, to confuse her romantic passion for learning with a tender feeling for the decaying carcass of some senior professor of reputation. She did give me great joy, on several occasions, and really turned my head. But I finally told her the facts of life and lent her my handkerchief until the fit had spent itself.

So I got used to solitude. Or rather, I filled it up.

I had long since ceased to think much about the *imperium intellectūs*—though I still got some excitement from a well-turned thought or a striking metaphor. I had lost the last dregs of my professional ambition, and the lust for fame. I had struggled for them, and had found some metaphysical justification in them—even while sneering at myself. But now my research and writing, like women, became valuable to me as a way to fill up time, and as I had more time to fill I had more fame. I tried to be kind to my students, but to bear down on them. I still had one belief, held with some passion, that good technicians—and you notice my choice of the term, for what it is worth—are better than bad ones.

And the young are very appealing. Particularly if you are inclined to brood over what is likely to happen to them along the rocky road.

．　　．　　．

I loved Ephraim with a greater passion, the kind that made me wake up in the night and want to pray. Even though I did not know how to pray.

In any case, Ephraim did not seem to be the kind of boy who needs much praying for, he was tearing up M.I.T. by the roots, and the only trouble was that, when he did have time to come see me, we didn't have much to talk about, I was so ignorant. But he still might bait me into a philosophical argument. He liked nothing better than to tease me about my absurd notion of the nature of scientific belief.

I almost forgot to say that something very important did happen to me during this period. I made a friend. I have already mentioned him as the *sandik* who held my son on his lap, a role of greatest honor at the circumcision. He was the much younger brother of my ex-mother-in-law, a Polish Jew, a young scholar of science who had fought against the Russians in 1939, and had been captured but twice escaped. After the second recapture, in 1941, in what amounted to a death camp on the island of Ostov Bezimienny (which quaintly means No-Name Island), he was given the option of fighting the Germans or remaining in the camp, and being about as happy to kill Krauts as Russians, made a reasonable choice. So, as he was later to say to me in his excessively correct and very unnatural English, he had a "delectable war": all enemies, no friends, no grief no matter who got the chop. Indeed, he killed Krauts so well that, after the war, he was allowed to proceed with his mathematical studies, an advantage made easier, no doubt, by the fact that the bookkeeping of No-Name Island was so slovenly that when a certain Pole, Casimir Borowski, died, the name struck off was that of Stephan Mostoski, my Jewish friend to be, who henceforward remained gentile until he reached the Land of the Free and the Home of the Brave, and, as a professor of physics, resumed his Jewish identity and name.

My new friend Stephan Mostoski and I had nothing in common, it would seem, and yet we were true friends. Or perhaps because we had nothing in common, we would be true friends. No, we did have one thing in common: solitude. So each could tell the other all the things that had happened to him over the years to create the solitude. I told him of all my early years in Alabama, how my father fell to his death to become a legend and a joke, of all the schoolyard fistfights, of my crazy dream that you could peep through a word in a foreign language into a redeemed world. I told him that I had now lost that faith.

I told him how, hating the South, I had fled it, and ever afterwards blamed my solitude on that fact. I had fled but had found nowhere to flee to. I told him how I had tried to buy my way out of solitude by supporting the causes of virtue, but I felt isolated even from that virtue, an interloper, one might say, into Yankee virtue.

At this point, one night, Stephan lifted up his hand. "You fought a war for your country," he declared.

"I fought a war," I admitted, "and I did not like Mr. Hitler, but if I was fighting a war for my country that was only a happy coincidence. I was fighting a war—as history will someday demonstrate—for the rationalization of power in the Western World. Which is, of course, unpredictable."

"As for me," he said, "I have no country that I recognize as my own, and I am trying to learn to be happy in that condition." And he began to speak of a countryless world to come: "We are merely feeling the first pangs of modernity," he affirmed, "the death of the self which has become placeless. We are to become enormously efficient and emotionless mechanisms, that will know—if 'know' is not too old-fashioned a word to use in this context—how to breed even more efficient and more emotionless mechanisms. Let us take another drink and drink to Perfection, and to laughter."

Which he immediately did.

So, since the data were inexhaustible, friendship could flourish forever in this pooling of the resources of solitude. Stephan, I must admit, had one advantage over me. Physics itself is a study of the vastness of solitude—infinite motion in infinite solitude. While I suffered the disadvantage that sometimes my professional subject matter, however much I and other scholars might bleach it, treated of moments of human communion, however delusive, and of human community, however imperfect.

In any case, Stephan and I often talked till near dawn and saw the bottle drained, like silly youths with all their lives and aspirations before them. More than once Stephan told me that I was the only person he had met in America who could really understand him. And he, I felt, understood my story—which I did not pretend to understand.

.   .   .

One other item I almost forgot to recount. On the twenty-fifth anniversary of the death of Agnes Andresen, I woke before dawn with a strange sense, not of sadness, not of loss, not of emptiness, but of disorientation and uncertainty. All day the feeling persisted, becoming more obsessive, gnawing, acute. It was not until 7:15 that evening, as I sat in a cafeteria, that I suddenly realized the truth, and, to the astonishment of neighboring feeders, I was saying aloud: "She will die tonight." And looked at my watch.

I got a night plane to Minneapolis, sat up hours in the airport there, and arrived at Ripley City in midmorning. The town was much bigger than before, with traffic lights for blocks and blocks, new elevators along the sidings, a couple of factories, developments of tiny, ranch-style houses nibbling out in all directions into the prairies, and now, of course, a real if not very big airport to replace the shack I had known years back.

I walked out to the cemetery. It, too, had partaken of the general prosperity—to such an extent that I had difficulty in finding the right Andresen plot. Even though there was a blank space by the side of Agnes and a blank space on the tombstone set to that side of her head, Agnes already had plenty of company. An older brother was there. Her father was there, her mother was there, and in my fancy she lay smiling within their protective arms, the finest little scholar, as the doddering old school principal had said to me at the funeral, ever to come out of Ripley City. I thought how the whole town, a little town then, most of them belonging to her father's congregation, had come down to the railroad station to see her off to college.

She should never have left, she should never have left! my heart, full of nameless emotions, cried out.

I did not feel like getting any lunch. I found the church where we had been married, and where, at the reception in the basement, a half-ton of cake and half an Esso tank car of coffee had been consumed. I found the parsonage, where, in the evening after the funeral, I had knelt and prayed with her father—or rather for her father—who had lost the power of prayer. I walked the streets and hunted for the tribal name on places of business. It occurred several times. I entered the least prosperous, a shoe-repair shop, and said that I was Agnes Andresen's husband, and the big bald-headed man with leather apron and gnarled, stained hands, and eyes the celestial Scandinavian blue like Agnes' own, said, ja, ja, he remember her right good, his cousin, in school together, pretty smart girl, folks they said, though he did not have no personal way to judge. He wished he could ask me home to supper, but his woman, she was not too well on her feet, but would I have a Coca-Cola with him.

Which I did, at the drugstore soda fountain two doors away. We shook hands, and I picked up a sandwich at an eatery, and walked back to the airport in time for the Minneapolis plane.

I looked down on the town named for the feckless Federal brigadier who had finally been outfoxed by the Oglala Sioux, and had the vision of the infant Agnes sitting forever on her father's knee, precociously pronouncing her ABC's beneath the eternal blessedness of his holy blue-eyed smile.

Even if I had never expected to come back here at the end, a slot had been reserved for me and the official invitation had, all the years, been held open. But now I knew that the invitation, uttered in all sincerity, had been mystically revoked.

There was no place for me in that charmed circle around the infant that would never grow up.

.   .   .

It was only a coincidence, but what do you call a coincidence that seems to conform to the inner logic of things and validate destiny? As I have said, my first essay, *Dante and the Metaphysics of Death,* the little work on which my career was to be founded, was written in an almost hypnotic state while poor Agnes was dying, and when it found unexpected acclaim, I began to feel that it had indeed been her death warrant. I began to feel that on some moonless midnight, on a desolate heath, while the great white outcroppings of stone reared up to grin skeletally in the dark, I had struck a bargain with the Prince of This World, and he, like a gentleman, had scrupulously fulfilled what I had taken to be his whole contract.

But now, twenty-five years after the death of Agnes, having been mysteriously stirred to return to the spot on the prairie of South Dakota where I had long ago left what remained of her tortured body, I returned to my attic, to find a most important-looking communication, on most elegant, official stationery, from the Università di Roma, Facoltà di Lettere e Filosofia. It began:

350

Illustre Professore,
    Il ministero della Publica Istruzioni ci ha
communicato il suo gradimento che . . .

and to cut courtesies and matters short, it was another honorary degree, and the years flooded back over me, the early years when I had tramped those ancient stones, lonely and nameless and full of humble curiosity, in a most untidy uniform—this long before I had ever laid eyes on Agnes Andresen or written that essay on Dante and the Metaphysics of Death.

It was as though whatever forces had led me to suffer my journey through those years had also reminded the Prince of This World of what must have been a further obligation to me, and he, like the gentleman he is, had coughed up the appropriate document into my mailbox.

The old pang struck, sharp as new, and I was about to tear the sheets across when I thought: A bargain is a bargain, isn't it? I had kept my side of the bargain, hadn't I?

.   .   .

The ceremony was to be in early June, 1976, but suddenly, even as I stared down for the first of many times at the splendid document, I knew the first stirrings of a need far deeper than my vanity for a return to Italy. So I arranged leave for the spring term. I had a fine official excuse to offer. A certain amount of checking at the British Museum was required, and then I could be in Italy for a time before the Prince of This World paid his latest installment.

Long ago, in the mountains, among my desperadoes, I had found something significant: that one does not have to be alone. So one morning, in the spring of 1976, mounted on a fifth- or sixth-hand Harley-Davidson (probably one originally lifted from the transportation pool of some U.S. outfit), beret on head, goggles at eyes, rucksack containing a suit of clothes in case need arose to turn respectable, I exploded out of the old Flaminian Gate of Rome and was on my way.

I had, it may be said, begun this journey before leaving Rome, by great good luck running across a newspaper note to the effect that the famous cartoonist "Carlo" was in real life named Giacomo Antonio

351

Rieti and had served with the Partisans—Giacomo being the name of the desperado whose robust wit had decorated the whitewashed interior of our little underground hideaway in a peculiar combination of the Sistine Chapel and a bordello on an especially manic Saturday night. I wrote "Carlo," identified myself as the timid American *capitano,* and asked for a meeting for old times' sake. Not only did he invite me to Milan, where he lived, but gave me names of other old comrades in wholly different walks of life, one of them being the Communist mechanic who sold me the Harley-Davidson on which I was soon wandering among the Sienese hills, the *creti sienesi,* that ordinarily are round-topped hills in a desert world, yellow or yellow-gray, whose blankness, like the blankness of life, is nowhere better caught than in Simone Martini's great fresco in the Palazzo Publico of Siena.

I would go directly there, to the Palazzo, I would go in the doorway and stare at the caparisoned knight riding across the stricken world, with the fortified gray toy cities, apparently unpopulated, in the background. So the knight rides across the stricken world, the only mark or source of life, and I remembered how, long back, when the war, my little war, had rumbled northward, I had stood in Siena and seen the picture and discovered the image of the empty world—with one difference, the knight in the picture is moving in the logic of his unidentified mission. The dusty observer standing in that noble chamber to gaze up at him did not have any mission. Until he remembered that soon he was to rejoin his desperadoes, his only friends.

And now—how many years later!—I headed for Siena, whirled past the *creti* that, in a brief season, were streaked green with gorse, the only plant hardy enough to grapple there, and the gold of its blossoms. After the long months of grim sterility just passed, and before the hot new summer grimness to come, the burst of green-gold seemed to promise that effort was not totally in vain.

Besides the visit to the picture, there was another to be made in Siena. To an old comrade-in-arms (thanks to "Carlo"). I found the address easily enough, an elegantly ambitious thriving business concerned with ocular work, and such apparatuses as microscopes, binoculars, and opera glasses, populated by employees in professional-looking white coats who treated my request to see *il Dottore* with the contempt it clearly deserved—until after a note had been delivered.

Then *il Dottore* did see me—seeing me quite literally from behind his own vast watery fish-eyes, his own best advertisement, which swam slowly, each in its own enormous aquarium of one-half of his spectacles. With the great fish-eyes (which I did not remember from thirty years earlier), he regarded me with as little sympathy as had his white-coated underlings, but at last did agree to have a drink with me after business hours. So for some two hours I sat on a café terrace and gave myself to the great tower across the Campo, which combines the grace of a lily on its stem with some mathematical ferocity of the builder's soul, meanwhile disposing of a certain amount of whiskey.

Precisely at 6 P.M., *il Dottore,* with an air that made me brace myself for an eye examination, appeared. But instead of my eyes, *il Dottore* examined my corduroys, my red shirt, my boots, my beret, deciding apparently that it was a loan, not an eye examination, I was up to. To put him at his ease, as well as soothe my vanity, I passed him a couple of clippings from the Rome papers. Muttering something polite, he clearly expressed relief, but the relief was short-lived when I took the bull by the horns and reminded him of our old association in the Partisans—this especially since the tables nearby were filling up with well-dressed non-Partisan types. He broke into a sweat when I said I was seeking out comrades-in-arms because that old period was of great importance to me and I was trying to recapture it's "feel," its spirit.

"The romance of youth is best put by," he managed to get out, and I was sure that I was seeing thick, slimy, translucent, algae-like green plants begin to climb up the inner glass walls of the aquariums that were the lenses of his spectacles. Out of a sudden sadism, I refreshed his memory in great detail and in a loud voice. He was weaving in his chair like a man having bladder trouble at a funeral, so I finally stuck money under my saucer and thanked him for seeing me. He rose with alacrity, and put out his hand, murmuring, *"Grazie, grazie mille."*

I seized his hand and said goodbye. But it quivered only weakly. Tears of self-pity gathered in the aquariums.

"Ciao!" I exclaimed, waved my hand, and uttered in a loud voice, *"Caro vecchio ammazzacristiano!"*

And so it was as I pursued my researches. Sometimes old chaps jawed with me about the good old days, as though we were concerned with a peculiarly successful Boy Scout camp. Or I sat on the terrace of a great villa looking over the starlit waters of Lago Maggiore and an old comrade-in-arms wept because his young wife had just taken a lover, and he, who, to my knowledge, had been a very brave man with the stride of a panther, was cursing himself for a coward because he could not shoot the lover and then himself, but drank all day long. Now he proclaimed that the world was foul and he was becoming a Maoist—which he became, as I was to learn from the papers—and got himself shot by the *poliziotti* in an attempt to blow up an express train.

I gorged a great meal with another comrade, swilled noble vintages, and heard him boast of the fortune he had made *all'americana* by building quickie slums around Rome, below the level of the Tiber. "The people!" he cried out. "One must labor for the people. That is the meaning of life!" And added: "A sacred meaning—for they say there's Vatican money in the same project." And he gave me a monumental wink.

But in Milan I found "Carlo," the serious young painter who had developed on the whitewashed walls of our hideaway what was to become his extremely well-paid-for talent for obscene wit and slashing social commentary, and who now put me on the track of my saint. "Not," he said, swaying his rotund weight on his graceful dancer-toes, and waving his Havana cigar in the middle of the conversation pit of his most elegant modern Milan apartment, "that a saint has any more place in our world than a painter. Look!"—and with that he stepped out of the pit to thrust the burning butt of his expensive cigar through the middle of a large and expensively framed painting on the wall of the apartment.

"That," he declared, "is the only one of my so-called serious works that I have preserved. I destroyed all the others but clung to this. I thought it had—shall we say?—*something*. Yes, perhaps it did—a fusion of the dedication and reverence of the old age for the world, along with something of the new post-Einsteinian vision. Yes—and that is why I now, at last, put the cigar butt to it—and a very good cigar it was. Look, the hole is enlarging. The canvas has caught, and glowing threads uncurl. Ah, Silvietta," he ordered his beautiful young *amica,* "turn down the lights, then we may see all the lovely little red worms squirm toward their eternity of darkness!"

She obeyed.

Then: "And tomorrow I go back to sex and politics, which never let you down because they are not only the most durable, they are the funniest things in the world."

Turning on the light, he said: "But back to our saint. I have sound report, and you, since you say you are trying to recover some old sense of meaning, must not miss him. He might even persuade you to become a saint, then we'd have two!"

He went to inspect the now splendid hole in his painting, lighted another Havana, and poured us each a noble French brandy.

"Saints," he said, "they are so unpredictable, so do be careful."

"I'll be as careful as necessary," I said.

"Who would have thought it!" he exclaimed. "It had to be our Gianluigi, our *bell'uomo,* whose cheeks the SS had so carefully turned into purple sausage, it had to be the fellow who got so many fingernails pulled out—it had to be the fellow to whom we always turned over the hero-cases that wouldn't talk and that he always made talk. You called him our secular arm—remember?—ha-ha! Well, he turns out to be our saint."

"You are sure I can find him?"

"Sure, just go to the village of Abbadia San Salvatore, and seek out the last four or five Cistercians left there, on Monte Amiata. The people there are bred of the *sangue bollente,* and there is little way to predict how the blood will boil, in politics, feud, or blessedness. Back in the last century there was even a certain Lazzaretti, who passed from homemade sainthood to the announcement that he represented the Second Coming. Eventually, in 1878, he got himself shot by the *carabinieri,* whose business it is to keep order.

"The people of Amiata were so ignorant and stubborn and so poor that even in the summer of 1948 they did not know that Italy had really gone Demochristian, so they had their own little revolution and had a *festa* in the piazza and there they tore limb from limb a young *carabiniere* who was trying to find out what was going on. Ha-ha, they thought he was a Cossack. Then the *poliziotti* came, too, and they can be very tough.

"As for our saint, this turned the tide for him. He cannot kill a fly

355

now. He is the Crazy Man Who Helps People. He lives in a hut in the woods and eats crusts and drinks cold water and prays a great deal and works very hard to aid the aged and sick and infirm. He is the Crazy Man."

So, by the direction of one of the last Cistercians, who dig up the eighth-century ruin of the crypt, I found our saint in that land of crests, ravines, forests, and abandoned or active cinnabar mines, and he explained to me how he lay awake at night to pray for the souls of men he had slain in war. He lived in a cave in the great band of conifers below where the beeches start on the mountain. He said to me: "I live as all men must who in doing what seems necessary have impaired their humanity. I have been chosen by God," he continued, "because I was proud of being called handsome of face, and my face God turned into repulsion to teach my soul humility. But for the sins of the flesh I committed I now do not dare to enter the church. I lie on the stone outside in rain or snow and pray to be made worthy of communion."

He honored me by dividing his crust with me and gave me a cup of cold water from his spring, and embraced me. I kissed the poor flesh of his cheeks that had been mangled and empurpled like old hamburger in the days before his saintliness.

I spent the night at the village hotel, at 6 A.M. drank what locally passed for coffee, and a half-hour later was tooling down the mountain on the old Harley-Davidson war surplus, feeling rather blank of heart and head. Whatever I had come in search of, I had, clearly, not found. And it might be added, whatever illusions I had started out with I had lost. I had only the old wisdom we all struggle so hard to get and always find we already had: every man has to lead his own life and has little chance of knowing what it means, anyway.

And, anyway, there was Rome to get through, and a Roman funeral, as Dr. Stahlmann had called such occasions, and I trusted my vanity to see me through. So I plunged into the traffic, and headed for my hotel, of whose hot and cold running water I had great need.

CHAPTER XVI

The desk clerk at the Hotel Inghilterra set a great stack of mail in front of me, with a smile of personal accomplishment as though by special *virtù* and *fortitudine* he had been able to outfox all railway workers, air pilots, and postal employees. Having received my thanks and my two thousand lire, he unveiled his masterpiece. He leaned more closely, and now with the smile one *bell'uomo* offers another on a coup, said that the *bella signora* had been telephoning almost every hour for three days, and had that very morning appeared in person at the hotel—and *veramente bella, veramente chic,* she was—to make sure that another message would be delivered immediately and personally, for she might have to leave Rome soon, and to do so without seeing *il Professore* (i.e., me) would be like death to her. With that, he thrust a sheet of paper at me with a number scribbled on it.

The number, he explained, was that of a suite at the nearby Hotel Hassler, at the *Trinità dei Monti*—this in a tone to congratulate me even more fully than he had in describing the lady as *veramenta bella* and *veramente chic,* for being *bella* and *chic* did not necessarily mean you could pay the bill at the Hassler.

I had already guessed what the name of the lady would be, and stood there wondering if—especially after my just-concluded plunge into the history of the peninsula and my small personal past therein—I could face this even more dramatic plunge. For I was at that moment seeing in my mind's eye the picture that I had last seen so long ago and far away—the body, face down on the tumbled bed, with the sheet stretched across the swell of buttocks, just below the point where the bifurcation first speaks to the deepest blood, the waist preternaturally narrowed by the thrust of the arms upward to clasp the pillow over which the bright hair was upflung and into which the face was to be forever and speechlessly hidden.

But just as I was about to say to myself, no, the past is what it is, I felt the old stigma appear on my right thigh, and knew that I would telephone, that the jig was up.

The jig was indeed up, for at that instant a voice was saying, in a stagey Southern accent, right there behind me: "Why, Lordy me, if it isn't the Ole Bum himself!"

I turned, and there she was, and just what the desk clerk had said she was, *bella* and *chic* and quite a lot more, in a sleeveless linen dress, as simple as could be, and an aquamarine silk scarf filmy about her neck, and a broad straw hat and her arms outstretched, saying, "Come kiss me!"

"I'm too dirty," I said. "I've come all the way from Monte Amiata this morning, on a war surplus Harley-Davidson, and God! am I dirty."

"You're dirty, all right," she said, "but you aren't half as dirty as you're wicked, and I'll even kiss you with the wickedness, for I just love seeing Dear Old Broke-Nose with a beret stiff with guck and your goggles pushed up." And she hugged my filth to her bosom and kissed me on both cheeks, and then really and truly on my mouth, very unritualistically.

"You tast-a good," she said, drawing back to appraise me, though still grasping my shoulders, "but—" and she rubbed her chin "—don't you ever shave?"

"Sometimes I have been known to," I said.

"I don't give a damn what your habits have been for the last quarter-century," she declared, "but—"

"It hasn't been quite that long," I said defensively.

"—but I have plans," she continued, "for the next few hours. For starters, there's a wonderful restaurant right near here called Ranieri's, and if you'll get decent so they'll let you in—just shave, put on a tie, and some kind of coat, and a pint of *eau de cologne,* and I'll get you in."

I looked down at my caked corduroys, my sweat-stained suede jacket, my red shirt, my boots.

"Get cleaned up quick," she commanded, "or I'll come help you! And Christ, then we might never get fed! Get the lead out! *Dépêche-toi!*"

I grabbed my rucksack from the floor and made a bolt for the lift, calling over my shoulder for the desk to send a *portiere* up with the mail.

"Don't you read a damned line!" she yelled at me as I was hoisted upward.

. . .

When I got back to the lobby, there she was, sitting cross-kneed, legs very bare, very tanned, and very much the same leggy legs, and arranged so that, on the upper foot, one blue-colored sandal, of the thinnest strap, hung loose from the toe, like the rhythm of a heartbeat; and the color of the nails of the foot were, I noticed, aquamarine to match the scarf and sandals, the same color of the nails as on that predinner evening so long ago, in the Carrington barn, by the studio side of the Carrington fireside, when I had watched the firelight play on that same, then-not-quite-so-tanned, but roundly molded and sinewy foot, from which a sandal then, too, dangled. That was the evening I had made the remark about Dugton's being the rock from which we both were hewn.

But this now, as she had said, was nearly a quarter-century later, and in Rome, a lot further from Dugton than even Nashville was. Or was it?

"Thank God," she said, popping to her feet, "I'm starving—" and she came at me "—but not so starving I'm not going to kiss you again."

Having done that, she led me down the street, clinging to my arm in a most defenseless and confiding fashion, to the promised restaurant, which could not have had more of an unostentatious, well-bred, and yet very businesslike air, and where she immediately received most decorous hospitality from the staff.

"You see," she said as soon as we were settled, and the apéritifs were on the way, "they like me here."

I grunted.

"They like me for a lot of reasons," she said, "and one of them— no, not number one, of course—is that they like me." And she smiled about her with precisely the benign smile of the Beauty Queen of Dugton High, and the smile was, I could see, taken personally by at least several waiters and one bus-boy, just as it used to be taken personally by every male student at Dugton High, excepting, of course, Yours Truly.

The smile was the same, but the face was different. Beautiful, yes, but in a more bony, carved way that, in collaboration with the very positive tan, made the amethystine eyes more than ever the center of life. I could not help examining whatever else was above the table edge, the now thinner edge of the breastbone below the throat, the faint lining of the throat itself where the filmy garroting of age was doing its almost imperceptible work, the fullness of veins on the backs of the vivacious hands that could suddenly go so still—the bruised-looking blueness of veins, there modified by sun tan but boldly accentuated by the big turquoise rings she wore on each hand. I was trying to imagine what things were like, officially visible or not, below the level of the table, how the honed-down boniness would give the honed-down female softnesses a special pathos of joy that no bouncing babe, not even Rozelle in her prime, could match.

"I do keep myself in shape, don't I?" Rozelle demanded, reading my mind and glancing across at a side mirror which showed us both in profile from head to heel.

"You sure do," I said.

"I'm not wearing a bra," she said, "and I bet you never guessed it."

I shook my head.

"You see," she said, "I lie on my back on the floor every morning and hold a five-pound dumbbell in each hand and stretch my arms fifty times over my head to touch the floor with them. Which, to judge from your shape," she said, giving me a quick appraisal, "is something you don't even think about."

Again I shook my head.

"With me," she said, "it's about the only thing I have to think about. I look at myself in the mirror every morning and ask if I were a man and not in love with me, just happening to be with me, what I'd find most fault with. This is what is called intellectual honesty. As time gets shorter, you see," she added didactically, "you have to get longer on intellectual honesty."

"I know all about that," I retorted.

"Well, what do you do about it?"

"Absolutely nothing," I said, and suddenly was as happy as though I were a cocaine addict and had just had a whiff of snow after a long drouth. "I mean," I said, "I work, and when I work I don't have to be intellectually honest. I don't have to care what the work means just so long as it's well done."

"I read the piece in *Il Messaggero* about that degree or whatever it is they're going to give you because you must have worked so very hard at not being intellectually honest."

The wine—the *Riserva*—had come, and we tried it.

"That, to resume the conversation," I said, "is only half true. I have been intellectually honest enough to recognize two facts, long back."

"It's good—the fettucine, I mean," she said, testing it. Then: "Go ahead, what facts?"

"Fact Number One. That the main function of work is to kill time. I mean time with a capital *t.*"

Having said that, I found myself very hungry. I began to eat, ravenously. When I had washed down the mound of *pasta* with the *Riserva,* I said: "Now for Fact Number Two."

"All right."

"Fact Number Two," I said, "is that I have never had the slightest notion of what happiness is—that what I had thought of all my life as happiness was only excitement. Of one kind or another."

Very daintily she touched the napkin to her lips. Carefully, she held up her wineglass, half full, as though to admire its color against the light. She spoke very impersonally, as though to the glass, or rather as though she were a medium or an oracle or something of the sort who was staring into a crystal ball swimming with the red brilliance.

"So," she was saying, in the oracle's whispery voice, "that is why you stood in the middle of the floor and looked down at a naked girl on a bed who was crying her heart out into a pillow because she believed in happiness, and then you just walked out the door?"

"Listen," I said, "at that point in my life I had made no generalizations about me or happiness. I merely knew what I knew—that I could not run off to Europe—without occupation—and live off your money—or to be more exact, Butler's money."

"In other words," she said, still staring into the swimming brilliance in the glass, "you lacked—somehow—any faith in me. I was, that is, just one more big chunk of excitement?"

She set her glass down, leaned at me, and said: "You know, Dear Old Broke-Nose, you never once tried to figure out what I was like. You didn't even try to help me find what I wanted to be."

I started to say something. But I had nothing to say.

"See!" she exclaimed, maliciously. "You haven't even got something to say about it. Maybe you even believed that Lawford was right, that all I wanted was to be respectable, to have position. Just Dugton."

As I felt flustered and overwhelmed by guilt, she gave me one of her old wicked, eye-sparkling grins, as though all the years were nothing. "But," she said, "don't you worry your pretty head about it, Old Broke-Nose."

Again I tried to answer, but her voice went on: "I didn't know what I was then, either. All I knew was that I loved you to wild distraction.

"You know, I used to wake up in the middle of the night and want to kill you dead because of the first time you ran away from me—that night at the Prom, back in Dugton. But your doing that—it might have been a favor. Suppose we had danced and then gone out to the falls by moonlight and started screwing like rabbits for Easter and I got knocked up and you married me and got yourself a regular job at the A&P, and got to be manager after ten years because you are so smart, but by that time I had three or four kids and looked like a hag every morning—oh, yeah, I was the Beauty Queen of All Hags! —and so one morning I just bummed a ride out of town with a paint salesman with a little black mustache and a new Pontiac, to Atlanta, or God knows where—with, of course, all there was in our savings account."

She looked down at her plate, giving some matter deep thought, then directly into my eyes. "But you did her a bigger favor, maybe, just walking out on that ass-naked girl and her desperate tears. Suppose she had gone off to some jerkwater college with you and went to pieces in some generally disastrous way? Or you had gone off to Europe with her to live on Butler's money and so had gone to pieces in your way? Oh yes, we'd have loved each other to distraction—to hell and damnation and busted bed-slats. But then what?"

She again studied her glass, and, not lifting her gaze, said: "There is, of course, one possibility we have not yet touched on. Have you ever thought that we might really have loved each other and been happy in that? For always?"

Before I could find an answer, she resumed: "No, Dear Old Broke-Nose, you sure did that girl a favor. When you walked out that door, with everything so coldly and capably arranged, that was what did it —she was cured. Yes, I'll tell you something. Right then, when she had cried all her tears, she masturbated. Are you shocked?"

"Scarcely."

"Well, you sure look it," she said. "For that was her first step to get good and cured, and never love anybody to distraction again. Love somebody so you wanted just to be soul and body with that person, just one flesh like the Bible used to say back in Dugton. Well, you cured her good.

"That girl jumped off that bed and went home and took the lay of the land, how that fool Amy girl had her eye on Carrington and how she was on dope she got from her swami who read that Hindi or whatever fool poetry to her, and so that girl you taught the lesson to knew how to make everything work out, just give water plenty of opportunity to run downhill, and even if J. Lawford now and then wanted to whack a piece off his legal wife because she was convenient, she never said no, for she had a secret trick, just roll over and pretend you're one of those inflated rubber dolls Japanese sea captains are said to carry on long voyages. Just hang on and wait for the other shoe to fall.

"And meanwhile, just to do what would give Lawford the biggest jitters—if he knew about it—I carefully drifted into an arrangement with the swami, who definitely was not on drugs, and who was one of the smartest men I ever knew and who—"

About this time waiters started laying out another course and more wine, and Rozelle, I could tell from old signs, got more and more glittery with what she had to tell me next.

"It's about the swami," she said, "and you'd never guess!"

"No," I said.

"He's a nigger—as they used to say down home," she said, and giggled, and thrust out her left hand at me with the ring on it, "and he's my husband!"

"Well," I said, as soon as I got my breath back, "you might have at least put the news in two separate sentences."

"Well, to take the nigger part first," she said, "he was a college boy, yes-indeedy, nothing but the best for me, at Jackson State, Mississippi —no less—and joined the Navy—back before we were in the war— and found himself a mess boy, and jumped ship in India and being the smartest man I ever knew, present company excepted maybe, learned the language, Hindi or whatever, and learned how to write poems in it and took up the swami stuff, too, and was in a monastery or something like that for a time, and then he got so he could speak real English like he had been to Oxford or something, and when he had all connections in order he got a fake passport—and put on a turban—and hit the U.S.A., including Nashville, for a high old time, till Amy and Lawford got romantic about dying together. I helped the swami on his way out of that mess fast. But long since he's straight. Now he's a big boy in arbitrage. Really big, and—"

"What's arbitrage?"

"Oh, you know, working with foreign exchanges, playing both ends against the middle, and all very legal. You see, he ain't no common disrespectable pusher. Really big and really clean—that's the motto. You'd never guess where we live—aside, I mean, from all the poshest places on the Continent when we're traveling."

I admitted that I couldn't guess.

"Morocco," she said. "And do we live like lords! In fact, we *are* lords. To hell with Dugton, Nashville, and respectability." She seemed to be seeing me from a great and marveling distance. Then, with a sad, sweet smile, she was saying: "When you walked out that door, you set me free. From so much, dear Old Broke-Nose."

"How do you make out?" I demanded. "Otherwise, I mean?"

"Just splendidly," she said, "if that is what you mean. He has to travel a lot—he's in Amsterdam right now, or says he is—but I never worry about him. Even if he may go Arab on me now and then. To tell the truth, getting married was my idea—after quite a spell, I mean. I enjoyed our goings-on and he's got a real sense of humor, and I wanted to crown the black boy's success by giving him legal as well as literal access to all the apertures on the fair white body of the Beauty Queen of Dugton High. I wanted him to feel truly appreciated, and in the mainstream of American life. Also, I didn't want him to think I might ever be in a position to testify against him. Also, you know, he's a pretty impressive guy from any angle."

"I imagine," I said.

"Back in Tuscaloosa, Alabama—" she began.

"I know about Alabama," I said.

"Well," she said, "I took a sociology course—it was a big fat green book—and it quoted some other sociologist who had called the Negro the 'lady of the races.' Meaning, I guess, that the colored folks like to sing and dance and wear bright colors. But if that is what that sociologist meant, he was superficial. The Negro," she said, pronouncing the word with an excessively long *e,* "if you are old-fashioned and square enough to use that locution—is, for my books, the gentleman of the races. Anyway, my specimen is. He is never flashy. Even when he tours the Continent in his Rolls, with his driver, everything is oh-so-genteel, and if I am the female ornament, I am very discreetly —some might even say dowdily—rigged out. Except for a king's ransom diamond—or emerald.

"But him—even without a turban! There's something about the guy. When we go into a three-star restaurant—say, outside Lyons or Les Baux or the Tour d'Argent—even with no reservation, and the place jammed, he just has the air that something is going to happen in a certain way. I mean, he is sort of self-defined, and that is what being a gentleman is, I guess. You know, he has that sense of power in not having to use power. I don't know anything about his business, but once I did catch a glimpse—well, to hell with that.

"I'm getting off the track. He's so self-contained, you'd think he had always been that way and no Jackson, Mississippi, ever. But he seems to need to remind himself now and then. There are signs I can see coming on. Watching is one of the things I long since learned how to do.

"And first, I noticed a long time back, he sort of loses his appetite. In Morocco we eat French, French being rich. When he begins to get picky, it means he wants me to cook something for him. What it amounts to is, I'm supposed to make things taste like a nigger shack in Jackson, Mississippi, and so I do what I can in place of sowbelly, chitlings, collards, corn meal, and sorghum. In other words, I'm what you might call his Ole White Mammy.

"But to come to fundamentals, we are more married than most people ever are, and like it. It maybe started out in a complex way because he had a yen for white girls like me that he, the black boy, used to see cruise by in a big Chrysler—"

"I can remember how a white boy felt," I said.

"I'm not talking about that," she said, "and anyway, you aren't black. And when he got hold of one, he must have had a mixture of interesting feelings which gave some extra tilts to the pinball game. I don't really know about him, but I do know about me. At first, it was a special way of foxing Lawford, and, I might say, Nashville, Tennessee, to boot. And for added complications, I guess I was stuffed to the eyeballs, too, with all those notions about the way niggers are supposed to be in bed. So, in a sort of upside-down way, we have a really good old-fashioned Southern marriage blessed by God and Jeff Davis. Even if my husband talks Italian like a Tuscan, and Hindi like those folks who aren't really niggers after all, and French like a maharajah. By the way, I hope you noticed my Italian accent."

"I did," I said, "and I admired it."

"Well," she said, "you ought to hear my French, and I've read a lot of fancy books in French, too. I hope you remember that I was not dumb in Latin class."

"I devoutly remember," I said.

"Do you want me to tell you about Levi-Strauss and structuralism?"

"No, thanks," I said.

She fell thoughtful for a moment.

"We've been married a long time," she said then. "Not old exactly, but definitely slowed down. So, instead of ripping something off, sometimes we just get to talking about some special time in the past. Or we talk 'Ole-Timey down home' talk, about Dugton High and what happened, or nigger patois of what he, my husband, says white folks used to call Possum Prick Alley, which was where he lived. And the longer we live with Wops and Dagos and Wogs and Greasers and Frogs—and even Limeys—the more we have a real Ole-Timey Confederate marriage, with the Stars and Bars tacked on the wall above our bed."

I sang the first line of "Dixie" under my breath—or almost under it.

She looked assessingly at me across the debris of dessert and fruit and cheese and brandy glasses. "I don't seem to remember," she said, "that you were ever especially high on the Lost Cause."

"You are wrong," I said.

"Well, I don't seem to remember—"

"You remember very well," I asserted, "as far as crude objective facts are concerned. But the inner reality is different. I *am* the Lost Cause."

"Excuse me, Buster," she said, *"excusez-moi, excuses-moi, mon vieux, mon cher, mon petit chou,* but time she so fast fleet away, '*Ou sont les neiges d'antan,*' and '*les lauriers sont coupés,*' but if we had just one more brandy together—"

"We have had three," I said.

"And then," she said, ignoring me, "suppose we went up to *numero ventuno* or *ventidue* or what the hell number in your fleabag hotel, then we might find, even in *quest'ora del tramonto*—"

"But it's not sunset yet," I interposed.

"I speak metaphorically," she declared, in a flat, factual tone, not the slightest bit boozy, "and metaphorically speaking, you are wrong.

We both are approaching sunset. But do not forget that sunset—oh, *il tramonto!*—can be the glory of the day."

Suddenly she stood up, not boozily, very erect, chic and simple, breasts slightly shrunken under linen and slightly prolapsed, the aquamarine scarf hiding the marks of the filmy garrote, and the bony structure of her face and the shadowed amethystine glint of her eyes woke a sudden flash of beauty like the illusion created by a great actress in her absolutely last appearance, and in a clear, positive tone, she proclaimed, "Shit."

And, in the stunned silence, moved toward the door.

The waiter, who had been keeping a watchful eye on our shenanigans, appeared with miraculous speed to lay a bill before me. And miraculously, I had enough to pay up, though not to leave him bowing, and made the door.

A few meters away Rozelle's linen-colored flame flickered in the deserted street. I knew she could hear my step, for I was wearing heel-irons on my boots, but she did not turn. She did not even turn when I had caught up with her, merely began to move along beside me, though well apart, as I slowed to a possible pace.

The sky was painfully brilliant above the yellow-red tile roofs, but we were now walking the shadowed street, and her voice was saying, "I suppose you think I planned to leave you there with not enough cash, and so avenge myself for the times you left me."

I said nothing, listening to the click of heel-irons on Roman stone, thinking how I had heard that sound long ago multiplied as regiments swung past.

"I won't say," she was saying, "that such a thought did not cross my mind. Anything can cross your mind, but that doesn't mean you'd do it, does it?"

"I reckon not," I said.

"It was just the way everything felt as I sat there," the voice was now saying, "just like when I saw your name in the paper—like the time I saw it in the *Nashville Banner* long ago—it was like a sign that something was going to be—to be—"

There was no way for me to help her finish the sentence.

"—to be clean—to be final," she concluded. "Final and redemptive." Then, after a couple of steps: "Though how, I can't possibly imagine!"

Nor could I be of any help here.

"Not that I was lying about anything I was telling you. I was telling you how the story all really comes out and the exact truth about my life." She walked in silence, then lifted her gaze to me. "You know, back in Nashville, you were the only person I didn't have to lie to in some way. Oh, I'd told Lawford all the real dirt about me—I'm not that kind of a liar. But there was some little nest of unspoken lies. I even lied to myself—in a very deep and subtle way—when I was by myself. I didn't even know who I was."

"What does anybody know?" I asked, miserably. "About himself? And anyway, you were willing to go off to Europe with me. It was me who made the trouble there."

"And quite properly." She leaned back as though to admire me. "Look how great you are now!"

I don't know what expression my face wore at that moment, but it could not have been very happy, for she, grinning suddenly, said: "But you don't have to look so doleful. And don't worry about me, either. For one thing, I never have to worry about truth and lies any more. I can't think of anything I haven't told my husband. Except you —and somehow you don't count. You are real and not a charade, and with your kind help of long ago, I understood that everything was a charade for me. So to have my fun I rigged up, as I explained to you, my very complicated joke on just about everybody—my aunt, Dugton, J. Lawford, and Nashville—and maybe a little on you."

"Maybe," I said, "since all of my life seems to be a joke on me."

"And maybe," she added meditatively, "maybe on me, too. But at least I can laugh at it." She paused again, looking up at me, eyes independently shedding their strange light in the dark shadow of the hat.

"Listen," she said, "I can laugh because I've learned one trick. I used to say to myself, I've just got—for instance—seven more years. Then five. Then four. Do you know how I'd test myself?"

"No."

"Well, at a party, or somewhere—a bar or at a single table in a dining room—or even if I was sitting with somebody—I'd see if I could test myself. Was I hitting somebody where he really lived? Old guys are easy. I'd only test young ones, or at the prime. Oh, I don't mean I'm ever promiscuous. I am most definitely fastidious. I've never gone out for pick-ups—though now and then I have made them, oh, very subtly. But a woman can sense the impression she's making. A man is talking to his girl and his eyes begin to wander. And you give him just one fleeting but direct engagement of your glance. It's all you need to know. It's two years now I give myself—maybe three on good days."

After the heel-irons had clicked off half a minute, she demanded: "You know what then?"

"No," I said, staring into the world of shadow under the wide hat, where the eyes shed their piercing light.

"In our world," she said, "it's always easy to come by something. It doesn't hurt a bit!"

And she began to walk very fast, making me hurry to catch up.

Then, stopping abruptly, she said: "When I was propositioning you back there in the restaurant, all that horsing around about your room number and the hour of sunset—I wasn't trying to test anything. I swear it."

"You said the old guys are too easy," I said. "And I'm not so goddamned young any more." I hated the bravado in my voice that came out like forlornness.

"Not trying to test anything—no!" she said. "No—what I said just popped out—that was why I sounded drunk, I guess, and was doing all that horsing around. Because I was all torn up, in a dozen ways. Maybe you had obligations and—"

"No," I said. "Divorced. And a son near grown."

Ignoring that, she was plunging on: "—and if things had not turned out well—there in *quest'ora del tramonto*—I'd think nothing had ever been any good and then what good was all my life? But if things, even in that hour of metaphorical sunset, had turned out good, what then? All the old misery. And for what? Or just the new misery of living the old mistake. Unless we could treat it, like—like a footnote, no doubt you'd say. You must be great on footnotes."

I struggled to say something, but I was shivering, literally, with

370

fear. Not fear of one thing. Of a dozen things which I could not name. But I could name one. If things had happened and had turned out all right, how could I bear not having had the years I had thrown away?

But did I know the answer to that, either?

"Oh, don't say anything," she said, with social brightness, like putting a stupid stranger at his ease at a cocktail party. "Probably everything is, as I said at lunch—for which I do thank you—all for the best. Maybe even a telephone call I expect within the next hour or so will summon me to Amsterdam to resume real life, and that will be for the best. But I'll be in my suite between four and six, and if I am not summoned to Amsterdam, you are most definitely invited to join me for dinner."

Again she stopped, one hand clasping the edge of the broad hat, to tilt it properly, and the other, with a purse in it, pointing in a most unladylike fashion at my hotel across the street.

"There's your fleabag establishment," she said, "which you so rudely did not invite me to enter with you in *quest'ora del tramonto.* No—don't kiss me goodbye. For—" and she gave her most wicked grin—"this may not be goodbye. If you call by six."

She wheeled like a drill sergeant, looked back to crook her hand at me and say, *"Ciao,"* and marched a few steps. Looking back, she said, "Hurry up and read all that mail you have stored up. I could tell all during lunch that you were just fidgeting to get at it."

With that she definitively did march off, through patches of shade and patches of dazzle, on into the distance of the ochre of Roman plaster and the iron-gray of Roman stone.

· · ·

Once in my room I saw the great stack of mail, idly glanced at a return address or two, and was all at once overcome by fatigue and sadness, which the stack of letters seemed to symbolize. I unpacked the suitcases that had been stored by the hotel to await my return, hanging up my clothes to get things ready for my academic festivities, and took a long bath. While I lay in the water and soaked off the grime, I could see nothing in my mind but the face of a great clock with the minute hand grinding from four to five. I simply saw the image.

When I got out of the tub, I lay naked on my bed, with the mail stacked on a couple of chairs nearby. I lay naked and began to work through the pile, first running through all to see if any bore the name of my son. Well, that was the way boys are, and without sadness or reproach, my heart filled with love.

A half-hour later I found the letter from Dugton. It was not in my mother's inimitably vigorous hand, which always gave the impression that she had slain the paper by each thrust of the pen. The return name on this letter was: Mr. Perk Simms, Jonquil Avenue, Dugton, Alabama, U.S.A. I lay there trying to get the courage to open it. Then, courage or not, my hands did it. There the words were:

Dear Perfesser:

With greeting heart I report that my Dear One and your fine Ma has passed to the Other Shore, where all tears, they shall be dried. She was strickened of a Friday Night—a bust appendicitus—and died Sunday. She was buried that Tuesday. We knowed we could not get at you in time for nuthen, and so put her in the ground. When she went to the hospital she kept them new photos of you. She said she hope she done right in raising you. When they taken her to the operation room to operate they had to take them photos from her hand. She talked a lot about you even weak like she was become, and left many word messages to be more personal. I will give them personal when you git back. Last thing she say to me to tell you she was sorry she bust yore nose, but she'd do it agin by God. It looked like she was trying to laugh.

Let me hear a word from you and yore fine accomplishments.

Respectfully,
Perk Simms

P.S.   Yore Ma died as easy as you kin expeck with perontinitus. I always tried to be a good husband, like the Lord would let me, and my heart it is broken. I got lot to tell personal when you are back. I know I aint yore blood father but I want to see you, she talked so much about you, and I feel like I got a claim on you too. And a man in my shape, not to start pity himself, needs some kind of claim.

.   .   .

So that was it, and as I lay back naked, waiting for the after-bath coolness, with the letter on my chest, it seemed to be as I had always known it would be. The woman had thrust a being forth from her body into the blaze and strangeness of the world, and now, half a century later and half a hemisphere away, a heavy, swarthy man, running to belly and getting a little bald on the top of his head, lay naked in a strange room in a strange country, and the voices rising from the street below, as the afternoon shadow lengthened, were in a tongue that, all at once, was strange to him. It was as though that man had never heard that tongue before.

I knew I was that man. Therefore, I leaped from the bed and looked at my watch. It was just past six o'clock, and I called the number at the Hassler. I would call and say that my mother was dead. No—I would go there for dinner and tell about my mother. Maybe I could wait and tell about her a little later. Then I could even weep if I wanted to and not be ashamed, and the language of comfort would be my own tongue.

I kept ringing the suite at the Hassler, but it was no use.

Rozelle had probably not received the summons to Amsterdam and perhaps at this moment was down in the discreet and expensive dungeon-like bar of her hotel and had just caught the eye of a rather handsome youngish man and now felt that Time had stopped and the moment for doing what she would do when Time had run a certain course had been indefinitely postponed, and I felt like praying that the man, even if he wasn't so very young after all, would be without vanity, and tender and aware of his great good fortune and would create all the illusions that we live for, even if illusions are only illusions, and none seemed to be handy for me that night. For my grief was not an illusion.

Then a thought popped into my head. Maybe Rozelle had found no man, young or old, in the bar. Maybe—maybe—she had suddenly felt that the time had come. And another kind of grief was thus grafted onto the grief I already had.

But then I had another thought. Maybe Rozelle, when the time actually came that she talked about, wouldn't do it after all, no matter how little it would hurt. Maybe she'd just drift on with her swami-husband, just like any old couple, talking things over, trying to remember how things were, having an occasional spat just for the hell of it, each watching over the other's diet, maybe holding hands in the sunset, just another old married couple, only richer—all legally married, with the special blessing of God, Ole Marse Robert, and Jefferson Davis.

And this thought brought another kind of elegiac dampness to my eyes. So I hastily dressed, went down for an indifferent and silent dinner, took a walk to look at the Campidoglio in moonlight, a place which at such an hour can persuade even a historian that our history is, as indeed the poet saith, grave, noble, and tragic, then home to bed and a brace of sleeping pills to be fresh as a daisy for the next day's festivities and the honor to be visited upon me simply because I had learned the elementary, but difficult, lesson that work will fill up Time.

Before I fell asleep I wondered how much the need to see Rozelle and talk to her about my mother's death had been merely a mask— oh, a most transparent mask. How clearly!—how clearly, in the depth of my being indeed—had I known how the comforting of grief and the wiping away of every tear would have wound up between the sheets. Yes, I had not read my Aristotle for nothing, for he, in the *Rhetoric,* points out that the awakening of an emotion of one genre evokes those of a similar genre. Tenderness calls forth tenderness.

Then, after this little example of characteristic and ironic self-flagellation, my last waking thought was a kind of laughter—a quiet laughter of the mind, shall we say?—at the image of how my mother, on the Other Shore, would have howled with mirth at the picture of me weeping away my grief for her death on the shoulder of "Miss Pritty-Pants," all the while slipping "Miss Pritty-Pants" the old meat.

.   .   .

But maybe, had the number at the Hassler answered, my mother would not, in the end, have howled with mirth. Long ago, true enough, in Dugton, she had recognized "Miss Pritty-Pants" as the characteristic temptation to her son and the natural threat to her deepest plans, but now, in the total knowledge and total wisdom of the Other Shore, she might merely have smiled sadly and pityingly at the thought that in the compulsive grapplings, confused struggles, and obsessive appetites of "Miss Pritty-Pants" and Old Broke-Nose something she might even have called love was making an effort to emerge.

With this thought my own variety of pitying sadness began to come over me. In the end it was a liberation.

Finally, I went to sleep.

CHAPTER XVII

After Rome I went back to Paris, to the libraries and solitude in restaurants (but with a wine that I could now afford) and a solitary walk along the Seine, or in a crooked street on the Left Bank, or in an avenue of the faubourgs, feeling myself caught more and more in a routine for which I could find no meaning. In those last listless weeks of early August in deserted Paris, when at night the premature dead leaves lay on the pavements of the faubourgs, awaiting the first seasonal wind to make them slide and rustle, I was sustained by the thought that Ephraim would soon join me in New York and he and I would have a beautiful ten days in a canoe on the bright maze of waterways of northern Ontario, watching the coniferous forests slide silently past in their subtly variable flux of green, watching a bear stand like prehistory on a great stone by the lake set against the evening sky. And all day I would be watching the tanned shoulders of polished muscle swing in Ephraim's tranceful rhythm, over and over, up to the moment when the blade lifted and the final silver drop fell; and at night, lying by the last glimmer of the campfire, I would listen while Ephraim's strong, sleeping breath came regular, slow, and deep, and listen, too, to the distant loons calling their amalgam of mirth, grief, and manic irony—in other words, to sink myself in a solitude that was the cure for other solitudes.

That was indeed what happened, plus the collecting of his specimens (he still followed entomology as his hobby), plus the fishing (which he did while I read), plus the eating of bass or walleyed pike (which he cooked magnificently), plus his voice by the fire while we drank whiskey and he quoted Baudelaire, Rimbaud, Vigny, Valéry, and Villon (which seemed to stuff infinitely his head, tucked away among his formulae), plus the fact that long after he was asleep I might crawl out of my bag for a last piss, and linger to look down at him, as I had years before when, wandering back to the nursery, I would stare down at the little blob of protoplasm zipped into the night garment. Even now, as the last glimmer from the coals touched his cheek, the man's cheek shaped with the same old innocent curve as the child's—the same curve shadowed by dark lashes, I would add to myself, with a slow, tearing wrench, that long ago I had learned to observe on the sleeping face of his mother.

This was our trip, the perfect trip, to the North, perfect except that an image and a conversation that were in my mind remained only there. In the streets of Paris I would find myself looking forward to a campfire so many thousand miles away, and I would hear my voice saying: "Son, my mother died last May. I had not seen her for more than twenty-five years. This fall I am going down to see her grave. Will you come with me?"

And I would feel the great rush of words to be said, the words that would tell everything—whatever *everything* was—and I would see myself pointing at the chinaberry tree under which I had stood and wept the morning of my father's death, pointing at the spot on the pike where the body had been found, pointing at his grave in the Heaven's Hope cemetery, pointing to the cannery where my mother had worked all the subsequent years, refusing to come to see me, sending back the torn-across checks, saying she better stay put for a spell longer, and she knowed how mortal ugly I was without looking one more time. I would point at the spot on the sidewalk on Jonquil Street where I had stood one June sunset.

Sometimes, in fact, in the back of my mind lurked the thought that I might write and ask him to go now—not to Ontario, but to Alabama. Of course—he would go! Then everything in my life would be different. Why wouldn't he go there, instead of to Canada? Then all my life would be in one piece, somehow. Everything would come together. I would no longer wake up at night and ask where I was, ask why I had come here (wherever here happened to be), ask why nothing I did, no matter how devotedly, seemed any more to have meaning, ask why sometimes I literally could not bring myself to think of the past or speculate about the future, when I had locked myself into my attic room.

I never had the courage, however, to ask him, and did not even tell him of my mother's death till after the trip was over, and then almost in passing. I had certainly not had the courage to suggest to him that he and I go to Alabama—and how ricidulous it would have been, in August, in the dry time when dust covers the ragweed by the side of the road whiter than hoarfrost and hotter than hominy grits in hell, and the moon comes up bigger than a barn and red as blood! How ridiculous at any time!

Back in Chicago, one night after Stephan had taken dinner with me at our faculty club and we retired to my old attic room to deal with a bottle of half-century-old calvados which he had brought along to celebrate my return, I told him of my mother's death, and even showed him the last letter from Perk Simms.

"How lucky you are!" he said, with the saddest and most ironic of his sad and suddenly Jewish smiles. "At least you know when she died, how, and where the body lies. I know nothing of what my late—" he spat symbolically from the side of his mouth "—comrades-in-arms did to my mother."

It was this, I presume, that made me then tell him of my fantasy of asking Ephraim to go with me to Alabama, and how my courage had failed.

"You did him a grave injustice," he said. "I can imagine his wanting to go, and for years now wondering why you did not ask him. I can imagine his wanting to go with you—to see you—his father—" and here, with a hint of irony, he paused "—be reborn."

"No, thanks," I said. "Once is enough."

He studied his calvados.

"I am not as sure as I once was," he said. "Even I, mind you, may someday pray to be reborn." He took a few drops, relished them, and said: "In the period when I was a Russian patriot dying for Stalingrad, and both my comrades-in-arms and the Nazis were dying like fruit flies caught in a blizzard, and I could not decide whose losses gave me the deeper satisfaction—well, in that period, just to be sure that I remained totally impartial and enjoyed to the fullest my private war, I developed the habit, to be practiced only with discretion, of course, of spitting on dead Russians. If you are fighting shoulder-to-shoulder with someone in a common cause, it is all too easy to forget to hate your comrades properly. It is so easy to slip into the habit of taking sides, and that habit is, as your great American sage Emerson points out, a mark of the little mind."

"You've got me licked," I said. "Proceed."

"No, my brother, I did not slip into little-mindedness and fail to spit on dead Russians. I continued to do so—as I said, with due discretion. But once I almost did slip into little-mindedness. I found a Russian infantryman freshly bayoneted, in a patch of ground we had just retaken, and so, as he lay there in the stained and trampled snow, I let him have it full in the defenseless face. Then I realized that it was the face of a young boy—sixteen, not more than seventeen. You know what I did?"

"No," I said, and poured him more calvados, to be sure I might come to know.

"The simplest thing in the world," Stephan said. "I simply leaned over and wiped his face. I possessed no such amenity as a handkerchief, so an old rag had to serve. Then I rubbed the spot with a little clean snow. I felt—"

He stopped, twirled the glass in his fingers, then lifted both hands to twirl his very Middle European-looking, military-looking, 1890's-looking black mustaches, this with the prideful gesture that he, at the age of eighteen or so, with his new lieutenant's stripes, must have employed.

379

He ceased twirling the mustaches. "I felt," he said, "rather a fool. Especially when tears came into my eyes. But—" He paused, and began again: "—my friend, my brother, my joint father of our great Ephraim, be not distressed. I soon returned to the large-minded and rational point of view endorsed by your sage Emerson, and spat with profound pleasure on my dead comrades-in-arms, that is, when convenient and safe. You wonder, good friend, why I tell you this?"

"Yes," I said.

"I tell you this because I think you did not ask your son to go with you to Alabama for the reason that in your deepest heart you knew his presence there on such an occasion—" and he swung into his elaborate syntax that always bemused me "—would deprive you, in your essence of being, of something, not easily namable, but necessary to your identity. It would deprive you of your solitude. Is not that the word we have agreed, in an almost technical sense, to use in referring to our common complaint?"

"It is a good word. Why seek further?"

"Did I ever tell you," he said, with seeming irrelevance, but leaning hard at me across the table, fixing me with eyes that, when not twinkling with wit or the joy of an idea, could go hard as blued steel, "how I finally understood and accepted my solitude? I have mentioned my wife, haven't I?"

"You have said a little of her," I said.

"What is there to say of a wife?" he demanded harshly, and drank. "A soft hairy hole in the dark." He set his glass down. "I do not wake at night and try to remember what my wife looked like. I do not try to imagine what she would look like now." He fell silent.

"Proceed," I said.

"I had found my plan to leave. So in the middle of the night I looked at her sleeping face, by the light of a candle shaded by one hand, and was gone. Do you know why I had no goodbye?"

"No."

"Because I did not trust her," he said. "That much I knew. But a deeper reason was that I had already withdrawn. From what? There had been nothing to withdraw from. Whatever affection was there between us, I had decided was only an accident, as the weather seems.

380

Certainly, she had nothing of that poetry of the flesh which you refer to in connection with—what is her name?"

"Rozelle," I said. "But I must add that your niece was not without that gift."

"I am glad to hear that," he said soberly.

"But," I went on, "out of that poetry of the flesh she always seemed to expect a cosmic truth I could not emit."

"I am sorry to hear of her lack of realism," Stephan said sympathetically. "But to continue my narrative. I said to myself that we are all accidents of history in accidental conjunction. All a matter of perspective, yes. So I pinched out the wick and set the candlestick down on the little table by the bed, thoughtfully laying a couple of matches in convenient position."

Now he was looking down at his right thumb and forefinger as though the black trace—or a blister—might yet be visible. Then, looking at me, he said: "It is odd."

"What is odd?" I asked.

"I was in the dark street," Stephan said, "before I realized—or did I merely imagine it, our poor minds being so complex and so befogged —that in the dim candlelight the sleeping face of my wife resembled the face of the bayoneted boy, on whom I had once spat and whose face I had then, in a moment of weakness, cleansed. The idea did give me a certain curious momentary pang, but I put it in its place. Anyway, the face of a Russian peasant boy, before his face hardens, and the face of the young peasant woman often look very much alike." He fell into meditation. Then: "She—my wife, I mean—was then pregnant."

"The tiger's chaudron," I remarked.

"A very apposite quotation," he said, "from that greatest of your English poets. Precisely. Not that I knew about the pregnancy at the time. If it was to be known at that date. The child—the son—appeared only later, and never with the explicit date of birth. But when, by correspondence, I was belatedly apprised of the birth of the child, I said to myself that the State would take care of its own in its own way. And what would a son—or daughter—be, in a certain perspective? How many stars in infinity are nameless? Do we need to know the

381

name of each grain of pollen shaken from the poplar bough?

"All I knew was, the grain of pollen known properly as Stephan Mostoski was on his way, and eventually he arrived at his heaven in this country where all men live in solitude, though of various dimensions and definitions. Are not all Americans great joiners, as you say? —and you join because you cannot bear your loneliness. You—we— Americans have made a religion of abstraction. And is not the air full of words and pictures all night to persuade you of your reality? And in this country I am honored for practicing a profession that raises nameless solitude to the level of mathematical clarity."

"You love Ephraim!" I said with sudden anger.

"Like my life," he declared, "for have I not sat in the seat of the *sandik* and seen the blade flash?" He stretched across the table to seize my wrist, saying, "And I love you, dear friend. Our souls speak in understanding, for we know that love is the poetry of substance and that poetry is the only language of value. Poetry, and the beautiful mathematical statement of what otherwise might not be statable."

.   .   .

When your parent dies—the last to survive, I mean, for I can speak only for myself and the death of my father occurred before I had reached the age of speculation—you begin to count deaths, even those on the obituary page of the *New York Times.* As long as you have a parent alive, you are the child; and mystically, the child is protected, the parent is an umbrella against the rain of fate. But when the umbrella is folded and laid away, all is different, you watch the weather with a different and more cunning eye, your bones ache when the wind shifts, all joy acquires a tinge of irony (even the joy of love for a child, for you feel yourself as the umbrella, or lightning rod if you will, and know the frailty of such devices). Furthermore, with the death of your parent you begin to see in each death the weight of "a tale told"—to quote the Prayer Book—and you begin to feel the fleeting impulse to verbally sum it up for yourself, or for some common acquaintance. "Poor John," you begin, "it's funny how things turned out—"

And my eyes fell on the notice of the death of David McInnis, and into my mind coming the glimpse I had had of the two faces swinging into conjunction as the hotel-room door closed, I felt the pathos of a life that so late, at the moment of sunset, had found happiness.

"But no, no," Mrs. McInnis said to me, months later, at dinner in her hotel suite, "it wasn't quite like that. David had all sorts of satisfactions—you might say he had the grim happiness of his rectitude. He was so old-fashioned—just as you are, Jed, in your own crazy way. David fought a good war—way back yonder in 1917 and '18, and he was proud of doing well. He had, too, a few good years with his first wife, Maria's mother."

This was two months after David's death, in early November, and she, back in Chicago on business, had invited me to dinner, and I had brought Ephraim along just for cocktails, to show him off—the showing off being a tremendous success.

Now still pursuing the item I had opened after Ephraim's departure, she was saying that, when she came back to Nashville, David was something like a dream come true—though, she said, "like a dream I didn't ever know I had dreamed.

"What a funny dream to have had," she added, after Radcliffe, then Cambridge, and my grand English marriage with the son of a lord—even if a younger son and the title being one of those nineteenth-century iron-puddler's titles. Oh yes, my husband was so brilliant—everybody said so, a double first at Oxford, one of the youngest dons at Cambridge, so flashy and full of paradoxes—son of a lord but in the Labor Party and big there, in the Labor Party and a Catholic convert, and then, me. I think I was his biggest paradox!—the poor little American girl whose French was so good and who would take any jump he would—oh, wasn't I a surprise to 'em! And how handsome he was, in that carved, Greek way of Lawford's. But later—once after we had been making love—I caught sight of him in his bathroom, naked, flexing his biceps and sucking in his guts and admiring his muscles. Well, thank God, Sergio had no paradoxes.

"Anyway," she said, "back to Nashville in the end. And there was David, who had no paradoxes, either. Just his rectitude. David was a rather young fellow, in the trust department of one of the banks, where my brother was his superior, too. Well, with the connivance of my brother, I'm sure—God help his soul!—the bank tried to divert my poor little inheritance for one last desperate scheme, and David just blew up. Nothing personal—didn't even know me. Just rectitude —of neither the mint-julep nor the New South variety. He made an awful fuss, and saved the inheritance, and got fired, and quietly went back to work on the family farm. Then, bingo! The Depression.

"So little David, the boy with galloping leprosy in Nashville financial circles, reemerges as the Boy Who Stood on the Burning Deck, and nothing was too good for him. And by the way, since he is—*was* —oh, I think I'm going to cry again—"

She managed to stop, and dab her eyes, but straightened herself in her chair and took command, saying, "No, by God, I won't!—Well, the long and the short of it, he did know a lot about the way things were going to develop, and he got very rich. And as a by-blow made me rich, too. Business machines, electronics, all that.

"Rich or not, it was rectitude, or old-fashioned honor, or whatever, and it's all so sad and funny—how Tennessee—Nashville—the whole South—wants to take on Yankee vices. As though they didn't have enough of their own, and plenty for export. But there were people in it like David, and your mother—oh, I'd love for you to send me a copy of the picture of her pointing at the new tooth. How David would have loved that!"

"They weren't exactly alike," I said.

"Of course," she said. "But they could recognize each other. They both had guts."

She got up and began to walk about, while the waiters cleared the cluttered table.

"Anyway," she finally said, "I went back there. And I built my allegorical whimsy. And there were the horses. And I wanted to do what I could for Lawford."

She paused.

"But all the time," she exclaimed, "there was David." Still standing, she seized a glass of brandy and lifted it. "To Happy Endings," she said, with a bright edge, like joy, in her voice.

We drank.

"And to Ephraim," she said, again lifting her glass, "and Happy Beginnings."

That done, she said what a beautiful boy Ephraim was.

Then, all at once, she looked very old.

384

"Forgive me, Jed," she said, "but I think I'll have to tell you goodbye. It looks like I'm only a quarterhorse now."

"Are you—" I began, in apprehension.

"*I* am all right," she said. "It's only the way *it* is. The only trouble is that when you suddenly get old and have to go to bed early, there's less and less reason for going to bed at all." Then, wryly: "I've taken up reading Gibbon—oh, what lovely, crystalline lava flowing over all the centuries up to your first old-lady snore when you drop the book."

She pulled herself together, raised her tilted cheek, touched a finger to the old spot she had touched when saying goodbye after the last of the Dante lessons.

"Right there," she said, in a strange mixture of schoolmarm severity and sudden gaiety, and stood very straight.

.   .   .

Maybe I would see her again, I thought as my train to the University rambled through the city which was—I always told myself with renewed marvel—my home. *My long home,* I sometimes thought in Biblical echo, as a sardonic jest, when I remembered how much of my life had been spent here in this benign and *fourmillante* hive of de-selfedness. But quickly I was wondering for what deep and perverse reason I had not asked about the Cudworths and what kind of a boy Jim was, and found myself, in the generosity of my joy in Ephraim, wishing them well with their Jim—red-headed and brawny and braw, no doubt. Then I was thinking that I did not even know whether Cud had made a go of his farm.

Or whether or not he was dead.

On impulse, well before my station, I got off the train. If I got off at this station I could, by a tangle of streets, go home to my attic by the street where the much diminished Castle of Otranto yet stood. I did not feel like going to bed and I wanted to walk. A long way.

.   .   .

The idea had been hardening well before I got off the train, so here I was back where I always started in my thoughts, at the Castle of Otranto. By this time I was moving down what had once been an old residential street but, with the yards gone, was now a real artery for traffic. A few trees, however, still grew in plots of ground left near the buildings, or had taken root in the allotted apertures in the sidewalk. Leaves still clung, and in the light stir of air and backwash of traffic there was a ripple and shudder of shadow on the pavement and even patches of swaying darkness.

The motor traffic was heavy, but the sidewalk almost deserted. In my meditations—or rather, drift of mind—I was vaguely aware of a figure some twenty-five paces ahead of me, now lost in deep shadow, then again emerging, a female figure, clearly old, a classic shape in the meaner streets of the American city—the immigrant grandmother whose breasts had suckled the brawny new man of tomorrow—a woman short, squat, excessively broad of bum, short-legged and the legs bowed with old rickets and seemingly frail beneath the weight, with a swaying sidewise motion, in one hand an enormous sack of something, like a stuffed shopping bag, in the other a smaller parcel and a heavy, shapeless purse, clad in black and topped by a shapeless black hat crammed on as though by a merciless hand that had set the whole apparatus to go on its darkling and merciless errand in which every side-sway promised to be the last.

As I have said, I was almost unaware of the listing and heaving patch of blackness going forward, in and out of blackness. But suddenly, in the deepest patch of blackness, I did sense an agitation, sensed other figures, and heard a muffled cry, and there I was, short-winded and middle-aged, at a pace that would not win me the silver cup in a foot race for paraplegics, hastening—*running* would scarcely seem the *mot juste*—toward the disturbance. Then, in some gusty shift of shadow, I saw two skinny youths struggling with the valiant broad-bottomed old crock, one after the heavy shopping bag, the other after the purse. All this now in full sight, while the traffic proceeded on its lawful and disdainful occasions.

Just then, in the light of a passing car, I saw the glint of a blade from the youth struggling for the purse.

"Stop it!" I yelled, almost on them.

I can't be quite sure of what happened next. I felt a sensation of little more significance than a bee sting, but when I touched my right hand to my left shoulder it was wet. I was by then at the curb, calling for help, for the police. I remember the outraged face of a driver glaring at me like the basilisk as he stepped on the gas.

Then I was lying on the pavement, and my last vision, before fading out, just at the moment when traffic was halted by a light ahead, was of the taller of the two assailants—a youth of, say, fourteen or fifteen —as he leaped, rather as he seemed to drift with ineffable, slow, floating godlike grace—godlike, truly, it seemed—to the hood of the nearest halted automobile, to stand beautifully balanced there with the purse—like Medusa's head hanging from the hand of Cellini's Perseus in Florence—but his pale yellow face lifted to the high stars, his lips open in a wildly beautiful, lyric, birdlike cry of triumph, an angelic, gratuitous and beautiful cry to the stars.

I remember thinking how beautiful, how redemptive, all seemed. It was as though I loved him. I thought how beautifully he had moved, like Ephraim, like a hawk in sunset flight. I thought how all the world was justified in that moment.

By then, of course, my head had gone very groggy.

.　　.　　.

The next thing I remember is being prodded by the night stick of an officer who, at a distance, was saying, "Drunker'n a hog."

And another voice: "Not before he done killed the old dame."

"Son of a bitch," the other was saying resentfully, leaning over me, "he been knifed, too."

"Son of a bitch," the other repeated, "nothing could you ever get easy."

I awoke in a hospital bed, where they told me not to worry, it was just a fainting fit from loss of blood. They even allowed me to get up and go to the toilet in my hospital robe and slip-slops, this with an orderly. Back at my bed a nurse with a face long from mechanical sympathy said my mother was in a serious condition and was calling for me.

I said that my mother was dead.

This brought on some confusion and dispute, for the nurse said her own mother was Italian and she understood the old lady was asking for her *figlio*. It seemed that I clearly had to be the *figlio*. The next thing I knew, I had been thrust into a wheelchair and was trundled off now, calm and accepting my fate, to the death-bed, where I held the hand of the dying *mamma*.

When I took the old lady's hand, she stared at me with eyes that I realized were blurred past sight, and called me *figlio mio*.

She called me *Giuseppino*, which is Little Joseph.

She called me *tesoro del cuore*, which means the heart's treasure.

She said she knew I had done *niente di cattivo, mai, in tutta la mia vita*—no, nothing bad in all my life—and she'd always known they'd let me come back to her.

And all the while I kept saying *sì, sì, sì*, which, as everybody knows, means simply yes, and saying that I'd seek to be always a *figlio buono*, and *non la lasciarei più, mai, mai*, which means I would never go away, never. I kept saying *mai* while the grip on my hand grew steadily weaker, and I was still saying *mai* when another hand, very hygienic, entered the range of my slightly blurred vision, and with the efficiency of a forceps grasped the old unhygienic hand and removed it.

For a moment, with a kind of numb wonder, I sat looking down at my own now empty hand.

But immediately ensued a hubbub. The impression was still current that the old lady was my mother, and I was rapidly approaching the stage of physical exhaustion and emotional confusion when I would plead guilty to anything, even sonhood. But, switching to the offensive, as offensively as possible, I demanded to know what would now be done with the body, first, if I refused kinship, and second, if no kin was found. I demanded that my lawyer (the only lawyer in my life, my divorce lawyer) be immediately called. They compromised by saying they would call him at home at 8 A.M., and I promised to make great difficulty for all and sundry if I was not on the line with him at that time.

I was trundled back to my own bed, leaving the old lady to be put in cold storage until morning. Then I was suddenly asleep.

.   .   .

They were as good as their word—the enemy in white, I mean—and at 8 A.M. I was on the wire with my very irate lawyer, who grew more irate when he learned that I didn't have another divorce proceeding for him to handle, and didn't even have the excuse of calling him from jail. What I wanted was for him to track the old lady down and, if, as I suspected (except for a son in the pen somewhere), she was without family and destitute, to arrange a decent Catholic funeral, which I would attend and pay for, with whatever friends the old girl may have happened to have. My divorce expert reminded me that this was not his specialty, nor was he an ambulance chaser, but out of friendship he would find some young squirt who would take charge. I promised to get married as soon as possible and be divorced immediately thereafter. He laughed hollowly, and hung up.

Two days later there was a proper funeral mass in the parish church of San Sebastiano, with candles and incense and the works. There were two mourners, me and the young squirt. I had been right in assuming that there was no kin—except, of course, for Giuseppino, who couldn't come. He was absent on business at San Quentin.

.   .   .

When I drove up to the gate of the house on Jonquil Street, he was already on the porch, and had on his blue Sunday suit—blue serge, as it predictably turned out to be—for my coming, and he must have been watching for hours through a chink in the same front-room lace curtains my mother had nursed through all the years. In any case, as I slowed down my U-Drive-It, rented at the Huntsville Airport, he was already on the front porch, with his right arm waving creakily in welcome. Then, making his way to the gate, his big-boned, liver-spotted, joint-swollen, strong old hand already thrust out on an inadequate wristbone from a too stiffly starched white cuff, he was saying, "I'm Perk Simms, I'm Perk what had the luck to find yore ma in this dark world and I declare I will love her till the day I die."

By this time, forgetting his abortive handshake, he was grappling for my neck like a spookily inept Strangler Lewis returned from the shades, the formidable old hands on their pipestem wrists finally getting a grip, and with both arms around my neck, he pressed one of his great, bony, leathery, and imperfectly shaven cheeks, as raw as a clutch of cockleburs, against my own, all the while saying it was God's blessing to see me, there was so much to tell piling up inside him, and he claimed me like a blood-kin son, with my kind permission, for he had loved her so. And meanwhile I felt the dampness on his cheek.

I muttered what seemed appropriate, and disentangled myself to get my suitcase out of the trunk. Thereupon another struggle ensued, between me and that ectoplasmic version of a man of power, and I won, and after he had opened the gate, I carried the suitcase up to the steps and through the door, one of his bony hands on my shoulder all the way as though he needed to be reassured of my literal presence.

Once we were inside the shadowy house, even as I waited there with the suitcase still in my hand, we both stood in a kind of daze. It was, literally, a daze for me. I kept trying to fix on some small object and claim old familiarity with it—on the black-and-white china bulldog on the mantel shelf that my mother once won in a street carnival raffle, on the crocheted antimacassar-shaped thing she had made to cover the threadbare spot in the headrest of the ritual overstuffed chair in the front room, on the stereopticon viewer and the box of cards I used to spend rainy Sunday afternoons lying on my stomach staring through, on all the wonders of the world beyond Dugton, on Niagara Falls, the Pyramids, and the dynamo of the Chicago World's Fair.

I stood there, clutching the suitcase, which I was afraid to set down, for that action might break the spell, and looked long and hard at each object, until another noiselessly summoned my devotion. Each object seemed to glow with a special assertion of its being—of my being, too, as though only now, after all the years, I was returning to my final self, long lost.

It was the assertion of indestructible and absolute identity, the fullness of being and possibility—the numinousness, one might say with more than etymological whimsy, its "noddingness" at me, its recognition—that gave each object its power to draw me forth from, as it were, the long drowse of my being.

Perk Simms, feet motionlessly planted in the great box-toed, highly polished shoes (polished every Sunday and every funeral) and preternatural Adam's apple tufted with bristly gray hairs sticking out motionless above a blue-and-crimson striped Christmas tie, seemed to respect the long experience through which I was passing. Perk watched my eyes find each object, now long familiar to him, too, but in a different way, and waited until my mystic transformation was finished. When the last was over, he came to take the suitcase from my woodenly unresisting hand. He had carried it into what had been my mother's (and his) room before I came out of my catatonia and followed him.

"You'll be comfortable here, I bet," he was saying pridefully. "You see, yore ma—now I doan mean she was ever a woman for complaining, she shore-God was not—but lately it got so her back warn't so good—standing all them years leanen over things at the can'ry, and I just went and got her the best mat-ter-ress I could learn about—it's all *or-to-peed-ic,* and it helped her good. You'll sleep good, I'll give you a certified and signed guarantee."

And he pretended to be fumbling for a fountain pen and contract. He grinned, and I grinned back the best I could.

"Much obliged, Perk," I said, "but it'll be wasted on me. I can sleep anywhere." Then, realizing that this was not the most graceful ploy, I said: "You see, Perk, I want to sleep in my old bed tonight. For old times' sake."

At that he nodded, not saying a word. He just picked up the suitcase, beating me to it, and led me to the little room I had occupied so many years and where I had lain laughing my drunk-fool head off while my ma did her work on my nose with the shoe.

"The bed's all made up," Perk said. "I don't mean just for me tonight, though I was going to sleep in here. I mean she always kept it made up. Except when she'd pull it apart for a good airen. I'd catch her at it and I used to laugh at her, before I caught on good how it was a-tween you. I'd say, 'So he's comen tonight!' 'Naw, you clabber-headed hoot owl,' she'd say, she liked to make up names to call me for fun. 'Catch him comen to Dugton, I'll break his durn neck, after all the trouble I taken to git him out. It's only I like to make a bed fer him. It's a way of sayen there's a place fer him in my heart. But he shore better stay out of town.' "

"I guess I'll unpack," I said, and got very busy with the process until he had withdrawn.

.   .   .

Perk said we were going to eat out—at a right new place on the highway, he said—and added he'd be eating enough of his own cooking from now on not to jump at a chance to get some other vittles. My "ma," as he always called her, she had been mighty handy at the stove and liked to see a man eat, he'd say that for her, and said it.

So we went out to the new place on the highway, where, in fact, the steaks were good and the pecan pies homemade. Several people from Dugton came in to get supper, and for each one known to Perk we had a little occasion. Perk introduced the Perfesser, who got told what a fine mother he had had and how sad he must be, and they were sorry for me and glad to see me even on a sad occasion, and were proud of me being from Dugton and being a perfesser at Chicago— or was it Kansas City?

Then we went home, and Perk poked up a coal fire in the grate, before which we drank a quantity of black coffee. Then Perk broke out the bourbon. He carefully poured himself two measured ounces, that being Ma's allowance for Sundays and holidays. He said he knowed I was a grown man and to do what I liked, but I poured myself two ounces.

Perk said that five days after the funeral he was sitting here one night about to go to pieces. Said that with the funeral and all and the next day or two with people talking to you on the street, you sort of forgot how it was going to be. Just sitting in the house at night. Said he tried to pray but he never had no sleight at it. All he could say was "God, God, God," and he felt like something was gonna bust in him. Said he tried to cry but the tears locked up inside. He had slipped, he said, when he seen me that afternoon, and he begged my pardon. But he did have some excuse. Before my mother had died, just before, she said for him to kiss her boy for her.

He said he knew a man had to learn to live by himself, but he said it was a sort of mean joke how the better a man's wife was for him and the more he appreciated her, the worse it was when she left him, you just couldn't win in that raffle. He had had the other kind of wife once, with his kid rotten, his boy shot by the cops in a stolen car, and no trouble getting a divorce the way his wife carried on.

"Then," he said, "yore ma come along and I began to like to open my eyes in the morning, there being something in the world to pleasure 'em. She sort of took me in hand. Give me a way to live and a thing to live for. And me, I'd lay awake sometimes at night trying to figger out something I could fix about the house, build a cabinet or fix a loose step or something, and wondering how she'd grin and what kind of a joke she'd make, her being so long on jokes."

It gave him something to think about now at night, he said, trying to remember the times he'd fixed something she really liked. He'd always been pretty apt with his toolbox, and even now he'd remember something at night and git up. He was trying to hold on to the habit, he said, and keep the house in shape. The house warn't his no ways he said, just for his life, it was mine by will, but he prayed God to keep strength to respect it. She's always respected the house. No matter how hard she worked at the can'ry, she always was spick-and-span.

He almost let the fire go out, staring at it, having let the conversation die off. Then he put some coal on, and apparently catching sight of himself in a side mirror on the wall, went over there and carefully retied his striped Christmas tie, which had been climbing up his neck and over his Adam's apple like a tropical liana of peculiarly brilliant blossoms. It was as though he had suddenly heard a voice saying, "Git up, Clabber-Head, and go fix yore tie afore it bites you in yore ear like a spreaden adder."

Having subdued the gaudy spreading adder, he returned to his chair, and downed the last watery dregs in his glass. "She had the gift," he said. "She had the sleight."

"What?" I demanded.

"All her funning and all," he said, "she had the sleight. To make a man always feel like a man. She could stop anything she was doing —washing dishes or anything—and just for a second give you a look that made you feel you and her had a wonderful secret. Sometimes I might be helping her make up a bed on Saturday and she'd give me a wink, and then pretend she hadn't never. She never come home and found me in the house without taking on over me like I was a surprise package—a big fuss, then she'd turn that into a joke, too."

He paused, looking into the fire.

"We was married a long time, son. I mean, Perfesser."

"I wish you'd make it son," I said.

"Thank you kindly," he said. "As I was saying, we was married a long time," he repeated, like a lesson, "ever since before you got your growth good, and she never lost the sleight to make a man feel like a man, like she set store by him."

Then: "A man gets old, he ain't what he was. Ain't worth powder and lead to perish. Ain't nothing but spindle bones stuck in a pair of pants. But living with a woman like yore ma—" and here he stopped, twisted in his chair, and seemed to be physically struggling to phrase something just right "—it is like you was living in a—a dream—and time ain't gone by, the way she could make you feel that everything kept on being the truth."

The next pause was a long one. Twice he picked up the empty glass from the floor beside him, tightened his grip on it, and set it back down.

"All she done for me—" he burst out, croakingly.

I waited, for I caught the peculiar inflection.

"And then what she did," he said, "and on her dying bed."

I waited, for I now could tell that whatever it was, it had to come.

"Holding her hand," he said, "setting close to the bed, that's where I was, and she said it. Ast me did I know she loved me. I nodded my head, being a-sudden choked up. Then you know what she said?"

I shook my head.

"She said for me to forgive her," he managed to get out, "she loved me and declared she never knowed a better man and more fitter for her, and she said she prayed God I'd come to know it was not to kick up dirt in my—in my—" He did a few contortions in his chair, then took it head on: "To kick up dirt in my—in my sweet ole face—no, don't make no mistake. Perfesser, them was the words she spoke, not me."

After a little: "Do you know what it was on her mind?"

"No."

"She wanted to be buried out in Heaven's Hope graveyard," he said. "Next to—to you know who." Then: "What kin a man do! You do the best the Lord let's you, and it is like all yore love, it is in vain. All I could do was git out of that hospital chair and git out in the hall, and find a settee in the room at the end. I got there just in time to set."

After a long pause he managed to continue: "When I sort of taken holt, I come back. And she said, did I understand, and I could not say yes, and I could not say no. I was froze. She said, please, to understand, that if something in yore past time was good even a little time, it deserves you not to spit on it, no matter how bad it turned out, and she did not want to see anything good ever happened to her throwed away like dirt. And she said: 'Both the happiness and the miserableness I learned when I was young, it was that that made me ready to set all my heart on you when you come by, Pore Ole Clabber-Head.' "

He turned at me in an awful voice of chill fury, saying: "What's a man to do?"

The nurse, Perk said, had come in by now and she motioned to him. My mother was sure weak by this time, Perk said, and the words faint. But seeing the nurse, she got stronger, Perk said, like a last thing that had to be said. "You'll understand," she said to him, "for I'll be with you in the house, helping you understand all day, and I'll be laying by yore side a-nights."

Then the doctor came and motioned to Perk.

That was the last time except for a minute or two that Perk saw her. They let him go back in to hold her hand. "I understood it was sort of goodbye," Perk said. "Her eyes was closed, but now and then she sort of gripped my hand, and I let her know I felt it. Then I did the foolest thing of my life. I leaned over and said right soft, 'Don't you be afraid. I'm here, and I doan want you afraid.'

"And you know what? The God-durnedest thing happened. Soon as I got them fool words out, her eyes popped wide open, bright and shiny black like when she was excited or full of fun, and her voice was a-sudden strong, almost like usual, and she said: 'Dying—shucks! If you kin handle the living, what's to be afraid of the dying?' "

.　　.　　.

We sat by the smoldering fire another half-hour or so. Then Perk said he reckoned we might go to bed. So we shook hands good night.

He said if I heard a noise, it was him wandering around. But he'd be as still as he could.

So I said good night again and went into the bathroom to do my duties and on to bed.

My light had been out a time and I was staring up at the dark when the knock came at my door. I called, and Perk entered, turning on the switch by the door to make the top light blaze. He had a great lot of papers under his left arm, various manila files with rubber bands around them and stacks of letters tied in old ribbons of different colors.

"Something I forgot," he said sheepishly.

I sat up in bed and he pulled up a chair. He carefully laid aside the files, which seemed to be of newspaper clippings, and nursed the pile of letters in his lap.

"She set by the fire a-nights," he said, "and read these here letters. I'd be a-reading the paper. Then she'd come acrost something she'd forgot, and she'd slap herself on the thigh and bust out laughing, a-saying, 'Now listen, will ye, ain't he a rooster!' "

So now I sat propped in my bed, while he read, as he said she had done, and listened to some fool insanity of my own, some description of somebody, some joke, some remarks about a dumb class, some lie I had written to please her, now sitting there trying to remember where, when, why I had written each stupid item, feeling my life go by me like a black blast of wind of mounting intensity and from a quarter undefined, until I said, "Excuse me," and took my suitcase and went to the bathroom and exhumed my private supply and took three long gulps of whiskey, and came back, and got propped in bed to resume the inquisitorial infliction.

Superfluously inquisitorial, I may add, for I was long since prepared to confess to anything whatsoever. But I did not know what the Inquisitor wanted me to confess to in particular.

The only thing I could think of confessing was that I was I.

.   .   .

It had flurried snow during the night, and though my rented car was parked out there by a road of blacktop shiny in the sun, here in Heaven's Hope graveyard the snow was still powdery white on fallen leaves, like sugar sprinkled on cornflakes. The last time I had traveled this road, I had been a little snot-nose sprig lost in the world, on a wagon stuffed with our meager household gear, and the iron tires of the wagon wheels had seemed to grind the gravel on forever on the way to Dugton and the shadowy future. Now, standing in the graveyard, I remembered how the snot-nose sprig had stolen one look, like crime or not-yet-developed masturbation, toward the spot of heaped raw ground where lay the father he would never see again.

This return trip had taken only twenty-five minutes on blacktop, and a quarter of a mile up the road toward Dugton there was already a real development started—two split-level ranch-type houses glittering with new and untarnished mortgages; and the kind of people who used to sweat and moan in anguish for their salvation in the little goods-box-sized church, and bury their dead in the Heaven's Hope graveyard, were long since gone, or had transmogrified themselves into another kind of people.

I knew what the church was like now. I had just inspected it. The steeple, never too steady on its pins, had long back definitively collapsed, and the bell had been made off with. Wind, weather, and wandering fowl of the air now made entrance and exit at will through apertures once covered by colored paper on window glass to shed a dim religious light. The little pump-organ, which had suffered some random mayhem from hands of the unGodly, had now taken a thirty-five-degree header at the corner where the floor had finally rotted out. The scene was the same as that of one of the more famous photographs by Walker Evans, but a generation of damage later. Walker Evans should have hung on to take the valedictory view, for now the last soul had been saved here and the last flesh committed to the process of nature.

No—my mother's body might not be the last thus consigned. I had that very morning promised Perk that when he died and got cremated, I would personally see that his ashes got stuck in the ground out here. "Just anywheres, not too unhandy to Ma," he had said. "And no stone —no funeral, no nothing. Whatever my life was, there warn't nothing to brag on but her, and that don't belong on no stone. Just here, it belongs—here—" he had burst out, and struck himself on the chest with such vigor as to upset his coffee cup.

After a moment, having wiped up the coffee and replenished the cup, he had said: "What's writing for, no ways, on a stone in a place like this, all ruint. Nothing but common folks to begin with, and now who comes? I say, let folks lay with what's in they hearts."

Later, having extracted my solemn promise, he added that, when the time came, I would find a spade in the cellar with his garden tools. He was one, he said, always believed in keeping a man's tools in order.

So now I wandered around and idly tried to decide on a good, not too unhandy place for Perk's ashes, Perk not having come with me, saying he believed a man sometimes wanted to be by himself.

Yes, I had wanted to be alone. And now I was. I was alone with what Perk Simms had told me: "You know, she said she done the best she knowed to raise you right and git you out of Dugton, and keep you out."

And: "She kept that bed fresh ever night. Said it was the least she could do."

And: "When that photo-shot of yore boy Eph—that's what we calls him—come, she kiss it ever night, and say, 'Now, ain't he a rooster?' And she'd grin. And one time she said she'd give a million dollars to have holt of him in her arms not more'n five minutes."

And: "Gittin on later, when come a photo-shot of Eph sort of growed up, she kept looking at it, a-saying, 'You know, if I could only be behind a post or something or in a crowd and only look at him to the content of my heart and him not know! That would be enough,' she said."

And: "Time that letter come about you and Eph's mother split up, looked like she couldn't believe it. That night, us in bed, she put her head on my shoulder to cry, a-saying: 'Don't my boy ever have no luck? Gits his name in the papers, makes good money, but don't he know nothing's no good when the lonesome time come?'"

Ah, but I knew about the lonesome time!

I sat on a moss-grown, fallen tombstone, and thought how all things I did to ward off the lonesome time seemed to come to nothing. I had not been found worthy to sit on the placeless, sunlit lawn of Dante's vision and listen to the blessèd music that was the language uttered by the saints and sages—or, at least, I had brought back no fair report to open the ears of others. I was no citizen, after all, of the *imperium intellectūs.* My naturalization papers were forged. And as for the kindly thought that Dr. Stahlmann had long ago held out to me—the hope that out of my anger, my innocence, what he called my *sancta simplicitas*—I might write a worthy thing—what a comedy!

The mysterious anger was there, and unannealed, God knew. But my *simplicitas* was not *sancta*. My *simplicitas* had lost the blessèdness of knowing that men were real, and brothers in their reality. And all I had in place of that was a vast number of cards that measured three by five inches, with notes in my large and legible script. But could not a man pray?

Was all too late? Was all too late, after all?

I had the wild impulse to lie on the earth between the two graves, the old and the new, and stretch out a hand to each. I thought that if I could do that, I might be able to weep, and if I could weep, something warm and blessèd might happen. But I did not lie down. The trouble was, I was afraid that nothing might happen, and I was afraid to take the risk.

And I had the notion of coming back when Perk died—that shouldn't be too long now and I'd be getting toward retirement. I would come back and live alone in that house on Jonquil Street, that Perk, handy with tools as he was, would have left in good shape, and at night, in winter, I would sit by the fire and try to figure out why things had all turned out the way they had. And later, not being able to sleep, I might get up and wander about with a dimming flashlight in my hand to touch familiar objects.

.   .   .

Well, I couldn't stay here all day. I had a plane to catch. After a last look at the graves, I went and started up the car. All very business-like, with squared shoulders.

Then it came to mind that I had one further piece of business. To see the spot where Buck Tewksbury had taken his lethal header with the noble dong in clutch. It was just beyond the old iron bridge, "t'other side o' the church." That was what a man had said, standing under the chinaberry tree, long ago, but the voice was clear in my ear.

I was at the church now, so that meant toward Dugton. The trouble was, there wasn't any old iron bridge. There wasn't even a creek now.

Podmore Creek, I suddenly remembered its name—the creek my mother had thrown the saber into. Now only a couple of big culverts went under the road, and so it must have been along here before they drained for the new development and the untarnished mortgages. But there was no marker, nothing to inform the tourist that at this spot Buck Tewksbury—remarkable man that he was—did so-and-so.

I drove on and thought that the only thing wrong with Buck was he was born out of phase. If he had been born in 1840, he would have been just ripe for sergeant in a troop of Alabama cavalry. You could see him, high in stirrups, black mustaches parted to expose white teeth and emit the great yell, the saber, light as a toy in his big hand, flashing like flame. Buck leading the charge, Buck breveted rank by rank, Buck the darling of his tattered wolfish crew, Buck in some last action under Forrest—say, in the last breakthrough into Tennessee—meeting lead as the saber flashes and the yell fades from his throat.

Poor Buck, I thought.

Then I said out loud: "Poor Buck."

.   .   .

A month later, back in Chicago, I wrote the letter:

Dear Dauphine:

You have known me a long time and know what I am, too, for it is unlikely that we change much. But perhaps, in what little growth of wisdom is granted us, I am wiser than when, a thousand years ago, in our ignorance, we quarreled over politics, or even a little wiser than when years later you said everything was wrong and wept in despair. And we do have Ephraim. And his gloriousness may give some indication that his father may not be entirely without worth.

It would be disingenuous of me to appeal to your feelings by saying that you and I should be together to rejoice in him. I ask for your company because it is what I feel myself most deeply craving.

At this point I laid down my pen and stared into distance for a long time. Then I resumed:

It is not that I cannot stand solitude. Perhaps I stand it all too easily, and have been, far beyond my own knowing, solitary all my life.

I ask for your company for what blessèdness it is. But I say also that in it I may learn, even as the light fails, a little of what I need to know.

In all hope,

Your (whether you like it or not) JED.

It was night, but I did not want to wait until morning to post the letter. I went out, found a mailbox, and then walked for a long time. In the course of my wanderings, I fell into the fantasy that someday —perhaps on the mission to put the ashes of Pore Ole Perk in the ground, unmarked, but not too unhandy to the spot where Ma lay— I would be accompanied by Ephraim, and I could point out to him all the spots that I had dreamed of pointing out to him.

ABOUT THE AUTHOR

ROBERT PENN WARREN was born in Guthrie, Kentucky, in 1905.
After graduating summa cum laude from Vanderbilt University
(1925), he received a master's degree from the University of California
(1927) and did graduate work at Yale University (1927–28) and at
Oxford as a Rhodes Scholar (B. Litt., 1930).

Mr. Warren has published many books, including ten novels, eleven
volumes of poetry, a volume of short stories, a play, a collection of
critical essays, a biography, two historical essays, and two studies of
race relations in America. This body of work has been published in
a period of forty-seven years—a period during which Mr. Warren has
also had an active career as a professor of English.

All the King's Men (1946) was awarded the Pulitzer Prize for Fiction. *Promises* (1957) won the Pulitzer Prize for Poetry, the Edna St.
Vincent Millay Prize of the Poetry Society of America, and the National Book Award. In 1944 Mr. Warren occupied the Chair of Poetry
of the Library of Congress. In 1952 he was elected to the American

Philosophical Society; in 1959 to the American Academy of Arts and Letters; and in 1975 to the American Academy of Arts and Sciences. In 1967 he received the Bollingen Prize in Poetry for *Selected Poems: New and Old, 1923–1966,* and in 1970 the National Medal for Literature and the Van Wyck Brooks Award for the book-length poem *Audubon*. In 1974 he was chosen by the National Endowment for the Humanities to deliver the third Annual Jefferson Lecture in the Humanities. In 1975 he received the Emerson-Thoreau Award of the American Academy of Arts and Sciences. In 1976 he received the Copernicus Award from the Academy of American Poets, in recognition of his career but with special notice of *Or Else—Poem/Poems 1968–1974.*

Mr. Warren lives in Connecticut with his wife, Eleanor Clark (author of *Rome and a Villa, The Oysters of Locmariaquer* and *Baldur's Gate*), and their two children, Rosanna and Gabriel.